OUTGUNNED!

"We wasn't doing nothing but riding out on a hunt," Michael said to the hidalgo.

"How unfortunate for you," the officer replied coldly, "that the truth no longer matters. What does matter is that you have seen what you should not see." He looked up at his corporal. "Kill them."

With the addition of the bunch in front of them, Michael and his party were surrounded by nine armed men. The odds now were anything but even. The men in the camp closed in around the riders.

"Four against nine," Michael said calmly in Spanish for all to hear as he laid a hand on the wrist of his rifle stock, his thumb falling close to the curved firecock of the old weapon. "But who wants to be the first to die?"

All around there was a clatter of rifle hammers being drawn back and locking noisily into a position to fire.

Muskets roared . . .

Berkley Books by Tom Early

The SONS OF TEXAS Series

SONS OF TEXAS
THE RAIDERS
THE REBELS
THE PROUD

TOM EARLY

SONS OF TEXAS

Book Four

THE PROUD

BERKLEY BOOKS, NEW YORK

SONS OF TEXAS: THE PROUD

A Berkley Book / published by arrangement with
the author

PRINTING HISTORY
Berkley edition / January 1992

ISBN: 0-425-12967-5

A BERKLEY BOOK ® TM 757,375
Berkley Books are published by The Berkley Publishing Group,
200 Madison Avenue, New York, New York 10016.
The name "BERKLEY" and the "B" logo
are trademarks belonging to Berkley Publishing Corporation.

PRINTED IN THE UNITED STATES OF AMERICA

10 9 8 7 6 5 4 3 2 1

TEXAS

December, 1838

☆ Chapter ☆

1

"James? James Lewis. If you're going to change out of that patched shirt, James Lewis, you'd best be getting yourself inside. Come you in this minute now, hear?"

"I won't be much longer," he called.

"You'd best not be, James Lewis, or my corn pudding will be burnt to a crisp before ever we start."

"Then take it out of the oven, old woman."

"And have it be cold afore we ever start out? No thank you, James Lewis. And you'll not be calling me old woman no more or I'll knot the side of your head, mister."

James chuckled. "I won't be but a minute, Libby. Really."

"Well thank the Lord for small favors." Elizabeth Caldwell Lewis disappeared inside the living-quarters half of their cabin, and James stood, scratched himself, and picked up the bridle he'd been working at mending. It wasn't like there was any hurry to complete the project. It was just that at this time of year, when harvest was no more than memory and planting was a far distant hope, a man had to take advantage of any chance he got to make himself usefully busy. None of the Lewis boys had ever been noted for their laziness, and James had no intention of changing that.

He stepped up onto the puncheon flooring inside the dogtrot breezeway that separated the two halves of the cabin, hung the newly repaired bridle back onto the peg where it belonged, and then walked on through to the backyard. It was early yet, but he needed to confine the chickens in their coop now, or the foolish creatures would surely choose to roost where some passing night predator could reach them. Rather than bother chasing the hens,

James took a handful of cracked corn from the bin at the back of the dogtrot and used that to toll the birds into the tight-built coop. He used a peg to wedge the coop door closed, then brushed his hands vigorously. For a moment he stood where he was, head tipped back and eyes reaching toward the horizon. At his back were the fields that James Lewis himself first put to plow. Before him were the wooded banks of the Colorado River. Beyond that lay a thousand miles or more of Texas, grand and glorious Texas. Great grasslands and rolling hillsides and clear-running streams. It was country big enough for a man to breathe in, Texas. James wouldn't have left it to return to Tennessee now, not for anything.

Why, with so very much of Texas already his by right of grant and title, James Lewis could count himself among the most fortunate of men. He owned more of the rich Texas soil than any number of sons could ever help him to farm, and he had a handsome woman waiting for him inside that cabin who this very moment was busy nurturing their firstborn within herself. That thought alone was enough to make James swell with pride and satisfaction. It . . .

"James!" Libby was commencing to sound exasperated. Really and truly peeved this time.

"Coming." Even so he paused a moment longer, drew in one more deep breath, the air chill as it filled his lungs and filled his being, the air here as clear and tasty as springwater spilling from a Tennessee mountainside. "Coming, Libby." He turned back to the cabin.

Libby stood in the dogtrot waiting for him. She was a pert and perky little slip of a redheaded thing, her waist barely beginning to thicken this early into her condition. James slowed his pace just a trifle so that he could watch her that little bit longer. Two years they'd been married now, since the winter following San Jacinto and independence, and still James enjoyed the sight of his wife.

"You have that clean shirt ready for me, old woman?" he asked as he stepped up beside her and reached down—Libby was so small, and James towered so above her that he had to bend at the knees to reach her—and gave her a pinch on the bottom.

"James!" she squealed. She bolted forward and he gave chase.

"We don't really *have* to be there so early, you know."

"James Lewis, quit your shenanigans and get that shirt changed this minute. Of course we have to be there early. I promised Petra a corn pudding, and a corn pudding she shall have. Or else."

James feigned a pout. But he went inside and changed his shirt as Libby asked. The cabin was filled with the warm, rich scents of a good woman's baking, the contrast between that and the chill outdoors making the warmth inside especially welcome.

"Best take your heavy wrap," he suggested. "It'll be cold after the sun goes down. We don't want you t' catch something."

"It's already laid out over there, mister. You mind your knitting and I shall tend to mine." Libby tended more faithfully to the Dutch oven that held her corn pudding, rich with fresh eggs and laced with hidden nuggets of cracklin's, than to herself. She wrapped the cast iron pot in layer after layer of cloth before she consented to turn it over to her husband for the carrying and finally fetched her cloak and drew it about her shoulders. James waited patiently by the door, his arms filled with the padded bulk of the Dutch oven.

Libby paused for a moment to cast her eyes about the room, obviously checking to see what she might have forgotten. Then she picked up a cunningly woven willow basket filled with eggs and cradled that in one arm. With her free hand she took up their largest crockery jug.

"What's all that?"

"The eggs are for Petra." James grunted. A coon had gotten into his brother Andrew's coop several nights ago. It was only proper that James and Libby share. "And the milk is for Annie," Libby rambled on while she headed toward the door, still peering back over her shoulder as if sure she'd forgotten something but mystified as to what the lack might be. "That old cow of theirs won't freshen for another month. Not that she is any great shakes even when she's fresh. Annie needs the milk for the baby." Annie was James's sister, two years older than he and married to Sly Shipman. Like the rest of the Lewis clan, Annie and her husband had taken up land on the Colorado, on the westernmost fringes of the old Austin colony. The closely grouped holdings lay beyond the now nearly abandoned colony headquarters at San Felipe de Austin on the Brazos River.

More than half the Lewises lived here now, James reflected, near enough to enjoy each other's company, near enough to draw strength and comfort from one another, near enough to share triumph and tragedy alike. Tonight's gathering, thank goodness, was more in the triumph category.

Of the boys who had been sired by Mordecai Lewis, only the eldest son, Joseph, had chosen to remain back in Tennessee. Joseph was still there, farming the last of the land that their father had taken up, the last of several fruitless attempts he'd made to settle in one spot and till the ground when his restless spirit demanded that he rove the far horizons instead. Joseph stayed back, and so did Heather and Dora with their stay-at-home husbands. But all the others had followed Mordecai's example and given in to the lure of space and freedom that was Texas.

Old Mordecai had been the first to cross the Sabine into Texas, back when it was still Spanish. Back when it was both harsh and hateful to Americans. Mordecai had died at a Spanish officer's hand on his second journey into Texas. His son Michael—as much James's idol as brother—had been with their father that time in 1816. Michael was wounded and nearly killed too. But he had lived, and the magic of Texas was too strong within him even for his memories to keep him away. Michael returned to Texas and took his next younger brother Andrew with him. They were among Moses and Stephen Austin's early colonists, taking up their grants and honestly attempting to obey the harsh laws of Spain yet rejoicing when Mexico declared her independence and promised fair treatment for all. When fairness proved impossible, though, the Lewises, by then including James and Annie newly emigrated from Tennessee, declared for freedom and stood on the side of the republic.

Stephen Austin lived to see the land he helped create become a proud republic that bowed to no authority and to no will but its own. The little man whose vision gave so much to others lived to become secretary of state of the new nation—and then died so early, too early. Michael and Andrew, who had known him much better than James, grieved for him, and they argued afterward about politics and policy. Michael and Andrew cared about such; James cared about family and field. He was perfectly willing to let others do the work of . . . whatever work it was that politicians did.

That was the reason for this evening's gathering at the home shared by Andrew and Petra and their children: Andrew Lewis, who had been one of the Austin colony representatives at the council that first declared Texas must break from Mexico, had been elected to the Texas Congress during the recent elections, which elevated Mirabeau Lamar from vice-president to president of the young nation.

Likely Sam Houston would have been able to win reelection except that the constitution prohibited a president from succeeding himself. So now Houston was out and Lamar was in, and Andrew

Lewis was on his way to the capital at Houston—the new town named for the recent president and general—to take up political office in the service of the republic.

It was all very exciting stuff, James was sure—to those who cared about such things, anyway.

For the moment, though, his interest was in matters somewhat more mundane than great political movements. "Don't forget t' take up my rifle, Libby. I got my arms full here."

"And you think I don't? You see what I have to carry, James. And it isn't like you will need it for anything. There hasn't been any sort of raid on this part of the Colorado, not Indian nor Mexican either one, in all the time I've lived here. Leave it be, James."

Never mind that it was his own beloved wife he was talking to; for the first time since she'd begun pestering him earlier, James frowned. "I'll leave the corn pudding if I must, Libby, but the rifle goes with me."

"You Lewises," Libby Lewis complained.

"It goes," he said, his tone of voice even and low, and verging on cold. He would happily take his direction from his wife most of the time. But there were some things a man did not do.

The Lewises, since old Mordecai and likely long before him too, were men of the forest as much as they were men of the field. They had won through too much to take life for granted now. And no Lewis was likely to allow himself ever to be far from his long rifle and bullet pouch.

James smiled, wanting to offer compromise in the wake of his comment lest this minor nothing work itself into something. "If you like, Libby, I'll carry the milk over to Annie come the morrow. First thing. And you know there will be milk for the little one at Andrew's tonight. Annie won't have need until tomorrow."

"But I promised . . ."

"Tomorrow," James said gently but firmly.

Libby obviously did not like it, but she set the jug of milk back into a pail of river water and used that hand instead to take up James's rifle and pouch.

"Good. Now let's go to a party," James said, genuinely cheerful again. As Libby passed him he bent to deliver a peck on the side of her forehead, but she ducked away from him and headed grumpily out into the slanting golden sunshine of a winter's late afternoon.

☆ Chapter ☆ 2

James ambled away from the noise and confusion surrounding Andrew's cabin, where the women clucked and fluttered over their preparations and the smaller children ran, climbed, crawled, drooled, and in general enjoyed themselves underfoot. It was a loud, laughing, happy occasion when the Lewises gathered together, and this evening would be no exception. James spotted the menfolk perched on upended wood chunks beyond the long trestle table that soon would be groaning from the weight of food. He veered toward them.

As guest of honor—never mind that this was his own home—Andrew held forth at the center of things. Cousin Frank, whose farm lay beyond Michael's, was seated nearby. His older sons, James saw, were being allowed to sit on the fringes and listen in to the talk of their elders. Edward was soon seventeen and David two years younger. Their father had always been a reader and a charmer yet a solid and stable man in spite of that. The boys showed promise of having Frank's same quickness of mind, although they both seemed more serious than their father generally cared to be.

Seated opposite Andrew and holding the inevitable jug of mellow corn was Annie's husband, Sly Shipman. Before Annie tamed him—as much, that is, as he was ever apt to be tamed, which was considerably more than anyone ever expected he would be—Sly had been a merchant of the night-traveling variety. That was a time when trade between the United States and Mexico was forbidden. The American colonists in theory were allowed to buy only merchandise that came to them by way of Mexico and was subject to usurious tariffs. Sly Shipman and men like him who ought their wares in Louisiana and brought their mule trains cross the Sabine behind the backs of Mexican army patrols made fe easier, and goods cheaper, for the colonists during those years. Now, though, Sly was retired from the trade, more or less. He still onducted a little business now and then, the primary difference eing that the business was no longer illegal, Texans having no eluctance whatsoever to trade with Americans across the border.

For that matter, most Texans felt that the border itself should be abolished and the young republic annexed into the union of states. n a referendum election taken on the heels of independence, the Texans had overwhelmingly voted in favor of annexation. James had no firm feelings on the subject himself. When the vote was taken those two years past he had been more interested in courting Libby Caldwell than in worrying about politics. He hadn't bothered to ride all the way back to San Felipe to vote—not when Libby's kisses tasted so sweet, and the journey back would have meant being apart from her for several whole days.

As for now, well, that was the sort of decision Andrew was being sent off to Houston to fret about. James and other honest men like him had different fish to fry.

Sly Shipman wordlessly handed the whiskey jug to James and tipped up a chunk of unsplit wood for him to light on.

"Ah, now that's good," James said once he got his breath back. "Aged all o', what, a week and a half?"

Sly chuckled. "Aged long enough to get all the way down from Kentucky. Beyond that, I give you no guarantee."

James grinned and took a second, smaller sip before he returned the jug to Sly. "Where's Michael?"

"Likely waiting for Angeline to brush her hair again," Andrew suggested, his eyes pinned on Frank's eldest as he said it.

The boy squirmed and blushed. "We're cousins, dang it," he protested.

"And a shame for you that you are," Andrew sympathized. It was true that Michael and Marie's daughter was beginning to bloom. But then Marie, with her French and Spanish ancestry, was a true beauty herself. It only stood to reason that Angeline would be too. The girl would soon be fourteen and saw herself as a scrawny, ugly lump . . . to the great amusement of everyone else in the family, since Angeline was the only one who seemed not to know how very pretty she was becoming.

Edward was in no humor to be teased about his own budding impulses, particularly as they might apply to his cousin. He stood and tugged at his brother David's sleeve. "C'mon. Let's go see can we knock down a fat deer." The boy picked up a slim rifle that was nearly as long as he was tall and headed for the timbered riverbank with his brother close behind.

"That boy's a Lewis, all right," Shipman observed.

"How's that?" Frank asked.

"Any excuse, you-all slip off into the woods with a rifle on your arm."

"There's worse things a body could do," Frank said, his tone of voice poised somewhere between defensiveness and pique.

"I wasn't criticizing. Just observing. There ain't a thing wrong about that boy, Frank. Not that I ever yet seen."

Frank grunted, mollified by the compliment to his son.

"Is that a new rifle he's got?" Andrew asked, changing the subject.

Frank grinned. "Sure is. Got one of those new cap-fire locks too. It's three, four times quicker to shoot. You won't believe it. Why, I daresay now anybody can draw a steady bead."

"I've heard they don't shoot as hard as the flint," James said.

"No difference that I can see," Frank told them. "Wait till you try it."

"Not me," Andrew said. He reached into his pocket and fetched out a pipe and tobacco, crossing his legs and commencing the pleasant chore of loading and tamping the bowl. "Flint's been good enough all my life. I wouldn't want to try and take up something new now."

"I'd give it a try," James said.

"What about you, Sly?"

"Oh, I've tried it already. I have a pair of cap-lock pistols that I been known to carry now and then. I got no quarrel with new ways."

"I'll call the boys back while we still got a little light to shoot by," Frank offered. "They won't find no game anyhow."

"That's for sure." James frowned. It had been weeks, perhaps longer than that, since anyone took a deer within five miles of the Lewis farms. But then the whole reach of the Colorado for miles in either direction was taken up and occupied now as more and more people swarmed into Texas seeking the free land the republic was offering to immigrants. In some places even small game like squirrels and rabbits were becoming scarce. "Don't call them in," James said when Frank stood and turned to look in the direction his sons had taken. "It ain't game they're out there for. Leave them be, Frank. Better if we let them show off the rifle when Edward feels like crowing about it."

"That's thoughtful of you, James. You were asking about Michael? There he comes yonder. Wonder why Marie isn't with him." Frank pointed down the river, then shaded his eyes and shook his head. "No, by Godfrey, that ain't Michael. It's Mordecai coming by himself." He chuckled. "The boy's getting so tall I mistook him for Michael."

Michael's boy Mordecai, named for his grandfather, who lay buried in an unmarked grave on some empty Texas prairie, or at this point like as not buried beneath some farmer's newly broken field, was nearly the same age as Frank's son Edward, but Mordecai was a good half a head taller than his cousin and showed promise of someday reaching Michael's height.

"Hell," Sly Shipman observed, "anybody could mistake any one of you Lewises for any other. Put you all side by side in a pea pod and you couldn't be told apart."

That was an exaggeration, but not much. Some long-gone Lewis had left his stamp on all the sons who came after and the sons' sons and their sons in turn. Just as Michael looked like his father Mordecai so did Mordecai the son look like Michael. And Andrew and James too. The older Mordecai had looked much like his brother Benjamin, who was Frank's father, and the stamp was on Frank's sons too.

The Lewis men to one degree or another were all tall men, lean and wiry, their builds seemingly slight. But slight in their case did not equate to fragile, no more than the lash of a whip is delicate merely because it is slender.

Their faces tended to be long and their jaws sharply defined. They were high of forehead and cheekbone alike, and their mouths were thin without being cruel.

Their hair color varied to some extent, Benjamin's side of the family and therefore Frank's running to lighter shades than old Mordecai's, but all of them with hair that was straight and lank and resistant to civilized fussiness.

The most striking feature of the Lewises, and the one mark that seemed unvarying, was their eyes. James could look at Michael's eyes or at Andrew's and see the same that he found in his own shaving mirror, eyes a startling pale blue, clear as springwater and bright as a buttermilk sky in summertime. Annie had the Lewis eyes too although, mercifully, she lacked some of the other physical traits. And Angeline had them also; combined with her mother's dark hair and golden complexion, Angeline's bright blue eyes were hypnotically intense. They contributed much to the beauty that was forming within her.

But for Frank to mistake a youngster like Mordecai for his father . . . ? James took a look for himself, and danged if he couldn't see it too. Mordecai came stepping along at the edge of the woods with a rifle lying in the crook of his arm as natural as if it had grown there and a brace of squirrels dangling from his free hand. Lordy, if that didn't look just like Michael as James remembered him from when they were boys.

"I'll carry these t' the house and be right back," Mordecai said as he passed. "Mama and Pap will be along in another minute."

"Your cousins are down in the woods somewhere," Frank told him.

"Seen 'em already, thank you." He marched on toward Andrew's cabin to deliver the meat that was his contribution to the party.

"There they come," Andrew said, pointing.

Michael, Marie, and Angeline were in sight now, coming along the path that would take them past Petra's garden. The path was the shorter route but being in the open offered no last-moment opportunity to take game, which was probably why Mordecai had chosen to leave early and go out of his way. The boy did indeed take after his father, James thought, and he could not help but wonder what sort of man his own son would prove to be.

His own son. For some reason—for many reasons—he was convinced, had convinced himself that is, that the child who lay within Libby's swelling belly was a boychild. Another Lewis boy who in his time would become another Lewis man.

Lordy, Lordy. Just thinking about that was enough to give James the shivers.

A son of his own—thinking about that was enough to make him feel proud, of course. But solemn too. Teaching a son, guiding him, raising him up to be tall and true: that was a serious responsibility, a special sort of thing indeed. He looked at young Mordecai disappearing into the dogtrot of Andrew's place and then back across the field toward Michael and Marie. They were managing well enough with Mordecai and with Angeline. James figured he could do his damn-sure best too. He supposed that was about all a man could do.

"Is one of you coffee coolers gonna come help me tote all this or are you just gonna watch?" Michael called when he was close enough to be heard. He was heavily laden with pots and bundles, mostly Marie's last-second additions, or else Mordecai would have been burdened with a share of the chore.

"Reckon we'll watch, thanks," Andrew drawled. But then he and James both hurried to meet their older brother and take part of the load from him.

James sniffed at the aroma rising out of a covered pottery bowl he was handed. Whatever it was smelled wonderful. And all the family, all that were in Texas anyway, gathered together here to see Andrew off to the capital. Life itself was pretty dang wonderful.

☆ Chapter ☆

3

"Stab me a chunk o' that ham, would you, Mordecai? No, no need to pass the whole plate, just spear me that chunk on top there. Thanks." James grinned at his nephew and held his plate for the slice of home-cured ham. The hogs they'd brought in had established well in the woods along the river, where they were allowed to run free in search of their groceries. Now that the game had been cleaned out of the country so thoroughly, the only natural enemies that hogs had to worry about were the Blackwood brothers, who lived on the other side of the river. The Blackwoods were noted for a tendency to help themselves to whatever was loose. Except for that, the hogs were doing well, and tasted mighty fine the way Annie cured them in the mud-chinked smokehouse the men had gotten together to build for her.

"Blackwood," Michael said. Michael was seated just the other side of Mordecai, and for a moment James thought his older brother had somehow been reading his mind when he gave thought to the Blackwoods and their hog stealing. Then he looked up and saw that that wasn't it at all.

"H'lo, Cyrus," James said with a smile. "If you're hungry, son, grab you a plate and find a place to light. Mordecai, whyn't you shift over just a bit so Cyrus can get in between us."

The boy stood where he was, glancing nervously back and forth between smiling James and scowling Michael. He obviously didn't know whether he was being welcomed here or resented. The truth, of course, was that both applied. Michael hated the child as he hated all Blackwoods; James insisted on being hopeful that Cyrus might yet take after his dead uncle—possibly his father—Isaac.

The Blackwoods had been neighbors of the Lewises back in Tennessee. There had been bad blood between the families for many years, all the more so after old Cyrus Blackwood, namesake of the youngster who had walked up the path from the river just now, first came to Texas with James's father, Mordecai, and with Michael on that ill-fated expedition. Cyrus Blackwood showed his true colors after Mordecai was murdered by the Spanish and Michael was grievously wounded. Blackwood abandoned Michael on the prairie and left him to die. Only the help of another survivor and the nursing care of a Mexican family—Petra's family—enabled Michael to live, and to return to Tennessee to become a thorn in the Blackwoods' sides.

The Lewises thought they were shut of the Blackwood tribe until like bad pennies they showed up in Texas and for some reason, likely simple meanness, chose to take up land within stone-tossing distance of the Lewises again.

By then the old man was dead, survived by one-armed Finis—the arm was lost to Michael's bullet on an occasion when Finis tried to murder Michael from hiding but succeeded only in wounding Benjamin Lewis—and half-witted Luke, and by the youngest boy, Isaac.

Despite the lack of any semblance of decency in his upbringing, Isaac had been as honest as his brothers would allow. If Isaac had lived, James still believed, there might have been real hope that young Cyrus would be raised to become the best of all the Blackwoods. There was considerable room for doubt about the boy's parentage, and Isaac had admitted to James that he thought of himself as Cyrus's father. During the recent war for independence, he had also gotten James to promise that he would keep an eye on the boy as much as possible if anything happened to Isaac. Isaac and James had spoken more intimately then than any Lewis and Blackwood likely ever had. Then James had ridden off to look for his own fight while Isaac remained behind—at the Alamo.

Now Finis and Luke remained along with a passel of children, with Cyrus at thirteen or thereabouts being the eldest. The children's mothers were a line of slatternly women with so little self-respect that they would take up with a Blackwood. James had heard that the latest had run off, and the Blackwoods were bachelors again. If that was so then Libby and Annie could probably expect to see dirty faces in the yards now and then in the silent entreaty that was the Blackwoods' preferred method of begging. The kids would start showing up soon, and likely the women would feed them, Libby and Annie the most because they were closest, Petra and Marie and Frank's wife, Hope, somewhat less often. Not that James blamed or begrudged. A man couldn't let children starve no matter their name. But a man could resent the kind of neighbor who would make such a thing necessary.

"Go on, Cyrus, it's all right. Ain't it, Michael?" James frowned. More loudly this time he drawled, "I said ain't it all right for the boy to set and have something to eat, Michael?"

"Yes, that's right, Cyrus. Have you something to eat."

Only when Michael spoke did Mordecai comply with his uncle's wish and slide over to make room for Cyrus.

"I didn't . . . . I didn't come here t' ask nothing t' eat, Mister Lewis," the boy stammered.

"Oh?"

"No, sir. I come with a message. From my pa. For Mister Andrew."

Andrew had been sitting quietly nearby. He had little more use for any Blackwood than Michael did. Now he leaned forward and showed some interest. "What message would that be, boy?"

"It's t' do with you going off t' the congress, Mister Andrew. My pa says that you're t' mind you represent the all o' us, sir. An' not do what you want but what we'uns wants you t' do down there."

"Your papa said all that, did he?"

"Yes, sir. He says I'm t' tell you, sir, that him and all the other voters o' this here county, sir, they're all for holding the spending down, sir, an' not wasting money on all them ranging companies, sir. An' that's what I'm supposed t' tell you, sir." The boy bobbed his head, and a look of intense concentration eased as he reviewed what he'd said and decided he had remembered to tell all that he was instructed.

Andrew laughed. "Boy, if your papa and your uncle want the ranging companies reduced then they're sure up to something that they oughtn't be. Thank you for letting us know."

"I wouldn't know about that, sir."

Andrew grunted, not bothering to hide his sarcasm. Michael snorted and paid no more attention to the young Blackwood.

"You said what you were told to, Cyrus, and you did just fine with it," James said. "Now you can relax and have yourself that bite to eat."

"I dunno, Mister Lewis."

"Are you hungry, Cyrus?"

The look in the boy's eyes was answer enough. James could as good as see the saliva commence to flow in his mouth at the sight and smell of all the good food that was piled from one end of the long table to the other.

"We have more'n enough, son. Come share it with us."

James expected that Cyrus would dig into the meal, as he did. But James was saddened yet at the same time encouraged to observe the youngster sneaking choice bits of meat and pone inside his shirt to carry away, saddened that such a deception was necessary but encouraged to see that Cyrus was looking out for his younger brothers and sisters enough to steal food for them. And wasn't it a helluva note when seeing a child steal food could be thought any sort of a good thing.

James finished his meal quickly after that, much of his appetite killed by Cyrus's visit. Later, after the boy had gone, the Lewis men and Sly Shipman repaired to the woodpile and Sly's jug of Kentucky corn. Mordecai and Frank's boys sat quiet nearby but weren't offered the jug and weren't expected to participate in the talk.

"Those Blackwoods are up to something illegal," Andrew said.

"That's about the same thing as saying those Blackwoods are still alive and breathing, isn't it?" Michael observed.

"Point is, I'd like to know what it is. I won't mind if they get their own tails caught in a crack, but they usually spread their troubles around for all to share. Whatever they're doing, I just hope it ain't something that will come back on those of us as lives this side o' the river."

Shipman helped himself to a swallow of his own product and said, "I'll look into it. I can still find answers in places where you boys can't even find the questions. If you know what I mean."

"You do that, Sly. And if they're up to something . . ." Andrew closed his mouth and sadly shook his head. There was no sense in adding more. The Lewises were entering a third generation without being able to find any satisfactory deterrent to the Blackwood's inclinations.

"Come on now, boys," Michael said loudly. "We didn't come here to fret about Blackwoods. We came here to give our congressional kinsman a send-off. So are we gonna do that or not?" He grinned and stood. "Frank, where's your banjo?"

"I'll get it for you, Daddy," David volunteered.

"Somebody build that fire up good and bright so we can see what we're doing. And bring those women out here to where we can get at them too. They been hiding in that house there telling gossip long enough. It's time we get down to some serious celebrating," Michael announced.

Michael commenced to clapping, then Andrew did, and pretty soon the children took it up, which brought the women smiling out into the dogtrot to see what the excitement was. The few moments of concern caused by poor Cyrus were quickly forgotten.

☆ Chapter ☆

4

James ambled along at Libby's side, enjoying the clean smell of the night air—morning air was closer to the mark really, it being so late by the time the party broke up—and the feel of it crisp and cool against his skin. He walked with his coat and shirt unbuttoned so the cold air could reach his sweat-slippery ribs, overheated by the exertions of the drinking and the gorging and the dancing that they'd been doing all evening long. He carried his rifle in one hand and Libby's Dutch oven in the other. The iron vessel was empty and scrubbed. The corn pudding had been a success, and so Libby seemed every bit as pleased tonight as James felt.

He edged a little closer to Libby and then closer yet, bumping into her hip just a little as they walked and staying close so that his hip began to nudge hers with each matching step they took.

"James!" she whispered as if fearful she might be overheard.

"That's me," he answered cheerfully.

"Don't be doing that, James."

If he'd had a hand free he would have put an arm around her. Or taken her hand. Or something. But he didn't. He bumped her with his hip again.

"No," she snapped quite sharply.

"I just . . ."

"I know what you 'just,' mister. What you can 'just' is to just leave me be tonight. Aside from being in the family way with your child, James Lewis, I'm 'just' having a headache, a truly horrid headache, and I 'just' can't handle but so much at one time. All right?"

"I'm sorry, Libby, why didn't you tell me? The way you were

dancing right up to the very end there I never suspected that . . ."

"What are you accusing me of, James?" Her pace quickened and she stepped a little to the side as well, putting distance between them.

"Nothing." His tone of voice was perplexed, and quite genuinely so: he was concerned about her. He certainly hadn't meant to accuse her of anything.

"I have a headache, I tell you," Libby said peevishly.

"Of course you do, dear. Tell you what, soon as we get home I'll build a nice fire in the stove and put you on some comfrey tea. Would you like that?"

Libby paused for a moment before she answered, "Yes, James, I think I would like some comfrey tonight." Her voice was softer now and she walked a little closer to him again, no longer seeming in such a hurry to draw away.

"Quick as we're home," he promised. "I sure wish you'd told me, Libby. I surely do."

"You know I never want to burden you, James. You know I try to be a good wife to you."

"I know you do, Libby. I surely know that."

Libby moved closer yet so that they were making slight contact at hip and shoulder as they walked side by side in the night.

Michael Lewis walked slowly, one arm around his wife's waist and his hand riding lightly on her hip. Marie moved beside him as smoothly and as naturally as if they were joined together. But then, he reminded himself, they were.

Angeline walked a few paces ahead of her parents, on feet so light and lively she looked as if she was still dancing—or floating. Sometimes she seemed graceful as a bird in flight. Angeline had enjoyed the evening as much as any of them, Michael thought, with the pleasure he so often had when he observed his own children.

Mordecai wasn't going home with them. He and Frank's eldest boy, Edward, had put their heads together this evening and plotted an excursion of some sort. Their stated purpose was to go off in search of game, but that was merely an excuse. What they really wanted was to go off somewhere with a rifle in hand and a blanket over the shoulder and nothing else to burden them. Where they went and what they did mattered little; the freedom to take up a rifle and move along was what they craved. It was a feeling

Michael could well understand, for such a feeling had nagged and gnawed at him all his life. But then, it was a feeling that had given him a deep and abiding joy too. There was nothing else quite like the sight of the far slope on that next hill over.

Angeline reached the step that led onto the dogtrot of their cabin. She went up it as if she were rising on the air itself and disappeared into the half-cabin side that she shared with her parents. Mordecai's often empty bed was in the kitchen side of the cabin, which was built in typical fashion with two small log structures set facing each other and joined into one unit by the dogtrot and a roof that was common to all three sections.

Michael slowed and came to a halt in front of the cabin that had been their home for so many years now. Marie stayed warm and close at his side. She lifted her face to look at him, and there was moonlight enough that he could see how pretty she remained after all this time.

"What are you thinking, Michael?" Her voice was as soft as the look in her eyes.

"'Bout how handsome a woman you are," he answered truthfully.

"Pooh."

"I mean it."

"Good. I am glad that you do. But pooh." She smiled.

"There's something I keep forgetting t' tell you to do, Marie."

"And what is that, Michael?"

"You need t' find something heavy. A sadiron, maybe. An' you need t' set that thing plumb atop your daughter's head. Keep that young 'un from growing any more. I say she's growed enough now. Time she slacks off and stays just like she is for the next eight, ten years. Give me time to collect my strength before all the eager bucks come snorting around the door."

"You should have thought of this long ago, Michael. I fear it is much too late now. Angeline is soon a woman, no?"

"No," Michael said. "No, dang it, she ain't."

"But *oui*, Michael, she is," Marie said simply. "Very soon."

"I ain't ready for this, Marie."

"No father has ever been ready for this. Did you not know? Never in all of time. But never has this stopped daughters from becoming women."

"I wish . . ." He stopped and shrugged. He didn't honestly know what he wished. Not on this subject, he didn't. Marie seemed to understand. That was no surprise; Marie nearly always understood. No matter what his feelings, she sensed them. She laid a fingertip gently over his lips to shush him and then laid her cheek just as gently against his chest, both her arms slipping around his waist as she held herself pressed warm and secure to her husband's body. They stood in the night like that for several minutes, Marie offering unspoken comfort while Michael stroked the back of her head and enjoyed the silky feel of her hair beneath his palm. There were a few streaks of bright gray amid the raven softness now. Those bits of contrast only seemed to make her the more beautiful to him. And he was in no position to judge harshly on that score anyway: his own hair was quite liberally laced with gray nowadays. There were so very many things that were changing, just all of a sudden like—and none of them for the good, either.

"Come to bed, my Michael. It is late."

"Yeah." But when Marie drew away from him and they both went up onto the dogtrot, Michael paused at the door. "Go on inside. I want to walk out and see that everything's all right."

Marie offered no protest. She went up onto tiptoes to give him a peck on the shelf of his jaw and then disappeared inside the warm cabin.

Michael settled his old rifle in the crook of his arm and went through the dogtrot to the back. A dry branch cracked loudly in the night, followed instantly by a scuffling noise in the loose bark and wood chips that surrounded the woodpile. Most likely a hog brave enough to come scavenge for tidbits close to the house but not brave enough to want to be seen doing it. Michael smiled a little.

He stepped down off the dogtrot floor and, with Marie not here to observe, allowed himself the luxury of a wince. His knees pained him these days, not constant pain and not acute, but too frequent and too sharp for comfort. And it wasn't only his knees that hurt, either. Both hips were getting bad, and there was a near-constant dull aching in his wrists and knuckles. It was getting so it was uncomfortable to sit a horse, dammit, or to climb things or stand too long or walk too long or . . . or do most anything like a man ought, it sometimes seemed to him.

He wasn't old, dammit. He really wasn't. Just in his middle years, that was all. So why all of a sudden was he falling to pieces? All those years, all those countless nights of sleeping on hard ground with a scattering of stars to serve as a blanket and a chunk of wood for a pillow, that was probably what this was, all of it catching up with him now. He clenched his teeth—the way things were going lately, they would probably be the next thing to go—and turned away from the woodpile, silent now, to peer off into the night toward the river and the beckoning horizon beyond it.

Mordecai was out there somewhere, out awandering with a rifle and a blanket and all the vigor and freedom of youth. He was a good boy, Mordecai. A wonderful son. And right at this moment Michael Lewis wished he too was out there in the night, out there young and strong and with a horizon to pull him forward. It had been a long time since Michael left hearth and home to take himself a sashay away from the sight of chimney smoke and plowed fields. An awful long time. He would never have admitted it to Marie nor to anyone else in the family, but the biggest part of the reason why he'd been staying home so faithfully of late was that the aches and pains made it hard for him to travel these days. It wasn't like it used to be. Nothing was.

He sighed. Some things were the same. Inside, underneath all those stupid impediments posed by his own aging and long-abused body, deep inside where the real Michael Lewis lived, *nothing* had changed.

Deep inside he still felt as strong and as vital as when he was Mordecai's age. Did old men feel that way too? Not that he was old yet, of course. But really old men, did they remain young down deep inside? Michael was beginning to suspect that maybe they did.

Aw, this kind of thinking wasn't getting him anywhere. He chided himself for wasting his time like this and turned his back on the vast emptiness that lay far off to the west, out there where his Mordecai was roaming now. It was warm inside the cabin, and Marie was waiting for him there.

Michael winced only a little at the pain in his knee when he climbed back onto the dogtrot and went to join his wife in the bed they had shared for all these years.

Andrew waited in silence while Petra went to check one last time on the pile of tangled limbs and cherubic faces that had grown on the spare cornshuck mattress as first one child and then another gave up sleepy-eyed wonder and exchanged it for slumber. Every child in the clan under the age of twelve or thereabouts was lying now on the floor in front of the stove in Andrew's cabin. His and Petra's own two, eleven-year-old Ben and motherly—ofttimes bossy, but you'd get an argument started if she ever heard that opinion expressed—Rose, who was nine, were somewhere in amongst the nest of wiggle-worms.

He hadn't even left yet, and already Andrew was missing the children.

And Petra.

She came back to his side and eyed the freshly filled pipe he was holding. "You are not tired, Andrew?"

"A little," he admitted, "but there'll be time enough for sleeping after I get to Houston."

"I have not changed my mind," she said, guessing what he wanted to talk about in the middle of what might be their last night together for some months.

"I know." He nodded agreeably enough but was not inclined to give in without one more try.

"We should go outside. Not to wake the children, you know?"

Again Andrew nodded. He squeezed Petra's hand and left her standing where she was while he made his way silently around the sleeping children to the stove. He plucked a wisp of straw off one of the fresh-made brooms he had fashioned for her and touched the straw to a coal. The dull cherry light given off by the bed of coals flared bright yellow as the straw burst into flame. Andrew cupped the flame with his hand so the sudden light would not disturb the children. He held it to his pipe and lighted the tobacco surface, then dropped the straw back into the stove, where it blazed briefly and was quickly consumed. Andrew had to stay where he was a moment longer while his vision adjusted to dim light once more, then he was able to edge past the children without stepping on any stray fingers. Petra stood waiting by the door. Her expression at the moment showed more stubbornness than affection. He took her shawl down off its peg and draped it about her shoulders before they went out into the predawn cold.

They sat on a split log bench that young Ben had proudly made for them this summer past. For a time they sat there in silence, shoulder pressed warm against shoulder, the only sound the bubbling hiss of the burning tobacco in the bowl of Andrew's pipe.

After a while Petra leaned her head against her husband's shoulder, and he put his arm around her. "I have not changed my mind," she repeated in a whisper.

"I know," he said again.

This obliquely hinted disagreement was as close as either of them wanted to come to a fight on this last night.

Not that they had fought about the subject before, either—not xactly. But they certainly disagreed about it.

Andrew wanted Petra and the children to move to Houston with him. He wanted, in fact, for the family to make their home there now that he was a member of Congress. They would keep the farm, of course. They would want to come back to it to visit, often. And Michael and James and Frank and Sly could use any part of it they wished and be welcome to the fruits of their labors. It was just that Andrew had been too many places now, had seen too many wondrous sights, to be so easily contented as in the past. He had been traveling a great deal since the republic was declared, had become more and more involved in the politics of creating a new nation. It was exciting stuff, he had learned. And his newfound knowledge had shown him fresh horizons that he had never before suspected, much less thought about.

During the election campaign, and all the more so after it, he had spent nights in fine hotels where the suppers were cooked and delivered by smiling servants, where there were rugs on smooth polished floors, and clean sheets every night, and candles made of scented wax instead of guttering tallow. He had eaten his meals off of elegant china and been served brandy and cigars afterward.

And there were homes that were every bit as grand and as elegant as any of those hotels, private homes. Homes owned by men who were little different, and certainly not a lick better, than Andrew Lewis. Homes kept by women who weren't half so pretty or half so fine as Petra Lewis.

And after all, there wasn't a thing wrong with a man wanting to better himself. That was what freedom was all about, wasn't it? That was the very reason Texas had fought and won its independence and the reason why Texas might, or might not, want to join itself to the States now.

Bettering himself and his family was all Andrew was trying to do here.

But Petra was balking. She was afraid of change, untrusting of city people and city ways. Petra hadn't seen all the wonderful things that Andrew had. She had little concept of how grand things could be. Petra had grown up on a dirt-poor farm near Nacogdoches and after her marriage lived on another dirt-poor farm near San Felipe de Austin. She had had so very little chance to come up in the world. Andrew tried to explain it all to her. But she kept insisting that she and the children belonged here on the farm, that Andrew's place was indeed in Houston, but only when Congress was in session, that he should hire a room, not a house, when he got there and then hurry home to his family—and his constituents—as quickly as the session ended. She believed that this farm was enough for happiness—this farm and her family, that is.

Petra feared the city would be unhealthful for the children, citing over and over to him Houston's reputation as a dismal and pestilential swampland. And health was only the half of it, she insisted, refusing to enumerate her other fears but trembling and shuddering over them. It was almost as if she thought Houston an immoral place. No matter what he tried, Andrew had been unable to shake Petra's conviction on this subject. Whenever he tried to discuss it with her of late she became so agitated that she lost her English and lapsed back into the Spanish that was her first and still foremost tongue. He should go off to the capital alone, she insisted hotly; she and the children would remain here on the farm awaiting his return. She would love him, she would miss him, she would be here whenever he found time to return.

Now husband and wife sat silent in the night, Andrew smoking his pipe and Petra thinking her unvoiced thoughts. In a few more hours the sun would rise, and it would be time for Andrew to saddle his horse and ride east to the new, still very raw and growing capital at the city named for Sam Houston.

Until then, dang it, he could still hope she would yet change her mind and agree to move to Houston with him.

And after that, no matter what, he would love her then as much as he had for all these years they'd shared.

Andrew smoked his pipe in the silence of the night and knew that things really were not so very bad after all. Not so long as he had Petra and the children, one place or another.

"It is late," Petra said once, her hand creeping into his and their fingers lacing tight together.

"Yes," he agreed.

But neither of them moved, as if both were suddenly afraid to let go of the sense of closeness that so unexpectedly wrapped itself around them.

☆ Chapter ☆

5

Houston was raw but plenty exciting. In the eight months or so since Andrew last saw the capital of the young republic, new buildings had sprung up like mushrooms—Petra would've said toadstools—after a spring rain. The streets came one of two ways, depending on the weather: knee-deep ruts or hip-deep mud. There wasn't enough timber available to build with logs here, so lumber was cut and sold as fast as sweating workmen in the sawpits could strip one saleable log into half a dozen even more saleable boards. The uncured boards were spiked or pegged in place and almost immediately began to warp and spring. There was no paint to slap onto the boards and no time to fret over such trivialities even if there had been paint available; after all, a wall already in place was yesterday's wage. Today was what mattered. And tomorrow.

Representative Andrew Lewis walked the streets and the pine-slash corduroy sidewalks and marveled at all the bustle and excitement he could feel in the air about him.

Houston felt alive with possibilities. New nation, new city, new opportunities. Houston felt like a place where anything might happen.

"Congressman. Yo there. Congressman."

A man wearing a carpenter's apron and wielding a maul nudged Andrew and said, "Hey, bub, I think it's you that man wants."

"Mmm? Oh, thanks." Andrew grinned. "I was woolgathering."

"Yeah sure," the carpenter said without interest. He marched off down a side street. Andrew stood on the corner and waited for a fellow who was scurrying toward him, dodging traffic and leaping ruts and breathing rather heavily. That carpenter might have thought the man wanted Andrew, but Andrew had never seen him before and could not imagine why a stranger would be approaching him on the streets now. Still, it did indeed appear as if it was Andrew whom the fellow wanted with all the frantic gesturing.

"Congressman Lewis?" the wheezing, panting messenger gasped when finally he did reach Andrew.

"That's right."

The man smiled broadly and extended his hand. "What a pleasure to meet you at last, Congressman."

"Really?" Andrew was confused, but willing enough. He shook the fellow's hand and took a moment to assess the stranger.

From a distance he had given an impression of youth. Up close, though, Andrew could see that he was at least in his thirties, possibly even his forties. His small stature made him appear younger than he was, for he probably stood no more than five foot three and was roundly plump. Anyone observing this man next to lanky Andrew in his rough homespun was no doubt amused by the contrasts between them, because it was every bit as apparent in the two men's mode of dress as in their height and build. The stranger wore a beaver hat that was too large for him and a cutaway coat that had seen better days, but his clothing had been rather fine in its day and still was more presentable in polite company than Andrew's ill-fitting garments and floppy hat.

"A pleasure indeed," the little man said, pumping Andrew's hand with vigor.

"I reckon you have the advantage of me then, neighbor," Andrew said mildly, wanting to extricate his hand from the little man's grip but not quite sure how to go about it without giving offense.

"I do? I mean . . . dear me. Ha ha, how stupid of me. Allow me to introduce myself, Congressman Lewis. I am, sir"—at which point he finally let go of Andrew's hand and swept his beaver off, following the gesture through into an actual bow, quite certainly the only time Andrew Lewis had ever been bowed to—"Christopher Columbus Campodoro."

"Well I'm right sure I'm pleased t' meet you, Mr. Campodoro."

"Please, Congressman. The pleasure is mine. And it will be my pleasure to make sure that your visit to the capital is as enjoyable as possible for you."

Andrew lifted an eyebrow at that odd statement. Whoever this

Christopher Columbus etc. fella was, Andrew couldn't see much reason for him to take on to any such extent as that.

"I see that once again, sir, I assume too much. I am not making myself clear. I am a, um, what you might call a personal assistant to the president of our republic, sir. And as President Lamar is particularly anxious to have the benefit of your counsel, Congressman Lewis, I have been asked to see that you are established in such a way that nothing will, shall we say, interfere with your concentration on the matters of state."

"That's a mouthful, Mr. Campodoro—"

"Christopher to you, sir," the little man corrected.

"That's real nice, I'm sure, Christopher. An' I'm Andrew. But I think maybe I'm not following all o' this as close as I ought."

Campodoro smiled. He had an absolutely beatific smile, wide and bright and filled with joy. It was the sort of smile that no one could fail to respond to favorably. When Campodoro smiled like that he looked years younger, young and innocent and open to all the joys this world has to offer. It was the sort of smile that no one could look at and fail to trust. Andrew was no exception to that rule.

"But you see, Congressman, you are a *most* valued representative. Your advice and your goodwill are important to the president. And he, or actually some of his close friends and advisors whom it is my privilege to help from time to time, they have asked me to see to your comfort and your, um, successful introduction into the ways of getting things done here in the capital."

"Meaning?"

"Meaning, Congressman, that I shall be pleased to assist you in any way that I can."

During this conversation, Christopher Columbus Campodoro had grasped Andrew by the elbow and turned him so that they were headed now toward a quarter of the city with which Andrew was as yet unfamiliar. With Campodoro urging him along, Andrew and the presidential aide began to stroll in that direction.

"For instance," Campodoro was saying, "I learned this morning that you took a room with Mrs. Enriquez, mmm?"

"That's right, I did. Nice lady."

"Yes she is," Campodoro agreed. "But she charges much too much for her rooms, we've found."

Now that, finally, was a subject on which Andrew had some definite thoughts of his own. "Ain't that the truth," he said forcefully. "Why, that woman was wantin' near all my day-rate just for a room. No board, mind. Just the one room. And I was lucky t' find it, or so everybody says. Rooms, they ain't easy t' come by in Houston, Mr. Campodoro."

"Please call me Christopher, Congressman. And I sympathize with your plight. Everyone new has the same trouble. By the time the new members arrive, all the available rooms have been spoken for. Which is why the president's advisors wanted to make sure you manage to escape that trap. Before you ever arrived, you see, these gentlemen asked me to arrange for you to stay at my own boardinghouse."

"Really?"

"Yes, indeed, Congressman. I engaged a very nice room for you. Second story, overlooking the street. And the rate, you will find, is less per week than Mrs. Enriquez charges per night."

"No!"

"Oh, I mean it, Congressman. I wouldn't fun you about that."

"But Mrs. Enriquez—"

"Now, Congressman, don't you worry about a thing. I've already explained the situation to Mrs. Enriquez. I went there first, you see, when I was looking for you. She's the one who told me which direction you'd gone off in. So while I was there, Congressman, I cleared that little matter up. She didn't mind. She already had a waiting list of clients. In fact, as I was leaving I heard her tell a boy, cute little big-eyed tad of eight or so . . ."

"That'd be her grandson Jose," Andrew put in.

"Right. Whatever. Anyway, Congressman, as I was leaving, Mrs. Enriquez was already sending little Jose out to find another gentleman whose name was next on the list and give him your room."

"But—"

"Now don't you worry. Haven't I made that clear? There isn't a thing you need to worry about. By now your things have already been taken to your new room. Probably by now Lexie has everything unpacked and freshly brushed and put away again."

"Lexie?"

"Later. You'll meet Lexie and the others later." Campodoro smiled that smile again, and Andrew felt much better even if he remained somewhat confused. "You're going to just love Lexie. I guarantee it."

"But—"

"You still have questions. Of course you do. Can't blame you a bit for that." Campodoro still had Andrew by the elbow. Now he was steering him off the street and into a doorway. There was no sign posted, but once inside it was clear what the place was. A salon, Andrew understood them to be called. One of those establishments where gentlemen meet to sit and talk and read and drink and whatever else gents do in such places. Andrew knew of salons but had never actually been inside one. He'd seen his share of cantinas and the like, but never a salon. This one had lamps that were fringed with red crystal drops like so many rubies, and bright polished brass spittoons, and a long bar at the back with a mirror on the wall behind it, and so many glasses and bottles and fancy jugs that it was a wonder a body could keep track of them all.

"You're a gentleman who appreciates a dram now and again, aren't you, Congressman?" Campodoro asked with a boyishly cheerful smile.

"I been known to enjoy a snort, sure. Nothin' serious, but a little now an' then never hurts."

"Splendid," Campodoro cried as if that news were quite wonderful indeed. "Then why don't we sit, Congressman . . . no, over there, that chair will be much more comfortable for you, I think . . . why don't we sit and share some spirits while I answer every tiny question you might have, mmm?"

Andrew hardly had time to seat himself before there was a bald man in an apron standing there asking what the gentlemen's pleasure might be and behind him a colored girl carrying a tray of sweetmeats to offer and . . . hell, Andrew Lewis was commencing to know what royalty must feel like when they walked into a place and got fawned over.

He was commencing to know that feeling for the first time in his life and, truth be told, to discover that it wasn't all that bad a dang feeling.

For a fleeting moment he wondered how Petra would respond to this kind of high-blown treatment. Lordy, this was the way a woman as beautiful and as dear as Petra deserved to be treated. Each and every day she deserved that, Andrew thought. Then that nice little man Christopher Columbus Campodoro was talking again, and there wasn't time enough for Andrew to be thinking about the wife and family he'd left back at the farm. He sipped from the glass that was put down for him, nibbled at one of the tasty sweetmeats, and listened to what-all Chris was telling him.

☆ Chapter ☆

6

Andrew yawned, stretched, and reached underneath the sheet to scratch himself. Heavy draperies were hung over the window which, as promised, fronted the busy street below, but the folds of cloth failed to block all the bright daylight beyond. Andrew had no idea what time it was but knew it was well past the dawning—hours past, quite possibly. He had never slept so late in his life as he was beginning to do here.

He smiled a little, thinking about the reaction he would get from his brothers if this proved to be a habit that would be carried home with him. Oh, wouldn't they rag him about it.

He stretched again, scratched again. The thing was, while he was doing all this pondering and imagining he was yet lying slugabed with his eyes squeezed tight shut against the bit of light at the edges of the drapes. It felt so nice just to lie right there. It did.

And there wasn't any reason why he should have to leap out of bed, was there?

None, and that was the truth. No reason at all. No cow to milk nor flock to feed. No ox to yoke or mule to harness. No field to plant nor row to tend.

Here a man could lie abed until noon and yet get all his day's work done. And wasn't that a fearsome strange thing to recognize.

The way his functions as a representative in the lower house were evolving, Andrew had until past noon to get himself around. Then half a dozen or so of the more favored congressmen—Andrew Lewis among them—would gather for a brief caucus. On rare occasions President Lamar might join them. More often the president's views would be put forward by Christopher or by

Junius Randal, who was an exceptionally close personal friend and advisor to the president and well above Christopher Campodoro in the order of things. At least one of those gentlemen would be on hand, however, to present the president's wishes to the caucus. Then late in the afternoon there might be a vote, Andrew and his new friends voting as a bloc. And then they would all be free to repair to supper and brandy and the rounds of late caucuses that often ran far into the night.

It was exciting, this being at the center of things, Andrew silently conceded to himself now in the privacy of his bedroom. Certainly more exciting than bucking the handles of a plow and watching the backside of an ox day in and day out.

It was exciting and it was important. Why, the things they were deciding here and now were things that would affect the citizens of the republic for years and years to come.

Education, for instance: that was one of the issues President Lamar campaigned upon. President Lamar intended Texas to be a leader among nations when it came to the education of its citizens. Already plans were being laid to provide land grants for the establishment of colleges, and soon each individual county would be given grant lands also to provide for free schools, open to the children of every citizen.

Money was a problem, of course. But Texas was rich in land if not in cash. And back in the United States there were thousands upon thousands of men who yearned for just such farmlands as Texas had to offer them. President Lamar wanted to encourage immigration at a level even greater than former president Sam Houston envisioned.

Houston, Andrew thought sleepily. The republic owed the old campaigner much, there was no denying that. But now that he was on the inside, Andrew was learning that Houston had been about as poor a president as he was grand a general. All Andrew's friends in Congress understood that, and explained it to him. President Lamar, that good man, was steadfastly at odds with Houston. It must have been awful for Mirabeau Lamar, having to serve Houston as vice-president for a full term of office. Now, of course, Lamar was free to correct Houston's mistakes—if he could get the votes he needed in the house and senate, that is.

And that right there was where Andrew Lewis and others of the president's good and true supporters came in. That right there was the reason for all the caucuses and the late nights and the whispered consultations. In Congress there still were some shortsighted men who would cling to the Houston policies if they were able. Andrew and forward-thinking men like him had to stand fast for Lamar if they hoped to take Texas on to the position of leadership and prosperity that was its due.

Andrew yawned again and rolled over, burrowing his cheek into the feather-stuffed pillow. He was undecided. If he got up now he might still be in time to take breakfast with the other early-rising gentlemen in the house. But if he dozed, well, he was sure he could manage a breakfast anytime. They were so accommodating here. So considerate. Why, . . .

The click of the door latch brought him out of his state of half-sleep with a heart-pounding leap.

His eyes came open and he began to sit upright in the rumpled bed.

Quite as quickly as he'd begun to rise, Andrew flung himself backward onto the mattress and grabbed for the covers, pulling them tight to his chin in an effort to make sure he was covered. After all, dang it, he was wearing only his smallclothes to sleep in. He wasn't at all decent.

"Lexie!" he bawled.

The girl covered her face with her hands to hide a giggle. Andrew wouldn't have said she was particularly successful at it. "I am sorry, Andrew."

"You don't sound very sorry."

"That is because I am not very sorry. But I will try to be more sorry if it makes you happy." She giggled again.

"Lexie," he admonished. "Darn it anyhow."

"I will try to remember, Andrew." She smiled. "I am getting better, am I not? I remember to call you Andrew, do I not?"

"You do," he agreed.

"That is better, no?"

"That is better, yes."

Lexie beamed as if she'd been paid a compliment. In a manner of speaking she had. It had taken Andrew more than a week to convince her that she should refer to him informally. At first she'd insisted on "Congressman" or "sir" or worse. It had made him uncomfortable.

Well, that hadn't been anything like the discomfort he was experiencing now, with Lexie parading about inside his room while Andrew lay here with hardly anything on beneath the covers. Even with the door standing open, that wasn't right. Particularly when Lexie was such an undeniably pretty thing.

She was, he guessed, eighteen or twenty, with a flawless olive complexion, flashing dark eyes, and hair as black and shiny as a raven's wing. She wore her hair loose and allowed it to flow shimmering down her back. Her figure—not a subject Andrew wanted to dwell upon but one that was impossible for a man to fail to notice, considering the poor and flimsy garments Lexie possessed—was sleek and trim in some places but rounded and lush in others. And everywhere it was, quite frankly, exciting. Her face was heart shaped, her lips full, and her cheekbones high. She was a real beauty. Not in Petra's class, of course. But then no woman was. In some ways, though, Lexie reminded Andrew of Petra as his wife had been when she was Lexie's age. Both were dark beauties and both had a lithe and graceful way of moving.

On the other hand something about Lexie was lacking, some inner fire or resolve, perhaps. Lexie seemed as eager as a pup to please the boarders, but if she had any preferences or opinions of her own they were never voiced, never even intimated. Andrew was unused to being around women who were as completely submissive as this servant girl. He smiled a little, thinking about that. Not used to being around submissive women? Now wasn't *that* the natural truth. His own Petra, Michael's lovely Marie, James's sharp-tongued Libby: nobody was ever going to accuse any of them of lacking say-so.

"What is it you're doing here, Lexie?"

"I am bringing the tub and the water for you to take the bath, Andrew."

"Bath? What ba . . ." By then he was speaking to an empty doorway. Lexie had already set down the bundle she'd brought in with her—he could see now that it was a wad of fluffy cloth, towels perhaps—and disappeared into the hallway. He could hear the thump and clang of the heavy copper tub being dragged out of the hall closet and toward his room. Normally Andrew would have been inclined to go help the girl with the awkwardly heavy object. But not while he was undressed like this. He would have been mortified to be seen without proper covering.

He muttered a little in the Spanish he'd learned from Petra, secure in the knowledge that no one in this house would understand even if they heard.

Lexie, it seemed, spoke English and French but no Spanish. Andrew spoke English and a little Spanish but no French. Michael, of course, would have gotten along famously with

Lexie, because his Marie was of mixed French and Spanish origin and spoke all three languages. So did young Mordecai.

But no one here except Andrew spoke any Spanish, or admitted to it if they understood any. In the wake of the massacres at Goliad and the Alamo even the other congressmen, it seemed, professed hatred for all things Mexican and therefore for all things Spanish.

That was one of the few areas in which Andrew disagreed with them. After all, a heavy percentage of their own constituencies had to be Texans of Mexican ancestry. And surely the other men must have friendships with Mexican families, as the Lewises certainly did. But then likely most of the congressmen were not married to women of Spanish descent as Andrew and Michael were. And none could have friends as true as the Moreno and the Zaragosa families. Andrew tried to understand and make allowances. But sometimes that was hard for him to do.

Lexie dragged the bathtub into Andrew's room and quickly hurried off again, returning this time with ewers of steaming hot water that must have taken her hours at the stove to prepare for him.

"Hey, not so fast, Lexie."

"Oui, m'su?"

"Why are you bringing me a bath this morning?"

"You do not know, Andrew?"

"Lexie, I promise I wouldn't be asking you now if I already knew."

There was a moment's pause before she giggled, the time probably having to do with her need to translate from one language to another before she fully understood, even though her English was excellent. "It is because of the tailors, Andrew."

"Tailors?"

"You know, Andrew. Measure you all over. Cut the cloth." She grinned and made a snipping motion with her fingers like scissors coming together through a bolt of imaginary material. "Make the suit of fine clothing. You know."

"I don't know about any suit of clothes, Lexie."

"No? M'su Campodoro he say, Andrew. I am to wake you and have you ready this morning. For the tailors." She shrugged, and smiled.

Andrew grunted. There was no point in worrying Lexie with more questions, that was plain. The girl was only doing as she had been instructed. "Okay, then. If it's a bath I'm to have then it's a bath I shall take."

Lexie bobbed her head and finished filling the tub. She had towels laid out close by and a porcelain bowl of soft, sweet-smelling white soap at hand. She pushed the door closed behind her and smiled. "You come get in now please, Andrew."

"Lexie, no."

She was advancing toward him, obviously with all the intention in the world of stripping the covers back off him and helping him into the bathtub.

"Lexie!" Andrew yelled.

"Is something wrong?"

"You can't . . . I ain't dressed, Lexie."

"But of course you cannot be dressed to be in the tub, Andrew. That would be silly."

"But you can't . . . that is t' say . . ."

"You do not want me to wash your back, Andrew?" She made a pouting face, then giggled again and winked at him.

Andrew blushed. He could feel the heat burning in his cheeks like a lantern flame and felt the fire of it infuse his flesh down his neck and far beyond.

Lexie giggled again. "You are nice, Andrew. You are sure you do not want . . . anything of me?" That slight pause was disquieting to Andrew. It seemed to imply . . . but he was being stupid, wasn't he. Of course it wasn't implying anything. Lexie was just being kind and thoughtful, that was all. And dumb Andrew was imagining more than was there. He felt like several kinds of a fool for ever thinking such an ungenerous thing as he'd just then thought about this pleasant, helpful girl. This pleasant, helpful, dark-eyed, young, and beautiful girl. With the figure that . . .

He scowled and motioned Lexie away. "I don't want anything else, Lexie. Please leave now so I can take that bath before the water gets cold."

"Whatever you wish, Andrew. I do anything you say."

"Leave now. Please."

She smiled and nodded and walked away with a light, springing step.

Andrew waited until she had time to get well away, then jumped out from beneath the covers and scurried quickly to slide the bolt home on the door.

He shivered once, then told himself what a fool he was being and peeled out of his undergarments so he could step into the hot bathwater and prepare for whatever this tailor thing was. He was certainly going to have to ask Christopher about that. But he would not say anything to Christopher about the foolish imaginings he'd had concerning Lexie. Not even in jest with the other members of the caucus would he want to do that.

The water closed around him, so hot it took his breath away. And it took his thoughts away too. The discomfort of the overly hot water proved much easier to deal with than that other discomfort had been.

☆ Chapter ☆

7

"Why'n't we all just move down to the parlor, dang it," Andrew grumbled aloud. "Or better yet out onto the street. Make it easier for folks to come an' gawk."

Christopher, smiling as always, only chuckled at the absurdity of that. The tailor, a burly fellow who looked more suited to blacksmithing than wielding needle and thread, gave Andrew a dark look and jerked impatiently on Andrew's wrist to bring the arm back into the desired position.

The measurements were being taken in Andrew's room, and if unwanted guests continued to arrive they would soon fill the place beyond its capacity to accommodate them. In addition to Christopher and the tailor there were three other boarders present and a senator who lived a block over. Andrew was a man who normally enjoyed company, but he could have done without quite so much of it this morning. He'd never been measured for a suit of clothing before and was finding it to be an experience that did not leave a man much room for dignity. At the moment he was naked except for his smallclothes—clean ones; Lexie had seen to that—and was standing barefoot and embarrassed atop an overturned washtub, being pulled and turned and pushed in one direction after another while the tailor measured and mumbled and wrote down arcane scribbles that meant nothing at all to Andrew's untrained eye. Dignity under circumstances like that? Andrew hadn't a shred of it remaining, or so he felt. The experience was made all the worse by having an audience.

"Hold still," the tailor snapped when Andrew tried to lift a hand so he could scratch his nose. Naturally enough now that he was not supposed to move he was finding himself alive with itches and annoying, crawly sensations.

"Sorry," Andrew said. He didn't mean it in the slightest. Christopher laughed again.

"You and me, Christopher. We got to talk."

"Later," Christopher promised. He sounded as if he meant the promise just about as much as Andrew had meant his apology to the tailor.

Christopher knew what Andrew's complaint was, of course. Andrew had been trying to voice it—and to get a satisfactory explanation in return—practically since the moment Christopher walked in. Andrew suspected Christopher did not want to discuss, while these others were present to overhear, the question of just why Congressman Lewis needed this set of finery, and at whose expense the suit was being made. All the tailor said when Andrew asked him about it was that there would be no bill, everything had already been tended to.

"So, Andrew," piped in Johnny Troy, a congressman from Velasco and a gentleman who enjoyed his cup more than most, "are you coming with us for the special caucus during the recess?" Johnny winked when he said "special caucus."

"I dunno anything about that, Johnny," Andrew said quite honestly.

"Andrew is a married man," Christopher chided. "You know that, Johnny. He wouldn't want to join that party."

"Party?"

"It isn't anything we thought you would, um, want to do, Andrew. Although you're certainly welcome if you want to come along, of course. It's just a bunch of the boys getting together in Galveston over the Christmas recess. You understand—the fellows who live too far to go home easily, and those with no one to go home to. Not like you. We know how much stock you put in family." Christopher smiled.

"I've been wanting to see the new port at Galveston. They say the construction is coming along nicely. But I wouldn't want t' go for no reason like that," Andrew conceded. "Not if . . . you know." Andrew felt himself almost going warm in the face again. There were occasions when he was almost embarrassed by the activities of his fellow congressmen. Sometimes their revelries, even among the married men, went beyond the bounds of propriety. Not that Andrew wanted to place himself above those men or act as judge and jury. But there were some things that he imply did not approve and couldn't bring himself to condone. He adn't tried to hide that from anyone.

"If you don't hold still, mister, you will end up looking a erfect scarecrow," the tailor warned sharply.

"Then have at it," Andrew told him. "It'd be the first time I ver been a perfect anything."

The others members of the caucus found that amusing. The ailor did not.

The tailor's assistant, who had been sent rushing away after the ery first preliminary measurements were taken, returned, crowd-ng into the small room with wads of cloth over his arm. Andrew's ed was already covered with bolts and bits of sturdy cloth from which selections might be made.

The tailor grumbled at his assistant too—apparently sourness was a matter of routine disposition with the man and not a trait eserved exclusively for Congressman Lewis—and directed the crawny apprentice to help the gentleman down.

"You mean that's it? 'Bout time," Andrew said as he stepped ff the washtub with considerable relief.

"I mean nothing of the kind," the tailor returned. "Albert, help e gent into his things." Albert began shaking out the bundles of cloth" he had brought back. They proved to be garments already ewn. To Andrew the tailor explained, "This won't fit right until 's altered, you understand, but it will have to do. The dimensions re close enough but the cut isn't quite right for your shape, you ee. What I suggest, mister, is that you leave it like it is until I ave your good suit finished. Then you can wear that one while I dy up this everyday thing."

"But . . ."

By then the apprentice was already helping Andrew into a fresh nen shirt with a new collar attached. Broadcloth trousers ollowed and a lightly embroidered vest, a swallowtail coat, a uffy cravat, and spats that transformed Andrew's rough-made old hoes into something almost acceptable. And topping it all off a ow-crowned, wide-brimmed gray hat of what surely must have een the very finest quality beaver.

The apprentice had forgotten nothing. Studs for the shirt, tockings and garters, even a silk handkerchief to tuck into a ocket of the swallowtail.

The tailor grumbled and groaned at what he was seeing, but veryone else in the room nodded and effused over how handsome e gentleman from the old Austin colony looked now.

Andrew felt awkward and shy, until the tailor's apprentic dragged in a tall mirror and adjusted it so the gentleman could se himself.

Andrew gaped. Why he looked . . . quite the grand gentleman. He really did. He looked as well set up as anybody.

He permitted himself a tentative grin, and the room full of hi new friends laughed in their shared pleasure and applaude Andrew's approval.

Andrew smoothed the lapels of the coat, admired himself in th mirror, turned first one way to inspect himself and then the other Apart from hardly recognizing himself in that mirror, why, he ha to admit that he looked fine, mighty damn fine.

No more homespun. No more linsey-woolsey. No more baggy shapeless droop to clothes and hat brim alike. Andrew Lewis, if h did say so himself, looked every inch the gentleman.

Lord, wouldn't his old father have marveled if he'd ever see his son like this. Old Mordecai, who probably hadn't ever once i his life had so much as ten gold dollars in his pocket all at on time, would surely have marveled if he could see Andrew now.

For one fleeting instant it occurred to Andrew that Michae owned no such suit of clothing and likely never would. Nor Josep nor James nor any other Lewis.

Quickly Andrew set that ungenerous thought aside. But h couldn't help admiring himself in the mirror a moment longer. H looked good. He really did.

And it was his new friends at the seat of government whom h had to thank for this revelation.

Andrew turned to Christopher and winked.

Christopher Columbus Campodoro, the president's man behin the scenes, threw his head back and roared with pleasure. Th other gentlemen in the room couldn't possibly understand wha that was all about, but they contributed their applause to th moment, and even the dour tailor unbent enough to nod and if no actually smile then at the least relax his scowl into an expressio of neutrality.

Of a sudden Andrew found himself thinking about the impression he would make when he went riding home for the Christma holiday. Why, he would be the envy of the colony. And wouldn Petra be proud to see her husband cutting so fine and gentlemanl a figure as this. Andrew looked into the mirror again and wa pleased.

In this getup even he had to admit that he looked the part of congressman and gentleman. Much more of this and he might actually start to feel like he belonged amongst these people at the capital.

Was that the reason the president of the republic—for surely it was he who was responsible—arranged for the new congressman to experience this oddly personal, oddly affecting revelation?

Andrew felt a warm glow at the thought that President Lamar should think so highly of him. Why, the president graciously presented this gift yet was asking nothing in return for it. That was not the sort of compliment a man was likely to forget. Andrew found himself wanting to repay the president's generosity in the coin of loyalty.

And Petra was going to be so pleased. He just knew she would be. Why, he could scarcely wait now for the recess so he could start for home wearing his brand-new finery. He hoped the custom suit would be ready by then too. Andrew grinned, practically aquiver with eager anticipation.

☆ Chapter ☆

8

Michael stood for a moment peering into the shadows. He had come over here only for a moment, to look in and make sure Angeline was safely asleep so he could ask Marie's opinion about something. But the sight of his sleeping daughter, so lovely looking now so very young and so childishly innocent, caught and held him. As she slept he could see her as she had been only a very few years ago, round cheeked and round eyed, back then the baby spoiled by all the clan. And as she slept he could see her too as she soon would be when she matured and was a woman with a woman's grace and beauty. Right now Angeline was a child of promise, promise kept and promise yet to be fulfilled. Michael smiled at her and felt his heart fill with an emotion he would not have felt comfortable to describe or even acknowledge but a feeling he could in no way deny at this moment.

As if she knew what he was feeling and would share it with him—so often he had the sense that she knew anything, every thing he thought or felt or did—Marie came barefoot and beautiful in her nightdress to slide inside the curl of his arm and press her cheek to his chest.

"She's growin' so fast," he whispered.

"Soon she will have babies of her own," Marie said.

"Don't say no such thing. She's still too much the baby her own self for that."

"But soon."

"Too soon," Michael said. He gave Marie an abrupt, almost embarrassed squeeze and turned away.

Marie followed him across the room, lighted only by a faint glow escaping from the firebox of the stove. She sat beside him a the table Michael's own hands had built for their use. "She would be ten now," Marie said. She didn't have to explain who she meant. Michael's thoughts too had traveled from their beloved Angeline to their equally beloved but long, long gone Prudence, who had been sickly from the day of her birthing and who clung to life for only a few months before the family gathered to mourn and to place her tiny coffin into the soil on a slight rise overlooking the river and the Lewis farms. Michael suspected that Marie still blamed herself for the infant's death, thinking there should have been something, anything, that she might have done to save the child, but if so she never spoke of it.

"Aw, think about it, Marie. It'll be kinda nice when it's just you an' me again. Won't have to think about one o' the kids coming in t' ask a fool question or show off a frog they just caught. Why, I might get t' feeling like a young'un again myself." He chuckled and winked at his wife of many years.

"You are my young and handsome hero still, Michael dearest."

"Nonsense."

"You think I should not talk so?"

"I didn't say that."

"Oh, now I understand. You say no so I will insist it is yes. Michael, Michael. What am I to do with you, my Michael?" She laughed and took his big hand between both of hers, raising it to her lips and kissing it.

Again, much as when he'd looked in on his sleeping daughter, a sharp pang of—something—shot through Michael's chest. It filled his throat, and stung his eyes, and fair made him weak and foolish.

"I love you, Michael."

"I . . ." He nodded and turned his head away.

Marie, bless her, sensed his discomfort. "The stove is still hot, Michael. Do you want me to put the coffee to warm?"

"Is there any left?"

"A little."

"That'd be nice then."

She rose and bustled about in the near-dark kitchen, never once looking back in his direction until she was done with her few tasks and her husband had had time to compose himself.

Lordy, though, Michael didn't know what was the matter with him anymore. Seemed like instead of doing things he spent all his time fretting about things not done. Worrying what would happen if Mordecai in his near-constant woods roaming ran up against a band of wandering Indians—Michael felt confident that he could handle something like that himself but was sure his son hadn't experience enough yet to know when to stand and when to parley and when to run like hell—or if little Angeline's head could be turned by sweet-talking boys with smiles on their faces and nastiness in their thoughts. If Mordecai was handicapped by not having had experience with Indians, he at least had had the benefit of hearing talk about the raiders that used to come through from time to time. Angeline not only lacked personal experience, there was no way she could be prepared for the way boys are. Some things it simply wasn't decent to discuss.

Michael sighed. It seemed there were more than aches and pains to tell him that his youth was no longer something to use. At this point it was something for him to remember.

"You wanted to talk with me, Michael?" Marie asked when she came back to the table with a cup of bitter, barely warm coffee for him.

Michael nodded. No point in asking her how she'd known what he wanted. Likely, though, she'd known even before he walked over to check on Angeline while he tried to gather his thoughts. And hadn't *that* been a wasted effort. Why, ever since he done that he'd been thinking about everything except what he intended. He sipped at the coffee, so distracted that he didn't even make a face at the awful stuff, and tried once more to marshal his thoughts and feelings.

"It is Andrew, yes?" Marie said from out of the blue.

Michael frowned, and nodded.

"Make to me a promise, Michael?"

"What?"

"Promise to me you will never ask me to move with you to the city. Cities, they do bad things to people, I think."

Michael's frown deepened. That, in a nutshell, was what was worrying him the most right now.

Lordy, but Andrew had changed. Weeks, that was all he'd been gone, but he came home dressed up like a damn popinjay. Worse, he acted like one. Michael's own brother Andrew was acting like he thought he was some punkin, all full of big plans and bigger talk, mostly about people nobody in the family or anywhere else around the home place had ever heard of.

Except for Lamar, of course. Lordy, by now they'd all had a bellyful of listening to "the president said . . ." and "I told the president that . . ." and "the president asked me . . ." Why, it was most enough to make a fellow puke. Michael's own brother Andrew was talking like President Lamar's personal toady. That was the truth of the matter.

And the sonuvabitch wasn't even right. That was what made it really so frustrating. President Lamar wasn't even right about what he was trying to do, especially with the Indians.

According to what Andrew said, right out front for God and everybody to look at, Lamar was abandoning all the hard work and goodwill that General Houston accomplished during his entire term of office. Instead of trade and treaties, Lamar was wanting to handle Indian policy by way of whip and sword.

Well, Michael knew better'n that. Anybody should, and any Lewis more than most. Any male Lewis ought to understand what it was for a man to be a brother to the wolf. Lord knew Michael sure did—and Andrew should too.

Those Indians, they were all just as wild and free as a wolf. But there wasn't nothing wrong with a man being like that. Wasn't that very thing what led to the Texans rising up and fighting for independence from Mexico? 'Course it was, and not but a few years ago too. Much too recent for anybody down there at their fancy new capital city to forget already. Texas and Texans only wanted freedom. So did the Indians, whether they be Caddo or Cherokee or Comanche.

Treat a man decent and he'd treat you decent back, that was the ticket. That was what General Houston proposed, and it was paying off too. Up north right this minute there were Cherokee settlers who farmed and dressed and acted hardly different from Michael and James and Frank Lewis. Plenty different from Andrew Lewis of late, but that was Andrew's problem. Those Cherokee paid their land fees just the same as anybody else and built their homes the same as anybody else and were even said to be bringing in a press to start up a newspaper. Yet from what Andrew said, that damned fool Lamar intended to treat the Cherokee the same as if they were marauders, order them off their farms and back into the United States. Which wasn't any smarter than Texas these days, since the States didn't seem to want Cherokee farmers neither. Well, General Houston understood. And so did Michael Lewis. The pity, dang it, was that President Lamar didn't understand. And neither did Andrew Lewis.

Michael sighed and frowned and finished off the last of the bitter, leftover coffee.

Marie squeezed his hand. "Come to bed now, my Michael."

He nodded and leaned over to kiss her on the forehead. "Thanks for talkin' this through with me." It did not occur to him that most of the "talk" and all the unresolved worry had taken place entirely within his own brooding thoughts. Nor did Marie correct him. She rose, lithe and graceful and very nearly as slender as when she was a young and lovely girl in Natchitoches, and led him off to the warmth and the comforts of the bed they had shared through good years and bad.

Michael paused in his work, frankly grateful for a reason to stop for a few moments, and dropped the head of the heavy maul to the ground amid the splinters and sawdust that lay thick around the woodpile. Mordecai had cut all the remaining log sections into stove lengths some time ago. Now Michael was using the maul and wedges to split them.

The late December day felt cold as a Tennessee January, but there was no snow on the ground. They hadn't seen snow yet this year and might not at all; there was no way to know in advance. Unless he kept himself warmed with exertion, the cold alone was enough to drive daggers of pain into Michael's hip joints and back, and swinging a twenty-pound maul did nothing to ease any of that. As soon as he stopped working he reached for his coat, pulling it quickly on lest the chill cut through his sweat-dampened shirt and lodge deep inside his body. He leaned backward, stretching, and lifted a hand to shade his eyes against bright sun-glare. After only a moment he commenced to grin.

"Marie!"

"Yes?" She appeared in the dogtrot opening, a smudge of flour on her cheek and a towel in her hands.

"Put some coffee on, woman."

"We still have a little left from this morning."

"Put on fresh anyway. Company." He pointed, but from the back end of the dogtrot Marie could not see the road from San Felipe.

"Who?"

Michael smiled. "Looks like Sly Shipman's mule string t' me."

Marie let out a tiny, glad cry and clapped her hands before she spun and hurried off to put the coffee on. Shipman had gone to Natchitoches on what he liked to call a business trip, whose exact nature was perhaps best left unsaid. In the old days when Spain and then Mexico ruled, Sly had been one of the more successful smugglers whose forays kept settlers in Texas supplied with untaxed, and therefore affordable, goods. Worse even than the taxes was the government edict that said goods should come only through Mexico. The merchants to the south did not bother to do business as far away as Texas; had the settlers tried to obey the rulings they would have had no imported goods at any price.

All of that, fortunately, had changed. It was no longer necessary for Texans to smuggle goods in from the United States. Trade was virtually unrestricted. But Sly sometimes acted as if very little had changed. Marie's excitement at his return now, however, had nothing to do with merchandise of whatever sort. Whenever Sly went to Natchitoches he carried letters between Marie and her parents in the old Louisiana border town.

Michael was pleased to see such joy in Marie now. Whatever pleased her was a pleasure to him as well. He looked off toward the east, to where the mule string had fully emerged now from the leafless gray and black maze of the forest. It was Sly's string, he was sure. Michael's joints might be failing him, but there was nothing wrong with his eyesight. He recognized Sly's loose, easy posture on the saddle mule at the head of the string and the glint of sunlight on metal at the rider's waist. Unlike most men of Michael's acquaintance, Shipman liked to carry a brace of pistols on his belt.

Sly should reach the house within fifteen minutes at the speed his mules were traveling, Michael judged. There was time enough to split a few more stove lengths before he arrived. Michael shrugged out of his coat and tossed it onto the wood-pile, then bent over and with a grimace picked up the heavy maul once again.

"Will you unsaddle?"

"Thanks, but I won't. Reckon you understand why," Sly said.

Michael chuckled and nodded. His little sister—if she ever knew he thought of her that way there'd be hell to pay—Annie was at home not a mile and a half distant awaiting her husband's return. And Sly had been away for more than a week. Had Michael been apart from Marie that long he would be anxious to reach home too. The men settled for tying Sly's string of tall and powerful American mules—not such easy foragers as the smaller Spanish mule but considerably stronger—and leaving their pack frames in place. Michael couldn't help but notice that only one mule carried any appreciable burden. Whatever Sly was up to these days it wasn't anything that he brought home with him.

Unlike most of the Anglo settlers, who preferred knit caps or wool felt slouch hats or, like Michael, the coon and skunk and badger-skin hats they had always known back in the States, Sly Shipman affected a Mexican-style sombrero with its wide brim and tall crown. Michael had to admit that on Sly the big hat looked gay and dashing. Sly pushed the sombrero back on his head now and winked at his brother-in-law as Marie and Angeline came bursting out of the house to greet their visitor.

Sly accepted hugs from both and a kiss on the cheek from Angeline, then said, "I swear, child, you're getting pretty as your mother." Angeline blushed and shook her head furiously, but it was plain to see that the compliment pleased her.

"It is too cold for syrup to flow so easy out here, Sly. Come inside and warm yourself if you want to pour any more of it," Marie said, taking both of his hands and trying to draw him toward the cabin. "I have dinner nearly ready now and the coffee it is hot."

"A little o' that coffee I'd welcome but I'll wait t' eat till I get home, thanks."

"I understand. You come in now. It is cold out."

"And you ladies without no wraps. Hurry on in. Michael and me will be right behind."

"Is something wrong, Sly?"

"No. I just gotta get something out of this pack here. Won't take us a minute." He turned the women around and sent them off toward the house, then began loosening one of the sturdy canvas sacks that was slung onto the pack frame of his lead mule.

"Everything all right, Sly?" Michael asked.

"Pretty much. But I wanted t' ask you something before I went in' opened my mouth in front o' Marie." He pulled out a bundle that had been wrapped in oilcloth and carefully tied. He handed the package to Michael and began remaking the mule's pack. "Christmas presents," he said.

Michael nodded. A similar package had been carried east to the Villaret family when Sly left for Natchitoches. That was of little interest now, though. It sounded as if Sly had the sort of news that would not be welcome.

"I'll not say anything if you don't want me to," Sly offered, "but old Baptiste is going downhill, Michael. Getting real feeble. He's lost s' much weight he don't look like the same man, and he coughs all the time. I'll be surprised if he lives to see another spring." Baptiste, Marie's father, was Michael's friend as well as father-in-law. The Villarets had been a godsend to the Lewises in the early days.

"Whyever would I not want you to tell Marie, Sly?"

"Oh, some men might want their women not t' know stuff. Keep 'em protected, like. Or just keep 'em at home. If Marie knows 'bout her papa she might wanta rush off to Natchitoches."

"Why, I expect she will want to go help," Michael said. Her mother was no younger than Baptiste and likely needed help if the old man was failing. There were other children near, but they were all boys and not yet married. Marie's mother would need help all the more with her sons to tend to while her husband was nursed through his final days. "Lord knows I been the kind o' husband that left home to wander the woods often enough an' long enough. Reckon it'd be poor recompense for me t' resent Marie having needs of her own now."

Sly nodded. "I figured. Didn't want to take nothing for granted though."

"Thanks for asking."

Sly started toward the house, then snapped his fingers and stopped abruptly, almost causing Michael to walk over him from behind. "Almost forgot something else," Sly said.

"What's that?"

"You know how I said I'd ask around about your old friends the Blackwoods."

Michael grunted.

"You ain't gonna believe what I heard in Natchitoches."

"Sly, when it comes to Finis Blackwood and that half-wit brother of his, I'll believe most anything."

"Not this you won't," Sly promised. "Michael, them two been offering to buy up all the guns they can get hold of."

"What?"

"You heard me. Guns. Rifles or shotguns either one. But get this. They want old guns. Cheap. And they're offering to pay cash on the barrelhead for whatever is brought in to them. Hard money, Michael, not promises. Not even Texas scrip neither but gold and silver coin. They're being real firm 'bout that. I take it them two like to got themselves hanged in some past deal of theirs that went our when they tried to pay something off with republic land aper. This time they swear they got cash."

"If Finis Blackwood had any cash he'd use it to buy a jug of vhiskey with and he wouldn't have it any longer than it took for im to get good drunk," Michael protested.

"That's what I'da thought too, Michael, but I'm telling you vhat the word around Natchitoches is. In Nacogdoches too. They ot cash and they're buying guns. Whatever that means, well,"—ly shrugged—"maybe you got some ideas 'bout that. I sure lon't."

Michael frowned. Then he too shrugged. At the moment there vere much more pressing matters than whatever the Blackwoods vere up to. First and foremost would be for Sly to break the news o Marie about her father's failing health. The way Michael saw it, hey could spend Christmas together with the family all at home, hen Marie and the children could make the journey to Natchioches. Marie needed to have what time she could with her father, nd with her mother too, for that matter. There was no reason why Aichael couldn't manage alone here for a spell, particularly at this ime of year when there was no garden to be tended and even the ens weren't laying heavily. There wouldn't ever be a better time or Marie to be away. And if she delayed going now there might ever be another opportunity good or bad for her to visit with Baptiste.

With that settled in his own mind, Michael followed Sly into the varmth and homey kitchen smells indoors.

☆ Chapter ☆

10

"You are sure, my Michael? You will not miss me?"

"Not miss you? Now that's something else entire, woman 'Course I'll miss you. But I won't mind. You got to go see your papa while you can an' help your mother. It couldn't be any other way."

Marie frowned, then nodded. Michael understood what she was going through, of course. She was torn, her loyalties pulling her in two directions at once, but there was no contest. She decided as she had to, agreeing to what was right and necessary, and for the first time in all the years of marriage and motherhood determined to leave her responsibilities of hearth and home so she could help her parents.

"On the day following the Christmas we will go," she said slowly, as if working it out in her own mind even as she spoke "The sooner is the better, yes? So we go early in the morning just after the Christmas. We will take the wagon. Mordecai can drive me." She gave her son a sharp look, cutting off the protest that sprang immediately to the boy's lips. "Angeline I will leave here, Michael. She can cook for you. Child, it is time you learned to run a household anyway. You start by taking care of your papa while Mordecai and I are away."

It was Michael who shook his head, not Angeline. "I can tend t' myself, Marie. Angeline needs t' see her grandparents while she yet can. She seen them, what—once when she was five or thereabouts an' one other time when everybody was running from Santa Anna's army? Person needs better memories o' their own kin than that. She goes with you. If I get t' wanting better cooking than I can manage for my own self I'll walk over and set at

Andrew's table or James's or Sly's or somebody's. Won't be no need for me t' go hungry. You know that."

"Don't you think I oughta stay here too, Mama?" Mordecai pleaded. "Papa and me could manage."

Never mind which of them the question was addressed to, it was Michael who answered. "Your mama and sister can't be traveling all the way to Natchitoches without a man to watch over them, Mordecai. I count on you for that."

It was an argument to which young Mordecai could have no rebuttal, and at the same time it bolstered his pride. "Yes, Papa."

Michael smiled. "It's all settled then. You leave in four days."

"Four days," Marie exclaimed, as if she had never conceived of leaving so soon even though the date was of her own choosing. "But there is so much to be *done*!"

Angeline too seemed suddenly all adither. The two females began fluttering and squawking at each other as they planned what to pack, what to leave, what they could carry as keepsakes and little gifts. The conversation was a fast and fluid mixture of English, French, and Spanish, neither party much concerned, nor seemingly paying much attention, to which was being used at any given moment.

Michael smiled and winked at Mordecai. He pulled a pipe from his pocket and inclined his head in the direction of the door. Mordecai left the table, which Marie and Angeline would get around to clearing sooner or later, and went to fetch his father's heavy woolen blanket coat and his own. The nights were plenty cold at this time of year.

Before he went outside Michael filled his pipe and used a broom straw lighted from the cooking fire to set the tobacco burning. Then he let himself out with Mordecai following close at his heels. "Them two won't slow down now till you're two miles down the road," Michael observed.

"Yes, Papa." The boy seemed a bit troubled, as if he wanted to say something but knew he should not. Michael suspected he knew what was on his son's mind.

"I know you aren't anxious to go visiting in the city, Mordecai. You'd be happier saddling a horse and riding out to the west than driving a farm wagon off to the east. So would I. But your mama and your sister need you. I wasn't funning you 'bout that. There's people in this country that can't be trusted, and I'll be expecting you to ride with your rifle loaded and kept close under your hand.

Why, without you to protect them, son, I couldn't let your mama and Angeline go. I couldn't risk them like that."

"Yes, Papa."

"Besides, this may be the last chance you ever have to get better acquainted with your grampa Villaret and your uncles. The last time you saw them you were just a button. This time you're 'most a man. This time you'll get to know them in a way you couldn't before."

"Yes, Papa." He sighed, resigned to the inevitable. After a moment he brightened. "Does grampa still have his store?"

"Far as I know. If he's too sick to manage it I'd reckon one of the boys would take over an' run it for him." Marie's father was, or at least had been, a merchant in Natchitoches since long before there was a Republic of Texas. Villaret had done business across the border with Spanish Texas and Mexican Texas before the republic ever existed.

"Do you think he might have some of them new pistols like Uncle Sly carries?"

"New pistols?"

"Papa!" The boy sounded quite completely exasperated, as if his father were the most unbelievably dense creature that ever yet drew breath. "Don't tell me you didn't notice them when he was here this afternoon."

"If you don't want me t' tell you that, son, then I reckon I won't. But I will repeat my question: what pistols?"

"Revolving cylinder pistols, Papa. Colt's patent revolving cylinder pistols. Uncle Sly was carrying a pair of them in his sash when he come back from Natchitoches. You have to've saw them."

"I saw he had some pistols, son, but he always carries those."

"But these ones are new, Papa. The very newest thing almost. Why, I bet there aren't a dozen like these in all of Texas."

"Revolving cylinder pistols, you say."

"Yes, sir," Mordecai said with considerable animation. "They fire five shots between loadings. Five. Just about as quick as you can cock and fire."

"Cap locks, are they?"

"Oh, Papa. You aren't gonna bring that up again, are you? Cap locks are much quicker an' surer too."

"So you tell me, son. Me, I always been happy with my flint. And mounted on a rifle, I might add. Flint rifle shoots hard and rue. Kept me and your grampa Lewis and your uncles alive often nough."

"Yes, sir, and Grampa Lewis might not've been killed by those panish that time if there'd been revolving cylinder pistols for you fight them off with."

"That's something we'll never know."

"No, sir, I reckon not."

"As for your question, son, I wouldn't know what your grampa 'illaret might have in his store these days."

"If he has the Colt's patent pistols can I get me some?"

Michael couldn't help but smile a little. "Some? Now you not nly want this latest newfangled thing you want more'n one of nem?"

"Just two, that's all."

"So you can wear a brace of them in your sash like Sly does?"

Mordecai blushed. His father chuckled and sucked on the stem f his pipe. "If Baptiste has any such thing as those new pistols to ell, son, they're bound to be dear, and we don't have any cash noney to spare."

"I just thought . . ."

"You just thought that if he does have any then maybe he'd sell nem to his only grandson at a bargain. Or maybe give you a ouple of them. Is that it?" This time Michael laughed out loud. God love you, son, you ain't backward about reaching out for vhatever you can get."

"I didn't mean . . ."

"Whoa there, Mordecai. I never said there was anything wrong 'ith that. A man ought t' reach out for what he wants. That ain't say that he oughta trample over others t' get it. But there's no urt in a man striving for what he sees as better. Don't you never pologize for that, not to me nor any other."

Mordecai began to smile then too. "I could protect Mama and ngeline better if I had a pair of them revolving cylinder pistols."

"Then talk to your grampa about that. I don't have any of the nings to give nor to sell."

"Yes, sir."

"Tell you what I do have, though."

"Yes, sir?"

"What I do have is a hankering to cover some country again real oon. Maybe the two of us together, mm? Sometime after you get ack from Natchitoches," he grinned, "with or without pistols, I'd like it real well if the two of us put saddles onto some stout horse and took a look t' see what lays over the horizon."

"I'd like that, Papa."

"So would I, son. So would I." He sighed, suddenly consciou of a feeling of peaceful well-being. "So would I," he repeated softly.

Michael walked over to the end of the dogtrot and tapped hi pipe against the corner of the cabin, knocking the dottle out onto the ground. He stepped down and carefully trod on the ashes to make sure no live coal lingered, then tipped his head back and peered up toward a sky that was sprinkled thick with bright white pinpoints of light. "Gonna be frost on the punkin tomorrow."

"Yes, sir."

"Reckon things have settled down enough we can go back inside without getting bowled over?"

"You go ahead in, Papa. I'll talk a little walk around first Sometimes at night . . . I dunno . . . sometimes I get a feeling like the place is being watched."

Michael frowned. He'd never said anything to Mordecai about it. But that was a feeling he had himself quite often of late. Ye there were no Indians raiding along the Colorado. Apart from the fact that this wasn't the season for raiding parties, graze and forage for the horse herds being so poor now, it had been a very long time since there was trouble in so civilized and settled an area as thi had become over the past few years. And anyway with Andrew in Congress and James active in the militia, the Lewises would have been among the first to hear if there were any hostile bands on the move.

"Go ahead then, son, but carry your rifle with you." Michae grinned and squeezed his son's shoulder affectionately. "That ol thing might not be a fancy new revolving pistol, but at least it's a gun you own an' not just a notion to moon about."

"Yes, sir," Mordecai said.

"One thing more before I go in," Michael said.

"Yes, sir?"

"I'm counting on you to keep your mama and your sister safe I already told you that. What I reckon I didn't tell you out loud an maybe ought to, well, it's just that I'm proud of you. Proud it's you will carry my name on when I'm gone."

Mordecai looked about as embarrassed to hear the comment as Michael felt in voicing it. But Michael was glad he'd said it nonetheless. He cleared his throat loudly and beat a retreat for the warmth of the cabin where Marie and Angeline were still nattering about what to pack and what—if anything—to leave behind. Michael figured he would be lucky if they left a pot for him to cook in and a blanket for him to wrap himself into at night. Probably everything else the family owned would be loaded into the wagon and carried east.

☆ Chapter ☆

11

It was barely daylight, the sun not yet visible over the horizon to the southeast, when Marie's wagon rolled out of the yard, yet even so the entire Lewis clan had gathered to see the travelers on their way.

Mordecai sat proudly on the driving seat, his neck and ears swaddled in the bright red muffler that Angeline had knitted him for Christmas and his rifle secured under his knee. Angeline and Marie were nearly out of sight in a deep nest of blankets and pillows and skins placed behind the seat where the women would be out of the wind but could receive the warming benefit of the sun once it was up. The wood bows and canvas wagon cover would not be erected unless the weather turned inclement. All the remaining space inside the narrow wagon box was filled with boxes and bundles. In the end the women had chosen to take with them nearly every stitch of clothing they owned and foodstuffs enough to last the three of them at least through the next two months. Marie hadn't wanted to become a burden on her parents when she visited, nor did Michael want her to roll into Natchitoches empty-handed.

Michael considered it something of a blessing that they chose to leave his old plow behind.

But then perhaps that was explained by the fact that it would be several months still before plowing could begin.

At the moment of departure Michael turned suddenly shy about showing the wrenching emotions of this separation. He hemmed and hawed and dug at the hard-packed earth with the toe of his right shoe.

This was different, dammit, from all the times he'd ridden away on his own journeys.

That had been . . . well, then he had known where he was and how he was and that Marie and the children were safe at home and surrounded by friends and family.

Now it was occurring to Michael that he would be the one who was safe at home while Marie and the children were out on the road somewhere, out of the reach of family or friend either one, out there surrounded by people neither they nor Michael knew.

Anything might happen to them on the road like that—accidents, brigands, even worse than accidents or brigands—and back here no one would so much as know that there was trouble.

Michael discovered that he did not like the kind of worries that beset a person staying at home while a loved one traveled.

He cleared his throat and approached the side of the wagon for the last time. "Marie," he said gruffly. He couldn't put into words any of the things he was feeling. But he could hope that Marie was able to read in his eyes all of that and anything more that might comfort and sustain her while they were apart.

She nodded, just as if she truly had seen the message of his love and his concern, and lifted her face to his for a final kiss.

Michael bussed Angeline on the cheek, having to pull back a layer of scarf to reach it, and gave his daughter a hug.

Then he reached a hand up to Mordecai, seated so tall and erect on the hard, bare plank that would be his perch for many miles and many days. Michael wanted to give Mordecai a hug too but knew better than to embarrass the boy in front of everyone else. "Good-bye, son. You know what t' do."

"I'll take care of 'em, Papa. I promise I will."

"I know you will. Remember what-all I told you." The two of them had stayed up the night before, even after Marie's excitement was finally bludgeoned into silence by fatigue. Michael had talked too much, delivering warnings and instructions and cautions about every danger he ever experienced or ever thought of and some that had never occurred to him before that moment. He had talked on and on and knew at the time that he was worrying overmuch, but Mordecai had humored him and never so much as hinted that his father should hush up and go to bed.

"I will, Papa."

"Yes, well . . ." There wasn't anything more to be said now, and delaying the start would serve no purpose for anyone. Michael stepped back away from the wagon, and Mordecai adjusted the lines in his hands, taking up a light contact with the bits of the harnessed team.

Michael felt a pang of regret as Mordecai put the team into motion, and the wagon tires crunched loudly on the frozen, gravel-strewn soil. He attributed the sharp jab in his chest to the cold of the air he was breathing.

Marie and Angeline waved gaily from the depths of their warm nest, and Michael felt his own hand rise in automatic response.

"Good-bye, everyone. We will soon be back," Marie called. She blew a kiss off the tips of her gloved fingers, and Michael knew the kiss was meant for him alone.

"Good-bye," Angeline shouted.

Michael felt a catch in his throat, and there was a hollow sensation deep inside his belly.

"They're gonna be fine." The voice was James's; he had come up on Michael's left side and was standing close.

"They really will," Annie said from Michael's right. She moved over so that she was standing tight against him. Andrew and Frank and their families were nearby.

"I know that, dang it."

"O' course you do."

Michael lifted his arm and waved again, vigorously this time, meaning it. "Take care," he shouted across the distance that already—so very quickly—separated them.

Marie and Angeline waved back, but Mordecai was intent on his driving and did not take time for such frivolity.

Michael sighed and allowed his arm to drop to his side.

"Come along down t' the house," James said. "You can take your breakfast with me and Libby."

"He can eat with us," Annie protested. "I already have things ready."

"I ain't going noplace until that wagon's out o' sight," Michael growled.

"And then you will be coming to our house," Annie said, her voice dangerously sweet and syrupy. "Won't you, Michael?"

Michael looked from Annie to James and back again. Then he chuckled. "Why'n't you-all work out a schedule. Then tell me where I'm s'posed to be, and I won't have t' get in trouble for picking and choosing."

When he looked toward the road again the wagon was rolling at a swift clip toward the smoke-gray wall that was the forest in winter. Just a little while more and it would be out of sight. Already Marie and Angeline had stopped waving, and already Frank and his family had turned and were straggling off toward home. Now Andrew and Petra and their two were doing the same. Michael felt Annie's arm come around his waist and lightly squeeze.

"Just till they're out o' sight. You know?"

"Of course, Michael. We'll wait right here till you're ready."

He nodded, grateful that he had family to keep the loneliness from being complete but knowing nevertheless that there was a void inside him that no one but Marie and those young'uns could fill.

Michael did not turn away until the wagon was several minutes out of view.

☆ Chapter ☆

12

Michael's nose wrinkled in distaste as he shoved his hand beneath the speckled black-and-white chicken. The hen grumbled and fluttered in feeble protest but gave way. He felt of the packed straw, surprisingly warm from the body heat of the hen, and found a recently laid egg. He pulled it out amid louder clucks and mutterings from the bird and placed it carefully into the basket that was suspended from his left wrist. There were very few chores that Michael truly detested, but this was one of them. He did not at all mind the few minutes it took to gather eggs each day, but there was something about the heavy, ammoniac stink of the coop that caught in his chest and threatened to choke him, as if the very air that would carry such a smell should be considered unclean and rejected by the body.

That was all perfectly ridiculous, of course. Michael knew that. Anyone would. But knowing it did not make him enjoy the chore. Didn't keep his throat from constricting against the stench either. He gathered the last of the day's laying—eight eggs today, not bad at all considering the time of year—and with no small sense of relief let himself out of the rude shack that protected the laying flock from predators.

"Michael?"

"Back here," he called.

Andrew appeared at the rear of the dogtrot. Michael was pleased to see that his brother had empty hands. Petra and Annie and even James's wife, Libby, kept loading him down with comestibles no matter how loudly he hollered Whoa. Between the meals he took at other tables and all the food that already had been sent home with him, Michael likely could get along without having to cook for himself for the next, oh, six or eight months. Or so it seemed sometimes. Today maybe he could get a little back on Petra. He'd send the day's egg gather home with Andrew for Petra to use.

"What brings you?" he asked, kicking the chicken coop door closed behind him. The flimsy panel of lashed saplings clattered shut on its leather hinges. "And dressed like regular folks for a change too," Michael added, noting that for practically the first time since he came back from Houston Andrew had put aside his finery and was wearing homespun britches and a blanket coat. He looked like the old Andrew again instead of the near-stranger who'd been off to Congress. "You, uh, haven't come t' invite me to eat more, have you?"

Andrew laughed. "No. Better'n that."

"Good, " Michael said with perhaps more emphasis than was polite. After all, Petra and the others were only wanting to be helpful. He quickly began to stammer an apology, but Andrew cut him off.

"You don't hafta explain. I understand what you mean."

"Thanks." Michael stepped up onto the dogtrot beside his brother, careful not to limp even though a jolt of pain stabbed through his left hip. He winked and handed Andrew the egg basket. "Come inside where it's warm. I got something that'll warm your belly from the inside too."

Andrew trailed him into the cabin—rather untidy now without Marie there and distinctly silent and empty too—and closed the door to hold the warmth inside.

"Keep them eggs by your coat," Michael said. "I'll want you t' carry 'em home with you. I sure cain't keep up with what-all are laid, not by myself."

Andrew nodded and set both the egg basket and his heavy woolen coat on a nearby bench. While he was doing that Michael took a moment to add a chunk of wood to the fire, then fetched out the crockery jug that Sly Shipman had packed in so very carefully from the east. The colorless liquor likely originated in Kentucky or Tennessee and, every bit as likely, hadn't had the U.S. taxes paid on it. That might have made it illegal back in the States, but it made no nevermind to Texas or to Texans. Didn't make a fine product taste any different neither, the way Michael saw it. Whoever made this batch was a craftsman to be honored and cherished. The corn whiskey tasted something like drinking a warm cloud when it was going down, it was truly that smooth an mellow.

None of the Lewises was much for hard liquor or debauchery though. Andrew and Michael each had one swallow and then se the quart jug aside. They were seated at the homemade oak tabl that dominated the living quarters of Michael's home.

"You never got around t' mentioning what you come over her for," Michael prompted now that the amenities were out of th way. It wasn't much like Andrew to pussyfoot around the side o things. Like the rest of them Andrew was more in the habit o going straight ahead. This time, though, Michael thought Andrev looked almost . . . It took him a moment to decide wha Andrew's expression was giving off, the fidgeting and th downcast eyes and the Adam's apple bobbing up and down like frog with its foot caught in something, then it came to him: dange if Andrew didn't look almost shy today for some reason.

"I, uh, I was thinking you might wanta ride out with me Michael. I mean, with Marie away and everything there's n reason why you couldn't. Except for the chores around the place tending the hens and that. I've already talked to Frank's boys, an they'd take care o' that stuff."

"You say you already talked to 'em?"

"You don't mind, do you?"

"Mind? 'Course I don't mind. I'm just surprised, that's all. S what is there behind this that I ain't seeing, Andrew? There' something. We both know that."

"Yeah, well, I know you and the rest o' the family think tha General Houston walks on water. I know you get a mite fussed u with me for being so strong for the president now that I been dow t' Houston and seen the government firsthand."

"Andrew, whatever could politics have t' do with you and m riding out? Unless it's the capital you're wanting me t' ride to. I ain't that, is it, 'cause you know I'm not one for city stuff. I' rather stay here an' gather eggs as go down to Houston an' watc the swells roll past in their fancy carriages."

"I'm not wanting you t' go t' Houston with me, Michael. Bu I was hoping . . . well . . . President Lamar and some of th fellas, they'll be coming north on a buff'lo hunting trip. I got wor about it today. They were, well, they were asking me to join u with them. And I got to thinking, if you and James and Sly too if you-all was to come along with me, meet these fellas from al over Texas, these friends of mine who're senators and congressmen and the like, well, I was thinking maybe you'd understand better why it is I'm thinking like I am." Andrew shrugged. After a moment he lifted his chin and grinned and once again seemed the old Andrew. "'Sides, Michael, we haven't all of us been off running the woods together in an awful long spell. I say it's about time we up an' do it again."

Andrew's expression now was a mixture of doubt and excitement, excitement at the idea of them all taking a sashay away from the sight of chimney smoke and doubt that Michael would agree to go along and meet the president of the republic.

In truth Michael had his own doubts, doubts seated in his worries over whether he could keep up his own end of things without letting anybody see how stove up and creaky he'd become these days. But, dang it, Andrew's excitement was catching. It had been an awful long time since they'd all got off together. And it would be mighty nice for a change. "How long d'you figure?"

"A week, not more'n two. We won't be gone long enough for it to be a worry. The president's party is gathering in Houston now. They'll come west along the San Jacinto an' cross the Brazos at Groce's Ferry, then move on to the Colorado from there. I figure we can meet them somewhere around Mina. That's where they'll stop to see if the folks there've seen buffalo. We can meet up with them there, I'd think."

Michael smiled. "It's been s' long since my rifle brought down any meat that I wonder if I can still shoot."

"Smoked tongue," Andrew crooned enticingly. "Fresh hump meat. Ribs roasted over mesquite coals. Plenty meat t' dry and keep. Maybe some extra robes to lay over your beds when the nights get deep cold. There's a lot o' use a man can get from a buffalo, Michael."

"Maybe . . . if my rifle barrel hasn't rusted through . . ." His nagging dang pains weren't all *that* bad. He could manage. Besides, he'd gone and promised Mordecai a trip. This would give Michael a chance to freshen the old skills. And to tell the rest of the truth, it would give him a chance to work out what he could or maybe could not manage nowadays and do it at a time when his son wasn't watching his every move. A practice run, so to speak. Michael grimaced, but so briefly he was sure the expression went undetected, and then nodded. "Why not?"

Andrew laughed and slapped his thigh. "All right then." After just a moment he sobered. "You'll help me talk James and Sly into it too?"

"Won't be any convincing necessary, I'd bet."

"But if there is?" Andrew looked worried again.

"We'll go all together, Andrew. Count on it."

A smile returned to Andrew's lean features once more, and he reached forward to take up the liquor for a drink to seal the bargain, if bargain it was.

"Y'know," Michael mused out loud while the whiskey was spreading its heat through his belly, "y'know, Andrew, this is gonna be more fun than I can remember having in ever so long. I'll just bet it will be."

"And I'll bet you're right about that," Andrew agreed, sounding genuinely at ease now for the first time since he'd come. "I just bet you are."

☆ Chapter ☆

13

Michael raised up in his stirrups and braced himself against the cantle of the heavy saddle as the horse swayed and fidgeted beneath him. He kept his hand firm but gentle on the reins to hold the animal in place while he breathed deep of the sweet, clean Texas air. It infused his lungs and made him giddy in ways that Sly Shipman's whiskey never could. He tipped his head back and breathed extra deep, then once more bumped the horse into a smooth and easy singlefoot.

The last of the chimneys and the barnyard smells were far behind now. Ahead lay silent woodlots and rolling, winter-brown grasslands. All about them there was freedom. And most of all there was a sense of joyous release that filled Michael's chest right along with the sweet nature-scents on the unsullied air.

He hadn't known how very much he missed this feeling of freedom and anticipation a man got when he was astride a good horse and moving beyond the constraints of civilization.

There just was nothing else that could compare with this, never mind some minor aches and irritations. Nothing, nothing could compare with this. Michael smiled silently to himself and rode, chin high and shoulders back, at the head of a short column of his own kin. No, sir. Nothing could be better than this.

Michael and Andrew and James and Sly Shipman were moving relaxed and easy. There was always a theoretical danger from passing hostiles. But that was unlikely at this time of year. And anyway a man can't walk scared all his life. There is trouble enough in anyone's life without borrowing more by way of one's own imagination.

Michael heard a shuffle of hoofs in the grass as someone

behind trotted forward to come beside and match his horse's stride. He turned to see Andrew on the long-legged bay that he had ridden home from Houston last month.

"What d'you think, Michael?"

"'Bout what?"

"'Bout a place to light for the night. Should we angle back toward the river, d'you think?" They had left the Colorado almost as quickly as they crossed it back at their own farms. The banks of the Colorado River were flanked on both sides by farmsteads and newly erected cabins for miles and miles upstream and down. Michael had wanted to get away from all that as quickly as they possibly could and so had led them immediately away from the settlement-attracting flow of water. Two or three hours' ride to the east would put them back within sight and sound of settlers, but here they might as well be a thousand miles from civilization for all anyone could tell. Michael was enjoying that fact and did not want to give it up again so quickly.

He shook his head. "No, let's keep headin' north. I know a couple places we can water." He grinned. "If I'm remembering a'right from the last time I came this way."

"And if your memory's wrong?"

"Aw, you've had some dry camps before this, Andrew. 'Nother won't hurt you."

Neither of them entertained the slightest belief that Michael could be wrong in his memories, even though it had been years since he had passed this way. Michael had the long hunter's gift when it came to the terrain he crossed: once seen, always known. The notion that anyone could ever become lost, at least in country that he'd been awake and conscious when he was brought into it, was quite simply inconceivable to him, as incomprehensible as a lecture delivered in Greek or Latin would have been.

"There's a creek bottom we should reach before dark," Michael elaborated, "with a rock bluff that'll stop any wind that comes up in the night and a nice pool where a fella might wanta drop a hook, see if he can't manage some fresh fish for breakfast."

"Fresh fish, soft beds." Andrew glanced back toward the pack mule that Sly was leading, loaded with bedrolls and provender enough for a month. "I'd say we're fixing to have it mighty soft. Not like in the old times, eh Michael?"

"Everything easier now except finding meat," Michael agreed. He patted the buttstock of the old flintlock that lay across his pommel.

"We'll find buffalo above Mina," Andrew promised. "Meantime, well, you and me have et squirrel often enough before. Reckon we can handle it again if need be."

Michael laughed. There had been a time, a good many years ago now, when he and Andrew subsisted almost exclusively on squirrel. That was when they'd been making their way from Tennessee to the fresher prospects of Texas. Squirrel for supper had become first a vexation and finally a joke to them, and Andrew swore at the time that he never wanted another mouthful of bushytail. Apparently he'd had a change of mind since.

"How far did you say this camp spot should be?"

"Oh, I dunno. Out o' this drainage and into the next one north o' here. Call it four hours. Why?"

"I was just wondering if them other folks might be headed for the same spot."

"Other folks?"

"Riders. Moving ahead of us. I thought you seen their sign and was following them deliberate, but I guess you ain't."

Michael shook his head. "I guess I sure ain't." James was trailing too far behind to have overheard, but Sly and his pack mule were close. He booted his horse nearer. "What was that, Andrew?"

"C'mon, Sly. I'm used to Michael not seeing what's under his nose, but surely you seen them tracks we been following."

"What tracks?"

Andrew chuckled. "I dunno 'bout you boys. You accuse me o' turning to city ways, then we ride out on a little bit of a hunt an' who is it has to watch out for who?"

"You always was the tracker in the family," Michael said. It was the simple truth. When they were both boys it sometimes used to gravel Michael that Andrew had an almost uncanny knack when it came to deciphering the tiniest and most insignificant of scrapes and scratches and making those things read like a book. And a weighty volume at that. Michael was the one with the itchy feet and the moving-on ways, but Andrew was the Lewis with the eye for tracking, becoming even more adept than their father had been when it came to trailing game. Michael could find game better, but once found it was Andrew who could follow it. Apparently it was a talent he had not lost.

"For the past half hour we been following close beside the trail these fellas left. You don't see it still?"

Neither Michael nor Sly did, which Andrew seemed to find amusing.

"We ain't following no Indians, are we?" Michael asked.

"I don't think so. Just a minute." Andrew swung his mount aside and moved over thirty yards or so, then moved forward again parallel to the line of travel Michael had taken. Michael still could see no hint of whatever it was Andrew had spotted over there. Andrew moving off by himself like that finally attracted James's attention too, and he caught up with the rest.

"It's no Indians," Andrew said after a few minutes. "Two riders mounted on horses with awful big feet. Big horses. Draft stock, I'd bet, that're being ridden under saddle for some reason."

"Two of 'em?"

"That's right."

"You don't suppose somebody might have had a breakdown with a wagon and be looking for help, do you?" Michael asked.

"If that's what it is," James said, "they got a long wait coming. There aint' anything straight north from here until you get to Missouri."

"Missouri's way east from here," Sly said.

"All right then, there ain't anything north from here a'tall," James corrected himself.

"Nothing but the Santa Fe trail," Sly agreed this time.

"Might be we should catch up with them just to make sure they're all right," Michael suggested.

"What if it isn't somebody in trouble? What if it's somebody that values his privacy?"

"Then we'll have our look-see and know we ain't leaving anybody stranded and ride wide around. Whoever it is don't ever have to know we're near."

"Sounds reasonable."

"Anybody say otherwise?" Michael asked.

No one spoke, so after a moment more he added, "Take the lead, Andrew. And mind we don't make ourselves obvious about it."

It was odd, but now there was a sense of purpose among them that hadn't been there before. Michael found himself riding more erect in his saddle and even leaning slightly forward in anticipation sometimes. Lordy, but it was good to be out again and moving.

☆ Chapter ☆
14

Pale smoke visible against the dark gray of clouds to the north ointed like a signpost in the sky. They would have been guided the scattered copses of scrub oak and cedar even if Andrew adn't been along to find the way. Michael motioned for silence nd let his horse advance at a slow walk, the others coming close t his heels. They didn't want to bother anyone. Just check and nake sure things were all right.

If possible though, Michael thought, they at the least should top and talk to these folks. Warn them that a smoke so easily seen nay attract more than passing hunters to the camp. Comanche laimed this part of the country, and the Comanche were testy bout who traveled in it. A party mounted on two heavy horses vasn't strong enough to defend against attack, never mind that vinter was not the time when bands of marauders were supposed be on the move. Likely these folks didn't know how easily isible their smoke was, else he doubted they would risk the fire.

Even as he thought this, though, the slender column was cut off t the bottom, the white candle shape growing smaller and smaller s it lifted higher into the sky and at the top dissipated. In a matter f moments there was nothing left to show where the pale beacon ad been, not even the smell of the fire, because the wind was rifting away from the Lewises' approach.

"They seen it," James said.

"Good," Andrew added.

"Pilgrims, though, or there wouldn't have been smoke t' begin vith," Sly said.

"Shh." Michael frowned at the others and forced his horse nrough a gap between two gnarled cedars. The going was slow here and louder than he would have liked. The ground was hard a flint and littered with loose rock. A horseshoe clattering on ston could be heard much too clearly and much too far.

The place where that smoke had been rising was less than a hal mile distant, and Michael did not want to be seen except b choice. He slowed the pace even more, so that the horses steppe one foot at a time in bored tolerance of the riders' wishes.

The stand of cedar and oak thinned, and their small train woun slowly up the side of a low hill. Michael stopped just short of th summit and dismounted, handing his reins to Andrew. He wen afoot through a clump of scrub oak, his moccasins making n sound on the winter-damp leaves that covered the ground here When he reached the far edge of the growth he frowned an pursed his lips.

From here Michael could see into a broad, shallow draw whe the column of smoke had originated. And presumably where h would find the horsemen Andrew had been tracking throughou much of the afternoon.

Two horses, Andrew said.

In the bottom of the draw beneath him, Michael could see eight ten, perhaps a dozen horses tied. Two of them were thick-bodie animals that looked as if they should have been in harness. Thos would be the horses Andrew tracked. The rest, though, were ligh saddle stock. They must have come by a different route or Andrev would have seen sign of their passage. That, or they were here t begin with and the two recently arrived horses joined them.

Oddly, the heavy horses bore saddles and the saddle horse stood with bare backs.

Odder yet, Michael could see no people nearby.

The grassy flat close to the horses showed the smolderin remains of the fire whose smoke they saw minutes earlier. Ye there was no sign of the men who had ridden these horses here an who had built the fire.

Whoever those people were, he realized, and whatever ha become of them, the people his party followed here were mo definitely not travelers whose wagon broke down. They were nc folks in need of rescue. Better then to simply turn and ride quietl away lest they give offense to whoever was out here. Micha turned back through the brush and walked, more quickly this time out of the thicket to his brothers and the horses.

"You will join us, yes?" The words were spoken in Spanish The man who spoke them was one of four. And all of four of th strangers carried rifles cocked and leveled and aimed very surely at the bellies of the Lewis brothers and Sly Shipman.

Michael stopped. He realized with a chill that he was already a good two steps from the scant cover of the winter-barren scrub oak. And anyway even if he were to bolt now that would only bring the wrath of these riflemen down on Andrew and James and Sly. Instead he showed his hands spread open and empty as if in innocence. "A simple invite would've been enough," he said, also in Spanish.

"If you say so," the Mexican with the rifle agreed without, however, shifting his point of aim. "Mount now, please. We will talk about this all together, eh?"

"Down there?"

"Si." The Mexican smiled. "You admit to spying upon our camp. Good."

"I admit to seeing your camp. Did you tell 'em, Andrew?" Andrew was the logical one to ask. His command of Spanish was much better than either James's or Sly's, better, in fact, than Michael's. Michael was careful, though, to pose his question to Andrew in Spanish. He did not know whether this young man, who he saw now was somewhere in his twenties, spoke any English and would not have wanted anyone to pull a trigger because they were worried about what might be said. Better to keep everything as open as possible.

"I did," Andrew said. "I don't think he believed me, Michael."

"Most assuredly I do not," the Mexican agreed. "You would follow two strange horses so far for so flimsy a reason? I do not believe this to be so. I say you came to spy upon us."

"But we really . . ."

"Enough." The Mexican scowled and jerked the muzzle of his rifle in the direction of Michael's horse. "You come with us or lie where you are, *si*? Now."

"We'll talk later," Michael agreed. He swung onto his saddle and nodded. "Lead on, mister."

"First you will give us your guns, one of you at a time, please. Then you may lead. You already know where it is that we go."

"I'll lead if you like. But me and my brothers are not giving up our guns. We have done nothing wrong here, and we're willing to come along and explain it to whoever you want. But we are not handing over our guns without a fight."

The young Mexican pondered that for a moment, then nodded. "You go in the lead. We will be close behind."

"Take your rifles down to half cock if you please."

"And if I do not please?"

Michael didn't bother to answer, just sat and waited. He didn't think that would be a point worth fighting over. And after a moment the Mexican agreed. He let his own hammer down to the safe-cock position, and the men with him did the same.

Michael took a moment to look at the rest of the men. They were all Mexican. But beyond that he wasn't sure. They were dressed much too well to be peons but much too poorly to be merchants or artisans. They certainly did not carry themselves like hidalgos or the sons of hidalgos either. They acted, if anything, like soldiers. But their clothes were ordinary, everyday civilian attire, not uniforms. He couldn't quite figure them out.

"Gracias," he said once his request had been met. "We will be pleased to accompany you now."

The young Mexican who seemed to be the leader of the small group grunted and motioned for Michael to lead away.

☆ Chapter ☆

15

"Hssst. Michael!" James's whisper was barely audible. "Over t' the right there. D'you see what I see?"

Michael cut his eyes in the direction James indicated. Beyond the line of picketed horses he could see a small grouping of men. Before them, in plain sight now, were several men dressed much like the ones who were riding behind them with the ready rifles. And now he could see this separate, smaller group partially hidden by a screen of intervening brush.

At the moment, however, Michael's attention was pretty much occupied by the sight of the Mexicans who were in plain view. They too were armed with large-caliber flint rifles.

In fact, Michael realized now, all the rifles he could see looked very much alike. Now that he thought on it, they looked like the sturdy *escopetas* that the Mexican army carried.

Yet that made no sense. This was no raiding party. No military intrusion could penetrate this far into Texas without being spotted and an alarm raised. For that matter, there was nothing out here for raiders to capture. There was simply nothing out here.

So why would a group of Mexican soldiers, in civilian clothing but carrying military arms, be here to begin with? If indeed they were soldiers.

"Hsst. Michael."

"What is it, James?"

"That fella over there. That ain't no Meskin."

Michael tried to see, but his line of sight was not clear. There were three men over there. No, four. Two appeared to be rather well dressed Mexicans despite what James was whispering about. The other two were standing with their backs toward the approaching riders. One of that pair was tall and burly, the other considerably smaller of stature. Michael could see now, though, why James thought they were not Mexicans. Their hats were not the broad-brimmed sombreros that Sly Shipman and most of these Mexicans favored nor the felt hats or woolen caps that one saw in towns. Instead they seemed to be fur caps like those Michael and his brothers had always worn. In fact, the hat the smaller of the two was wearing seemed . . . he wasn't sure. He caught only a glimpse, but it seemed familiar for some reason. Except that couldn't be. Now he was imagining things right along with James. Forget that. "I don't think . . ."

"You will be quiet now," the Mexican at Michael's back snapped.

"And you, sonny, will mind your manners. We came here without a fuss just to be agreeable. I don't say we have to keep on being so easy to get along with."

The Mexican snorted. "Up there, four against four, eh? Here . . ." He chuckled and looked around, inviting Michael to do the same.

With the addition of the bunch in front of them, Michael and his party were surrounded by nine armed men. The odds now were anything but even.

"Four against nine," Michael said calmly in Spanish loud enough for all to hear as the men closed in around the riders. "But who wants to be the first to die?" And this time he smiled too. "I believe this is what's called a standoff, is it not?"

"Nine against four, señor, you are sure to die."

"So are you, señor. I'll see to it personally." Michael laid a hand on the wrist of his rifle stock, his thumb falling close to the curved firecock of the old weapon. "So. Do we talk? Or do we fight?"

The young man licked his lips nervously. He seemed considerably relieved when one of the well dressed men from the other, more distant group walked out from behind the horses and came toward him.

This man, Michael saw at a glance, was a personage who thought himself important. Although whether he was remained to be seen. He walked with a swagger and, more than that, with a certain barely noticeable swing to his gait that suggested there should be a sword suspended from his sash even though there was no weapon of any sort there. Perhaps, Michael thought, it was the way he carried his left hand, as if he were accustomed to resting it on the hilt of a sword and now did not know quite what to do with it in the absence of the weapon.

"Who are these people, Corporal?" the hidalgo demanded, confirming one suspicion but raising many more questions than were answered.

The corporal stiffened to attention but remembered in time that he was not supposed to salute. "Spies, Your Excellency. They were on the hill there, looking down into our camp."

The officer's brow beetled into a dark scowl.

"We were doing nothing but riding out on a hunt," Michael drawled in English.

The officer's scowl deepened. "Spanish," he ordered. "Speak a civilized tongue, man."

"Well, what I was saying," Michael said, switching smoothly into Spanish, "is that we were riding out on a hunt when my brother saw . . ." He repeated the story—the truth, although that seemed hardly important at the moment—that Andrew already gave to the corporal.

"I did not believe what these men say, Your Excellency," the corporal added when Michael was done.

"We came along with this young hombre without a fuss in the belief that a gentleman of your wisdom and experience would know the truth when he hears it," Michael said, laying a bit of butter on in the hope that might do some good.

"How unfortunate for you," the officer responded coldly, "that the truth no longer matters. What does matter is that you have seen what you should not see." He looked up at the corporal. "Kill them."

All around there was a clatter of rifle hammers being drawn back and locking noisily into position to fire.

Michael felt a rush of heat into his chest and his cheeks, felt his neck and shoulder muscles swell with sudden tension. His mouth sprang open and before he knew himself what he intended he bellowed his defiance of this foppish Mexican's casual order for the destruction of the Lewis clan. In his sudden rage he did not even try to form words. He simply raised up and roared. And brought the muzzle of his rifle swinging fast around.

☆ Chapter ☆

16

Muskets roared, the sound of the shooting loud but dull, almost a hollow sound, most unlike the sharper crack that announced the discharge of a much smaller bored Tennessee rifle.

The first few nervous shots on the part of the Mexican soldiers were more a reflexive response to the officer's orders than they were an attempt to kill. Surely none of the men had had time to take aim before they fired.

Hastily directed perhaps but lethal nonetheless. Michael felt the hot breath of a musket fired from close range and heard something that could have been, but was not, the world's biggest bee drone past his ear with a sudden, ripping noise. Instinctively he ducked, knowing that it was too late to bother but unable to keep from it, and clutched at the reins of his suddenly plunging horse.

"No," he shouted, struggling to bring the animal's forefeet back to earth. "Wait."

Even now, even after having been fired upon, Michael's desire would have been for them all to talk this over, to convince the haughty Mexican that he should reconsider.

But there was no time. Not any longer.

Another musket bellowed, and James reeled drunkenly in his saddle, a streak of scarlet showing bright and bold on the back of his coat.

Michael heard the sharp bark of a rifle behind him as Sly Shipman returned the Mexicans' fire, and the young corporal who Michael had claimed he would kill crumpled and twisted with Sly's bullet instead in his chest. The corporal toppled backward out of his saddle, falling to earth underneath the skittish feet of the Mexicans' horses.

More muskets roared. A horse screamed and began pawing the air. Andrew shot a Mexican in the face from a distance of no more than five feet away, then spurred his horse to James's side. He righted James in the saddle and then snatched James's rifle out of his hand, dropping his own empty rifle and taking swift aim at another Mexican who has leveling a musket at Michael.

The moment of paralyzing amazement passed, and Michael fought once again to bring his horse under control.

Damn these people. Damn them anyway.

He stood in his stirrups, intent now, and saw the Mexican hidalgo scampering straight-backed and chin-high but nonetheless quick as he could go for the safety of distance. Now that he'd gotten this dance started he was wanting to leave the ball.

Michael's rifle came to his shoulder with the smooth speed of a lifetime's practice, and the pale blade of the front sight lined up on the small of the officer's back as if by its own volition.

There was a moment's hesitation as Michael realized he was going to shoot a man in the back.

But another musket roared, and Michael could not take the time to look and see if the shot hit some member of his family.

His finger gently squeezed—even now the long-learned injunctions against jerking a trigger could not be forgotten—and the rifle pushed sharply back against his shoulder.

Sixty or so yards in front of him the arrogant hidalgo flung his arms high and was driven face forward to the earth, the sight of him almost instantly obscured by a white veil that seemed to enclose Michael and his horse.

Pale smoke curled and eddied on what little breeze there was, he saw now, the stink of it acrid and unpleasant in this concentration. Michael had always thought the smell of burnt gunpowder one of the most pleasant scents there was. But that was only in small quantity. With this much of it surrounding them, so thick now that vision was blurred by the shifting, swirling, artificial white clouds, the stink of it filled his nose and seemed an almost tangible thing.

He ducked at the hollow sound of a musket's shot and came face to face with a mounted Mexican who materialized out of the smoke-mist like a ghost. But this ghost carried a musket, and the gun was aimed at Michael's belly.

With his rifle already emptied and having no time to do anything else, Michael spurred his horse straight at the Mexican and drove the hot, powder-blackened muzzle of his rifle hard into the man's teeth. Blood spurted and the Mexican, more startled than injured, fell out of his saddle, dropping his musket as he fell. Michael heard a sound that might have been the man screaming—perhaps a horse stepped on him—but had neither the time nor the interest in paying any more attention to the fellow.

Short, sharp, light gun-cracks kept sounding. The shots were neither musket nor rifle. Michael had no idea what they were until an eddy in the battle smoke gave him a brief glimpse of Sly Shipman standing on the ground with his feet braced wide apart and a revolving pistol held in each hand.

Ten shots Sly had in those two guns. Ten shots plus the charge in his rifle. The young Mexican had been wrong when he'd assessed the odds, Michael realized now. It wasn't nine men against four after all. Not when Sly alone commanded the armament of nearly a dozen.

Not that there was time to be thinking about that now. Michael's horse reared again. He kicked his feet out of the stirrups and dropped away from the terrified animal. He hit the ground awkwardly, lost his balance and fell. There was pain in his hip and knee and shoulder, but he knew no harm had been done. It was only the same dull, familiar pain he'd come to know so well these past few years. He rolled, came to his knees and was groping for his powder horn and bullet pouch even as he was rising.

A riderless horse thundered by, nearly knocking him over, but he got the flintlock reloaded and primed in near record time despite the distraction.

"James. Andrew. Where are you?"

A musket spoke. Then Andrew. "Here, Michael. Rally here."

Michael heard a grunt and then the snap of Sly's pistol again. He moved in the direction of Andrew's voice.

There was less firing going on now. The smoke was thinning.

James, Michael was relieved to see, was standing upright, wobbly but propped with his back against Andrew's, one arm hanging limp but the other busily engaged as he reloaded a rifle for Andrew.

A Mexican with a musket and bayonet was running toward James with the bayonet leveled and gleaming.

Michael shouldered his rifle and aimed with the practiced ease of a man who could knock a fleeing rabbit down in midstride. This much larger and slower target was no challenge. The Mexican, who looked no more than seventeen and would never live long enough to shave, fell a dozen paces short of James and Andrew, a bullet from Michael's rifle lodged in his breast.

"Look!" James pointed off in the direction of the picket line.

Beyond it, Michael could see now, there was one more handsomely dressed man. And beyond him the two Anglos who'd been in conference with him before the shooting started. Michael still could not get a good look at the men in the fur caps. But he could see that the taller of the two grabbed something—leather saddlebags, they looked like—from the Mexican, and then both Anglos began running.

One of the Anglos—Michael would almost have sworn it—had only one arm.

Finis Blackwood?

There were more men in this country who had only one arm than Finis. But . . .

Why would Finis and Luke, for surely if one was Finis the other was Luke, be out here in the middle of nowhere meeting with two hidalgos and an armed guard?

The answer had to be simple, Michael concluded. The only real likelihood was that it was not Finis and Luke he and James saw over there.

Whatever the meeting had been about, and whoever the participants, the Anglos were out of sight now. They'd left the Mexican officer alone.

A moment later Michael heard the sound of hoofbeats, and the two heavy-bodied horses they had trailed here burst out of the brush with the Anglos mounted on them. The men were urging the horses into a shambling run.

For a moment Michael thought about chasing them.

But there would have been no purpose to that. Whoever they were, if they were abandoning the fight that was all to the good.

Andrew's rifle barked once more. It was only then that Michael realized that for the past few moments the fury of battle had been replaced by blessed silence. It was quiet now. The shooting had stopped.

Automatically, even while he was thinking this, Michael dropped the butt of his rifle to the ground beside his right foot and began mechanically reloading. Pour powder into his palm, then down the barrel of the rifle. Bounce the buttstock lightly on the ground to settle the powder charge. Lay a greased patch over the muzzle and push a lead ball onto it. Use the short starter rod to compress the patch and force patch and ball into the barrel. Pull the ramrod from its ferrules and drive the ball the full length of the barrel to seat firmly against the powder. Then . . .

"Michael!"

Sly's voice barked in warning.

The Mexican officer, apparently the last Mexican alive now, had burst out from behind the tied horses and was charging at them with an upraised sword brandished wildly overhead.

"Michael! Help me."

There was alarm in Sly's voice now. Michael realized that Shipman finally had run out of loads in his weapons. His rifle and both revolving pistols were empty now. Andrew—Michael looked hastily around—Andrew was empty too. And James, slowed by his wound, had barely started the task of reloading his rifle for Andrew to use.

Michael's rifle was charged, but . . . never mind that.

He brought it to waist level, already running to place himself between Sly and the Mexican officer, and spilled gunpowder willy-nilly into the flash pan. He snapped the pan closed and dragged the cock back.

The officer wasn't more than ten paces away. He held his sword poised high overhead, ready for a slashing stroke that could cleave through flesh and bone.

Michael held his rifle leveled waist-high and pulled the trigger.

The unusually heavy recoil twisted the weapon and thrust it completely out of his hands. The gun clattered onto the ground in spite of Michael's efforts to hang on to it. He had never felt recoil so heavy.

But the faithful old rifle performed and, somehow, the barrel held together even though by all rights it should have burst wide open, for in addition to the normal and expected weight of ball and patch, the heavy powder charge this time was expanding against the great additional weight of the steel ramrod that remained inside the barrel. Michael hadn't had time to remove it.

There was an odd sound to the gunshot, and bullet and ramrod alike were flung out of the rifle, the ramrod twisting like a bit of straw being smashed with a maul. The curling length of distorted steel cut like a scythe into the officer's body.

The man dropped, his sword still clenched tight in his fist, and blood gushed out in torrents so great it seemed impossible that a single human body could have held so much.

"Not very tidy," Sly observed from behind Michael. "But damn-all effective."

Michael nodded and turned. He could see now why Sly hadn't tried to fight or run. Sly's left foot was drenched in blood, and he was having to balance himself on his one good foot while he disassembled his pistols and began the slow and laborious task of reloading each of the deep chambers.

"James?" Michael called anxiously.

"I'm all right."

"That's a lie," Andrew said.

"Well, I'm better off than any o' these fellows," James amended. The bullet that struck him had hit in the pad of thick muscle adjacent to his armpit, shocking his arm into numb uselessness and taking a chunk of flesh with it.

"Yeah."

"Anybody got any idea what this was about?" Michael asked. But no one did.

"Set down, Sly. Let's get you an' James patched up. Then, Andrew, me and you will see if we can find anything that'll make some sense o' this. Or leastways something t' tell us who t' notify. There's kin to these boys someplace, an' they'll be wondering, by an' by."

Andrew nodded and, congressman or not, began following his older brother's orders.

There was not, they soon discovered, a single Mexican survivor. At least none who showed himself. If there were any, and Michael found himself hoping that there might have been, he or they had gotten clean away and seemed intent on staying out of sight.

Sly's horse was dead. Andrew's handsome, fancy bay was so badly hurt that it had to be destroyed. Michael offered to do that for him but Andrew, his face set into a stony mask, performed the unpleasant chore himself.

They'd come out mighty lucky, Michael concluded, and that was thanks mostly to Sly and his newfangled revolving pistols. Maybe there was something to be said for new ideas after all.

"Set down, James, an' get your coat off. We'll have a look at that leaky hole in your hide."

"I'm all right. See t' Sly first."

"Uh huh."

James grinned—and sank into a cross-legged sitting position, probably without ever realizing that he was no longer standing upright. He was so pale and pasty complexioned that Michael felt a rush of renewed concern. He eased James onto his back and began unfastening James's coat.

It would be dark soon and there was still much to be done here. Michael found himself hoping now that there were no Mexican survivors from the fight lest they sneak back and launch an attack. As for the Anglos who certainly had survived and fled, they would not be coming back. Not if they really had been Finis and Luke Blackwood.

And if they *were* Finis and Luke . . .

Michael shook his head, annoyed with himself for allowing that distraction of his thoughts. There would be time enough later to think about things like that. Right now he had to see to James and to Sly and then to the horses. And there would be the bodies to bury and . . . too much, too much. He hadn't time now to be worrying about anything except what had to be done.

"Hold still, James. I gotta find something to bind you up with."

"I ain't going noplace, Michael," James assured him.

☆ Chapter ☆

17

"Let me have some of that medicine, will ya?"

Sly helped himself to another swallow from the small jug that had been concealed in his saddlebags, then handed the whiskey to James. Michael smiled. "You two the only ones that get medicine, are you?"

"We're the only ones wounded, aren't we?" James countered as he handed the jug on to Michael. "Where's Andrew?"

Michael shook his head. He didn't know. "Took off in that direction. He didn't say for what." He tipped the jug and took a little of the whiskey into his mouth, holding it there warm and biting on the tongue for a moment before he swallowed and allowed the heat to spread through his belly. Then he passed the liquor on to Sly. "You boys feeling all right?"

James nodded. Sly Shipman grumbled under his breath.

"What's that, Sly?"

"You know."

And indeed he did. Michael grinned. Sly had been wearing a favorite pair of fancy-stitched moccasins. Michael had had to cut the left one off of Sly's foot so he could reach the wound to clean and bind it. Now Sly had no mate to the pretty thing that still decorated his right foot. Not that he could have worn a left one at the moment anyway; his foot was so heavily bandaged that it looked like a shapeless lump. Sly had been lucky, though. He probably had some bones broken where the musket ball struck, but nothing was smashed beyond hope for a good recovery. Unless an infection set in, eventually he would be all right again, perhaps with a limp but even that remained to be seen. And if so, a limp was small price to pay. He could well have lost the foot instead.

James's wound, although undoubtedly painful, was even more straightforward. The ball had gone cleanly through, tearing at his flesh but striking no bone. There was no reason why James should not recover completely.

They heard footsteps from the direction of the picket line where the horses, their own and those of the Mexicans left, were tied. Michael didn't move, but he checked to make sure where his rifle lay, just in case. He noticed that Sly was casually scratching his belly, the movement placing his hand within inches of the butt of one of the revolving pistols in his sash.

"Did you save me any of that corn?" It was Andrew, coming back to the fire from a different direction.

"A little," Sly said.

Andrew grinned and sat cross-legged between James and Michael. "In that case I expect I'll share some of this with you." He held a flask up for them to see.

"What's that?"

"Brandy. Mighty good brandy too. Those officers had expensive tastes."

"Mexican officers can afford 'most anything they want," Sly observed, prompting the others to nod in agreement. Texans or Americans might find the Mexican system odd, but there would be few who did not envy the opportunities open to Mexican army officers. Few, that is, until they began thinking about the victims of that opportunity. Mexican officers, their commissions secured either by purchase or appointment, drew pay for the wages and the keep of the full complement of men they were authorized to command. If an officer received money enough to hire and provide for a hundred soldiers, he might choose—and likely would—to hire fifty instead and at that to hire the enlisted men at reduced rates of pay. He could save even more by giving his fifty soldiers barely enough food to sustain them and by clothing them in whatever rags were available, arming them with whatever battered muskets came cheaply to hand. And the officer, naturally enough, was entitled to pocket the difference between what the government gave him for his men and what he actually paid out to them. A commission in the Mexican army could be a lucrative opportunity indeed.

Andrew uncapped the flask and sampled the contents, then passed it around for everyone else to try. Michael found the brandy not as much to his liking as Sly's Kentucky-made whiskey. But then, Michael acknowledged, he hadn't all that much basis for comparison, and he certainly did not have sophisticated tastes as Andrew seemed to these days. All Michael knew was what he liked. He had no idea what things he was supposed to like instead.

"Let's see what else we have here," Andrew said, drawing a leather folio out from under his coat where he'd stuffed it behind his belt. "This was in the saddlebags too."

He unfastened the brass turnbutton that secured the flap and opened the folio. "Papers," he said. "Bunch of dang papers."

"What do they say?"

"I dunno yet, do I?"

"If it's anything about Finis Blackwood and Luke, I'd sure like to know about it," James said.

"Now whyever would a Mexican officer be carrying papers that would say anything about the Blackwoods?" Andrew demanded.

"Because Finis and Luke are who we followed here today, that's why," James snapped back at him. "Don't look at me like that, Andrew. Ask Michael if you don't believe me, dammit."

"Michael?"

Michael shrugged. "It looked like Finis and Luke. That doesn't mean I'd swear an oath it was them."

"You see 'em, Sly?"

Shipman shook his head.

"Couldn't have been," Andrew announced. "There couldn't be any reason why the Blackwoods would have anything to do with these Mexicans."

"Just because we don't know of a reason doesn't mean there couldn't be one," Michael reminded Andrew.

"Finis would do anything if it'd make him a dollar," James said.

"We know the Blackwoods are wanting to buy guns," Sly added.

"For the Mexican army? I don't think so," Andrew said.

"I agree with you about that," Sly said. "They're wanting to buy any old guns so long as they're cheap. But even a Mexican officer wouldn't want that for his men. They at least need muskets all the same size. Old Brown Bess castoffs, stuff like that. They couldn't use the kind of junk the Blackwoods are looking for."

"But they are looking for guns," James said. "That means they'll need money to buy them with. Could o' been money in the saddelbags Luke grabbed from that officer before they run off this afternoon."

"James," Michael warned, "we don't even know for sure that

those men were Finis and Luke, much less what they took fron the officer before they ran. That could've been their dinner for al we know."

"Sure it could. Or it could be a payoff too. And you know i your heart that them two was Finis and Luke. You know that a good as I do, Michael."

"I don't know it."

"But you're sure that it was. Just the same as me."

"Why don't you . . ." Sly began. He was interrupted by a lov whistle from Andrew, who while Michael and James bickered ha been reading through the papers that had belonged to one of th dead Mexican officers. "What?"

"This. Here." He thrust the paper at Sly, who only glanced a it and shook his head.

"I can't read no Spanish," Sly admitted. "Talk it some, but can't read a word of it. What's it say?"

"It's a letter sent from a General Filisola to some man calle Vicente Cordova."

Sly frowned. "I know Vicente Cordova. He lives near Nacog doches."

"That's the one," Andrew said. "This letter was being carrie to him by Manuel Flores."

"One of these dead men?"

Andrew shrugged. "Maybe. Or maybe these people wer carrying it to Flores for him to pass along. The point is, Cordov was supposed to receive a sum of money along with the letter. Th letter doesn't say how much, but it implies it's a lot of money. An Cordova is supposed to use that to buy guns . . . get thi now . . . to buy guns using 'the Texans you told me of' . . . n names, but I sure wish there had been . . . anyway, Cordova i supposed to give at least part of the money to two Texans who wi buy the guns for him and pass them along to Cordova." Andre frowned. "I suppose that's to keep Cordova out of sight, like in cas someone would wonder why he'd be wanting so many guns. An then when the guns are delivered, Cordova is supposed to distribut them and powder and ball to Chief Bowl for the Cherokee."

"The Cherokees. What the devil would they have to do wit this?" Michael asked.

"I'm afraid I can think of something," Sly said. "The Cheroke aren't at all happy with Lamar being president now. They dote o Houston. O' course he used to live with them. Always has got o good with them. But they're scared of Lamar."

"They ought to be," Andrew said. "The president understands Indians. He won't mollycoddle them the way Houston did."

Sly gave Andrew a look that said he didn't necessarily agree but wasn't going to get into a fuss about it now. "My point," he said, "is that the Mexicans surely know there's bad feelings between Lamar and the Cherokee. And they wouldn't for a minute be above trying to drive a wedge in between them. They might even give the Cherokee guns and try to get them to come in on their side in a Mexican attempt to take Texas back."

"The Cherokee won't fight," Andrew said. "It's a well known fact that they're cowards. Austin and Houston promised them all manner of things before, but they wouldn't help us fight the Mexicans in the War for Independence. That's one of the biggest reasons the president hates them so. They are cowards."

"He calls them cowards. Maybe they're just smart," Michael said. "It wasn't their fight."

Andrew glowered at his brother. He tapped the paper in his hand with a stiff finger and said, "It looks like they're willing to take up with the Mexicans now, dammit, even if they didn't think it was their fight then."

"Now dang it, Andrew, you said yourself that that ain't what that letter says. It says Cordova is to give guns to the Cherokee. It don't say that the Cherokee have promised to use the guns against Texans."

"Can you think of any other reason why Mexico would give guns away to an Indian tribe?"

Michael had no answer for that, unfortunately.

"I can't believe the Blackwoods would be involved in a rebellion against Texas," Sly said, returning to the original point.

"You don't know them as well as we do," James said.

"For that matter," Michael said, "they wouldn't necessarily have to know what the guns were intended for. Or who they would be given to. And the Blackwoods would certainly do almost anything if they thought they could come out a dollar ahead on the deal. Including giving guns to the Cherokees."

"Naw," James said. "If the Mexicans bought guns and told the Blackwoods to give them to the Cherokee, Finis would keep the money the Mexicans gave him and *sell* the guns to the Indians 'stead o' giving them away."

Michael and Sly laughed. Andrew did not. "Boys," Andrew said, "this is serious. This letter proves that Mexico is planning a fight to take Texas back. And that the Cherokee are lining up to side with the Mexicans when it happens."

"It don't prove any such thing," Michael said.

"It certainly indicates strongly that that's what they have in mind."

"But it don't prove it. We're reading a lot between the lines here, Andrew, and most of that because of what we know about the Blackwoods. Why, we ain't even all the way sure that it *was* Finis and Luke that we seen here today."

"Still and all," Andrew said, "I think it's a strong enough case that the president and his people need to see these papers as quickly as we can get them to him."

"If you think Lamar oughta see them, all right."

"You can manage to get James and Sly back without me, can't you, Michael?"

Michael chuckled. "I might."

"I didn't mean it like that," Andrew said.

"You better not have," James told him, "or me an' my one good arm will have to whup you, brother."

"I didn't. The point is, dang it, you need to turn for home. We aren't going to be having any buffalo hunt. Not until you fellows heal up, we won't. I just think come morning you boys ought to turn back while I take these letters and press on up the Colorado to meet President Lamar and his party. They need to see these. It's important."

"You think you can remember to pass the letters along without gilding the lily, Andrew?"

"What are you saying, Michael?"

"Just to . . . you know . . . t' not get anything stirred up without we're sure of what's going on."

"The president of the republic needs to see these letters, Michael. I'm not responsible for how they are viewed. Only for their successful delivery now that they've come into my hands."

"All right. But don't say anything about the Blackwoods. Okay?"

Andrew frowned. "I won't lie to President Lamar."

"Hell, Andrew, I wouldn't ask you t' lie. You know that. I'm only asking you t' not pass along guesses or b'goshes. Just facts. Will you do me that much, please?"

"I can do you that much, Michael. But if the president asks me a question I will certainly answer it."

"That's fair enough, Andrew. I got no quarrel with that."

"If you two are about done jawing," Sly said, "how's about you break out that flask again, Andrew. The little brown jug here seems to've run dry on us."

Michael settled back and tried not to worry about Andrew and the letters. No matter how hard he tried, though, Michael could not help fretting about it. For some reason he had a bad feeling about this.

☆ Chapter ☆ 18

James sat limp and dozing in a rocking chair on the dogtrot breezeway of his cabin, his feet propped atop a chunk of wood that needed splitting and his lean frame swaddled deep in a quilt. The chair was positioned to keep him out of the chill wind but where bright heat given off by the slanting winter sun could reach and warm him. The sun's heat was comforting, but even so he shivered now and again, his body racked and trembling from the ravages of a fever that had come over him just a few days after Michael brought him home.

Funny, but at the time of the fight with those Mexican boys they'd all thought Sly's foot wound the worst of their injuries by far. But that was two weeks ago. Now Sly was up and around with the help of a crutch Annie fashioned for him, but James was the one still laid up and miserable with an ague that he just couldn't seem to shake off, even though the bullet wound in his flesh looked to be healing pink and clean. Funny you bet, real funny indeed, James thought ruefully.

Behind him he heard the cabin door swing open and then slam loudly closed again. Those sounds were immediately followed by the sharp, staccato tap-tap-tap of Libby's footsteps as she came out into the dogtrot and marched rapidly out the other direction. She didn't speak and neither did James. He reached up from beneath the quilt that protected him and drew the puffy, thickly padded material closer to his throat. He wished . . . Abruptly he snatched hard rein on that thought, frowning and giving his head a shake of impatient annoyance with himself. Wishing won't put seed in the ground. That is something a grown man had best understand.

"I suppose now I'll have to cook for 'em."

James jumped, startled by the wholly unexpected sound of Libby's voice so close behind him. He hadn't heard her come back from the yard. He must have been dozing. Now the sudden movement jolted him and sent a fiery spear-point of pain through his side. The pain was strong enough to make him gasp, but he managed to keep from crying out even though sweat beaded cold and clammy on his forehead, and for a moment there he was holding himself so stiff he didn't dare to breathe. "Wha'?"

"Them riders," Libby snapped. "Andrew, looks like, an' whoever he's dragged along. I suppose now I'll have t' make them all welcome."

Her tone of voice was anything but welcoming. James thought about mentioning that, realized in time that that would be anything but wise, and instead said only, "I don't see them, Libby darlin'."

"Your eyes going weak as the rest of you, James Lewis? Right yonder they come." But she was still standing behind him, and if she was pointing he could not see in which direction. Nor did he see anything of Andrew or anyone else, dang it.

Libby made a sound that might have been disgust, or might not, and turned away. Before she disappeared into the cabin she mumbled something that James only partially heard, something to the effect that no Caldwell male would do . . . whatever. At that point James didn't want to hear any more anyway. Ever since he'd come home bullet-pierced and hurting, Libby'd been on her high horse about Lewis men being unreliable gallivanters and Caldwell men being superior in every way. Libby'd been a Caldwell before she married a Lewis. Some ways, James reluctantly admitted to himself, she still was a Caldwell and not a Lewis. Not that James Lewis had anything against Caldwell men, dammit. Not yet, anyhow. But sometimes . . .

He cleared his throat and leaned gingerly forward, striving for more height in the chair but quite frankly hoping that he wouldn't have to stand up. Not so soon again yet. It was frightening how very little moving around it took to sap all his strength clean away and leave him weak and shaking.

There. He could see figures moving now, coming down along the side of that winter-fallow field there. Libby'd been able to see them sooner than he because she'd been standing. There wasn't anything going wrong with his eyes after all. He was pleased to discover that. For just a moment there he'd been worried. Fevers can do strange things to a person. Weakness of vision is only one, and not the worst of them, bad though it would be. James was pleased to learn that so far none of that seemed to be afflicting him, anyway.

He smacked his lips and grunted a little, working up some saliva and swallowing it in an attempt to clear a buildup of phlegm from his throat. He was trying to avoid having to cough. Coughing cut bone-deep inside his chest and hurt like fire.

"Libby?"

"What?"

"We got any coffee on the stove, Libby?"

"I got no time to wait on you now, James Lewis."

"That ain't what I'm asking, dang it. Andrew and those men are turning this way."

"I knew I'd have to fix for them." Even as she complained he could hear the clang and rattle of pots and skillets being slapped onto the stove and a splashing of water being poured from the bucket into a metal container. James gathered that there hadn't been any coffee made and that now Libby was scurrying to put some on to boil. There was no telling what the rest of all that noise would be about. She couldn't expect Andrew to stop here to eat, not with his own home and family not a half mile distant across Sly and Annie's fields.

He heard the screech and creak of the firebox door hinges and the muted clunks of wood lengths being thrown in. James winced and wrinkled his forehead, physically trying to close off his ears in anticipation of Libby's oft-repeated complaints about the shortage of split wood. It was a chore he'd expected to complete when they got back from the hunt and now was unable to handle until his fever eased and the chest wound healed. This time she didn't bother going into it all over again, thank goodness.

"They're close now," he cautioned over his shoulder, not wanting his brother to overhear Libby complaining.

"What's that?"

He could hear from the sound of her voice that she was standing in the open doorway now. That meant she could see for herself how close Andrew and the other two men were. "Nothing," he muttered.

"Andrew." Libby's greeting was bright and cheerful and gay. "How nice t' see you, Andrew. An' you gentlemen too, I'm sure. Come set with James a minute, and I'll have you some lunch. The coffee's on the stove and I've got salt pork ready to fry. Got corn odgers mixing and the grease getting hot." She sounded absolutely delighted for the company.

Andrew and his companions dismounted. From the way they tood stiff-legged while they stretched and spat James could see hat they'd been steady in the saddle for a good many miles.

☆ Chapter ☆

19

Andrew and his two friends made an unlikely trio of travelers at least in James's opinion. There was lean and lanky Andrew looking pretty much his own homespun self after several rugge weeks out on the scout fighting Mexicans and doing who-knows what ever since. Then there was Christopher Campodoro, wh was plump and moon faced and who didn't come much higher t Andrew than his second or third shirt button. Campodoro, Jame thought, looked like an overaged little boy who'd dressed up t playact at being a woodsman but who got no closer to knowin how to act a woodsman than to smudge his cheeks with wood as and squint a lot so as to appear tough. Christopher Campodor looked about as much at home on this farm as James would fee himself to be if he was set into the rigging of a ship at sea. Finall there was Major Brown, first name unannounced, who wa introduced as being a special advisor to the president of th republic and commander of a militia company. Brown had col eyes, a crisp handshake, and no smile that James had yet seen The major wore a sword, carried a brace of pistols in holsters o his saddle, and looked as if he was more than passingly competen with either choice of weaponry. An odd trio indeed, Jame concluded.

Yet the truth was that his own brother Andrew really and trul did seem to fit in with these fellas. And wherever the three of the were off to, whatever business they were about, it was clearl Congressman Lewis who was the man in charge. Campodor deferred to Andrew shamelessly, and even the chill and humorles militia officer accepted Andrew's leadership. This was a side o Andrew that James had never seen before.

"We can't stay," Andrew said politely but firmly to Libby's near-frantic insistence that she finish cooking a dinner for them. "We'll eat at my place and stay the night there. I, uh, was expecting to have you come over this evening, James. Instead I take it you aren't feelin' up to a walk over to our place?"

James shrugged.

"No matter. We were just wanting a chance to talk."

"President Lamar is always interested in the views of his constituents," Campodoro put in. James was sure he was wrong about Campodoro—after all, the fellow was clearly a friend of Andrew's—but James's impression was that if Christopher Campodoro got any more oily-smooth you couldn't pat him on the back without your hand sliding off.

Major Brown sniffed but didn't say anything.

"You'll be here a few days, Andrew?" James asked. "I'm sure I'll be feeling better in another day or two. Just need a bit more time t' knock this."

"Sorry, brother, but we'll be riding on at first light tomorrow. The president's party is following. We need to get to Houston and begin pulling things together. The president wants to confer with the house and senate leadership and check on the preparedness of the militia. It seems our scrap with Flores has stirred up a hornet's nest."

"Flores?"

"That Mexican officer," Andrew said.

"We don't know for sure that he was Flores. Just that he was carrying a letter addressed to somebody named Flores," James corrected.

"That isn't the point," Andrew said. "The point is the intentions behind the plot we uncovered. Now we know the Mexican government is in collusion with the Cherokees, and—"

"You best talk to Michael about this some more, Andrew. Dang it anyhow, you know that ain't—"

"Do you have knowledge of this matter beyond the information in those captured documents?" Major Brown snapped.

"No, I do not. I'm only sayin' that you can't be sure o' all that stuff based on what we all read in that camp."

Brown ignored James's opinion and asked, "Have you seen the Blackwood brothers since you returned here?"

"Now mister, you take a close look an' see d'you think I been out makin' calls on my neighbors since Michael carried me home."

"It is Major Brown, if you please, sir. Not mister."

James didn't much cotton to folks who fretted more with titles than messages. But he wouldn't for the world have embarrassed Andrew by saying so, neither by word nor by deed. "Sorry," was all he said on that matter. "As for Finis an' Luke, no, Major, I ain't seen neither of them. Neither has anybody else that I know of. Annie stopped by here yesterday evening. She said that boy Cyrus is still coming regular to set to their table an' then sneak food out for his brothers an' sisters. That generally means that Finis an' Luke either are away or that they're home but laying up drunk. An' no Blackwood has ever had money enough to manage a two-week drunk, so I think it's safe t' say that they ain't home yet from wherever they been." He paused and eyed Andrew.

"I made it clear," Andrew asserted, "that we only suspect it was the Blackwoods we saw at that camp. We have no proof of it."

"You will inform us immediately the Blackwood brothers return?" Brown asked crisply, again choosing to allow parts of the conversation to pass by him untouched.

James tilted his head and looked the major over for a moment. He wished he was feeling up to getting onto his own hind legs so he could stare Brown direct in the eyes. But he wasn't. He just plain wasn't, dang it. He had to remain in the rocking chair, wrapped inside a quilt like some ancient dodderer. "It ain't much in me to stand up for no Blackwood, Major," James said. "But from the sound o' your voice whatever you got in mind for them ain't good. An' just this one time those boys may not be guilty of anything. For sure we don't know that they are. So I reckon I don't feel like taking part in it. D'you want Finis and Luke found, Major, you do it your own self. I won't be the one to sic you on 'em."

"James," Andrew protested. "Major Brown only wants—"

"Dammit, Andrew, I can see in his eyes what Major Brown wants. An' I don't think it's truth neither. Just confirmation o' whatever he already believes. Or wants t' believe. Well, I ain't gonna be the one to hand even a Blackwood over to that kind o' treatment."

"If you weren't a sick man . . ." Brown warned.

"If I wa'n't a sick man we'd sure as hell have t' find out." James finished the thought for him. "Wouldn't we? Major?" He managed to make the perfectly honorable military title sound like an accusation.

"James!" Andrew bleated.

"Dang it, Andrew. I'm sorry. Far as you an' this gentleman are concerned anyhow." James apologized with a wave in the direction of Christopher Campodoro, who, in truth, James didn't find to be all that much of an improvement over the major. "It's just that I can't see the whole congress an' militia o' this entire republic flying off the dang handle over a bunch of sheer supposition. Which these fellas sure seem t' be doing. What you need t' do, Andrew, is have you a talk with Michael before the bunch of you goes an' starts something you might regret later."

Andrew stiffened. "I don't need Michael's advice, James. Nor yours."

James felt hollow. He'd had perfectly good intentions, darn it. He'd tried to be polite. So how was everything going so horribly wrong now?

"Andrew . . ."

But Andrew had already taken Campodoro and Brown by the sleeves and was leading them back toward their horses. They weren't even going to stay long enough now to take a cup of that coffee Libby was preparing for them.

At least Andrew paused long enough to mumble a few platitudes and get-well wishes before he hurried to catch up with the other two and swing back into the saddle he had vacated only minutes earlier. Then the men were riding out of the yard toward Andrew's home, none of the three of them waving or looking back toward James in his rocking chair on the porch.

"I swear, James Lewis, sometimes you're crude as a boar hog in rut," Libby accused from close behind his chair. He hadn't heard her come outside again. "The one chance I've had to see some new faces at my table and enjoy some decent company for a change, the one and only chance I've had since I can't even remember how long ago, and what do you do, James Lewis? Darn you. You run them right off, that's what you do."

James said nothing. He knew better. If he opened his mouth at all, his comment would be taken as baiting or an insult, no matter what he said. Not that it was Libby's fault. She was only irritable because of being with child. He understood that. So for the time being it was better simply to say nothing than to try and correct her misinterpretations, some of which were so caustic and nasty as to make him think they had to be deliberate. This was just something a man had to learn to live with when his wife was expecting, James had long since concluded. So he sighed and slumped deeper into the rocking chair and waited for the relief of the solitude he would find once Andrew and Campodoro and Major Brown were out of sight and Libby was back inside the cabin. James sat in the light of the winter sun and wished he could doze off again, while behind him Libby complained and accused and loudly grumbled although her husband steadfastly ignored her, closing his ears to her nattering and allowing the sound of it to run off him like water off a well-shingled roof.

Eventually Libby ran down like a cheap clock unwinding. She went back into the cabin, and James was alone with a day that had turned gloomy and cheerless. Not that it had been so very grand to begin with. He sighed, closed his eyes, and hoped for the rejuvenating comforts a mindless sleep might provide.

☆ Chapter ☆

20

James looked up at the sound of footsteps in the dogtrot. It was late, a good three hours past daylight, but James was still sitting at the table with the leftover dregs of a cold cup of coffee in front of him. He hadn't yet felt up to going outside, and it would not have occurred to him to go back to bed, fever or no such; far as the Lewises were concerned a man didn't lay abed in the daytime unless his wife was already sewing him a shroud.

There was the sound of footsteps and then a faintly heard shuffle and stomp as the visitor wiped his feet on the square of burlap Libby laid down to keep mud or snow from being tracked in.

"Come in," James called through the closed door.

Daylight and chill air flooded the small cabin when the door was opened. "Michael," James said with a smile. Libby glanced up from the handwork she was doing in her lap, nodded once, and went back to the chore.

"Morning, Libby, James." Michael hung his cap on a peg beside the door and leaned his old rifle against the jamb. "Is there coffee left? I'm 'bout one cup short today."

"On the stove," Libby said without looking up again. She did not offer to fetch it for her guest. Michael acted as if that was the most normal thing there could be. He took a cup down off the shelf, poured coffee for himself, and while he was at it filled James's cup too.

"I don't need you two underfoot," Libby said. "Why don't you take him outside, Michael? The fresh air will do him good."

"James?"

"Sure thing." He was able to stand upright by himself today, although he was weak and wobbly and more than a little bit dizzy. When he looked down the floor seemed an awfully long way away. Still, it was better to be able to move than not. James was sure he was improving.

Michael took care of him while Libby worked on at whatever she was doing. He got James the quilt off the foot of the bed and a shawl to wrap close around his shoulders, then half supported him out to the rocking chair. He went back inside for the coffee and carried it out for the both of them.

"Thanks."

"You all right, James?" There was no other chair on the dogtrot, so Michael sat on the wood chunk that James had been using as a footstool.

"Better."

"You look pale."

"But better."

"If you say so."

"I do." James sipped at the coffee. It was strong and bitter and he enjoyed it thoroughly. Changing the subject, he asked, "Andrew and those men get off all right?"

Michael nodded. "I was just over to his place seeing them off. Figured if I was gonna be out anyhow I might 's well stop here an' see how my baby brother is doing."

"Then I expect you'd best write back home t' Tennessee an' ask," James said with a grin.

Michael hesitated for a split second before he too managed a smile, although a weak one, acknowledging James's intent if not all the details of what he was saying. James had forgotten that for some reason Michael never really had accepted Jonathan as their brother. It was a view James neither shared not understood. Jonathan was the baby of the family but only, if someone wanted to be picky about it, a half brother to the rest of them. Jonathan was their mother's youngest. His father was their pa's brother Benjamin, who had married Patience after Mordecai Lewis was killed. Michael inexplicably resented young Jonathan, even though their cousin Frank Lewis had always been one of Michael's favorite friends as well as kin. Why, the way James saw it little Jonathan was a brother and a cousin too, and surely that was close enough kinship as to not need any apologies. Michael never seemed to see things that way. Now James mildly regretted having brought it up, however fleetingly.

"You mean they just now got away?" James said, pouncing on

that as an excuse to once again change the subject. He glanced toward the sky, where the sun was well advanced in its climb off the eastern horizon.

"That little city fella was complaining 'bout it being so early, if you can believe that," Michael said with a chuckle.

"No."

"Truth. I swear it."

James grinned and shook his head. Why, by this hour a man ought to have all his chores complete and half an acre tilled. If he wasn't laid up like some useless invalid, that is.

"Tell you something else," Michael said. "That dang citified Andrew was 'bout as hard to get stirring as the little fella."

"No."

"Truth. It was the major as kept after the both of them. If it'd been up to Andrew and Campodoro I reckon they'd have stayed over another day or two."

"That major is a hard one," James said. "If I was asked, which I ain't been, I'd say that I didn't like him. There aren't so many that I feel that way about, but he's one of the few."

"I didn't like him neither," Michael admitted. "His kind only sees things from their own one side. Never seems t' occur to them that the other fella has a viewpoint of his own."

"Yet he's the one advising the president about military matters. Don't that give you hope an' confidence for a peaceful future, Michael?"

Michael snorted and shook his head. "With people like Brown in charge, we could have t' fight Mexico again. Indians too, maybe. I'd been hoping you and me done all the fighting that'd ever have t' be done for this republic an' that our sons wouldn't never have to take up arms against anything but a squirrel now an' then."

"Our sons?" James asked.

"Aw, if you don't get a boy the first time that's all right. You can always try again. An' there's a lot t' be said for having a little girl in the house too."

"You miss 'em, don't you?"

"Lordy, I reckon I do. I won't feel right again till they're home and I know they're safe. No telling how long that'll be though. I told Marie not t' rush. Now I'm hoping she won't take me at my word."

James laughed.

"Here's one you'll like, James, seein' as how you ain't any fonder o' the major than I am."

"Mm?"

"Last night Andrew had us all over to his place to meet those government fellas, so o' course Sly and Annie was there, and Frank and all his brood. I mean, there was pretty much a house full o' kids so that a stranger'd need a chart to keep 'em all straight even if he wanted to. Anyhow, that Campodoro fellow was making most of the talk. I got to admit that he has the gift o' gab about him an' can be funny. He got to imitating the president and poking fun at Sam Houston an' some o' his crowd, an' that was pretty good. And he done some imitations of how charged up Lamar was with his plans for the new capital city—"

"Capital city?" James interjected.

"Didn't nobody tell you?"

"They wasn't here very long."

"Oh. Well, yeah, new capital. Upriver on the Colorado there's a place they camped whilst they was on this buffalo hunt, and the president decided it'd be the most pretty an' perfect spot there could ever be for a new capital. Which he wants out of Houston on account partly that it's swampy and sickly but mostly on account of it's named for Sam Houston, and President Lamar can't hardly abide the thought of Sam Houston no more."

James grunted.

"Andrew says they'll get it through Congress easy enough an' be able to start building a brand-new capital city before this year is out. But anyway, what I been trying to tell you, the major last night spent pretty near all his time with his nose stuck high in the air an' wearing a frown. Petra told me in private that he showed up mad an' never seemed much interested in getting otherwise."

James supposed he would have to take the blame for that.

"What little the man said was all fuss an' bluster. Gonna fight these folks here an' attack them over there an' clean out 'bout every kind o' rascal there's ever been. Righteous SOB is what he is, I'd say. Part o' which is directed against Finis an' Luke Blackwood. Which is about the most sensible thing I've heard about Andrew's Major Brown."

"Michael," James cautioned in a low voice.

"I know, I know, they're human too. I never said I'd turn them over to Brown any more than you would."

James raised an eyebrow.

"Oh, we all heard 'bout the way you showed yourself yesterday. Andrew repeated it 'cause he was peeved with you for acting like that in front o' his mucky-muck friends. The rest o' the family thinks you done just fine, if you want to know."

"Reckon I wanted to know," James admitted.

"An' now you do. So we already knew something 'bout Brown and his views anyhow. And . . . and this is what I been trying to get at 'cept you keep interrupting me . . . your crazy sister put something over on Brown that the man still don't know nothing about."

"Annie?"

"You got any other sisters handy?"

"What'd Annie go an' do?"

"Remember how I told you there was all these kids running in an' out and getting underfoot and stuffing their faces whenever they weren't bawling or scrapping with one another?"

"Ayuh."

"Well, that dang Annie, she ups an' maneuvers your pal the major into a corner an' starts laying on the flattery to him. Batting her eyelashes something shameful an' shining right up to him while ol' Sly is off pretending like he don't know nothing about this. I mean, Annie was really egging that major on an' trying to get him to brag to her. Which he done. Any man would've, I reckon. She got him started on them Blackwood brothers an' what Brown figured he could prove about the Mexicans an' the Cherokees just as soon as he got hold o' them Blackwoods. And of course how there wasn't nobody, not a Blackwood nor nobody else could ever stay quiet when Major Norbert Grantham Brown got holt of them."

"Norbert Grantham Brown?"

"I ain't responsible for it, James. I'm only repeating what the man said. Now will you hush an' let me tell you about that sister o' yours?"

"Sorry."

"The thing she'd done, James, an' that I think was so dang funny is that she'd backed Brown around to the corner where there was this pile o' filthy dirty little varmints with grease running down their chins from the feed Andrew put on last night. An' what ol' Norbert didn't know was that that bunch o' kids was Blackwoods. Annie'd talked to Petra earlier an' made sure it was all right to bring them hungry children in to share the groceries. So there Brown was, bragging it up to Annie in front of him while behind him young Cyrus and all them little Blackwoods is getting their ears filled with this fella's threats to their pa and uncle. And Norbert, he didn't know then who any of them kids was and still don't know what happened."

James laughed. "Finis and Luke will hear every word of it repeated to them."

"Which is what Annie had in mind, o' course, an' what you would of done your own self if you'd been there, I suspect."

"What'd Andrew say?"

Michael chuckled. "I dunno if Andrew knows any more than Norbert 'bout it. He was off on the other side of the place being toadied to by the little fella. Had his chest puffed right full, in fact. So I dunno if he ever did get told. Petra knows, but she near had to stuff her hand down her throat to keep from giggling and giving something away. She sees things the same as you and Annie do."

"An' you, Michael?"

"Aw, I don't like no Blackwoods, James. You know that."

"Yes?"

"But I don't like other bullies any better than them. You and Annie done the right thing. We can't be turning meanness loose just on the basis o' suspicions. That'd make us every bit as bad as the Blackwoods. Maybe worse than them, seeing as how we was always taught right from wrong."

"That Annie," James marveled. "Making it so that Major Norbert Whatever Brown delivered his own warning to his own intended victims. I like that."

"Thought you might." Michael grinned and stood. "Your wife makes a right fine cup o' coffee, James. You want me t' fetch you a little more?"

"If there's some left, that'd be real nice."

Michael winked at his brother and carried both their cups back into the cabin. "We'll finish these," he said when he returned, "then I thought I'd split some o' them chunks for you."

"You don't have to do that."

"Oh yes I do. Andrew noticed yesterday that you was running low, an' Libby's in no condition to be splitting wood. Andrew made me promise last night that I'd see to it."

"I'll be damned."

"Brother Andrew has changed since he's gone off to Congress, James, but he's still a Lewis, you know, an' we've always hung right tight together. That part won't change no matter what."

James nodded and sipped at his coffee. He felt warmer now, but the feeling had nothing to do with the hot coffee he was drinking.

In fact, he decided, he was feeling better in a good many ways than he had been of late. With any kind of luck maybe this fever was whipped and he could think about getting on with things soon, getting his fields ready for sowing once the last frost danger was past—he reminded himself that he needed to check the almanac and see what the frost prediction was for this spring—and . . . Lord, there were a thousand things that needed to be done. There always were on a farm, even at this time of year.

James looked off over the acreage that was his, huge by Tennessee standards if nothing much by Texas count, and felt the strength well up within his wiry frame. He began to smile and for the first time in weeks to plan as well.

"Dang if you don't look some better, James."

"Dang if I don't feel some better now, Michael."

The brothers sat in the warmth of the winter sun and finished their coffee.

☆ Chapter ☆

21

Congressman Andrew Lewis sank into the overstuffed parlor chair and gratefully accepted the hot brandied cider Lexie made for him. The weather had turned poor these past few days, gray and gusty, the low clouds spitting cold rain and the nights brisk enough to freeze the roads solid. Trying to walk the streets of Houston was hazardous to wardrobe and dignity alike once the morning sun started the thawing process and created a film of slick mud over top of the ice. It had been almost as slippery coming home to the boardinghouse again this evening. Home. For a fleeting moment Andrew was conscious of a deep, aching void. For just a moment he felt incomplete.

Still, it was serious business they were engaged in here, and Andrew wouldn't have traded places with anybody. Not really. He missed Petra, all the more so for having seen her again so recently, but his place was here in Houston. He only wished she would relent and agree to join him in the city. Maybe, he hoped, she would come to the new capital when it was laid out and ready for people to start building homes. Austin, they'd decided to call it. Houston already had a city named for him. Not that President Lamar would have consented to anything honoring the general anyway. But this way, avoiding a name that would have tended to elevate Mirabeau Lamar, the president's people could reach a quick agreement on the new capital without alienating Houston's faction and making a long fight of it in house or senate or, more likely, both.

And Austin was to be built on the banks of the Colorado, not much more than an easy day's ride upriver from the Lewis farms. Surely Petra would be willing to come to Austin with him.

Andrew's lips thinned and twisted into a half-hidden smile as thoughts of Petra in Austin were briefly supplanted by thoughts of Michael in Austin. Just wait until Michael Lewis heard that the new capital city was being built *upriver* from his farm. If Andrew's woods-running brother needed any proof that civilization was passing him by, why, there couldn't be a much better one than that. They would all be lucky if Michael didn't up and demand that the whole Lewis clan pack their gear and move west once more. That Michael, he was a caution.

Andrew smiled again, thinking about his brother, then allowed his thoughts to return to Petra. Oh, he did miss her. He . . .

"Something funny, Andrew?"

"Mm? What?" He looked up. Christopher had come into the parlor unnoticed. The rotund little politician waggled a finger lazily, and Lexie hurried to bring him a toddy and a freshener for Andrew too.

"I asked if there was something funny. I thought you were smiling when I walked in," Campodoro said.

"Oh, uh, nothing important," Andrew mumbled. There were some thoughts that were no one's business but his own.

Christopher smiled and took a seat close beside Andrew without waiting for an invitation. "I suppose you know, Congressman, just how appreciative the president is for all your help," he said.

Andrew shrugged, his thoughts at the moment not really directed toward the political affairs of the republic. This evening he was, if the truth of it be known, more than just a little bit homesick.

"Not only that warning about General Filisola and his plans to stir up the Cherokees. Although that is of monumental importance, Congressman. The president, however, is beholden to you for a great deal, not the least of which is your support in lobbying some of the other members of, um, rural background, shall we say. You have a way with people, Congressman, a certain rapport with people of that, um, sort that I can envy but would never be able to duplicate. You speak their language."

Andrew shrugged. He really wasn't all that much interested in listening to Christopher's flatteries this evening. "Is there a point to this?"

"What?"

"Was there something in particular you wanted tonight, Christopher?"

"No, certainly not. Just thought I'd pass the time of evening with you."

"If you don't mind then, I'm feeling a trifle on the low side t'night. I think I'd like t' be alone for a spell if it's all the same to you."

Campodoro frowned but didn't press for more detail than was offered. "Of course. Whatever you prefer, yes?"

"Thanks, Christopher. I 'preciate it."

Campodoro smiled, patted Andrew's knee, and wandered away with his drink in hand. He stopped briefly to say something to Lexie and then ambled out of the parlor and out of Andrew's thoughts.

Petra. She seemed so very far away tonight. And Andrew missed her so very much. Her and Ben and little Rose, and Michael and James and Annie and . . . everybody. Lord, but he did miss them all tonight.

Andrew's eyes popped wide open in the darkness. He hadn't been sleeping, really. More like a shallow doze was all he could manage tonight. And he'd thought he'd heard . . . there it was again. Very faint. Very soft. The touch of a foot to the floor and an accompanying creaking of the boards. No sound of the door being opened though. That was odd. Or had that been what wakened him? He blinked and tried to peer into the nearly complete dark that surrounded him, but if there was any moonlight tonight it was blocked by the heavy curtains at his windows. Andrew could see nothing and could hear little more. Just that faint, repetitive series of tiny sounds that he thought might be footsteps.

And breathing? Could he hear someone breathing too? He honestly wasn't sure.

He lay stiffly in the softness of the boardinghouse bed, his thoughts and emotions racing.

Someone was inside the room with him. He was sure of that.

His rifle and knife were secured out of sight—and out of reach—in the big wardrobe in the corner. He had . . . he tried to think . . . there was nothing in reach that he could use as a club. Nothing that he could think of. But he was in the city. In his own bedroom. Who ever would have thought . . . ?

Andrew's hand clenched into a fist and he drew himself silently toward the side of the bed, wishing he'd thought to leave a lamp burning low, wishing his knife was ready at hand.

He had no enemies in Houston, dang it. Political opponents, perhaps, but no enemies. And the general's people were not so rabid in their politics as to begin attacking the president's supporters, surely.

Frowning, Andrew shifted nearer to the edge of the bed and swung his legs over, easing quietly into a sitting position there. The ropes that held the ticking suspended within the bed frame groaned in mild protest as they were stretched and pulled.

"Andrew?" It was a whisper, light and delicate and feminine. The voice seemed familiar and yet not. He tried to place it and failed. "Andrew? You are awake?"

The voice sounded almost like . . . Petra? Could it be? "Darlin'?"

She laughed softly in the darkness, and this time there was no doubt she was moving to him. She came toward the sound of his voice, stopped a tantalizing few feet away, and he could hear a faint hiss and slither that he recognized as the sound of cloth lightly rustling as it fell to the floor. Then a sigh. Now she was before him; he could sense more than see her, could feel the warmth of her body close the short gap between them. His arms went round her waist. Her flesh was soft and smooth and cool to the touch. She wore nothing.

"Oh, my. I . . . didn't expect . . . never thought." He hugged her tight and pressed his cheek against the softness of her belly. Her skin smelled of soap and lavender water.

She laughed. "Ah, Andrew. So long I wait. Wan' you. So long you don' let me come to you."

He frowned. There was something . . . "Petra?"

"*Oui, m'su,* if you wan' me to be."

"Good Lord," he blurted. He went cold, a chill shooting through his spine. "Lexie?"

"But of course, *ma' cher'*. Lexie, Petra, whate'er you wan', Andrew. I be whoe'er, whate'er you wan', do for you whate'er you say." She hugged him and ruffled his hair, but Andrew was trying to draw away. "Something is wrong, Andrew?"

"Lexie, I . . . I . . ." he stammered. "I can't—"

"Oh but Andrew. You are too much tense, too much worried. I would help you, Andrew. An' not because I must, no. With you, Andrew, I wan' to do this. I would do what I am told anyway, yes. But with you, Andrew, I wan' to be with. I am happy to—"

"But you don't understand. I'm married, Lexie."

The girl was still trying to hug and touch him. Andrew was

trapped on the side of the bed and was leaning back as far as he could, trying to pull away, trying to disengage himself from her persistent touching and fondling. Trying and yet . . . tempted too. There was no denying it. He was feeling temptation even as he tried to withdraw from her. Lexie was young and pretty—and here. Petra was very far away. If anything did happen here—it wasn't like he invited Lexie in; none of this had been his idea; she'd merely shown up in the night while he was already sleeping—Petra would never know. The rationalization, unwanted, ran rampant through his thoughts, and he tried to reject that unwelcome train of thinking even while he was trying to evade Lexie's insistent advances.

"Is all right, Andrew. Is different wit' a girl lak me, you know. An' I be very good for you, Andrew. I have much love in my heart for you. You don' never know that, eh? But is true, my Andrew. All the gentlemen, I never wan' to please nobody like I wan' to please you."

He reached out to ward her off, inadvertently touched her bare breast, and snatched his hand back like he'd been scalded. "Lexie! Please don't." He moved backward, scooting back onto the bed to try to get out of her reach. Lexie climbed onto the bed with him.

"Many night, *ma' cher'*, I dream. You know what I dream? I dream you buy me, eh? I dream I be . . ."

"*Buy* you?" He stopped trying to get away and sat where he was, rigid with shock. "Buy you?" he repeated.

"But yes, my Andrew. That is what I most wan', is what I think in my night thoughts. An' I know he would make for you a very good price now, Andrew. I am worth much, no? Everyone say Lexie is worth very much. But for you, the bargain, yes? Very good price. Very low. An' I would be for you so very good. Never give you no trouble. Do for you anything, my Andrew."

"Dear God, Lexie. I didn't know . . ."

"Didn' know? Then you didn' treat me so nice 'spite me bein' a slave girl. You didn' know." Her voice was sad now, a bleakness creeping in and replacing the innocent happiness that had been there before. She quit trying to force herself upon him and wound up sitting on the edge of the now thoroughly rumpled bed.

"I . . . it doesn't matter, Lexie. Not . . . that way. It's like I told you. I'm a married man. You being owned by somebody, that's got nothin' t' do with that. But . . . I dunno. I feel dumb now. I should have realized. Should have seen what was setting right there in front o' me. Not your fault that I didn't. Not your fault that I can be so dumb 'bout things. Who is your . . . that is t' say, who, uh . . ."

"Who own me? *M'su* Campodoro, Andrew. He buy me in N' Orleans. I be nice to his gentlemen friends, you see. But to you, Andrew, I wan' to be nice. An' you don' let me to be." She sighed. "One time it is what I wan', an' what happens? Ha! I should know better. Any girl should know better, but I am dumb, me. You, Andrew, an' me, we are sometimes pretty dumb, yes?"

"Pretty dumb, yes," Andrew agreed. He sighed and slipped off the far side of the bed. "I think, Lexie, that you'd better go now."

"If you say."

"I do." He heard the ropes creak again and knew the broad, empty bed kept them a safe distance apart now. "Christopher send you up here tonight, did he?"

"*Oui, m'su*. But he don' want to make you mad at him. He wan' to do for you a nice thing. Make you feel not so lonely, yes? Make you glad you are his fren'. He would not make you mad, not for nothing. An' Andrew. I would not make you mad neither. Not never. Not for nothing. Never. This I swear to you."

"Thank you, Lexie. You're sweet."

"If you wan' to change your mind, Andrew . . ." Her voice trailed suggestively away, the tone of it dropping easily into a sultry seductiveness.

"No," he said sharply.

"Good night, Andrew." And she was gone. This time he heard the sound of her footfalls and the sharp, distinct sound of the door opening. There was a candle burning in the hall. Dim light from it spilled into the room. He could hear Lexie pause, standing in the doorway there, no doubt outlined by the light beyond. She was a pretty girl. Too pretty. Andrew swallowed, hard, and stared resolutely away until the light diminished and then was pinched off completely as once again the door was firmly closed.

Andrew felt shaken as again he sought his bed. Lexie owned by Christopher. Lexie pliant. Sweet. Available. And Petra so very far away. Christopher so anxious to do favors for the congressman from the Colorado. Lexie so lithe and lovely. Andrew's flesh burned with lingering memory of the contact with hers. He groaned aloud, wadded his pillow into a ball, and punched it viciously, knowing even when he did that it would make him feel not the least bit better but making the effort nonetheless.

Damn it, anyway.

He should feel anger, Andrew thought. He had been offended, hadn't he? So now he should feel anger toward Christopher and toward Lexie too. So why didn't he? Was he harboring some sick desire to keep his options open lest he change his mind in the future? Damn his own dark soul if that was what he was doing.

Petra! Why wouldn't she agree to move to the city with him? None of this would ever have happened if Petra hadn't insisted on staying at the farm.

Andrew groaned with frustration and with a sudden, seething anger. He rolled back and forth, trying without success to find comfort in the lonely boardinghouse bed.

It was a very long time before he was able to sleep again.

☆ Chapter ☆

22

Life was almighty good, Michael Lewis reflected as he stopped, dropped the seed bag onto the ground to ease its weight from his shoulder, and took a moment to mop the sweat from his forehead. Life was almighty good indeed.

Over at the cabin he could see a flash of skirts in the shadows of the dogtrot, and seconds later Marie stepped out into the bright sunshine of this fine spring day. And that right there, Michael acknowledged, the fact that his beloved Marie was home again from Natchitoches, was the reason life was so especially good.

Marie and the children had returned two weeks earlier, in time for Mordecai to help him finish plowing and raking their fields. Now the oats were in, Marie's vegetable garden well started, and the beans already seeded in neat rows. At the moment Michael was broadcasting barley seed on a small patch that should produce enough for their own needs and a few bushels more. After this small field was done he would plant his buckwheat and some flax, then would have to wait for the warmer nights of early summer before he could put the corn in. All in all, though, things were well in hand, and he was pleased.

Marie left the house and walked out to him, carrying something carefully balanced in her hands. As she came nearer he could see it was a gourd. "How'd you know?" he asked as she reached his side and handed him the dipper of cool water.

"I always know," she teased. Or then again maybe she wasn't teasing. She always did seem to know when he wanted or needed something.

Michael smiled at his wife, gratefully drank the water she'd carried to him, and paid her with a kiss and a pat on her backside.

"Michael!" she chided. "The children could be watching."

"The children," he said, "could be sent off t' visit their cousins for a couple hours. Like till morning, woman."

"Michael." But she was smiling. It was good to see her smile like that again. She'd been altogether too solemn when she first came home. But then she'd buried her father back in Natchitoches and left her grieving mother with the oldest of her brothers. The only thing good about her trip was that it had enabled her to see her father again while there was time. Apart from that the journey had been a sad experience for her and for the children too. Still, it was good that they'd gone. And in Michael's view better yet that they were back. "Later," she said.

"Later," he agreed. He handed back the empty gourd.

"Who is that, Michael? It does not look like Frank or any of his boys, do you think?" She pointed with her chin in the direction of Frank Lewis's fields. A horse and rider were approaching, cutting across Frank's place instead of continuing up the old King's Highway from San Antonio to Nacogdoches.

Michael began to grin. "I can't see who 'tis yet neither. But I think I know."

"Yes?"

"That horse looks like one we sent down to Manuel. If I'm right I reckon we'll be having a visitor for a spell."

"Goodness. I must air out the blankets then, Michael. And Angeline can fill a ticking with fresh straw. And . . . oh, there is so much I must do. Good-bye." She raised up onto tiptoes and delivered a quick peck onto the side of his jaw—about all that she could reach without his cooperation even when she was on tiptoe—and hurried away toward the cabin to begin preparing for the arrival of a guest.

Michael had time enough to finish throwing the barley, he figured, then if Manuel hadn't yet reached them he would walk down to the river and tell Mordecai who was coming. Manuel was the eldest son of Elizandro Zaragosa. Elizandro had once been a soldier in the army of Spain serving under the officer who murdered Michael's father, and more than once Elizandro held Michael Lewis's life in his hands. Elizandro had been a fine man, though, and despite the gulf that separated him from Michael those long years ago the two eventually became friends. Elizandro was dead now—so very many were, Michael sometimes thought, so many killed in the fighting that had been necessary for freedom—but the Lewis and Zaragosa families remained close through the years and across the miles, the Lewises on their farms on the Colorado and the Zaragosas on a small place outside San Antonio de Bexar.

Manuel Zaragosa in particular had always been a favorite of Michael's and was a visitor here as often as circumstance permitted. If Michael remembered correctly, Manuel should be twenty now or close to it, a man grown, even if Michael did still think of him as a boy.

Mordecai would be especially pleased to see Manuel. Manuel's three-year advantage in age had been just enough to make him Mordecai's idol and mentor whenever the two boys had been together in the past. Michael was fairly sure it would have been Manuel who taught Mordecai the boyish secrets like those first sneaked smokes in bullrush pipes or the first giggle-whispered, and probably wildly inaccurate, facts of life. But then there are always some things that a man has to rely on others to teach to his son. And times when a man has to struggle to keep his expression neutral and his eyes down, like when a boy comes in from the shed looking green and woozy and you know he's gone and swallowed that chew instead of knowing enough to spit. It was that sort of close, if entirely too infrequent, relationship Mordecai and Michael had had through the years. They were still friends, and Michael knew that Mordecai would be delighted to see Manuel again now.

Michael hurried to finish tossing the barley seed in swift, fanlike sprays so that he could find Mordecai and tell him about the visitor.

"You are trying to tempt me," Manuel accused with a smile as he tried to decline the last of the honey-sweetened bread pudding that Marie was pressing upon him. "Truly I can hold no more, thank you. But you would enjoy it, Angelina? You take it. Please."

Angeline blushed and, like a young and inexperienced rabbit flushed from its cover, bolted from the table and began rattling plates inside the dish bucket, making a most unnecessary amount of noise and commotion as she did so. Michael could see with considerable amusement that the backs of Angeline's ears had turned a rather bright shade of pink, so she wasn't able to hide even with her back to the table.

Manuel blinked in confusion and looked as if he was wondering if he had just embarrassed himself. Mordecai, quite completely unaware of any sensitivity that might exist between his oldest and best friend and his common-as-grass little sister, resolved the bread pudding question by shoveling into his own dish the sweet, especially-for-company offering that Manuel had so foolishly rejected. But then his mother's special bread pudding, laced thick with dark raisins and scarlet currants and golden nuggets of dried peach and apple, was one of Mordecai's very favorite things in the whole world. And if a visit by Manuel Zaragosa could be combined with bread pudding for dessert, why, things just couldn't get much better than that.

"I don't see why you wanta go up to Austin anyhow," Mordecai complained around a bulging mouthful of the pudding.

"A man must work," Manuel explained for perhaps the tenth time since his arrival. "And they say there is much work to be had in Austin now. Any man who can use a shovel or a hammer is able to find work there."

"Aw, folks say lots o' things," Mordecai responded skeptically. "I say you oughta stay here a spell. You and me can go fishing. Don't that beat poking a shovel in the ground or swinging a dang old hammer?"

"It would be my choice, Mordecai, yes, but it would not put food on the table of my family, no."

Mordecai made a face and dug his spoon into the remains of the quickly disappearing bread pudding.

"Mind your manners, Mordecai. Manuel knows he is welcome in this house, but he must do as he must do," Marie put in.

"Yes, Mama."

"Surely though, Manuel," she went on, "you are not in so much a hurry to reach Austin that you will not stay for Angeline's party."

"Señora?"

"In three days we will celebrate the anniversary of our Angeline's birth, Manuel. Fourteen years it will have been then."

"Mama. Manuel doesn't care about that." An anguished voice reached them along with a louder than ever clatter of dishes in the bucket. Angeline spoke without turning to face the others at the table.

"But of course I would stay for this occasion, Angelina," Manuel said.

His daughter's ears became an even more violent shade of red, forcing Michael to duck his head and cover his grin behind a feigned cough lest he laugh out loud.

Angeline was so transparent—on the other hand, so was Manuel.

Twenty now, mm? And Angeline fourteen? He grunted softly to himself. Angeline was a long way from being old enough to be thinking about boys, that was for sure. Or about young men, which was what Manuel had become sometime when Michael wasn't looking.

When that time did come though, in another five or six years or perhaps a little longer, well, a girl—or a father—could do worse than a fine boy like Manuel Zaragosa.

And in the meantime Michael thought he'd best have a word with Marie and make sure she had a word with Angeline. Just to make sure the child really understood how different boys are from girls once they start getting to a certain age.

Michael sat back and watched with some amusement while Manuel helped clear the table and Angeline broke a perfectly good clay pot and Mordecai in blithe ignorance gobbled down the last scraps of bread pudding. Michael glanced at Marie, and she winked at him. Michael laced his hands over his belly in complete contentment and thought once again that life truly was very good indeed.

☆ Chapter ☆
23

Angeline wrapped a rag around the handle of the pot hook. The iron hook shouldn't be hot but it was probably dirty. Carefully holding her skirts back away from the coals in the fire pit she slipped the hook under the bail on the heavy bean pot and, straining, scooted the pot back until it rested more on the stones that rimmed the pit than on the dull gray and bright red hardwood coals.

"Thank you, dear."

"Yes, Mama." Angeline looked across the grove to the trestle tables where the menfolk were drinking and talking and smoking. Later, sometime after dark, someone would push the tables out of the way, someone else would produce the instruments, and there would be some dancing and hoorahing, all of it in her honor. That knowledge pleased Angeline, but not as much as the fact that Manuel had stayed just so he could attend this party given for her fourteenth birthday.

Manuel was so *handsome*. Not so tall as Papa, but lean and compact and very quick. Dark hair and dark eyes and a fine, olive skin and long, delicate fingers. He was tidy about his person too; his fingernails were always clean and carefully trimmed, not just bitten off like Mordecai's. And such thick, curling eyelashes. Angeline would have given anything to have eyelashes like Manuel Zaragosa's.

She looked across the way to where Manuel was sitting now with Mordecai, both of them close to Papa and Uncle James and Uncle Sly. She felt a rush of heat into her cheeks. She stepped back away from the fire pit, even though she recognized that the heat from the coals had nothing to do with the warmth she was now experiencing. It really couldn't, because heat from a fire wouldn't account for the squirmy, almost queasy feeling she was experiencing low in her tummy or the ragged fluttering that lodged in the back of her throat. Angeline stepped back and looked toward her mother, but she seemed to have noticed nothing. Angeline was glad. Not that Mama would have said anything to her if she had noticed. But Papa might, and wouldn't that be insufferably embarrassing, and Mordecai—Angeline rolled her eyes heavenward—Mordecai would blurt out anything that came into his head, darn him. She knew better than to ever let anything on to Mordecai.

"Are you all right, dear?" her mother asked from close beside her. Angeline had been so preoccupied with her thoughts that she hadn't noticed Mama come around the fire to her.

"Yes'm. I'm fine."

Her mother frowned and pressed the back of her hand to Angeline's forehead. "You feel warm to me. Why don't you get away from the fire a while. Take a little walk, dear. Get some fresh air. You've been hovering over this smoky fire ever since we started cooking."

"There's too much to do yet, Mama."

"Nonsense. There is only a little bit left to do and more than enough hands for the work. Go on now." She smiled and stroked Angeline's cheek. "Besides, this party is to celebrate you, dear, not work you to distraction. Go on now. No, I insist. Go on."

Angeline nodded, gathered her skirts in both hands, and walked quickly away in the direction of the river. She wanted to look back, but she didn't.

She was only being silly anyway.

She sighed and, once out of sight from everyone, slowed her pace to a stroll.

On a whim she straightened her back and lifted her chin. But with her eyes most carefully down. Yes, like that, she thought, and smiled to herself. Just like that. And the walk—very slow, rhythmic, but balanced. Oh yes, balanced. She held her left hand to her side and positioned her fingers daintily, primly, as if so very lightly touching a gallant gentleman's elbow. Her right hand she lifted slightly, fingers moving, as if she were twirling a parasol. She tilted her head, first this way and then that. She laughed aloud, softly, only a very little. A deliberately phony and almost falsetto ha-ha-ha, as if her imaginary companion had just that moment said something amusing, something that required the courtesy of a just-so response. "Ha-ha," she repeated. Didn't like the sound of that one. Frowned a little and tried it again. "Ha-ha-ha." Made a face. "Ho-ho-ho?"

"Ha-ha-ha." Now *that* laugh was genuine—and not hers.

"Oh, dear." Angeline froze in place, her eyes huge and the heat rushing into her cheeks so hot and sudden as to make her feel faint. "I didn't . . . oh, dear." She turned and would have bolted except that Manuel stepped in front of her to block her way.

"I didn't mean to frighten you," he sputtered. "Honestly I did not."

"Frighten me?" she exclaimed. "Frightening me I wouldn't mind so much. But did you have to make fun of me?" Embarrassment was replaced by a flash of anger that came just as quick as the other had been, and she stamped her foot and scowled up into the liquid brightness of Manuel's dark eyes.

"Make fun? Oh no, Angelina. Never. I swear it, I did not; I would not."

"You did to try and make fun of me."

"But I didn't mean . . . it was just . . . the way you were walking. Whatever you were doing, Angelina, you appeared to me like the most grand of most grand ladies taking the paseo in the square at Bexar. You looked . . . that is to say you sounded . . ." Manuel himself looked most thoroughly miserable at this moment. "I made a mistake. But I would never make fun of you, Angelina. Truly I would not."

She sniffed, loudly. But the truth was that what Manuel saw was precisely the event she had been imagining, herself taking the evening paseo on the arm of a most handsome gentleman—Manuel himself perhaps?—and most necessarily with a sharp-eyed duenna close behind.

"You were making fun," Angeline insisted, but not so forcefully this time. If marvelously handsome Manuel really wanted to persuade her otherwise . . .

Manuel stumbled with the English, tried again in Spanish, and was able to stammer out his apologies. Angeline allowed him to sputter on for some time before she relented and announced a willingness to believe him—conditionally, that is. Manuel seemed properly grateful for this favor.

"I should go now," Angeline suggested when all of that had been successfully concluded, not meaning a word of it.

"Please don't," Manuel blurted.

"No?" She looked into his eyes. That was a mistake. Manuel's eyes were deep, moist, and utterly gorgeous. Angeline felt a tightening, a certain electric excitement, inside her belly.

"Please." He appeared to be nervous. He licked his lips. She thought his lips were . . . oh, she should not have any thoughts about Manuel Zaragosa's lips. Really she should not. But how could she help herself when he stood so near, when his presence was so . . . commanding. She felt her breath become ragged, felt her knees go weak and begin to sag. A thin red haze began to creep over her vision.

"Angelina?" Manuel's voice was loud in her ear and almost frantic. Whyever should it be so loud? And why did he have his arm about her like this? He was supporting her with one arm, so strong, behind her shoulders. The other was at her waist. Her head was cradled tight against his chest. She could feel the warmth of him through the cloth of his shirt. The scent of him filled her nostrils. She breathed deep so as to take this essence of him into her lungs.

"I don't understand," she whispered.

"You went so pale you frightened me. You started to fall. I . . . I grabbed for you. I could not let you fall to the ground, no?"

"No," she agreed.

"No," Manuel said. "You are better now?"

"Yes." But he made no effort to let go of her. And Angeline made no attempt to pull away from Manuel's arms. Oh, he was so handsome. His eyes were so close above her, his lips so near to her own. She felt limp again, excited but faint.

Manuel held her tight, lifted her, dipped his face even nearer to hers, brushed his lips against hers. Angeline could feel the trembling in Manuel's lips, and felt tremors to match that through the core of her own body. A giddy, heady, loose and fuzzy sensation infused her. She felt as if she were floating. Her toes tingled and she felt that she was going to faint again, but this time she resisted fainting because she wanted to miss nothing of this extraordinary moment. She could taste Manuel's breath, and she knew he could taste hers. Her breath caught in her throat. For a moment she felt as if she might melt clean away into a warm, buttery puddle on the ground here beside the river.

For just a moment.

Angeline came reluctantly to her senses. She stiffened in Manuel's embrace and pulled herself away from him, stumbling backward several steps until she regained her balance and her propriety.

"I should slap your face, Manuel Zaragosa."

"Yes," he agreed.

But Angeline did not slap him. And this time Manuel did not apologize.

She took a shy, tentative step toward him. Manuel was, after all, quite devastatingly handsome. And Angeline was, after all, very much grown up now. A kiss—she really had been kissed, hadn't she? This remarkable knowledge would have to be savored slowly and in private some other time—wasn't so much. Not for a woman of fourteen. But she had scarcely been aware of Manuel's kiss at the time. She had been too faint to really experience it. But perhaps if they were to kiss again . . . ?

"Manuel."

"Yes, Angelina?"

She stepped boldly to him, smiled, touched his cheek, and drew him down to her. She could see his lips part to meet hers. And his eyes, those remarkable eyes—

"Hey! You." The male voice was harsh and accusing. "Leave her be, you greasy spic bastard."

Angeline gasped. There was a crashing in the brush nearby, and a huge, horrid, terrifying form burst out of it with upraised fists and a flying beard.

"Don't you never touch no white girl, you stinking spic you," the intruder roared.

Angeline put her hands to her throat and reeled back in horror as the man charged full tilt into unsuspecting Manuel.

Angeline cried out, shrill, loud. And again, louder this time, more frantic. She squeezed her eyes tight shut but was unable to block out the dull, ugly sounds of flesh battering flesh, the grunts and the anguished exhalations and the low, muted cries of pain.

Angeline screamed and screamed, even louder yet, trying to make them stop, trying to blot out the sounds of it, trying to will herself to faint again, this time dead away. She screamed until her throat was raw and she had no breath remaining in her body, but still she screamed.

☆ Chapter ☆

24

Michael raced along the foot-worn path to the riverbank. His heart was pumping madly, his fears spurred to a frenzy by his daughter's screams. Close at his heels and trying to elbow past him were James and Sly, with the others strung out behind them. Mordecai and the younger boys were much farther back but only because they had been standing farthest away from the river when Angeline's piercing shrieks began. Michael had no idea what her danger was—yes he did, but he could not bring himself to believe that of any son of Elizandro Zaragosa—and he really did not much care. Whatever was terrifying her, or whoever, would have a price to pay. Michael only wished he had his rifle in hand. But it was back at the cabin, leaning up against the dogtrot wall, out of reach. When Angeline screamed, Michael hadn't even thought of running back to get it. She had sounded so desperate, so terribly, terribly frightened.

His heart pumped madly now and his lungs were seared with sharp pain, but he would not slow nor move over to let James by. Whatever was attacking Angeline would have him to face and no other, by damn.

He could hear a crashing in the underbrush now as someone—Mordecai, he guessed—abandoned the crowded path and tried to forge ahead through the thick-growing bushes and low vines.

Ahead of him—he tried not to think about it, could not help thinking about it, could not help but feel every sound of it stab deep into his chest—Angeline screamed over and over and over again, her thin voice hoarse and labored now yet still she screamed and screamed.

Michael sprinted the last few yards and burst into the open glade where once he had taught Mordecai to hunt squirrels, close by the eddying backwater pool where he had taught both children to swim. There was no undergrowth here, only the massive cottonwoods forming a canopy over the riverbank.

He could see Angeline now. The child was on her knees, her face bloody. On the ground before her, Luke Blackwood was administering a vicious beating to a defenseless and apparently unconscious Manuel Zaragosa.

As Michael raced toward this odd tableau Angeline grabbed Luke's arm and tired to keep him from striking Manuel. Luke, maddened and probably not even knowing what he was doing, backhanded Angeline in an attempt to drive her away. He struck her in the chest and sent her tumbling backward. Then once more Luke turned his attentions to Manuel, raising a ham-sized, blood-spattered fist and driving it hard into Manuel's unprotected face. Michael saw blood fly and heard the muted crunch of breaking cartilage.

Michael continued to run full tilt, deliberately crashing into and over Luke before the big, dull-witted man knew he was there.

The force of Michael's charge drove Luke off of Manuel and sent both men rolling down the bank toward the slow-moving waters of the Colorado.

Before Luke had time to react, Michael spun about and came to his feet. As Luke rose to his knees, Michael delivered a sweeping blow with the back of his clenched fist. He hit Luke full in the face and again blood sprayed, but this time it was Luke's.

"'Ey!" Luke blinked.

Michael hit him again, a straight right punch this time. It was a mistake. The blow solidly delivered onto the shelf of Luke's massive jaw sent a sharp jolt of pain shooting up Michael's arm into his shoulder, and for just a moment he wondered if he might have broken his hand.

"Dammit," Luke mumbled. Blackwood lurched to his feet, swaying only a little.

Michael stepped in, throwing low, looping punches into Luke's midsection. Luke grunted and turned pale. His knees wobbled, and he gulped for air. Michael knew if he gave Luke time to recover wit and wind this could turn into a long afternoon, so he stepped to the side and again chopped at Luke with a clenched fist, this time battering the big man behind his right ear and then again on the bridge of his nose.

Luke staggered back a step and stood there swaying.

This was the man who had struck Angeline. Michael came forward, scarcely aware of what he was doing, and kicked Luke in the crotch just as hard and just as accurately as he knew how.

There was a roaring in Michael's ears that he did not comprehend, not until he tried to kick Luke again and discovered that he could not move. He was being held firmly by both arms, James on one side of him and Frank on the other.

"Lemme go, dammit."

"Leave be, Michael. He's out of it. Now leave be."

It wasn't until then that Michael realized the sounds he'd been hearing were the yammering shouts and instructions and screams of just about everybody who'd been at the birthday celebration. The women and children were mostly screaming, the menfolk shouting, and a couple dogs were barking.

About the only ones who didn't seem to be contributing to the commotion were Angeline, who was bent weeping over Manuel's motionless figure, and Luke Blackwood, who was writhing on the ground, rocking rapidly back and forth and seemingly making a great effort to draw himself into a knot the approximate size and shape of a washtub.

"Let me go," Michael ordered.

"You all right now? You got control o' yourself?"

"I'm fine. Just let me go, all right?"

"All right." Frank let go of him first. James hesitated a moment, then he too released his grip on Michael's upper arm.

Michael was belatedly conscious that his arms hurt where James and Frank had been holding on to him. His hand stung like crazy from punching Luke in the head, and every joint and muscle from his neck down ached as if they'd been stuffed with coals, from all the running and excitement. But his blood was up, dammit, and he could feel that swelling through his shoulders and across the back of his neck that tells a man he's ready for a fight if it's a fight that's needed.

"You sure you're all right, Michael?"

"Yeah. Sure." Michael pushed past the others and went over to kneel with Marie and Mordecai, who were on the ground beside a weeping but no longer hysterical Angeline. Annie was there with them, she and Angeline both working over Manuel's raw and bloody features. Annie had produced a wet cloth from somewhere and was using it to bathe the youngster's hurts, while Angeline sobbed and gasped and somehow managed to get a word out now and then, explaining to her mother as best she could what happened.

Michael knew there was something that Angeline was holding back, but from Marie's reactions he knew it was nothing bad, nothing that would have hurt Angeline. Marie seemed to know what it was the child was not saying, and likely she would fill Michael in on all of that later.

The gist of it all was that Luke had come roaring out of nowhere and attacked Manuel, for no reason at all or for reasons unspecified. The bedrock of the story was that Blackwood was at fault and Manuel wasn't.

Angeline needed a little cleaning up herself. Luke had punched her twice, it seemed, when she tried to intervene. The second blow was the one her father saw. The first time Luke had poked her in the nose inadvertently though, she was quick to point out. Luke hadn't known what he was doing at the time; she was positive about that.

Inadvertent or not, young Mordecai bristled and began to rise when Angeline said Luke hit her. Michael had to restrain him.

"But, Papa—"

"Leave it." Michael's voice was cold and sharp. There was no doubt that he meant what he was saying.

"Yes, sir." Mordecai didn't like it, but he did what he was told.

Michael motioned toward Luke, who was beginning to unwrap himself on the ground a few yards away. It was time they got Luke the hell out of there before someone lit into him again, possibly Michael himself if he let himself think about this very much more.

Sly Shipman saw Michael's signal. He ambled over to Luke, knelt, and whispered something into his ear. The big man's eyes went wide, and with Sly's help he struggled into a sitting position, then finally onto his feet, where he wobbled and swayed for a moment before he could be sure of his balance.

Without a backward glance at the unhappy scene he had created, Luke Blackwood squared his massive shoulders and began walking slowly upstream along the river, his ponderous gait taking him in the direction of the squatter's cabin he and Finis so rarely occupied nowadays. The Blackwoods had been mostly absent from their own home since the fight with the Mexicans this winter past and, more to the point, since Major Brown's interest in interrogating them on the subject of arms deliveries to the Cherokees. But they did come back now and then. Michael wished fervently that they'd stayed away just a little longer this time, damn them.

He turned back to the others in time to help Marie lift Angeline to her feet. Then Michael and the other men picked up Manuel, who was beginning to groan and mumble and stir, and carried him up the path to the house.

Angeline's birthday party had come to an end.

☆ Chapter ☆

25

"I dunno," Michael said with a grin. "I never figured you for being the same kind o' optimist as Frank."

"What do you mean?" Andrew asked.

"Putting your corn in so early. Me, I still want to wait another week or so before I start my planting. See do the nights stay warm."

Andrew flushed slightly and began to fumble with his pipe, nervously twisting the bowl around and around the stem. "I, uh, didn't come back to plant, Michael."

"No?"

"Uh, no." Andrew shifted position and reached into his vest pocket for a twist of tobacco. He brought out a tiny clasp knife and began shaving slivers of the dark, gummy tobacco into his pipe. It was a make-work excuse to be doing something with his hands, because he'd only minutes before finished a smoke; the pipe probably wasn't yet cooled off from that bowl and now here Andrew was filling it again.

Michael grunted but couldn't help wondering just why Andrew had come home for this visit if it wasn't to put seed in the ground. Lord knew Andrew came home seldom enough these days, so it wasn't any casual whim that'd brought him here.

At the moment Michael, Andrew, James, and Sly were sprawled in the shade of Michael's dogtrot. Marie and Angeline were out back near the woodpile boiling laundry, and there was no telling where Mordecai had got to this afternoon. The men could look across the field and see Frank and his boys busy planting the seed they'd saved from last year's corn crop. There was a jug of sweet cider on the ground but no one was much interested in it.

Flies—what a shame winter only sent the pests into hiding; it would've been nice if the cold killed them off instead—buzzed and flitted annoyingly. James and Sly had come over as soon as they heard that Andrew was home from Houston.

Andrew cleared his throat and frowned into the bowl of his pipe. "Actually, uh, I was thinking this year I might ought to, well, hire my planting done."

Michael stiffened.

"Dang it now, don't you look at me like that," Andrew protested.

"Hire your work, Andrew? Is that what I heard you say?"

Andrew looked at James as if for support, but he found none there either. Sly was carefully looking off toward Frank and his sons in the distance. "I have to be in Houston, Michael. I have to."

"All right, you have t' be in Houston. We ain't disputing that, Andrew. But . . . hire?"

"It wouldn't be right for me to burden anybody with my responsibilities," Andrew said.

"Just what the hell d'you think family is for?" James spat back at him.

"I don't think family is for taking for granted," Andrew returned.

"What's that s'posed to mean?"

"It means I won't come in here an' ask you to do my work for me an' then go off to a bunch of fancy dress balls while you stay here an' do it, that's what that means."

"Fancy dress balls? Is that really what we send you off t' Congress t' do for us?"

"Aw, you know what I mean."

"Yeah, but you'd better know that we won't take it very dang well if you pay out money for some stranger to come in here and work your fields. Not while there's a Lewis left standing, we won't."

"Now wait, Michael, maybe what Andrew is saying is that he ain't satisfied with the condition of his place. Maybe he thinks he could've done a better job of it."

Andrew gave James a slow smile and said, "Hell, brother, o' *course* I could have done a better job of plowing than that. But I'm grateful to y'all anyhow." The smile turned into a grin. "It ain't your fault that I'm a better farmer than any o' you will ever be."

Michael and James laughed. Sly snickered quietly, not that

anyone believed he hadn't been listening anyway. He was only trying to be polite.

"That settles it then," Michael said. "We divide up the labor. James, you can do the planting. Andrew, you keep the republic from falling apart. And me, I'll supervise the both o' you two."

Sly took the joshing as a signal he could turn back around and openly pay attention again. He reached into his pocket for a plug, then put it back when Andrew tossed him the twist he'd just been whittling on.

"Try this, Sly. Rum-cured. It's out of Jamaica."

"Jamaica?" Sly smelled of the tobacco suspiciously. "Where's that?"

"It's an island. In the South Seas or someplace like that. The point is, they make rum there, and mighty fine t'baccy. It's English."

"I didn't know the English grew tobacco."

"No, dang it, it's Jamaica that's English, not the tobacco. We're getting a lot o' English goods in through Galveston lately. For some reason they're taking a big interest in Texas now. Likely there's something they want from the States, and they're wanting to use this courtship with Texas for leverage to see that they get it. Which is fine by me just so long as we get the benefit of the trading."

Sly gave the twist another skeptical inspection, then fastidiously sliced a hunk off the end of it. "The part of it I care about right now is whether they pack a good quality t'bacco." He popped the chew into his jaw, waited a moment, and then nodded. "It's good, all right. Thanks."

"I'll bring you a keg of it next time I come home," Andrew offered.

"I don't need any whole keg of t'bacco," Sly said. "There's better things to spend money on than rum-soaked English twists."

"Who said anything about money? I get the stuff free, Sly. I'm always having to push folks away when they're trying to get me to take stuff from them. You know, wanting to get in good with a congressman. It don't mean anything. Next time I see John Bidwater I'll just tell him to drop me off a keg of that stuff for you."

"You sure that's a good thing to do, Andrew, taking stuff like that?"

"It doesn't mean anything, really. Why, everybody does it. Doesn't mean a thing."

Sly grunted. "It's good t'bacco, all right. I'd enjoy having some more of it."

"Then it's as good as done." Andrew smiled and gave James a wink. James was frowning but couldn't help smiling back at his older brother. "Tell me, Michael," Andrew went on, changing the subject. Now that he'd gotten past the discomfort of telling everyone that he wasn't going to be able to put his own seed in, he seemed to be feeling considerably more chipper. "You say I missed seeing Manuel by just a couple days?"

Michael nodded. They had all tried to get Manuel to stay longer. He was barely healed after the beating Luke Blackwood had given him, but the young man—Michael had to keep reminding himself that Manuel was in truth young but a man nonetheless—insisted on leaving just as soon as he was able to travel again. At that he had lain in Mordecai's bed for the better part of two weeks before he was able to hobble around the place without assistance. The injuries he had suffered would heal completely, Michael was sure. But he would always wear scars: a red, angry weal ran from the corner of Manuel's left eye to the side of his mouth and then zigzagged like a lightning bolt down onto the shelf of his jaw. He would never again be the handsome youth who had ridden in from San Antonio de Bexar that day. Worse, Michael feared, might be the scars that could not be seen. It was too soon really to tell—Michael hoped he was wrong—but Manuel seemed embittered by the beating. More than just his face and body seemed to have been broken, and this Michael could not understand. Certainly neither he nor Marie objected to Manuel as a suitor for Angeline when she was old enough to think about such things. But all during the time he was being nursed by Marie and by Angeline, Manuel had made it clear that he did not welcome Angeline's attentions. Michael could not understand that, and Manuel had not been willing to make explanations, not even when Michael pointedly asked. The youth had expressed perfunctory gratitude to the Lewises and then ridden away without a backward glance.

"He said he was going on to Austin. That's what he came up for," James said, "to work on the construction there."

"I'll have to put in a word for him," Andrew suggested. "Make sure he gets a good job."

"You can do things like that?"

Andrew winked at his brother again.

"Maybe you can clear something up for me then, Andrew," Sly said around his chew.

"If I can."

"Is it true that the Cherokees have been taking potshots at workmen in Austin?"

"It's true that the survey crews laying out the city were fired at," Andrew said. "But I don't think anyone is sure what tribe was doing the shooting. Some say Comanche, some Cherokee, some say it was Karankawa or Waco. Not that it really matters anyway. The president is determined to rid Texas of all the hostile tribes. And to tell you the truth, boys, you'll see things happen before this year is out."

Michael didn't like the sound of that. He leaned forward and tapped Andrew on the wrist. "Innocent and guilty alike, Andrew? Is Lamar going to rid Texas of the innocent too?"

"There aren't any innocent Indians, Michael. You can't trust any of them. You know as well as I do that we've lost good neighbors to raiding Indian tribes. Men we both know. Men whose funerals we've gone to and whose widows and children we've tried to comfort."

"I also know that not every Indian shot those neighbors, Andrew. There wasn't but a few in any raiding band that I've ever heard of. And except for rumor, which God help us you and me helped to start, I don't know of any raiding Cherokee at all. Those people are farmers, not raiders. Why, they've made treaties with this republic. Now you're telling us that Lamar wants to put them out of Texas? That ain't right, Andrew."

"First off, Michael, the Cherokee never made a treaty with the republic. They made one with General Houston, but it was never ratified by the senate. That was only an idea, not a treaty. As for rights, Cherokees don't have rights in Texas, no more than Comanches or any other tribe does. Texans have rights in Texas. Nobody else."

"Right and wrong don't change because of what a man looks like, Andrew."

"I couldn't agree more. And it isn't right for us to allow a bunch of thieving, backshooting Indians to stay here amongst us. It isn't right for us to risk the lives of our families by allowing Indians to live close. The president is right about this, Michael. You'll see."

"Some of those people have been in Texas near as long as we have, Andrew. They have families of their own. They've cleared ground and built farms and they've lived there in peace for years. Now you're saying we should throw them out, just like that?"

"Just like that," Andrew agreed. "It's self-defense, Michael. Plain and simple. The letter Flores was carrying—"

"Good Lord, Andrew, don't try an' tell *me* about that letter. I was there, remember? We don't even know that that dead man was Flores. Or much of anything else about what was planned there. If anything. This whole thing is just an excuse for Lamar to vent his hate for Indians."

"It isn't that at all, Michael. Truly."

Michael shook his head.

"Give the president a chance, Michael. You'll see that he's right."

"I can't believe that, Andrew. I'm sorry, but I just can't."

"And when the call goes out for the militia? What will you do then, Michael? If you're called out you have to go."

"I thought you people in Houston were forming another ranging company to take care of things like that."

"It's true that we're forming another ranging company. The one battalion has all it can handle down along the border. We need another to stand between us and the tribes out on the plains. But that won't be enough to manage the campaign the president has in mind for this summer. The militia will be called up too. That's all of us, Michael. Including you."

"If that happens, Andrew, I don't know that I'll go. I just don't know."

"Look, you fellas can talk out all this serious stuff without me," Sly said. "I got chores to do anyhow." He rose and stretched. "Thank you for the tobacco, Andrew. And the cider."

"Wait up," James said, rising. "I'll walk along with you. Andrew, you'll be here a few days, won't you?"

"A few days, sure."

"Then I'll see you tomorrow."

James and Sly left. Out back the women had finished the wash and were hanging the clothes on a rack to dry. Mordecai had shown up from his wanderings and been put to carrying wood inside for his mother.

"I didn't mean . . ."

"I'm sorry if I . . ."

Both Michael and Andrew tried to speak at once. Both stopped. Then both again tried to speak. They settled for chuckling at one another.

"No hard feelings," Michael said.

"None," Andrew agreed.

Michael nodded and leaned forward, dipping two fingers into Andrew's pocket and coming out with the twist of Jamaican tobacco.

"Help yourself," Andrew offered while Michael was already slicing a walnut-sized chunk off the dark twist.

"Reckon I will, thanks." Michael grinned and finished what he was doing, then returned the plug to the pocket where he'd found it.

"I ought to be getting back myself," Andrew said. "It's getting late, and Lord knows I put enough o' the work off onto poor Ben by not being here hardly ever." But he continued to sit where he was.

"There's something on your mind, Andrew," Michael said.

"Naw." Denial or no, Andrew stayed where he was.

"I dunno about you, but sometimes talking about something helps me to think it through."

"Ayuh, me too."

Michael waited, fairly certain now that there was a purpose to all of this, perhaps even the purpose that had brought Andrew all the way home from Houston. Whatever it was, now that the two of them were alone Andrew would get to it when he was ready, or not at all.

"You and me," Andrew said quietly after what seemed a very long time, "we been through a lot together, ain't we, Michael?"

Michael smiled. "We sure have." And that was sure enough the truth. When they'd been younger there had always been a special bond between Michael and Andrew. It was Andrew who had disobeyed everyone's wishes, including Michael's, and sneaked away from their home back in Tennessee to follow his big brother to Texas. They had shared hard times then and later, fought side by side, and protected each other from one sort of harm or another for virtually all their lives. No wonder Michael could sense now that something was troubling Andrew.

"Remember when you used to go off by yourself, Michael? Be gone for weeks and weeks sometimes."

"Sure I remember."

"Did you ever get lonely when you were away like that?"

"Oh, I s'pose you could say so, sort of. But the way I always looked at it, Andrew, even when I was a hundred miles from any settlement that I knew about, I always figured I was in pretty good company with me and a gun and all the things Pa taught us."

"That ain't exactly what I meant."

"You want to lay this out a little clearer, Andrew? I think I'm missing something here."

"Have you ever . . . I mean . . ." Andrew blushed. "Aw, never mind. I know the answer already."

"Little brother, I can't think of but one thing that'd make you get all red in the face an' embarrassed like that. And I reckon you do know the answer t' that particular question. No, Andrew, I ain't never cheated on Marie an' I ain't thinking of taking it up in the future neither. You, uh, have a woman problem back in Houston, do you?"

"No," Andrew said quickly. Too quickly? Michael heard what his brother said, but he heard the nervousness in Andrew's voice when he said it too.

"I'm real glad to hear that, Andrew, because I'm awful fond o' your Petra. I'd sure hate to see anything come between the two o' you."

"It isn't . . ." Andrew shook his head. He looked away, looked down at his hands, twisted his pipe as if it was a bird whose neck he was wringing, and spilled much of the tobacco he'd tamped into the bowl earlier. Andrew acted as if he didn't notice.

Michael waited silently, not wanting to press. He shifted his chew to one cheek and helped himself to a swallow of the sweetly tangy cider Andrew had brought. "That's pretty good," he ventured, but Andrew didn't respond and might not have heard.

"Tell me, Michael, what d'you think about slavery and . . . like that," Andrew blurted apropos of nothing.

"Damn, Andrew. You ain't gone and bought you a slave, have you?"

"No." But there was a certain hesitancy in Andrew's tone of voice that Michael didn't much care for.

"You asked me. All right, I'll tell you. It's like I said about the Indians earlier, Andrew. There is right an' there is wrong, and just because it's a government that does something that don't mean the something is necessarily right. Chasing folks off their land because they're Indians is wrong. Making slaves out o' other folks because they're nigras, that's wrong too."

"You ever know any slave owners, Michael?"

"Oh, I reckon I've met some. I can't say it's a subject I've ever thought to look at real close."

"Ever know any slaves?"

"Nope. Seen a few, o' course, just like anybody else. I wouldn't say I ever knowed any. Not to talk to."

"But you'd agree that a slave, a woman say, a bound woman wouldn't be the same as a regular sort of woman. I mean . . . if a man was to, well, if he was to be given the *use* of a nigra slave woman . . . wouldn't you agree that that wouldn't be the same thing as if he was, like, laying up with a white woman?"

Michael's expression hardened. "Dammit, Andrew, the way I see it, laying up with a woman is laying up with a woman. A man can't argue his way past that nor excuse it, an' never mind talk about what's legal or what ain't. Can't no law turn a woman into a thing and can't no law turn wrong into right. You know that as good as I do."

"Yes, of course I do, but—"

"Don't interrupt me, dammit. Let me get this out before I get so mad I can't. You came here wanting me to tell you that's all right? I can't do that, Andrew. I won't do it. Wouldn't do it if I could, damn you. And I resent you trying to make yourself feel better by asking me to be a party to it."

Andrew blanched. The stem of his pipe snapped in two as his hands clenched and twisted.

"Give a fella the *use* of a woman, is it?" Michael parroted in a taunting falsetto voice, his lip twisted into a sneer. "Sure, Andrew. Borrow a shirt. Borrow a shovel. Borrow some woman too." His voice hardened and grew deeper, stern and uncompromising. "Damn you, Andrew, don't you never again ask something like this o' me."

Michael stood and would have stormed away except that Andrew jumped up too and grabbed him by the arm. "One thing you got to know, Michael."

"Yes?"

"I never . . . that is nothing has happened . . . not ever. But . . . Lord God, I been tempted, Michael. I been so tempted."

Michael sighed and put an arm around Andrew's shoulders. In a much softer and gentler voice he said, "There's no shame in temptation, little brother. It's only human to be tempted. The shame only comes from giving in, not from feeling it."

Andrew nodded. He appeared thoroughly miserable now. "I'm sorry, Michael. I won't—"

"Hey, I'm sorry too. I jumped too quick. That's a bad habit o' mine. You know?" He smiled and squeezed Andrew's shoulder. "Forget what I said there. You come to me with any problem you ever have, Andrew. I mean that. Between us we can lick anything. Right?"

"You bet."

"All right then." After Andrew mumbled his good-byes and headed toward home Michael stood alone for a time, thinking, wishing it really was true that he and Andrew together could whip anything or anybody. Anybody, perhaps. But not always anything. There were limitations, much though they might hate to admit that.

With a sigh Michael tried to put Andrew and his problems out of mind. He went indoors to find Marie, to wrap his arms around her and hold her tight for a very long while.

☆ Chapter ☆

26

James stripped his shirt over his head and laid it aside. He paused for a moment to wipe away a trickle of the gritty sweat from his forehead, then plunged hands and arms and face into the basin of tepid water on the washstand. The water was refreshing, as much because it cleaned as because it cooled. A dry day spent inside the billows of dust that followed close behind a mule was a grimy day indeed. Just being able to get the caked dirt out from behind his ears was enough to make him feel better.

He rinsed everything he could reach, turned his head aside to blow his nose, and finally groped for the scrap of rag that served as a towel.

"James? James! Is that you, James?" Libby's voice was a querulous whine issuing from inside the cabin.

"Of course it's me," he said. He had to make a conscious effort to make his answer calm and patient. "What do you need?" Belatedly he thought to add, "dear?"

"Fetch some water in, James. An' if you want anything cooked for your supper you'd best carry some wood in too."

Meaning, he interpreted, Libby hadn't felt like dragging herself out of the rocking chair where she lived day in and day out these days. She hadn't brought in wood or water either one, and there wasn't any supper waiting for him at the end of a very long day.

Not that she was in much shape to be fetching and carrying, James acknowledged. Libby was weeks past the point when everyone had expected her to give birth. She'd gotten so large that it looked like she was carrying a litter 'stead of a son or a daughter. Annie suspected twins.

James dried his neck and hung the makeshift towel back onto its peg. "Right away," he called out to his wife. He tossed the now-gray water from the basin into the yard, momentarily scattering a clutch of curious hens. The water hadn't any more than quit flying than the hens squawked and clucked and charged in to examine the globules of fresh-made mud for something they might eat. James poured fresh water into the washbasin and decided there was enough water left in that bucket that he didn't need to fill it again quite yet. Then he went inside to get the house bucket Libby wanted him to fill.

" 'Lo, dear."

She nodded without bothering to look in his direction. She was swaddled chin-deep in a heavy quilt even though the day had been anything but cold. Even here indoors in the early evening—albeit without the heat of a fire in the stove—it was pleasantly warm. Yet Libby acted as if it was still the dead of deepest winter. She sat hidden within the quilt and slowly, with a relentless and sometimes quite perfectly maddening regularity, rocked forward and back, forward and back, the dull thud of her feet followed inexorably by the muted thump of the hickory rocker tail striking the oaken floor. It was a sound that had filled the cabin during all Libby's waking hours for weeks and weeks now.

Libby was miserable in these last stages of her pregnancy; James understood that. She was huge and bloated and had difficulty moving about. Her back hurt, her legs hurt, and no doubt other things hurt as well.

But that hardly seemed reason for her to withdraw to a rocking chair and hide under a quilt, James thought, though only to himself. His opinions about Libby and her pregnancy were not something he would ever want to discuss, not with anyone. But, darn it, he'd never known any other woman to act like this when she was fixing to have a babe.

Not that James Lewis was any sort of expert; he never claimed that. But he wasn't no stranger to birthings either. He'd been nigh when his own mother was big with child, and Petra, and Annie, and Lord knows how many different sorts of livestock. It wasn't like birthing was as big a mystery as womenfolk wanted men to believe.

But Libby, she was acting like she was the first female that'd ever gotten pregnant. Her tongue hadn't been soft or gentle to begin with, and it'd gotten sharper and sharper as Libby sat getting bigger and bigger. Maybe, James thought uncharitably, that was because Libby hadn't anything better to do with her time than to sharpen it. Sharpen her tongue, that is, and rock and moan.

James fashioned a smile that Libby didn't bother to look at. There wasn't anything to be said, he realized, and there wasn't any reason for him to be standing about feeling sorry for himself neither. Keep that up and he'd be finding himself as bad off in the ill-humor department as Libby was these days. He cleared his throat, still without drawing any particular attention from her, and walked around behind the rocker to get the chamber pot that she'd taken to keeping close by and to using even in the daytime, when one would normally go to the facility outdoors. She hadn't mentioned the pot but it needed emptying, as James could plainly tell from the strong odor that filled the tight-shuttered cabin. He wished he could air the place out some but knew that would only draw a squeal of protest from Libby. She would claim he was trying to give her her death of cold.

"Don't forget the water."

"I'll tend t' this first, then come back for the bucket."

"And wood, James. Don't forget some wood if you want somethin' t' eat."

"I won't forget the wood," he said with a somewhat exaggerated show of great patience.

"You're mad at me again," Libby complained.

"I'm not mad at you."

"I can hear it in your voice, James Lewis. You're mad at me. This here ain't my fault, James. I've swole up like a toad an' I got pains all over and it ain't any of it my fault, damn you. You're the one got me this way."

"Did I? Been so long I disremember."

She looked at him then, all right. She turned her head and gave him a look that was positively venomous.

"If looks could kill," he observed.

"If you are accusing me of anything, James Lewis—"

"I ain't accusing you o' anything, Libby. Who said anything 'bout accusing you?"

"You did and I heard it and you know I heard it and don't try and tell me I never. As if I hain't endured enough for you, James Lewis, now you're doubting that this child I'm carrying is even yours. What comes next, James? Will you throw me out? Is that it? Do you want me to go now? Or will you wait till the child is aborn 'fore you throw me out?"

"Libby . . ." She was off on a tear now. He shouldn't have said anything. He should've known better. Times she got to feeling really down on herself there wasn't anything he could safely say, wasn't any word or comment that she couldn't turn and make it sound like something it wasn't. And this time he'd gone and made it all too easy for her to sull up and turn snorty over. So to that extent and likely more this fuss really was his fault and not hers. "Libby," he repeated.

". . . as if anybody would *want* a no-'count thing like—"

"I'm sorry, Libby." He made his voice loud enough to drown out hers. If she heard or understood what he was saying, he couldn't tell it. She made no response except to keep on nattering—and rocking. That was kinda funny, James thought. Vexed and hateful though she was feeling right at this moment, the slow and rhythmic thump and thud of Libby's rocking never wavered, never varied, not by so much as a second it didn't. "I'm sorry, Libby," he half-shouted. "I'll empty this, dear, an' be right back for the water bucket. Then I'll get a fire going an' fry us up some ham, dear." Which was probably, he concluded, the best way to deal with Libby when she was running on like this. "Be right back, dear."

He carried the chamber pot out and tended to it, took a few moments more to rinse it clean, then carried the heavy pot and a few sticks of fat, fine-split kindling inside.

Libby had quit yammering by the time he went back indoors. She was rocking of course but had her eyes squeezed tight closed as if in deep concentration about something. She surely was aware that James was back, but she didn't choose to respond this time. He was grateful for that.

He put the chamber pot back in its place beside her rocker and the pitch-pine kindling into the open-topped old keg that they used for that specific purpose, the keg holding slivers of fat wood carefully separate from the regular burning chunks that had their own woodbox nearby. Then he took up the water bucket and started for the door. Outside the light was failing fast, and Libby hadn't lighted any candles yet, so the light indoors was poor. But he thought . . . "You all right, Libby? You look kinda pale."

She kept her eyes squeezed shut and her mouth—happily also closed now—clamped just as tight closed in a straight, prissy line. She did answer though, sort of. She shook her head abruptly, left and right and left again and no more than that, while she continued to rock forward and back, forward and back in that never-varying cadence.

"Whatever you say," he agreed, wanting of a sudden to make amends for having been the source of her vexation earlier. "If there's anything I can do . . ."

Libby didn't say anything, and after a few moments of watching her in silence James turned and carried the water bucket outside. He needed to hurry, he knew, if he expected to get everything done and get them fed—he would have to do the cooking again tonight; it was perfectly obvious that Libby wasn't feeling up to it—at anything like a reasonable hour.

It would help speed things along, he realized, if he brought the wood in first and got the fire started. That way the stove could get to heating while he brought in the water. James thought through the efficient sequence he should follow and then, pleased with himself, put the empty bucket down and went to collect a heaping armload of split wood. He carried the firewood inside and dropped it into the box with a clatter, then turned to the stove and pulled the firebox door open, reaching as he did so for one of the starter slivers. Now all he needed to do was to find a live coal inside the bed of gray ash that . . .

"James?"

"Yes, dear?"

"James!" Her voice was tight. Squeaky. She sounded . . . frightened.

"Dear?"

Libby's eyes were still squeezed tight shut. She had stopped rocking and was holding herself poised stiff and still, with her legs extended and the rocking chair pushed as far back as it would move. Her hands gripped the chair arms so tight they were white 'round the knuckles and the web of her thumb.

"Libby? What is it, dear?"

"James."

"I'm here, Libby. I'm right here with you." He rushed to her side, knelt there, tried to take her hand but could not get it loose from the chair arm and so settled for patting it. "What is it, dear?"

"I think . . ." She gasped and stiffened. Tendons corded at her throat and sweat beaded her forehead. In just these few seconds there was enough of it that it began to collect and run, but she seemed not to notice even when the sweat ran into the corners of her eyes. She began to pant and whimper.

"Libby!"

"I think . . . you should find . . . Annie now." She bit her lower lip as if to keep from crying out. "Go." She gulped for air. "Quick."

James sprang to his feet and bolted out into the evening shadows.

☆ Chapter ☆
27

James looked at Michael and at Sly and wasn't sure which he wanted to do more, grin or throw up. Before this night was ended he very likely might do both.

"Have another drink," Sly suggested, passing the jug to him.

James had another drink. The corn liquor had nothing to do with why he felt like puking. That reaction was pure nervousness.

Lordy, James hadn't ever felt so nervous. Not even when he was facing Mexican muskets he hadn't felt near this nervous.

But then he hadn't been waiting for the birth of his first child.

A boy, he hoped. A girl would be all right too.

He grinned.

"Go ahead. Help yourself."

James tipped the jug up and drank from it. The whiskey tasted flat. It had neither heat nor kick in it. He'd never known whiskey to be like this, unless someone had been into Sly's liquor and watered down what was left. Perhaps that was it. He tried one more swallow without achieving any particular effect, then gave the jug back to Sly.

James was trembling. He wasn't cold, but he was shaking as bad as if he was out in a norther with blowing snow an' no dang coat. Or else he was cold but so fussed up that he wasn't able to tell it. Like with the whiskey that wasn't really flat, or Sly and Michael would've noticed too and said something. To help warm himself and keep his circulation going, James flopped his arms up and down and started pacing rapidly between the woodpile, where they were sitting, and the henhouse.

Out of the corner of his eye James could see that Michael and Sly were winking and grinning and making fun of him. Well dammit, he bet they'd been plenty nervous when their first kids were being born too.

While he paced James glanced now and then, trying not to be obvious about it, toward the square of bright yellow that was the window he'd set into the back wall of his cabin. He couldn't hear anything from inside. And he knew better than to try and go ask again. Petra hadn't been any too gentle with him that last time he'd tapped on the closed and barred cabin door. She'd chased him in no uncertain terms and acted half mad. What was it about women that made them all get mad at a man just because that man's wife was having herself a baby?

If, that is, there was room in the cabin for a baby to be born into. Likely they'd have to chuck somebody out just to clear space enough for the newcomer. Why, Annie was in there of course. But Petra'd come, and Marie, and Angeline, who at fourteen was practically an old hand at assisting with births. And Frank's wife, Hope, and Andrew's ten-year-old Rose. 'Bout the only females within miles that *weren't* inside James's cabin were Annie's wee ones, and that was only because they were too little to be kept out late. They were both at home being tended by Andrew's son, Ben.

"This always take so long?" James asked of no one in particular.

"What it takes," Michael said, "is exactly long enough. Every time."

"But how long . . . ?"

"Go ask Petra if you want."

James grimaced and resumed his pacing.

Mordecai materialized out of the night, moving silent as a ghost to nod at his uncle James and grin at his father and help himself to a seat on the woodpile beside Sly. Mordecai leaned his long-barreled rifle against the stacked, split wood and shuddered as he tried to bite back a yawn. James acknowledged him with a wave. Sly handed the boy the whiskey jug, drawing a slightly startled look from Michael but no actual protest. Mordecai tasted of the liquor as if he was an old hand at drinking, then gasped and had to gulp for air. No one laughed, and after a moment he tried another taste before returning the jug to Sly, who once again tried to pass it to James. James, however, was too intent on trying to listen for sounds from the cabin to pay any attention.

"Been an awful long while," James said. He judged it would come dawn in another two hours or thereabouts.

"Catch anything?" Michael asked, ignoring James's plaintive observation.

"No, sir," Mordecai responded. "Lon Willet had his hound along, but it never took up a scent."

"That pup's got a cold nose," Sly accused. "It won't ever be the hound the sire was."

"He's just young yet," Mordecai said.

"Don't you think we oughta be hearing something?" James complained. "With all them women to make noise in there, you'd think it'd sound like a chicken coop with a weasel turned loose in it, but I ain't heard anything in a hour or more."

"James, you was pounding on the door not ten minutes ago. You must of heard that," Sly replied.

"I just wish they'd tell us something."

"I never cared that much for hunting coon when I was your age," Michael told his son. "But then back in Tennessee it was always food I had to look to first. We never had the luxury of hunting fur. Did we, James?"

"What? I, uh, wasn't listening."

Michael repeated his statement.

"Yeah. Right," James agreed automatically. He'd heard the words; he just hadn't comprehended them. They went into his head, swirled around in there, and then escaped again without making any impression whatsoever.

Sly winked at Michael and Mordecai and leaned forward. "Isn't it true that you seen a family of pink-an'-green geese nesting by the river yesterday, James?"

"Huh?"

"I asked wasn't that true."

"Oh. Right. It is."

Michael and Sly kept their expressions straight, but Mordecai laughed. James knew Sly'd just twisted his tail about something, but he didn't want to bother finding out how. It wasn't important anyway.

He looked at Mordecai, then at Michael, and then back again. Michael had his son, and Michael's son was most grown already. It didn't seem it'd taken all that long either. James couldn't help wondering if it would seem to happen so quick with his own son. If it was a son he had. He hoped so, and had believed so right along.

Of course a girl would be fine too.

Sam. That was what they'd name him if it was a boy. Sam

Houston Lewis. Andrew might think President Lamar could walk on water, but James had always favored General Houston, and still did. And he thought Sam Houston Lewis had a fine sound. A fine name for a fine son.

A fine son who, it occurred to James with something of a jolt of surprise, would one day be expected to become a fine man, all grown and independent and on his own. Looking at Mordecai was enough to remind him of that. James hoped he had it within himself to be as good a father to Sam as Michael had proved to be to Mordecai.

The closer the time got, the more James realized what a hellacious weight of responsibility there was upon a man when he had a son. Girls were mostly tended and taught by the women. But a son was a man's to guide. James shivered, thinking about that.

Maybe it wouldn't be such a bad thing for this first one to be a girl after all.

There was a clanging sound inside the cabin. The stove door banging shut, maybe.

Then a scream.

James stopped in midstride, frozen in place like a startled rabbit by the tearing, piercing sound of it.

"Any news when you were down to San Felipe, Sly?" Michael asked too loudly.

Libby screamed again, her pain knifing into James's gut and twisting there.

"Not much," Sly was saying. "Though they tell me Hal Rabe and Pat Winters are picking up and moving their families out. Many more and there won't be any town left down to San Felipe."

"Where is Rabe going?" Michael droned.

James tried to ignore the inane chatter. He knew good and well Michael and Sly were only trying to get him interested in something other than what was going on inside the cabin. He understood that. He appreciated them doing it for him. He wished the both of them would shut the hell up.

Libby shrieked again, and soon after there was a clang as something metal fell or was dropped.

Sly handed James the jug and he drank from it, hardly being aware that he was doing so.

Over at the cabin the door banged open and the dogtrot was flooded with light from inside. Angeline came running out, dashed into the chicken coop, and seconds later went running back to the cabin again with something clutched in one hand. The door banged closed, and the dogtrot became dark again.

James frowned. "What was all that? She wasn't collecting eggs."

"Looked like she got some cobweb, Uncle James," Mordecai said, earning a dirty look from both his father and Sly.

"Whyever would they need cobweb for a birthing?" James wondered aloud. "I don't remember anybody using cobweb ever before now. Not for no birthing."

"Aw, you dunno. Could be somebody was taking up a knife to cut the infant's cord or something an' cut themselves by accident," Michael suggested. Cobweb was a common poultice for the stopping of blood.

"Might not have nothing to do with Libby," Sly said.

Libby cried out again, but this time it was more an extended and half-muted groan than a scream.

"That's good, ain't it? She ain't hollering so loud now. Isn't that good?"

Sly shrugged. Michael said, "Could be, James, could be." Mordecai left the woodpile and began to pace alongside his uncle.

There was another cry from inside the cabin, this time low pitched.

"That wasn't Libby," James said. "I'm sure it wasn't her voice that time."

Nobody said anything. James quit pacing, but Mordecai kept going as if to finish whatever pacing was needed in James's place.

"Oh, dear." The voice from inside—it sounded like Annie's—was thin and mournful. Bleak, James thought.

Perhaps because of that he was almost prepared when again the door was opened and the dogtrot filled with candlelight from within.

Annie came out and stepped slowly into the yard. She stopped before her brother and wrapped her arms around him. "James, I'm so . . . so sorry."

"Libby?"

Annie nodded. "She was bleeding. We couldn't stop it. We tried everything we knew how, James. I promise you we tried everything we knew how to do."

"I know you did." James felt cold inside, empty, a husk without substance. If Annie hadn't been holding on to him he might've been lifted up on the breeze and blown away into the night. "The baby?"

"I . . . it was a boy."

"Was," he repeated slowly and distinctly, making an effort to form the words while trying to avoid the thoughts that went with them. "A boy. Dead though."

Annie began to cry. "Yes. It . . . had been. For a long time. Libby never said anything about it not moving inside her anymore?"

James shook his head woodenly. There was a dull roaring in his ears. He tried to get control of himself. There were things he needed to be doing. He had responsibilities, after all. It was his place to tend to these things, nobody else's. The empty feeling inside his belly flooded down into his legs and up through his chest to invade his head. He felt as if he might float right up off the ground. Just drift up into the sky and disappear. He wouldn't really mind if that did happen.

Dead. The both of them. Libby. Sam.

"I want t' see . . ."

"You will, James. I promise. Soon. They're being . . . cleaned now. But it won't be long. I promise." Tears streaked Annie's face and she was shaking. She wasn't all that big, but when James tried to pull away from her and go toward the cabin he found that he couldn't. Annie was stopping him. She had hold of him. And Michael and Sly and young Mordecai were pressed close too. He couldn't move. He had to, though. There were so many things he needed to do now. He had his responsibilities. To his wife. To his son. So many things to do. And the damned weather turning. A fog had come in from someplace. It clouded over his vision and kept him from seeing Annie's face very clear.

Dead. Libby. Sam. Dead.

James felt something lurch and turn inside his belly. Which was odd because he knew that he was hollowed out inside. There was nothing left inside him to roll over and churn like that.

He felt the fog closing the rest of the way in around him. Felt himself rise up and begin to float.

After that he didn't feel anything more.

☆ Chapter ☆ 28

"Thank you. Thanks for coming. Good to see you again, Martin. Miz Nathan. Thank you. She'd of been real proud to know you came all this way. George. Tom. Miz Willet. Thank you for coming." It was a blur and a nuisance but a welcome blur and a most necessary nuisance. Wagons full of neighbors, horsebackers, even whole families coming afoot from miles around had been pouring in the whole day long. It amazed James how quick the word had got out. It was only yesterday that Libby and little Sam died. There was only the one night and one full day for them to be laid out in the boxes Michael and Mordecai built for them, the boxes that were set up on the makeshift trestles with his cabin door laid across them. Little Sam's box was so tiny it fair broke a body's heart. That box was closed up. They'd stopped James from seeing—which was likely a blessing. He'd protested, but he hadn't truly insisted. Down deep he knew he was better off not having to remember his boy the way he looked now.

James stood at the front of the dogtrot and shook hands with the neighbors as they came, murmured words of sympathy, viewed Libby laid out in her good dress, and then went on past to the plank-and-sawhorse tables where the foods were laid out. From where he was at the other end of the dogtrot James could smell the aromas coming off the bean pots and casseroles and platters of chicken and steaming roasts and carefully smoked hams that folks were bringing and laying out. The food smelled good to him, reminding him that he hadn't eaten since . . . well, he couldn't recall exactly when he'd last eaten . . . and now it all smelled so good it made his mouth water and he felt guilty about that. Lord God, his wife and his only child had just died, and here he was thinking about something as petty as an empty belly. A man hadn't ought to be so selfish as that. Yet he smelled the food and wanted to go and eat instead of standing here listening to the same sad words being mumbled and stuttered and awkwardly stammered by folks who didn't much know how to express the shared pains they were feeling for him. No more than James really knew how to accept those well-intentioned sympathies.

"Thank you, Leo. Miz Johnston. Miz Holt. Ma'am. Thank you. Yes, ma'am. A Caldwell, she was. But there's no time for word to get there and any of her people get back for the burying. We can't wait for that. Yes, thank you. She'd of understood. Thank you."

He went on like that, and on, and incessantly on. He hadn't slept much last night, and now his eyes burned and stung, his legs ached, and his feet hurt from standing, but he knew it was his place, not anybody else's, to be the one to stand here and greet the folks as somehow the word passed along from one place to another and folks poured in from as far as fifteen, twenty miles away.

Along about midmorning Reverend Fairweather arrived astride a swaybacked and spavined nag, and that was good. The old preacher—Michael and Andrew still had doubts about the sincerity of Fairweather's call to the cloth; there'd been a time when the man was as bad as there was—was showing his age about as much as his horse. Fairweather's hair was long and unkempt and almost totally white, and there was a tremor in his hands that spoke of the infirmities of age. James was glad to see him, in spite of Michael's and Andrew's doubts. "Thank you for coming, Rev'rend."

The tall, gaunt old man answered with a sad shake of his leonine head and a quotation from the Book delivered in a fine and sonorous voice. Fairweather's body might be commencing to fail him, but his voice held all its old power and resonance, and that was all a preacher-man needed.

"Thank you. Thanks for coming. Yes, ma'am, she woulda been real proud to know you was here. Thank you."

Annie appeared at his side and tugged at him, pulling him down and back, and he discovered that she'd brought a stool from somewhere—Lord only knew where that might've come from—and was pushing him onto it. Bless her. It felt awful good to get off his feet like that.

Little Birdy Willet—there'd been a time when James might have sparked Birdy himself, but he'd taken a shine elsewhere and Birdy ended up marring Zeb Willet instead; Lordy, if things had been different then it would've been Birdy who was now laid out in that box over there, and wasn't *that* just awful to think about—little Birdy Willet took both James's hands in hers and cried for his pain and told him how sorry she was and then went on by with her burden of a stew pot and a bundle of corn dodgers wrapped in clean cloth.

Annie came back to him and pushed something into his hands. "Go on now, James."

He looked down, blinked; he had to concentrate on paying attention so he could get it through his mind what this was and what Annie wanted of him. It was a sandwich of some kind.

"You have to eat something, James. You just have to or you'll make yourself sick, and that won't do anybody any good, will it?"

Numbly, James shook his head and took a bite of the sandwich. The bread was made with some sort of hard flour—oat maybe or acorn, but for sure not cornmeal—spread thick with fresh butter and with a slab of salty ham in between. It should've been tasteless in his mouth, sawdust or worse, any grieving person shouldn't take pleasure in food, but in truth the sandwich was wonderful good to him, and he felt a flush of fresh shame that this was so. Yet the shame didn't keep him from gobbling down the sandwich nor from taking the mug of sweet cider that Angeline carried to him and gave him so he could wash down Annie's sandwich.

Libby wouldn't never again know the taste of earthly food, and tiny Sam wouldn't never know of any flavors or sights nor sounds, not none at all, wouldn't never suck at his mama's breast nor giggle and coo. Wouldn't never totter and fall taking those first awkward steps, nor walk through the woods at his papa's side with a rifle in his hands and his senses honed keen and pride in his heart.

Thinking about those things, knowing them, James felt mortal guilty for taking pleasure now in the taste of food and drink. But he did and couldn't deny it, and felt all the worse for trying and failing.

"Thank you, Arlen. Miz Kramer. Ma'am." Some of the folks who were coming now, the ones from farthest away, James recognized but just couldn't call their names to mind. Others he was pretty sure he'd never met before this day and likely wouldn't recall tomorrow. "Thank you. Yes. Thanks." He accepted the handshakes and the sympathies and sat on the stool Annie'd brought to him.

Sometime not long past noon the Reverend Fairweather had the boxes carried out into the yard in front of the cabin and called everyone to him. The flow of folks was pretty well stopped by then anyway, and it wouldn't do to let Libby lie in the heat any longer.

Somebody escorted James off his stool and out into the yard to stand beside Fairweather, as if he was as much on display there as Libby and baby Sam. The old preacher's voice thrummed and rolled in James's ears, but it was all a buzz to him with little of the meaning creeping through. A word here, a phrase there, not that that mattered. It wasn't the words that counted but the decency and goodwill of all these good neighbors who'd come to say how sorry they were for his loss.

The fog that James'd been in before threatened to close in on him again, and he didn't bother to struggle very much against it. That fog or maybe a good drunk would've been welcome about then.

Fairweather's voice rolled and thundered for a time, and then a light wagon was brought up and the boxes, Libby's big one and little Sam's tiny one, were loaded in and the wagon taken away in the fore. Reverend Fairweather walked right behind it with James beside him, and everybody else came shambling after, family closest behind James and then all the other folks in no particular order.

They went out to the knoll that was on Michael's land, where Michael and Marie had buried their baby Prudence years and years back. Without it ever being particularly planned that way Michael's knoll was more or less adopted as the Lewis burial plot. Michael'd kept it cleared and tidy all these years. James thought now that he might want to put a stone wall around it too. It helped him somehow to think about that now, and he determined to do it, to build the wall, the first chance he got, the first day he felt up to starting it.

There were already two graves dug out there—no telling who'd thought to go out and dig them; Michael and Mordecai, maybe, not that it truly mattered—and Reverend Fairweather said some more words, then the boxes were carried off the wagon and eased gently down into the deep holes.

James was jostled into place between the two graves, and somebody passed clods of dirt into his hands so he could drop the first coverings in. He felt groggy and his head hurt, but he knew what was wanted of him and he dropped the dirt where he needed to. He managed to avoid looking either down at the boxes or out at the crowd. The clods made a dull, ugly sound when they landed on the closed lids of the coffins.

Lordy, James realized, he hadn't ever gone over to take one last look at his Libby, hadn't even known when it was they'd closed the box and nailed the lid in place. Nobody'd told him. Or else maybe they had and he just hadn't recognized it at the time. That was a question he couldn't hardly ask now. But whatever, however, he'd missed his chance. He wouldn't never again see Libby's face. Wouldn't never again look at her smile or her freckles or the way the tip of her nose bobbed and quivered when she was talking. And little Sam . . . James wondered what his son would've looked like if he'd lived. He could wonder. He could guess. He wouldn't ever really know.

"Ashes to ashes. Dust to dust." Reverend Fairweather's voice was deep and rich but the words, so expected as to be mandatory, were as dry and meaningless to James as the dust the reverend spoke of. Maybe later James would remember them and take comfort or meaning from them. Today, right now, he couldn't.

The folks walked past; knelt; took up handfuls of earth and threw them onto the box lids below; walked on by. Soon there was a scattering of dirt thick enough almost to obscure the lids. The last of the neighbors went by, and Mordecai and Sly brought out shovels. Michael and Annie—there hadn't been time to get word down to Andrew, much less time for him to get home for the burying—took James by the arms and led him back to the house, where all the food was laid out and where all the crowd had reassembled now.

This time they put James on the stool in the backyard where the food was, and Marie fixed a plate for him and insisted that he eat now. He didn't want to, but he ate. He was famished and ate till he couldn't eat anymore, trying to fill the emptiness that was in him.

It was all of it, the talk and the shifting movements of the people, it was all of it a fuzzy blur to him. Most all of it. Snips and snatches stood out sharp and clear in his mind. Petra hugging a weeping, near-hysterical Rose, who was getting her first taste of grief close to home with the passing of members of her own family. Frank's boy David bursting into laughter at something someone said and then coming to a sharp, red-faced halt as he realized he was laughing aloud at a funeral and probably wasn't supposed to. Old Mrs. Willet, who'd been widowed in an Indian raid years back but who stayed and kept her farm going by herself until her sons were able to take over for her, putting her arms around Annie and Sly's Deborah and crooning something soft and comforting to the toddler, who at two was undoubtedly too little to understand what was taking place.

Sometime later—there was still good light, so it couldn't have been all that much later, though it seemed so at the time—there was a commotion off in the direction of the henhouse.

James couldn't see what was going on very well, but he saw a few glimpses of it. A fight was in progress, shouts and threats and flurries of fists and dust. People rushed in to break apart whoever was fighting and pretty soon there were more fights going. The combatants were pulled apart, one side being dragged away from James's sight altogether and another faction being muscled and pulled off toward the house. That pair consisted of Mordecai and his buddy Lon Willet. Mordecai was bloodied from a cut over his eye, and Lon had a lump alongside his jaw that by tomorrow would be purpled and painful. James had no idea what the fight'd been about, and no one bothered to explain it to him.

Marie took his emptied plate away and brought back another with a wedge of pecan pie and some honey cakes on it, and Angeline gave him coffee while Hope offered more of the cider.

Soon after the fight, almost as if that'd been a signal, the tide of visitors reversed itself and folks began drifting past James on his stool in the other direction from the one that'd brought them. They reaffirmed their condolences and offered sad handshakes or hugs or words of sympathy, then made their way off to their horses and their homes.

Soon they would all be gone, James knew, and they would leave him all alone.

He felt something lurch and clench inside his throat and a tightening deep in his chest.

Alone. Tonight, when everyone had cleaned up for him, as he knew they first would, and then gone away to their own homes and families, tonight James would be alone. Alone with his thoughts and his guilts and the knowledge that Libby and Sam were cold and moldering out on Michael's knoll, close beside the mortal remains of infant Prudence, who hadn't hardly lived longer than Sam Houston Lewis.

Alone.

James shuddered and hugged himself, wishing for a coat to wrap into even though the afternoon was yet warm, for of a sudden he felt chilled and empty although he'd eaten everything that was brought to him all this day long.

For the first time since Annie'd told him the news he felt like crying, although of course he did not.

"Thank you, George. Miz Kramer. Thank you for coming." He shook the hands and acknowledged the words, but it was all of it wooden and mechanical, and James wished he was man enough to take this better but at the same time was pleased that his senses were dulled and blurry and was shamed by the realization that this was so.

Alone. Tonight he would be alone. And tomorrow. And for all the tomorrows to come. James felt bleak and hollow and shook the hands that were extended to him, hardly bothering to register whose hands he shook or whose words he nodded in response to.

He'd never felt lonely before, although he'd often enough been alone. Tonight he knew that alone would also mean lonely, and he was frightened of this that he knew would come.

"Good-bye. Thank you for coming." He shook the hands and now and then even tried to smile. "Good-bye, Martin. Thank you. Good-bye."

☆ Chapter ☆

29

Mordecai was enjoying himself. He knew he shouldn't; it wa a genuinely awful thing that had brought them all together lik this. But he just couldn't help it. He'd never seen so many peopl all in one place before, unless you wanted to count camp meeting when a circuit preacher came by, and then everybody had to si quiet and pay attention. Today old Reverend Fairweather wa more interested in putting food into his mouth than sendin words out of it, and everyone was having a fine time despite th sadness of the occasion.

Now that the burying was over things were loosening up eve more. There were some liquor jars circulating around the fringe of the gathering, and most of the menfolk were drifting off tha way and then back again. Mordecai stayed close to the food. H hadn't much liked the few tastes he'd had of whiskey, although h did enjoy cider whether it was sweet or hard.

"Have you tried this stuff?" his friend Lon asked, pushin between Mrs. Kramer and Mrs. Wollock. Lon was carrying a sla of freshly split wood. Split flat and thin from the right-sized chun of pine the small, shinglelike slabs made dandy makeshift plate that could be used as fire starters after their original purpose wa served.

"What is it?" Mordecai asked.

Lon glanced down at his rough wood plate, but it held only few dark crumbs now. He grinned and shrugged. "I dunno wh you'd call it. But it was awful good." There were smears aroun Lon's mouth of a color to match the crumbs that were left on hi plate.

"Then I reckon I tried it." Mordecai smiled at his pal. "I cain believe you're still eating. Me, I'm stuffed up to here." He tapped his chin to demonstrate.

"That's 'cause you're littler an' easier to fill," Lon teased. Even though Lon Willet was almost a full year younger than Mordecai he was much heavier, his build chunky and low to the ground where Mordecai had the Lewis trait of sinewy leanness. Lon had been able to whip Mordecai in wrestling contests for as long as either of them could remember. On the other hand, Mordecai could outrun his friend without breaking a sweat. "I don't suppose you got a chew on you," Lon ventured.

"You know I don't." Chewing tobacco, like whiskey, was a taste Mordecai hadn't acquired yet.

"Then let's go find one. I got a bad hankering for a chaw."

Mordecai nodded and swung in beside Lon. The two of them wended through the crowd, having to avoid skirts in the middle of the crowd and then grown men as they moved farther away from the tables toward Uncle James's chicken coop.

At one point Lon let out a barely audible squeal that was part whistle and part groan. Mordecai knew why too. That was when they were passing behind Amber Holt and her mother. Amber had yellow hair and dimples and a sunny disposition. At thirteen she was grown enough to begin looking mighty interesting but wasn't yet old enough to be sparked by the young men who were commencing to think in terms of marriage. This made her about the prettiest and most desirable possibility there was to Lon and to Mordecai and to the other fellows of about their same age and limited experience. Mordecai poked Lon in the ribs lest the younger boy get carried away and do something to make Mrs. Holt notice where their attention was directed. Amber had already noticed, of course, but she didn't seem to mind overmuch. She blushed prettily and looked away real quick. But she didn't turn her back, and after a few seconds she looked up again. Mordecai and Lon went on toward the coop, where Hardy Brown and Eric Torsten were. Hardy and Eric were slightly older than Mordecai and Lon, almost grown in fact, but they weren't unfriendly or highfalutin about it. They could be counted on to give Lon his chew.

As he and Lon walked up behind the older pair Mordecai heard Eric saying, "I tell you, Hardy, she'll let you feel of her. Maybe more'n that."

"No."

"It's gospel, Hardy. She let that greaser feel her top an' under her skirt too. She's loose, Hardy. Hot for it. She don't care who it is wants to kiss on her an' whatever else. She *likes* it, I tell you."

"You really think so?"

"He seen it, didn't he? He told me so his own self, Hardy. He seen the two of them with his own eyes. An' he swears there would've been more to see if them two hadn't got broke apart just then. He swears she woulda let that greaser do it."

"I'd sure like to do it with her," Hardy said with considerable feeling. He shivered slightly just from thinking about it.

Mordecai couldn't help but wonder who they were talking about, and apparently Lon couldn't either. The younger boys had both come to a halt and were standing silently behind Eric and Hardy waiting for them to finish their conversation before they interrupted.

It was a puzzlement, though. Nearly every girl old enough for serious sparking was already married, practically every one for miles and miles in any direction. With girls in short supply out here on the Colorado, any girl who wanted herself a husband could have one. An unmarried girl older than sixteen was a mighty picky one indeed, and never mind what she looked like. There wasn't any such thing as a female too ugly to find herself a man. Not out here there wasn't.

As for the rest of it, well, Mordecai had to take that talk with a grain of salt. There wasn't a single eligible girl he could think of who could be called genuinely loose. Not even Delia Upton, who was positively known to have let Eric's younger brother Clay kiss her at a Christmas gala even though there hadn't been any mistletoe handy for an excuse. But Delia wouldn't actually *do* anything; Mordecai felt sure about that.

"You think she'd let the both of us do it?" Hardy asked.

"Bet she would," Eric stated.

"Man." Hardy chuckled and rubbed at the fly of his britches. "Look at 'er, Eric. Look at 'er when she bends over like that."

Mordecai moved over a bit so he could see where Hardy and Eric were staring. Across the way beside one of the food tables he could see a girl's trim but admittedly nicely rounded rump as, facing away from the boys, she was bending over tending to something in a tub on the ground. She wasn't being provocative about it though. She was busy washing something in the tub.

Mordecai frowned. That dress was familiar. And just a minute ago at that tub he'd seen . . .

The blood rushed from his head, and he felt a sharply urgent sense of fullness in his neck and shoulders. His nape tingled, and his hands balled into fists before he was conscious of them doing so.

That was his little sister Angeline that Hardy and Eric were leering at, damn them; lusting after; worse, saying things about.

"You take that back, Eric," Mordecai spat. He stepped forward, grabbed Eric by the shoulder, and spun him half around.

"Huh?"

"You're a liar, Eric Torsten. A liar and a sonuvabitch."

"Dang it, Mordecai, I never meant for you to—"

Eric hadn't time to finish whatever he wanted to say. Mordecai's right hand shot forward and pulped Eric's lips against his teeth. Blood flew and Eric was rocked back a step. He shook his head to clear it. Eric Torsten was older than Mordecai and heavier. But he wasn't anything like so angry. Before Eric could think of any sort of retaliation—or of defense, for that matter—Mordecai was on him with his arms pumping and his fists flailing.

Hardy Brown tried to intervene but Lon Willet, who as yet had no idea what the fight was about, sailed into Hardy in support of Mordecai. If Mordecai wanted to fight, that was quite good enough for Lon.

Mordecai knocked Eric to the ground, where Eric's greater weight and strength were all the more an advantage. The two rolled and pummeled, Mordecai snarling and scrapping and trying to bite Eric anytime any exposed portion of Eric's flesh came near. Mordecai was still kicking and hitting when someone pulled him away and broke up the fight.

Mordecai and Lon were led off in one direction and Hardy and Eric in another. In a matter of seconds Mordecai forced himself to pretend a show of calm. He accepted a bit of cloth from someone's helping hand and used that to staunch the flow of blood from a split over his left eye where Eric had managed to hit him. Hopefully, he thought, Eric would have suffered worse damage than that.

"Are you all right now?"

"Yeah. Sure," Mordecai grumped. He would have gotten up—he discovered he was seated on the back step leading into James's dogtrot—but he was being held down by Sly Shipman, he saw, once he bothered to pay attention. It was Sly who'd handed him the cloth so he could stop his bleeding and clean himself. "I'm fine, thanks."

"Uh-huh. What was that about, Mordecai?"

"Nothing."

Sly raised an eyebrow.

"Nothing worth repeating," Mordecai insisted.

"Alonso?"

"Yes, sir?"

"What were you boys fighting about?"

Lon gave Mordecai an apologetic look, then told Sly what they'd overheard.

"And it was Angeline they were saying those things about, Alonso?"

"Yes, sir, it was."

Sly grunted and looked down at Mordecai. "I'd have done the same thing myself at your age, I suppose. But don't you think it might've been sensible to find out where they heard such filth as that, Mordecai?"

"Yes, sir. Now that I think on it."

"Wait here. No, now don't you be getting up, either one of you, or you'll have more to worry about than a fight with Hardy and Eric. You wait right here. Both of you. I'll be right back." Sly turned and went off into the crowd.

"Sorry," Lon mumbled.

"It's all right." Mordecai sighed. "Thanks for keeping Hardy off my back."

"I wish I coulda done more."

"You done fine."

"I never did get my chaw."

"You can ask Sly for one when he gets back."

Lon appeared happier after Mordecai mentioned that.

Sly was gone at least ten minutes, but Mordecai never considered leaving the spot where Sly had told him to stay. He doubted that such would have occurred to Lon either.

"Now ain't this interesting," Sly said when he finally did return.

"What's that?"

"It seems the Blackwoods are back. Eric and his father saw them the day before yesterday and stopped to pass the time and ask for a drink of water. It's them who are rumoring filth about Angeline. No doubt they're still mad because of the whipping Luke took after he beat Manuel."

"But Angeline never—"

"Of course she didn't. Don't be silly. But then when was the truth ever necessary to a Blackwood, hmm? They're mad at your family, always have been for that matter, and now they're hurting all of you the worst way they can think of. And there isn't much anybody can do about it, I'm afraid. You can't stop a rumor, Mordecai, any more than you can stop a cloud from crossing the sky. Once one exists it just goes wherever it's a mind to, and there isn't anything mortal man can to do to stop it from traveling or so much as change its course."

"But if people think—"

"Most people will know better," Sly said. "Truth is, Eric knew better. He admitted as much. He was just being stupid, Mordecai. Running off at the mouth and pretending, like. Wishful thinking, I suppose you could call it. Your sister is an uncommon pretty girl, Mordecai. That's something you'll have to come to grips with pretty soon or else resign yourself to fighting every boy between Bexar and Natchitoches."

"Yes, sir. I s'pose so."

"Believe me, Mordecai. It's true. Ask Alonso."

"Lon?"

"I ain't saying nothing, Mordecai. No sir, not me."

"But if Angeline wasn't my sister?"

"Then I might think she was awful pretty too."

"But you wouldn't—"

"Gosh, no. Not hardly."

Mordecai grimaced. The possibility that Angeline might be thought of as an actual girl, subject to kissing and courting and . . . all those other things . . . That hadn't really occurred to Mordecai before today. "Dammit, Sly, there's gotta be something to be done about them damned Blackwoods an' their lies."

"Short of killing them, Mordecai, there isn't a thing can be done about them. And I don't guess any of us is up to committing murder. Not even 'bout this."

"No, sir, I reckon not." But Mordecai's jaw firmed and he sat up straighter now, his eyes unfocused and his thoughts quite obviously distant—and serious.

☆ Chapter ☆
30

Angeline was up in the loft in her bed. Mordecai could hear her up there, crying, so apparently somebody'd been dumb enough and insensitive enough to tell her what the fight had been about. His guess was reinforced by the fact that his mother was over in the corner trying to mend some things. She was having a devil of a time of it, though, because she couldn't seem to get her needle threaded. Mordecai could see, though he knew he wasn't supposed to, that she couldn't thread the needle because of the tears filming her eyes. So she'd heard too.

Not that anybody'd said anything to him about it. Not even Papa had said anything about the cause of the fight. That meant they'd all of them heard and approved of what he'd done but weren't gonna actually say so because fighting was supposed to be wrong.

Except, Mordecai knew, sometimes.

So now Angeline and Mama were upset because folks were thinking ugly thoughts about Angeline, and Papa would be upset about that and probably other things too, and the whole darn thing was just one big mess. Mordecai wished they hadn't been told. But he didn't regret laying into Eric this afternoon. He'd do that again or worse if he had to.

He stood, yawned hugely, and ambled toward the door. "Reckon I'll go down the river tonight, Papa, and see can I spot a possum or something." Possum roasted up awful tasty, and Mordecai had never known it better than the way his mama fixed it. It was almost a shame, now he was thinking on it and commencing to hanker after some of Mama's roast possum, because there wasn't no chance whatsoever that he'd be coming home later with a possum to show for his hunt.

"You going over to Frank's to take his boys with you?" his papa asked.

"Oh, I dunno. I'll be going by there so I might. Depends if they're still showing a lamp in the window or not." He knew he would have to make a detour later on or else prove to've been lying, which he didn't want. Better to walk a little piece out of his way, and really and truly go by cousin Frank's as he'd just said, than to lie. There wasn't no chance though that he was gonna ask Eddie and Dave to come. Neither one of them could keep his mouth shut good enough.

"Good luck."

"Thanks, Papa. G'night, Mama, Papa." In a louder voice he called, "G'night, Angie." She didn't answer, but that was all right. He picked up his rifle and went out into the dogtrot, crossed over to the side where he lived, and took his possibles pouch down off its peg. A few paper-wrapped cartridges made up ahead of time with powder and ball and the paper for wadding were all he generally carried, but tonight he might want more ammunition with him than that.

Cousin Frank's place lay in one direction and Aunt Annie's in another. Mordecai slipped quietly out into the night and turned upriver, toward Annie and Sly's place, instead of down toward Frank's.

Annie and Sly's was dark, but Mordecai turned up the path to their cabin anyhow. A guinea hen roosting somewhere near shrilled its warning, and the whistling calls were repeated by its companions. The hens were as alert as geese and better than watchdogs. By the time Mordecai reached Sly's cabin he knew they were awake inside.

"It's me," he said softly.

The door swung open and Sly came out into the dogtrot. "Mordecai?"

"Yes, sir. I'm sorry if I woke you."

"It's all right. We weren't asleep yet. Come in, son. Are you hungry? Want something to drink?"

"No, sir, I'm fine. I, uh, came t' ask the loan of something. If it isn't too much trouble."

"Oh?"

"Yes, sir. I kinda thought I'd go upriver a piece t'night and see can I tree some bobcats. I got a den of 'em spotted, I think. But there's a whole family of them, you see. And I only got the one shot in this rifle. So what I was thinking, instead of having to take somebody along, you know, like maybe somebody else wouldn't go after 'em as quiet as me an' then I'd get mad about it, so what I was thinking, Sly, is if I could borry those old pistols o' yours, well, I could handle the dam an' the sire of those cats by my own self. Not your new Colt's pistols, mind. Just the old ones you used to carry before you got you the revolving ones. If, uh, you wouldn't mind."

Sly smiled and used the palm of one hand to vigorously scrub at his face as if wiping sleep out of his eyes and kneading fresh life into his flesh. "I see, Mordecai. You want to take this den of cats by yourself."

"I never done anything like that before. This one time I'd sure like t' try it."

"That sounds reasonable."

"Then you'd lend me them pistols?"

"Don't see any reason why not, son. Wait here. I know right where they are."

"Gee, thanks." Mordecai grinned and waited where he was told.

Sly went inside and was gone only a matter of moments before he was back with a bundle of oiled cloth in his hands. He unwrapped the packet and brought out the pair of heavy, percussion horse pistols that he'd carried for some years before buying the repeating revolvers that had stood them in such good stead during the fight with the Mexicans. He handed the pistols to Mordecai, then handed over the belt that went with them. The belt held a pair of brass eyes that matched brass hooks affixed to the lock plates of each pistol. The single-shot pistols could be attached to the belt for safekeeping, one on either side of the wearer. There was also a small pouch on the belt that held powder, wadding, ball, and fire caps. "They aren't loaded yet," Sly said. "Mind you clean the oil out of the touch holes before you load them. Excuse me if I'm telling you what you already know, son, but your daddy is such a stodgy rascal when it comes to his flint guns that I don't know what he's taught you 'bout percussion. The easiest way to clean the oil out is to fire a couple caps before you go an' load in any powder. The fire from the cap is enough to burn out any oil."

"Yes, sir, thank you." Mordecai strapped the belt around his lean hips. It sagged some even buckled into the last hole, but it didn't feel as if it was going to fall off. Actually, Mordecai thought, the belt with its pair of pistols hanging at a jaunty angle over each hip felt kinda dashing and dangerous and good. It wasn't at all the same feeling as carrying a rifle in your hands.

"There's balls in the pouch there. If you want shot instead I can give you some."

"Ball will be fine, thanks."

"A cat's pretty easy to kill, son. And shot is easier to aim with at night. You might want to think about carrying the shot along."

"Don't bother. The ball is fine. Really."

"All right then." Sly smiled. "Good luck, Mordecai."

"Thank you, sir. G'night."

"Good night."

Sly went inside, and Mordecai walked silently into the shadows toward the river. The pistols at his sides made him feel somehow taller than usual. And tougher.

He supposed he should have felt bad now. But he didn't. It wasn't near as bad a feeling lying to Sly as it would've been lying to Papa or to Mama. That really would have bothered him. This didn't.

Mordecai reached the riverbank and, nearly invisible in the dark, headed upriver, just as he'd told Sly he would do.

☆ Chapter ☆
31

There was a breeze, which was a mixed blessing. The night wind cut and chilled Mordecai, knifing into his trousers where they were wet to midthigh. On the other hand, the rattle of the branches around him caused by the same wind made noise enough that the dogs didn't hear him coming. He passed through the corral and reached the side wall of the shed without rousing the dogs. There weren't any guineas or geese here, and the few chickens didn't matter. Chickens will sleep through anything short of a fox's running amok in their coop.

Mordecai ducked under a corral fence rail and leaned his rifle against the side of the flimsy post-and-sapling shed. He reached inside his shirt and brought out the things he'd scrounged behind James's cabin.

First there was the broken piece of bottle. It held a swatch of rotting burlap that he'd soaked in the grease left behind from cooking half a dozen hams. The rough cloth smelled good enough to eat, but it was probably a good thing that he couldn't see what it looked like. No doubt it was right nasty.

He wrapped the oil-drenched cloth around a yard-long stick that he pulled off the side of the shed, the dried-out sapling old and easy to break. He wrapped the cloth just at the end of the stick so that it formed a knot there the size of a large rat. When he was satisfied with his handiwork Mordecai leaned the stick against the shed next to his rifle, being careful to keep the one from touching the other lest he smear the rifle with the filth on the burlap.

Next he spread open the puffball toadstool he'd found on his way to James's. He held the puffball close to his face and blew. His reward was a bright red glow as the coal he'd gotten out of the firepit, left there from the cooking the women had done before the burying, received the fresh air he blew onto it. A coal could smolder almost dormant but still active inside a puffball for the better part of a day if need be. Mordecai hadn't needed to carry it anywhere near that long.

He felt on the ground, found some wisps of dried grass, and applied them to the coal. This time when he blew the cherry red of the coal was quickly followed by a leap of yellow flame as the grass stems took fire and flared.

He grabbed for the oiled burlap torch, but his burning grass stems died away into curls of gray ash before he could touch their flame to the torch head.

Mordecai cussed a little under his breath and tried again. This time he built a small mound of grass and straw on the ground, lighted bits of grass with the coal, then immediately used that flame to ignite his tinder. That was better. He had plenty of time then to take the torch and hold it over the tiny fire. The oil caught and took flame, dark smoke rolling off it as it popped and sputtered. As a light it was poor, but it should safely burn for fifteen minutes or maybe even more, Mordecai judged.

Finally he took the torch in his left hand and cradled his rifle in the crook of his left arm, leaving his right hand free. With that hand he picked up a chunk of rock and stepped out from beside the shed.

A hound's sleepy head raised up from the stoop nearby, and the dog let out a belated woof, much too late to warn anything or anybody.

"Yo! Inside the house. Wake up." Mordecai took aim and threw the rock through the open doorway to clunk and clatter about inside. "Wake up, Blackwoods. Come out an' talk to me." He picked up another rock and threw it.

☆ Chapter ☆
32

Luke and Finis looked mean enough to bite snakes. It was pretty clear they didn't like being waked in the middle of the night. Likely it was even truer that they didn't like being found at home this way. If a button like Mordecai Lewis could find them, so could that Major Brown or a ranging company.

"What the hell d'you want?" Finis demanded. He didn't sound very welcoming about it neither.

Mordecai stood his ground before the men, squared off in front of them in their own yard with his torch held high so everybody could see. The bare, trampled earth of the yard between Mordecai and the Blackwoods' front stoop was illuminated by the flickering yellow light from his torch.

"I come here to have a word with you," Mordecai announced.

"Dammit, boy, don't you know better'n to bother folks in the middle of the night. I oughta have Luke here give you a whupping, boy. Teach you some o' the manners that no-good daddy o' yours shoulda give you a long time ago."

"Step out here yourself if you want, Finis Blackwood. Or the both of you come. It don't make no nevermind to me. I know 'bout how you two are. I know you think you can get away with anything you like. An' all these years gone, my family has tried to be fair with you. That's been their mistake. I reckon it's time you hear from me now, Finis Blackwood."

"From a kid like you? Go t' hell, boy. An' go off to do it quick else I'll tell Luke to jump you. He'll give you a licking worse than that greaser got, too."

"I don't aim to take no licking, Finis Blackwood. Not from Luke nor from you neither one. That's why I brought these pistols along. There's two of you, Finis. And I got me three shots here. I expect I can shoot the both o' you if I have to an' still have a charge left over. Now are you gonna listen to what I have to say or are you gonna tell Luke to step out here and get himself shot?"

Luke frowned and turned to say something to Finis in a voice too low for Mordecai to hear. Finis grunted, and Luke stepped off the stoop to the ground.

Mordecai raised the first pistol and held it level, the muzzle bead that was all it had for sights held square and steady on Luke's breastbone. A ball placed there would crush the life out of a man before he could take five steps. It would shatter heart and lungs alike. And Luke would know that every bit as well as Mordecai did.

Luke stepped hesitantly forward. Mordecai took his time, drawing the pistol hammer back to full cock and allowing his finger to rest on the trigger guard. His eyes did not waver any more than the pistol barrel did.

"Finis. I think he'd shoot, Finis," Luke said in a whisper that this time was loud enough for Mordecai to hear.

"Believe him, Finis. I ain't bluffing. I'll shoot down the both of you before I take a beating. Won't be any trouble with a claim of self-defense. Not with my uncle bein' in the congress. An' you won't even be able to come to court and tell no lies on me or they'll arrest you and take you in for questioning about them dead Mexicans my papa and uncles all seen you with. There's a major who wants real bad to talk to you 'bout that, Finis Blackwood. And Luke, he'll be dead. Won't neither one of you be able to say nothing against my word."

"Are you gonna shoot or talk, boy?"

Mordecai motioned with the barrel of the pistol, and Luke scooted quick back onto the stoop at the front of the house. Mordecai obliged by taking the pistol hammer down to safe cock and fixing the pistol back into its belt keeper. He thought both Luke and Finis looked less nervous once he'd done that.

"I won't take up much o' your time," Mordecai told them. "I just wanted you both t' know something. Like I said before, my family's been trying for years to play fair with you Blackwoods. All it gets us is lies and meanness. To your kind, fair is just a excuse for you t' run roughshod over top of us. You think you can do whatever you want an' we won't backshoot you nor jump you outa the shadows or lie about you or anything. Well, gentlemen, I been thinking on that some. I reached me some conclusions."

Mordecai moved around a bit. His arm was starting to tremble and sag from the strain of holding the torch aloft so long.

"You Blackwoods been saying bad things about my sister."

Finis's mouth opened, but Mordecai cut him short. "Don't deny it. I know what you'll say, and I won't believe it anyhow so don't waste your time or mine trying to lie your way past me. It won't work. But it might make me mad, and I'm the Lewis that you don't wanta have get mad at you."

Behind the grown Blackwoods, Mordecai could see the wide, staring eyes of Cyrus and all his younger brothers and sisters or half-brothers and half-sisters. Rumor had it that nobody knew how any of them were kinned anyway, their fathers uncertain and maybe even some of the mothers mostly forgotten. They were more like a pack of wild animals than a family. Still and all, they were children too. And Mordecai tried to ignore them by concentrating on their elders.

"The thing is," Mordecai went on, reciting the argument he'd spent the whole of the late afternoon and evening working out in his mind, "the thing is, I know an' you know that I can't be all the time on the lookout atrying to protect my sister an' keep folks from saying anything about her."

Mordecai grinned and gave that a moment to sink in while he shifted the torch from hand to hand so as to rest his arm. "So what I think you and me had best do," he said, "is work together on this thing."

Finis snorted. Mordecai didn't mind that at all. If anything it was a more honest reaction than he'd ever expected from the oldest Blackwood.

"That's right, Finis. You and me and Luke. From this minute on, we all of us got the self-same aim with this thing."

"Do tell," Finis sneered.

"That's right," Mordecai said calmly. "I *am* telling you. From now on, you see, you are as interested in keeping my sister safe, and her name unsullied, as me and my folks are. You want to know why that's so, Finis?"

"Boy, you're so funny about this that you're starting to interest me. Sure, go ahead an' tell me why me and Luke should be wanting to be all that sweet to your sister."

"It's simple, Finis. I can't watch over her all the time, so what I reckon I will do is make you responsible for her. From this minute on, Finis, if anything happens to Angeline, I am gonna hold you and Luke to account for it. And I mean if *any*-damn-thing happens. Even if you ain't in the same county and something happens to her. Even if a mule kicks her in the head, Finis. Anything happens to her at all, and I hold you to account for it. It's just that simple."

Finis laughed. He seemed genuinely amused by the sight of this youngster who was making threats in the middle of the night.

"I don't blame you, Finis. All your life, ever since both our families was neighbors back in Tennessee, you been able to cackle and play hell with the Lewises because we're a fair people." Mordecai's smile was tight and calm. "That was before, Finis. Me, I see things a little different from what Papa does. Could be the Creole blood, eh, m'sieur? But whatever, mister, I ain't lying an' I won't hesitate. Anything bad happens to Angeline then something bad happens to you an' to Luke. Just as sure as the rain falls cold in winter, Finis, I will rain all over you. No warning. No fuss about is it fair. I'll just up and do it. Do we understand each other?"

Finis chuckled. "Sure, boy, sure. I believe you."

"No, I reckon you don't. Was I you I wouldn't believe a Lewis saying something like that neither. But you ought to. You best learn to." Mordecai walked the few paces to the shed. "I see you got a bunch of stuff in here, Finis. Harness, tools, is that a bag of seed there? Not that it matters. You don't believe I'm anything more than a boy and you don't believe I'm any different from my papa. Believe it, Finis. I ain't lying and I ain't playing with you. I'm just telling you the way things are gonna be from now on. And if you wanta object to that, why, feel free. You can come at me any time you feel lucky, and we'll see which of us is alive afterward."

Still smiling, Mordecai tossed the torch into the Blackwoods' shed. The old, sun-dried saplings caught fire with a roar. In less than a minute the shed was engulfed in a huge, billowing fire that lighted up the clearing all the way to the tree line and the river. The flames crackled and spat, and nothing that had been inside the shed would ever be useful again. Even steel would be twisted and destroyed by heat that intense.

Finis and Luke stood on their stoop, the children clearly visible behind them now in the bright light from this conflagration. Both men seemed to be staring at the pistol that Mordecai once again was holding.

"Believe it, Finis. I meant every word I said." Mordecai turned and began walking toward the river. He felt a tightening in the small of his back, just about the point where a rifle shot might be aimed, but he refused to give them the satisfaction of seeing him check his backside. He squared his shoulders and sauntered slow and insolent to the trees that lined the Colorado here.

By the time he reached the protection of shadows again he was drenched with cold sweat and felt weak and shaky.

But he meant it, dammit. He meant every word. And he would protect Angeline's name and honor if it meant backshooting every Blackwood from here to Tennessee and back again.

He hadn't been bluffing, not the least little bit.

He was about half scared, though. It was an awesome step he'd just taken, one he hoped Papa never found out about, because it was something Papa would never understand.

Still a little shaky, and eager now to get home, Mordecai almost jumped out of his skin when a dark figure stepped from the shadows into his path.

"Wha—"

"It's just me, Mordecai."

"Sly?"

Shipman grinned. "You didn't think I bought that story abou the bobcats, did you?"

"Oh."

Sly laughed. "It's all right, son. Honest."

"You won't tell Papa?"

"Not if you don't want me to."

"Please don't. He wouldn't . . . I mean . . ."

"I understand. And you're right. He wouldn't." Sly offered a chew, but Mordecai declined it. "You have grit, Mordecai. I can' say that what you done tonight was the same as I had in mind. Bu it wasn't real far off."

Off beyond the Blackwoods' clearing the fire still blazed, bu not so high now. The dry wood of the storage shed was quickly being consumed.

"You know you'll have to watch your back from now on," Sly said in a conversational tone of voice, as if concern about ambush were the most normal thing possible.

"Yes, sir, I figured on that."

"Those pistols, Mordecai."

"Yes, sir?"

"I think they'd best be a gift instead of a loan."

"But I couldn't . . ."

"Don't turn stupid now, son. You not only can, you damn wel better. If the Blackwoods come at you they won't do it fair. You'l need more than the one shot in your rifle if that ever happens. I want you to have the pistols. I have my revolving pistols, and I certainly don't need those old things anymore. Be my pleasure to make a gift of them to you. Matter of fact, Mordecai, you'd best stop by my place on your way home now. I'll get you the bullet mold to go with those, and a tin of percussion caps. Always carry plenty of caps, Mordecai. That's the one weakness of percussion against your daddy's flint. A man can't bend over and pick up a fresh lot of caps off the ground if he runs short, the way he can most always replace his flint. Be that as it may, son, I've found over the years that percussion is quick and reliable and shoots just as hard as anything. And I've found that pistols are almighty handy things. A rifle will feed you, but there's times when a pistol is better for keeping you alive and hungry."

"I . . . don't hardly know what t' say. I don't have no money to pay you with."

"I don't recall your daddy ever teaching you that a gift has to be paid for."

"No, sir."

"Then don't insult me by suggesting no such." Sly looked over his shoulder. "That fire's going down already. I hope Finis Blackwood's memory about it isn't as brief."

"I meant what I said, Sly. I'd do it."

"I believe you, Mordecai, but it ain't me that has to, it's Finis. And that's what we won't know until time proves it out one way or t' other."

Mordecai reached down and touched the butt of the pistol on his belt. The feel of it there was reassuring. They reached the ford across the Colorado and waded into the cold, slowly swirling water. Mordecai thought about the Blackwoods, who were somewhere on the riverbank behind him, and he felt a chill race up his spine. It was only from the cold of the water, though. He almost was able to make himself believe that.

☆ Chapter ☆
33

Mordecai stopped, dropped the blade of the hoe—Lordy, how he despised that hoe—into the dry, crumbly earth between the corn hills, and gave himself a moment's rest. His father was working the next row and Angeline beyond that. Mama was back at the house and soon, the sooner the better, would be calling them to dinner. Mordecai's job wasn't made any easier by having to wear his pistols even in the field, a newly adopted habit that Papa disapproved and that Mordecai himself would have been much happier without. Happier but not safer. He wasn't going to get sloppy-lazy about this and start taking chances less than a week after delivering his ultimatum to the Blackwoods. Doing that would be almost the same thing as backing off and saying he hadn't really meant it.

He stretched, easing tired muscles in the small of his back, and saw movement down toward the house. "Yonder, Papa. Looks like Sly is coming to pay a visit."

Michael stopped chopping at the earth and looked across the field. "So 'tis." He wiped his brow with the back of his wrist, rearranging the sweat and dirt there but not otherwise accomplishing much. "Tell you what, let's do the decent thing and go talk to our guest." He winked at his children. Apparently he was as ready for a break as Mordecai felt. The three of them took their hoes and walked back through the corn patch, where bright emerald shoots were sprouting strong and healthy in the rich Texas soil.

"Howdy," Sly greeted as they came near. He'd seen them coming in and was waiting for them out front, Marie behind him in the shade of the dogtrot.

"Howdy yourself." Michael shook Sly's hand, then Sly came

over and shook with Mordecai too. Mordecai was pretty sure that it wasn't just wishful thinking on his part. Sly Shipman really did seem to be treating him more like a man and less the boy these days.

"I see you're wearing those old pistols. Have you been practicing with them like I suggested?"

"No, sir."

"No powder?"

"We got powder. It just seems an awful shame to waste it shooting at clods o' dirt." He could hear Angeline and Papa splashing in the water basin, cleaning up ready for dinner. Mama had gone back inside already.

"I thought maybe that was why I hadn't heard any noise from down this way," Sly said. "But I think you'll find that a pistol ain't much the same as a rifle. It takes almost a different way of looking at things before a man can handle a pistol right. It ain't half as easy as it looks. I really think you oughta practice more."

"Yes, sir," Mordecai said, accepting the advice but not actually making any promises to follow it.

"Here." Sly bent down and took up a package he'd set on the breezeway floor. Mordecai found that it was heavier than it looked. "There's a pig o' lead there and a tin of English powder. I got them cheap, and I want you to have them, Mordecai. I truly think it's important for you to practice with those guns. Wearing them won't do you much good if you can't hit what you need to."

"Whyever would he need a pistol anyway, Sly?" Michael asked, coming up beside them with his face and hands clean and water running down into his shirt. He looked refreshed now. "It was real nice o' you to give them to him, but I ain't yet figured out why he insists on wearing them all the time. And now you're saying he could need them? What is it, Sly?"

"You know how it is, Michael. A man never knows when trouble will find him. I just want Mordecai to be ready when that day comes to him."

Michael grunted and refrained from arguing the point.

"Anyway, I had that lead and powder and thought I'd bring them by," Sly said, turning back toward the path that led north past Andrew's to his place and James's.

"You'll stay to dinner, I hope," Michael said.

"Thanks, but Annie will have ours waiting before I get home."

"You know you're welcome."

"I know I'm welcome, Michael, and I thank you."

"'Bye," Mordecai said. "And thanks."

"You'll practice with those guns?"

"Yes, sir."

"Promise?"

There it was. A promise made was a promise to be kept. "Yes, sir. I promise."

"All right then." Sly touched the wide brim of his sombrero and took a few steps toward home, then turned back and said, "Oh, by the way. Did either o' you notice any smoke or hear anything unusual lately?"

"I didn't," Michael said. "Son?"

"No, sir. Something happen?"

Sly grinned. "Something must've. James was across the river this morning. He said he smelled hot ash and followed it up. Found that the Blackwood place was burnt down, burnt clear to the ground, he said. Shed, house, everything."

"No."

"That's what James said. I didn't see it for myself." Sly was looking at Mordecai and for a moment Mordecai wondered if there was a question in his look. But there wasn't, not really. Sly knew good and well it hadn't been him that burned the house. Not without there being a fight. "He said it looked like they'd cleaned the house out, carried off everything worth taking, an' then burned it their own selves so nobody else could have the comfort of using it."

"That sounds like something a Blackwood would do, all right," Michael said.

"Ayuh."

"Did James say how long ago?" Mordecai asked.

"A day or two. Hot coals under the ash and in some of the heavier timbers."

"The wind was from the east the past couple nights. They could've burned it without us noticing, I suppose," Michael said. "No sign of where they went or why?"

"James didn't say anything about that."

"Well, I have to say that I can stand the notion of living without any Blackwoods near. Funny, though, that they'd just uproot and move on. Since Isaac died there hasn't been any of them with gumption enough to look for an honest living." Michael shook his head and shrugged.

"They got something in mind. You can count on that."

"Prob'ly something illegal," Mordecai put in.

"Prob'ly," Sly agreed.

"That's all right as long as it ain't around here and it ain't involving any of us or our'n," Michael said.

"The amazement is that none of them has hung yet."

"Give 'em time."

"Yeah, well, I better get back now." Sly chuckled. "And I mean it this time."

"Sure you won't stay to dinner?"

"Positive, thanks." Sly looked off beyond Mordecai and his father, coming onto tiptoes and staring away into the distance. "Looks like you might be having somebody else for company, though."

Mordecai turned. There toward the big pasture and the public road beyond it there was a rider, sure enough, and the rider seemed to be heading their way.

"Dinnertime," Michael said. "Whoever it is will be welcome. Son, run in an' tell your mama to set out another plate. That'll tickle her. She always does like company."

"Yes, sir. 'Bye now." Mordecai waved a sketchy good-bye—there were things he wanted to ask Sly and things he might say, but this was not the time to be getting into any of that—and went to do as his father bid.

☆ Chapter ☆
34

Michael waited out front to greet the visitor. There was plenty of time between when the rider was first seen and when he finally reached the yard. By then the entire family was outside, waiting and staring and ready to offer a welcome. With the old Royal Highway linking San Antonio de Bexar and Nacogdoches so close it wasn't unknown for them to have visitors. But it was a rarity and becoming even more so now that the country along the Colorado was filling up with farms and there were several equally welcoming places between the highway and the Lewis farms. Having company at the table always gave a boost to Marie's spirits.

As the man came nearer, Michael looked this guest over. Some travelers a man might want to invite to stay over. Others it was better to feed and let move on. No one, of course, would go away hungry.

This man, Michael saw, seemed presentable enough—ragged and dusty from travel but with a lively twinkle in his pale eyes and a lean and lanky build. Once he got close enough that he could be seen underneath the dirt of hard travel, he proved to be young, a little older than Mordecai but not much. If he tried to grow a beard yet he was likely to be disappointed.

He wore rough clothing made of a cloth that had been woven on some woman's own loom and dyed the peculiar shade given by homemade hickory nut dyes. Michael hadn't seen cloth like that in years, but he remembered it well from his youth. Here in Texas there were brighter and better dyes available from the native materials, but hickory was what they'd always used back in Tennessee.

The young man didn't seem to own a coat or a hat, and there

was no blanket rolled behind his saddle. In fact, his saddle looked like something he might've picked up off a trash heap. There was a burlap sack tied at the pommel and a blanket carefully folded and placed underneath the saddle to protect the horse's back. These seemed to constitute the bulk of his worldly possessions.

The horse itself was one eyed but stout. The rider—he was barefoot, Michael saw now—used a scrap of rope for suspenders and was traveling unarmed so far as Michael could tell. Certainly he had no rifle or shotgun, and Sly's influence on Mordecai apart, it was rare to see anyone carry a pistol in these parts.

Both horse and rider looked as if they had come a long way. Of the two the horse was in the better flesh. The rider hadn't any to spare. Michael could practically feel Marie's response to that. She would be determined to fatten this boy by a good five pounds before she let him walk away from her table this noontime.

"Step down and welcome," Michael invited when the young fellow drew rein and gave them all a smile that lighted his thin face bright as a lantern on a dark night. "Dinner's on the table an' there's a place set for you there. Mordecai, take care o' the gentleman's horse, if you please."

"Mordecai?" the visitor repeated.

"That's right. That's my son, Mordecai Lewis. I'm Michael Lewis. This is my wife, Marie, an' our daughter, Angeline."

The visitor's grin got bigger. "I thought this was Frank's place, but I guess I heard wrong. That must be Frank's over there. And that'd make that one Andrew's. And then Mr. Shipman's who I'm told married Annie an' then off up there would be James's. Do I have it now?"

"I don't . . . that is to say, well, yes. But . . . we haven't met before now, have we? How do you know us?"

The young rider laughed, the sound of it bell-like and exuberant. He pulled his right leg across the pommel of his ratty old saddle and perched sideways for a moment, just sitting and grinning down at them fit to bust, then slid lightly to the ground with a spring and a bounce. "We've met, Michael, but it's been an awful long time ago. I expect I've growed some since."

"We have?"

The boy yelped with a joy too great to contain. "It's me, Michael. Your brother Jonathan."

☆ Chapter ☆

35

Michael couldn't exactly understand it, the way everybody was carrying on over Jonathan. Jonathan Lewis wasn't no prodigal son, and this wasn't his home to be coming back to. These were his people, Michael admitted that. But it wasn't like he was a real brother or anything. More like a cousin, never mind that they had the same mother. Pa's brother Benjamin hadn't been any father to Michael and hadn't been welcome to try and act like one, not before Michael's father was killed and not afterward neither, when he up and married Mordecai Lewis's widow. Far as Michael was concerned, his mother's last child wasn't and never would be a true brother. For that matter, Michael didn't feel as close to Jonathan as he did to Frank, who was also his cousin.

Everybody else, though, was fawning and fussing and acting like Jonathan was their long-lost and oh how glad they all were to see him. The way Michael looked at it, Jonathan was acting like he was *every*body's brother, Michael's and James's and Annie's and Frank's too. It was enough to curdle Michael's juices, just about.

They'd all of them gathered—at Michael's house, dang it—quick as the word went around, and now a body would think there was cause for celebration or something.

Shucks, they were all so happy to see Jonathan that it wasn't even occurring to anybody, or so it seemed, to think on how bad was the news he carried.

Ma was dead. Uncle Benjamin had died a while back, and now Ma was gone too, put into the ground beside her second husband, Jonathan said. Michael didn't much like that notion neither. He knew she couldn't be buried with Mordecai. Even Michael couldn't find his father's grave, somewhere on a grassy flat west of the Sabine where Spanish soldiers had murdered him. But it graveled Michael anyway to know that she was buried on one side of Benjamin and Uncle Benjamin's first wife, Nancy, on the other side of him. That just didn't set right.

As for Jonathan himself, Michael found him to be too much the grasshopper and too little the ant.

Jonathan made no bones about it. After Ma died, the farm and stock were sold and the money divided amongst Benjamin Lewis's children. Jonathan—Michael gave him what credit was due him—delivered Frank's share and handed it over along with a paper from the magistrate back home. $21.80 it'd been, the same share as all the children got, the girls and their husbands and Jonathan and now Frank. Jonathan never said what he done with his share of his father's estate, but he sure hadn't had it with him by the time he got to Texas. He even said something about selling his rifle along the way. If there was anything in this world calculated to confound Michael Lewis, it would be the notion of a grown man selling his rifle.

Still and all, the pup had got here, and now they were all expected to put him up and tend to him.

Well, he was going to find it different in Texas than he must've in Tennessee, at least if Michael had anything to say about it. Jonathan could darn well earn his keep here. There wouldn't be any laying in bed till noon or expecting to eat what he wasn't willing to help provide.

The boy was a dang moth dancing and fluttering around a flame, that was exactly what he was, all smiles and charm and silliness.

He might've got along on that back home, but not here. No, sir, not here.

Michael sat quiet to one side and sucked on the stem of his pipe and let all the rest of the family carry on over Jonathan.

☆ Chapter ☆

36

"You come bunk in with me," James invited. It was late, and Jonathan was going to have to move in someplace. It might as well be with him as anybody; he sure had unused room enough. And a lot better with him too than for Jonathan to try and stay here with Michael. James had no idea what was chewing on Michael so hard this evening, but Michael surely was in a dark humor about something. Tonight Michael was grumpy as a sore-footed bear.

Jonathan beamed and bobbed his head in ready assent. Which, James suspected, he would grant in response to nearly any suggestion. Jonathan seemed just plain game for anything. He was a likable youngster too. There couldn't anybody help but be infected by his enthusiasm and his grins.

"I'd like that, James," he said. "If it wouldn't put you out."

"It wouldn't. Be nice to have somebody else in the place to talk to again. It's been kinda lonely over there since Libby and my son . . ." James stopped, hesitated. He hadn't meant to say anything like that, hadn't meant to whimper and complain so. The words were out almost before he'd known he was gonna say them. It was just that in talking with Jonathan now it'd seemed sort of natural to be open and honest like Jonathan was.

"I don't want to hold you up, James," Jonathan said, quick to cover over James's embarrassment lest anyone else notice the older brother's sudden discomfort. "All I need to do is find out what Mordecai done with my blanket. I expect the saddle's outside, but I ain't seen the blanket since I come in."

"That's outside too, Uncle Jonathan," Mordecai put in. "I draped it over your saddle to dry."

"Now that was real thoughtful of you, nephew," Jonathan said.

Both youths grinned. There were only a few years separating them, and both were very much the same in size and looks, both stamped with the Lewis traits. An instant rapport formed between them from the moment of their meeting, and now they both laughed at the silly idea that "old" Jonathan was "little" Mordecai's uncle.

"You aren't leaving so early, are you?" Annie complained with a frown that was matched by Angeline and Hope and Petra. "It isn't hardly late yet."

"I'd stay and jabber the whole night through if it was left up to me, but James is tired," Jonathan said with a wink.

"We'll forgive you if we have to," Annie said, "but there is so much you haven't told us yet. How are Heather and Dora, Jonathan? Are their husbands good to them? Do they have children?"

James had scant hope that he or Annie or any of them here in Texas would ever see their stay-at-home sisters again. That didn't keep him from caring about them every bit as much as he did Annie or Andrew or Michael.

"They're fine. I'll tell you all about them tomorrow," Jonathan promised. Then he grinned and added, "Before I left, though, Dora said she'd write when she has time. But I don't think you oughta start looking for her letter real soon. She already has four kids and another on the way when I left, so it might be five by now."

"No! Little *Dora*? What are all their names, Jonathan? I want to write them all down in my Bible."

"Tomorrow, Annie. I'll catch you up on everything tomorrow, I promise." Jonathan made the rounds from person to person, distributing hugs and squeezes indiscriminately among young and old, all those who were awake and some of the smallest Lewises who weren't. Michael avoided Jonathan's hug but accepted his handshake.

"Thank you, Michael. Thank you for having me in like this." He turned to Marie and gave her the hug Michael hadn't wanted. "That was a wonderful supper, Marie. The best meal I've eat since Ma passed, I swear it was, thank you, an' fixed by the prettiest sister I ever . . . oops, better be careful what I say there." He grinned at Marie and rubbed his stomach to display his appreciation, hugged Angeline, and then with a laugh made a big show of shaking Mordecai's hand. Then he had to go and finish his round of good-byes, leaving out no one whatsoever. James felt most wore out by all of Jonathan's good-byeing but didn't really mind waiting through it. The wonder of it all to him was that Jonathan could feel so comfortable and easy among them, since most of the people in this room he hadn't ever met before today, and many of them he wouldn't even have heard about. But Jonathan had a knack to him and never got so much as the least child's name wrong when he was doing his kissing and patting of the young'uns.

"Whenever you're ready, brother James."

"Whenever you are, brother Jonathan."

"You lead then an' I'll follow."

James waved a casual good-bye—it didn't feel such a big ceremony sort of thing to him—and went out into the dark.

"Should I saddle the horse and take him along?" Jonathan asked.

"Just leave him in Michael's pen for now. We'll move him tomorrow. What about the rest of your things?"

Jonathan laughed. "That *is* the rest of my things. All I had was that bag, and the money in it that belonged to Frank. Boy, I sure am glad I don't have t' worry about keeping care of that anymore. It fretted me, let me tell you. It's a lot better this way. Say James, d'you know where Mordecai might've put that saddle and blanket?"

"In the shed, I'd guess. But I told you, we can move the horse tomorrow."

"Oh, it ain't the horse or saddle I'm wanting. It's the blanket. That's all I got for bedding."

"I got bedding, Jonathan, and a bed. They won't smell of horse sweat neither." Something lurched inside James's chest as he realized that the bedding might well smell of human sweat, though. He hadn't done any washing since Libby and little Sam died. How had he gotten all that sort of thing done before? He couldn't actually recall right now. Annie, he supposed—poor, dear, thoughtful Annie. He was an awful burden to her, he was sure, and all the more so now. He felt that constriction in his chest again and a sudden, unwelcome heat behind his eyelids.

"I sure do thank you, James," Jonathan was saying.

"Sure. Sure thing." James rubbed at his eyes and tried not to think about Libby and Sam.

Lordy, but he missed them.

He hadn't thought he would, not this much, that is. No, that wasn't what he meant either. He'd known he would miss them—

Sam, anyway. Libby he'd been peeved with so much there at the end that he hadn't given real thought to missing her so much. And now he felt guilty as all billy hell about the callousness he'd displayed toward her. But he had known all along that he would miss baby Sam forever and would miss Libby to some extent. It was just that he hadn't realized quite how he would miss them. How sometimes he would see something or think of something and find that he was turning around and his mouth coming open to speak, to tell Libby what he'd seen or what he'd thought, and then he'd realize that there wasn't nobody there to tell, that he was all alone now and there never again would be anybody for him to tell things to. Or he would wake up in the night and find he was sleeping on the edge of their bed and that somehow in his sleep he'd moved all the way over onto the side that had always been hers, as if he was looking for her, hunting for the warmth of her hip against his in the night or the feel of her breath cool on his cheek. And there he'd be, about to fall off the edge of the damned bed on her side because she wasn't there for him to find anymore and never would be.

Come to think of it, James realized, what he'd best do tonight would be to put Jonathan in on his own side and him get in on what had been Libby's. Otherwise he might wake up in the middle of the night and find himself cuddled up to his baby brother, and wouldn't that be a nuisance to have to explain.

"You do travel light, don't you?" he teased.

"Light but easy," Jonathan said happily. "No weight to bow my back nor worries to make me frown, James."

"I got to admit to you, Jonathan, right at this minute your way sounds kinda appealing."

"It is, brother. It really is." As if to demonstrate the truth of his opinion, Jonathan began to whistle a jaunty air as they crossed Andrew's yard, guided by the light of the small lamp Petra had left in the window there, and went on to James's place.

James sighed and led Jonathan into his own dark and lonely home.

☆ Chapter ☆

37

The ground was cold and gritty underfoot as James came back to the house from the privy. Off beyond his oat patch there was a salmon tint in the sky announcing that the dawn wasn't but a little ways off. He'd slept late this morning, no doubt because of being up so late last night talking with everyone, and thinking. Jonathan must've been almighty tired too. The boy hadn't moved when James slipped outa bed this morning and set about the necessities.

When James eased inside, though, Jonathan was awake and sitting on the side of the bed with a shadow of whiskers on his chin and a grin on his lean face. "G'morning, brother James."

"Good morning yourself, brother Jonathan."

James knelt beside the stove and took up some starter slivers. He poked through the ashes until he found some coals to tickle—a couple times since Libby was gone he'd let the dang fire go out and'd had to go over to Annie's to get more—and gently blew on them until the pitch-sticky slivers were aflame and he could begin building a fire. "The necessary is out behind the shed," he said over his shoulder, "and there's water and a basin against the back wall there. If there's anything you can't find, holler."

"I'll manage," Jonathan said.

"And if you got objection to fried food, you'd best speak up now. Me, I figure there ain't all that much of a secret to this cooking business. Fella puts enough grease in his skillet an' gets his fire hot enough, he can fry up a mess o' sawdust so's it'd taste all right."

"Anything that ain't too tough to chew will be fine by me." Jonathan grinned some more. But then a wide and unaffected grin seemed to be his normal expression. "You shoulda seen some of the things I wrapped myself around on the way out here."

"You really came all this way without any money?"

The boy laughed. "Aw, I was holding back some when I told that last night. On account o' the ladies, y'see. I had my share of the farm money when I started off." He stepped into his pants and pulled the makeshift galluses over his thin shoulders without bothering with the shirt yet. "I come across a pretty girl in Vicksburg. You ever been there?"

James nodded. "I been there." He'd made that same trip from Tennessee to Texas once.

"Mighty nice," Jonathan said. James wasn't sure if he meant the girl or the town. Then he grinned and rolled his eyes toward the ceiling, and James knew which Jonathan was talking about.

"Struck some sparks, we did. 'Course it turned out she was more interested in my purse than my person." He laughed. "But I don't begrudge the price o' the lesson. If I had the money I'd go back an' do it all over again." And still laughing he went outside. James shook his head, although fondly, and added some fuel to the fire.

Later, over the remains of fried mush swimming in grease and honey, Jonathan expanded on the details of his trip. "It's a thing to remember," he said. "Folks are awful nice most times. All the way from the Mississippi to right here on the Colorado I never had anything to pay anybody but a smile and a thank-you, but I never went any hungrier than I could stand it, an' I never once woulda had to sleep without a roof if I didn't want to. I turned down more invites to sleep over and to work than I took the time to accept, and I never once had to worry 'bout being robbed or set upon. Some of them people and me didn't hardly speak any words the same, but there wasn't a one of 'em that wasn't kind an' helpful an' fine." He sat back from his plate with a belch and a smile and said, "I'm awful glad I came."

"We're glad too," James said, and found that he meant it. He hadn't taken the time or the thought to be glad about much of anything since Libby and Sam died. It seemed even when he was busy he was moping, inside his head if not out where it would show. Nights since they'd been gone he laid awake with his eyes burning from lack of sleep, but even so he couldn't sleep until sheer exhaustion made him senseless for a very few hours. Then he'd be up and starting it over again. Chop weeds through the day and think about Sam. Go to bed with an emptiness gnawing at his belly and think about Libby.

Damn her, anyhow. She hadn't been all that good a damned old wife to begin with. She was snippy and a complainer and a lousy cook. He really oughtn't to miss her at all.

But he did.

And little Sam Houston Lewis. Lordy. All the things James would never see his son grow up to do. James never even got to see the little fella sucking at his mama's breast. Nor smile nor coo nor flap his arms about and giggle. It wasn't fair. Not a bit of this was any kind of fair.

"James?"

"Huh?" He blinked. Jonathan had got up from his chair and was bending over James now with a worried look on him.

"You all right, James?"

"Fine. Sure."

"For a minute there you looked . . . I dunno."

"Oh, I was just woolgathering. Sorry." He forced a smile. "Wait till Andrew hears 'bout you being here, Jonathan. He's gonna be pleased."

"I'm looking forward to seeing him too, y'know. Next to Michael I guess he's the most famous of us Lewises, him being so early to come out here an' all. But a congressman? Whyn't anybody write an' tell us about that?"

"I guess we never thought. Annie writes sometimes, don't she?"

"We got a letter from her not quite two years ago. It told all about how everyone out here was doing. I don't know how many times Ma read that letter. She carried it with her all folded and kept safe between two pieces of leather until the paper it was wrote on most wore out. When she died we found it tucked inside the pages of her Bible. In Ephesians, Heather said it was, if that makes a difference."

"I wouldn't know."

"Me neither." He snorted. "Heather wouldn't neither, really. She just likes to take on airs sometimes and pretend she knows more'n she does." Jonathan laughed. "Heather'd really puff up if she knew she was sister to a congressman."

"The girls marry all right, did they?"

"Pretty much. You remember a family named Doble?"

"A smith, wasn't he?"

"That's the ones. Well, his middle boy Joshua is who Heather married. Josh has a store. To look at Heather now you wouldn't think she ever walked barefoot through a hog wallow. An' she wouldn't want you to know it neither. Dora, she married Anthony Wainwright."

"I don't recall anybody by that name."

"Maybe they come after you left the country. He farms an' raises a real nice strain o' beeves that he trains as oxen. He's a good hand with them and I think does better from selling his oxen than he does from his farming. I think mostly the farming gives him a way to work the steers an' teach them. And o' course that way he's raising feed for them too. Folks come from far off to buy off him when a good ox is wanted. But he ain't as gentle with Dora as he is with his livestock. Whenever he gets drunk he goes to hitting. He's bad for hitting, that one."

James felt his dander rise. The idea of a man hitting on a woman, and that woman one of his own sisters: it was unsettling. Even if there wasn't anything wrong with that just in and of itself, James thought, a man who was lucky enough to have him a wife shouldn't be so quick to take her for granted. He should be glad of his good fortune and act like he was. There hadn't been a time, no matter how mad he sometimes got at her, that he would've considered hitting Libby.

And Sam. The boy never got old enough to do anything wrong. There never was a switch taken to his backside. He never . . .

James felt hollow. Thoughts twisted and churned inside him sometimes, and sometimes he couldn't look at the things around him without being reminded of Libby and Sam both lying cold in the ground on Michael's knoll.

The littlest and the stupidest things could set him off. He'd take the lid off a jar and realize that Libby had ground the meal it contained. Or he'd pick up a piece of clothing and know that Libby had folded and laid it there on the shelf for him. The mug he drank his coffee from was a wedding gift from Libby's Caldwell kin. Piled by the head of the bed right this minute was a stack of cloths that'd been washed and fluffed and carefully checked to make sure they were soft and nice and ready to be used for diapers. He really ought to do something about those, give them to Annie or something. That was among the things he hadn't yet got around to.

There were so many things he hadn't got around to.

So many things that he didn't *want* to get around to, because they'd just remind him all over again of what-all was missing from this lousy, miserable, empty damned house.

"James?"

He blinked.

Jonathan was staring at him again. He looked worried.

"Sorry."

Jonathan frowned but didn't say anything more.

James got up from the table and dropped his plate into the bucket. One of these times he'd get around to heating some water and doing the washing up. "You promised to tell Annie about the girls today. Why don't you go on over there, else she'll start to think we're sleeping the day away."

"You won't be coming?"

"You know the way, don't you?"

"Be kinda hard to get lost between here and Annie's place, wouldn't it?"

"Yeah, even for a dumb ol' boy from Tennessee. But mind you keep a watch out for Indians." There hadn't been an Indian this far down the Colorado in almost three years, as far as James knew.

Jonathan's eyes grew wide.

"I don't have a rifle to spare or I'd loan you one," James went on just natural and matter-of-fact as he could manage. "Just mind your step an' be ready to run if you got to. You'll be all right."

"James, you're funning me—aren't you?"

"Just mind what I say, that's all. You'll be all right." James fiddled with the shaker bar on the stove grate, as if attentive to that chore while he went on talking over his shoulder. "Indians are hell for long distance, but they ain't much for speed in the short run. I promise you can outrun them an' get to one of us that has a rifle handy. You'll be fine."

With that James turned, touched Jonathan lightly on the shoulder, and left the house to get about his morning chores much, much later than usual.

For the next twenty minutes or more he was so pleased with himself and so intent on visualizing Jonathan's consternation on the short and entirely harmless walk between James's place and Sly's that James very nearly forgot the anguish that lay like a hard, cold knot inside his chest through all his waking hours these days.

☆ Chapter ☆

38

The first hard, cold droplets struck across Michael's shoulders and back like so many pellets of birdshot fired from a great distance away. They startled him, and then brought a quick smile onto his lean, weathered features. He turned and lifted his face to the rain that had drifted onto him from behind. He stood there with his eyes closed, soaking the moisture into his pores, as the rainfall intensified and steadied. The soil was in need of moisture. The smell of rainwater striking clean, sunbaked earth lifted off the ground and filled Michael's nostrils with a scent that was most welcome. This rain should make certain the success of his crop and the safety of his family for yet another year, and so he was grateful for it.

After only a few moments but already soaked to the skin he turned and began walking swiftly out of the cornfield and back to the house and shelter. There was a time when he would have run the distance, but while his wind was still good his joints were not and so it was easier now to walk. Mordecai, hoe in one hand and hat in the other, was whooping and leaping and racing on ahead. Michael smiled. He wasn't sure if Mordecai was more glad for the rain or for the excuse to quit chopping weeds. Likely the latter, Michael decided. Not that he could blame Mordecai. At his age Michael would have felt the same.

As Michael reached the sanctuary of the dogtrot porch he heard a drumming of hoofs on the wet ground, and a rider came out of the trees by the river at a high lope. Mordecai recognized the rider before Michael did and began to wave.

Michael poked his head inside the open doorway of the cabin. Marie was bent over in front of her stove checking the progress of something she was baking. Angeline was at the table frowning at an unmarked slate and holding a chalk stick in her hand. "Company coming," Michael said. "It's Manuel."

"How nice," Marie said, closing the oven door and rising.

Angeline's reaction was somewhat more dramatic. She let out a squeal of alarm and, abandoning slate and chalk alike, raced in a most undignified and unladylike manner toward the trunk where she kept her best clothes. "He can't see me like this, Mama—don't you dare let him in yet, Daddy—Mama, have you seen my comb?"

Michael smiled and pulled the door closed behind him as he went back outdoors. It couldn't hurt anything if he made sure the boys took their time about getting Manuel's horse settled in the pen and his things put away under cover.

The rain, he was pleased to see, may have slipped up on him without warning, but now it looked as if it might turn into a good one. Where before there had been only a thin, pale overcast there now was dark, heavy cloud overhead, and the rain was falling hard enough to obscure one's view. Michael could hardly see anything past the far limits of Andrew's land. This was exactly the kind of rain they'd been needing.

"Welcome," Michael said as Manuel and Mordecai dashed from the shed to the covered porch. He gave his old friend's son a warm *abrazo* and then stepped back to look at him. "It looks good," he said.

Manuel had grown a beard since he left to go to Austin. The reason for that was obvious enough. The beard, dark and thick but close trimmed and neat in appearance, hid most of the vivid scar that would forever mar Manuel's once-handsome face. Now only a jagged portion crossing his cheekbone to the corner of his eye remained visible. The improvement was marked. And apart from partially covering the scar, the beard made Manuel look older and more mature. He looked a man grown now, where before he had seemed a boy on the verge of manhood.

Manuel mumbled something, perhaps a bit embarrassed, and dropped his eyes..

"No, I mean it. It looks really good. Not many young men your age could carry it off." He smiled and poked his son on the arm. "This one couldn't grow a brush of any sort, much less one that fine. I'd be willing to wager Angeline favors it too."

The merriment went out of Manuel's eyes, to be replaced there by a bleak and hopeless pain. "I was thinking . . . I must hurry," Manuel said. "I only stopped to deliver to you a message."

"And what message would that be, Manuel?"

"It is from Andrew. He said to tell you that he would be home soon. He has news but he did not say what, only that he will soon be coming."

"You rode all the way down from Austin to tell us that, Manuel?"

"But of course I did not. I told Andrew that I would be leaving. Going home, you understand. And he said as I would pass so near I must stop and give to you the message. Now"—Manuel shrugged—"I must go."

"Go? Manuel, don't be foolish. It's raining frogs an' frog-stickers out there an' figures to keep it up a spell. Maybe this whole night long. You can't be in such a hurry that you'd be rushing off into rain like this. Besides, when have you ever been shy about staying here? This is your home, Manuel. It always has been an' always will be."

Manuel blushed and looked toward his toes.

"Surely you don't think . . ." Michael motioned for Mordecai to go inside. "Tell Mama to put a lunch out, son. Manuel's bound t' be hungry after his ride." Marie would already have something laid out, Michael was sure. But then that wasn't the point. As soon as Mordecai took the hint and went indoors, Michael said, "I know what's fretting you, son. You think Angeline won't care for you now that there's a wrinkle in the side of your face."

Manuel gave Michael a sullen look that was more discouraging to Michael than a response of fury would have been.

"I hope you know Angeline better than that, Manuel. I hope you know all of us better than to think that. You're still the fine, handsome young man you always been. And Marie and me still feel that if someday it's you who Angeline wants to make her life with, well, we'd both be proud and pleased. For the both of you. I never said that t' you before. Not in so many words. But I've felt it for a long time now. So has Angeline's mama. We've spoke of it often. And there ain't no reason we'd want to change our minds on the subject."

"You are being foolish, Señor Lewis. Angeline, she will want a white man for a husband. She will not want some dirty greaser to touch her."

"Dammit, Manuel, where'd you ever hear such an idea as that? Not in this house. I know that. And where d'you get off calling me señor? When you was little it was *papacita* you called me. Now it's señor? I don't like that, Manuel."

"There are many things in life that a man does not like," Manuel spat. "This I have learned."

"Not so good for you up in Austin, eh?"

For an instant, but no longer, Manuel looked as if he might let his guard down and let go of his emotions with this man who truly had been a second father to him. But the instant was fleeting and then the opportunity was lost. The young man's expression hardened. "Let us say that I have learned many lessons from your people. Now I go home to where I belong and remain with my own kind."

"I don't like hearing you say that, Manuel. I'd like t' think that we're your family too. I'd hate t' think that's all changed now."

Manuel sighed. "I . . . not all, perhaps. Perhaps not quite all has changed, no."

"I hope not." Michael put a hand on Manuel's shoulder and gently squeezed. "Let's go in now. Angeline will want to see you. No, don't stiffen up like that. She'll want t' see you whether you want t' see her or not. It won't hurt you none to be polite to her. Then you can eat an' we'll talk." Michael started the bitter and confused young man in the direction of the door. "And something I know Mordecai will want will be to introduce you to his cousin Jonathan. Jonathan came out from Tennessee a couple weeks ago, and him and Mordecai have got thick as thieves. Helluva likable cuss, Jonathan. I expect you'll like him too."

They reached the door and Michael paused there for a moment. "Don't make any big decisions just yet, Manuel. Would you do that for me, please? No, you don't have t' say nothing. Just think about it now an' then when you're feeling upset 'bout things and might wanta fly off. Just try and let things slide easy for a spell instead. Sometimes it takes time for things to heal."

Manuel reached up, the movement appearing to be an unconscious gesture, and touched his cheek.

"Not that," Michael said. "That is as healed as it ever will be. No, what I had in mind was something more important than that. An' that something ain't hardly begun to heal yet." He smiled. "Which I reckon you know even better'n I do right now."

"*Si, Papacita*. This I know to be true."

Michael laughed. "You ain't called me that in an awful long time. I have to admit that I kinda like hearing it again."

And this time Manuel smiled too. "I will try, *Papacita*. For you, eh? For my other family."

"You do that, son. Now come on in before Angeline an' her mama come grab hold o' you an' drag you in to the table."

Chapter 39

Mordecai broke a twig in two. One half he began to chew on, the other he tossed into the fire in the pit. Mordecai felt good tonight, contented. And why shouldn't he: there was a mess of fat squirrel baking on rocks near the fire, a can of coffee boiling on the coals, and the best company anybody could hope to find with Jonathan on one side of him and Manuel on the other. That was a mighty fine threesome, the way Mordecai saw it.

They'd crossed the river early in the afternoon and hunted the woods for several miles downstream and back again, so that now they were almost directly across the Colorado from home. If the weather turned bad tonight or they just plain took a notion they could go back to the house to sleep. Otherwise they could lay out in the woods and take life easy until they heard Mama clang the gong to call them in to breakfast. There wasn't much could be any better than that.

"James, he is all right, Jonathan?" Manuel was asking. Uncle James had been asked to come along with them today but he hadn't wanted to. Hadn't been doing any work either, so that wasn't the reason he stayed behind. But then James had been notional since Libby died. Mordecai hadn't liked Libby overmuch—not that he ever would admit that out loud, not to anybody—but he was awful fond of James and wouldn't have wanted to see him hurt, not for anything. And now James was hurting, that was for sure. Mordecai supposed James had a right to be notional now if he took a mind to.

"I dunno," Jonathan said. "He doesn't say much , but you can see he ain't happy. He should of come with us today. It woulda been good for him."

"He has shadows in his eyes," Manuel said.

"Bags," Mordecai corrected. "The term is bags under his eyes, not shadows in them."

"No," Manuel insisted. "I mean shadows in the eyes, not the bags beneath them. Dark shadows moving there. He is seeing bad things, memories and sadness, I think. But I agree with Jonathan. It would be good for him to get away. I would wish that he had come today."

"Yeah, well, Uncle James didn't, but I'm having a fine time," Mordecai said, wanting to change things to a lighter note. "Jonathan, reach down an' turn that tree rat around a little, will you? That shoulder is gettin' too done. No, that big one on the left. Yeah, that's the one I meant, thanks."

Mordecai had been pleased with how well Manuel and Jonathan were getting along. He'd always been fond of Manuel. And he thought his newfound uncle was awful good company too. You couldn't always count on two people you liked also turning out to like each other, though, so Mordecai was tickled to discover that in this case things were smooth and easy in all directions. Maybe mostly because Jonathan could get along with just about everybody. Except maybe Papa, and only someone as close to Papa as Mordecai was would even be able to spot that. Papa was careful to try and not show that he wasn't real fond of Jonathan. Mordecai didn't understand how or why that could be so and didn't want to ask. But it puzzled him, and he thought about it now and then. But not, he decided, right now. He winked at Jonathan and leaned down to poke one of the squirrels with the end of the stick he'd been chewing on, testing to see if the meat felt done yet or if they should give it more time to bake. More time, he decided, but not too much. His mouth was already watering in anticipation of the sweet, dark meat.

"You like to run coons, Jonathan?" Mordecai asked.

"You bet."

"So does Manuel. The next day or two whyn't I see if we can get some fellows together and have us a coon hunt. Lon Willet has a hound and the Uptons have a couple that I think we could borrow. Mr. Upton would wanta come along with them, o' course. I've never known him to stay home from a coon hunt. And George Peters has a real fine redbone bitch. If she ain't in season he'll want to run her. So what d'you think?"

"I'd like it fine," Jonathan said with his customary enthusiasm.

"Manuel?"

"Don't ask me, I will not be here."

Mordecai frowned. "What d'you mean not be here?"

"Very much like I say, no? You don't speak English now, Mordy? I will not be here. Because I will be going home. So now you understand, *si*? Very simple."

"You can't go home, Manuel. Not when we're fixing to have a coon hunt."

"I will go."

"Look, if you don't wanta hunt coons, why, we won't hunt no damn coons. It's no big thing. Just an idea. You don't feel like it, why, we won't do it."

"Please, Mordecai. I do not want to stop you from your fun. It is just . . . it is time for me to go. I did not intend to stay at all. I would not have but your father asked. How could I refuse when he asks, eh?"

"Huh. You don't seem t' be having no trouble refusing when I ask something of you."

"Please, Mordy. It is not you. You know this."

"Is it Angeline then? I noticed you been staying shy o' her this visit. Did she go an' say something, Manuel? If she did . . . well, never you mind what. But if she did, you just tell me. I'll fix it."

Manuel smiled. "Your sister has said nothing."

Mordecai sniffed. "I don't know if you already figured this out, Manuel, but sometimes I think ol' Angeline is soft on you."

Jonathan made a noise that sounded at first like a laugh but turned out to be a cough instead.

"What's that?" Mordecai asked.

"I didn't say nothing."

Mordecai turned his attention back to Manuel again. "Anyhow, like I was saying . . . uh, what was it I was saying?"

Manuel smiled. "You were planning to hunt a raccoon."

"No, dang it, I was planning some fun. Doesn't have nothing to do with hunting coons, and you know it. I was planning to have some fun with my old uncle there an' with you. But if you don't wanta hunt coons an' you don't wanta be anywheres around my little sister, what do you want t' do?"

"I want to go home, Mordy. I want to be among my own people."

"We ain't your people, dammit? Is that what you're saying now?"

"You know I am not," Manuel said patiently.

"What then? Them Blackwoods pulled out, you know. Left the country altogether an' we don't expect t' see them back. Not after they burnt their own place down."

"I have been told this, yes."

"Well then?"

"It is not something you would understand, my friend. But just now I do not wish to see any other of your white Texas friends. Not just now, please."

"Oh." Mordecai frowned. "I didn't . . ."

"I know you did not." Manuel was able to smile. "Anyway, Mordy, I must soon go home regardless. My family will need the wages I saved from the working. It is selfish of me to stay here any longer."

"Jonathan," Mordecai said after several minutes of thoughtful silence, "didn't you tell me the other day that you was looking for some way t' make you some cash money?"

"Cash money? I've about forgot what that is."

"What about you, Manuel? Or are you so rich from working up in Austin that you don't need no more?"

"Ha. Is there such a thing as too much? I do not think so. But I do have money. If you need some, Mordy, ask. Or you, Jonathan. What I have is also yours."

"Oh, I ain't asking for no loan. I reckon my old uncle there—"

"Mordecai!"

Mordecai grinned but otherwise ignored the warning from his "old" uncle Jonathan, who in fact wasn't quite to his twenty-first birthday yet. "Like I was saying, Manuel, my elderly uncle there ain't asking for charity neither. But what I just now thought of, since you don't wanta go on a coon hunt that'd involve a whole bunch o' people, an' since you need to be getting on home pretty soon anyhow, an' since the old man there is broke and looking for a way to correct that, an' since I never turned down free money in my life . . ."

"Dang it, Mordecai, get to the point."

"Yes, Uncle. The point is, y'all, why don't the three of us make an adventure outa Manuel having to go home. We could all go. But instead o' taking the highway, we could swing north an' west a piece and see can we chase up some wild cows outa the brush. If we was to yoke them down and gentle them enough to drive, we could take them on to Bexar and sell them there, then visit with Manuel's people for a spell." He grinned at Manuel. "My skinny baby sister ain't so much, but Manuel, he's got a younger sister so pretty she's been known to make growed men stand up in church an' howl like dogs."

Manuel laughed. "He is teasing you, Jonathan."

"You don't have no pretty sisters?"

"To the contrary, señor, I have very pretty sisters. They are all married now an' have fat babies. But there are other pretty girls in Bexar. Besides, if you court a girl who is not my sister I will not have to cut your heart out and feed it to the pigs. And it would please me to know that the cutting out of the heart is the duty of someone else than me, Jonathan."

"How come I'm the only one you're warning, Manuel?"

"Because Mordy is too young to court pretty girls or to need his heart removed. A boy of Mordy's years is of no threat to the protectors of the young women, eh?"

Mordecai launched himself across the fire and began a mock-ferocious wrestling match with Manuel. They were stopped after only a few moments, though, by Jonathan's reminder that the squirrels were done and would scorch if they were left by the fire too long.

Later, when all of them were full and the bones were charring in the fire, Mordecai again raised the suggestion he'd made. "So what do you think, fellas?"

"About what?"

"Does anybody want to ride west an' hunt the thickets for wild cattle?"

"You can really do that?" Jonathan asked.

"Lord, yes. Wild cows an' wild horses too."

"Manuel?"

"For this one time, Jonathan, Mordy tells you the truth. There are many wild creatures in the brush."

"How come nobody catches them all and claims them?"

Manuel looked at Mordecai and laughed. "He will know soon, eh?"

"Does that mean you'll go in on it with me?"

"But of course."

"Jonathan?"

"Hey, I'm game. But will one o' you please tell me what was so dang funny 'bout my question?"

Neither of them would. "You'll see" was as much of an answer as Jonathan could pry out of them.

☆ Chapter ☆

40

Michael winced at the dead weight of the water buckets he carried in each hand. He edged up the steps sideways, taking them one at a time in deference to the pain that was almost constant these days in his hips, knees, shoulders, even down into his feet and ankles. Fortunately Marie and Angeline were inside and Mordecai was off gallivanting and so he did not have to make a show of being spry and able. On the other hand, if Mordecai had been at home it wouldn't be Michael who was having to haul water this morning.

He took care of the water and the firewood, then washed and shaved while Marie finished preparing their breakfast. "Michael, where are you?"

"Right here, dear."

"I have some scraps here. Throw them to the chickens, would you, please?" She held out a basin containing a most unappetizing assortment of vegetable peelings, nut hulls, and other items that Michael felt he was probably better off not being able to identify.

"Woman, if you've gone and made my breakfast from whatever caused this mess . . ."

She smiled and slapped him lightly on the head, and he took the basin out into the yard, calling, "Here, chicka-chicka-chick, heeee-re, chick." The feisty hens clucked and fluttered and pushed in to be the first in line for whatever was coming. Michael broadcast the mess over the ground with a practiced sweep and yelped as an overexcited hen pecked the side of his ankle instead of the bit of gristle it'd been aiming at. "Ouch, dang it."

Michael limped out of the line of fire in a hurry and examined the inside of Marie's basin to make sure there were no sticky lumps or residues still in it. This time there weren't. He grunted and circled wide around the noisy chickens and the dust cloud they were raising.

"Now what have we here?" he mumbled to himself as something caught his eye. He had to squint and tilt his head a bit before he was sure, because the area in question was in shadow and there wasn't much light in the sky yet. But once he was sure of what had seemed out of place he smiled.

"Andrew is home," he announced when he went inside and returned the basin to Marie. Angeline was busy collecting linens off the beds. This was wash day, so she and her mother would be busy with that the whole day long, boiling clothes and linens, scrubbing them, boiling them again in rinse water, and finally wringing them out and hanging them.

"How nice. Is he coming over?"

"Not that I know of. I saw his horse in the pen when I took your stuff out. He must've got in some time last night."

"Andrew works too hard. How long has it been since he was home, Michael? Months. I do not think he should run again for Congress."

"You don't think he should? Or Petra don't?"

"Is it a crime for both of us to think the same thing?"

"I was gonna complain that you didn't answer my question. But come to think of it I reckon you did. Now where's my breakfast, woman?"

"Calm yourself. Andrew will still be there when the meal is done. You can wait that long before you go to see him, I think."

"Yes, ma'am," Michael said meekly.

Marie smiled and rose up on tiptoes to kiss the side of his jaw. "Sit. I am getting your breakfast now."

"You've put on weight," Michael said.

"You haven't. You look good, though." Andrew smiled. "I think I actually missed you this trip."

"You always miss me. You just won't always admit it."

"So you believe. I won't do anything to let you know otherwise."

"Damn, it's good to see you, Andrew. I'm glad you were able to come home."

"So am I, Michael. So am I." The two brothers had walked down by the river and were perched on a fallen log.

"Have you had a chance to, uh, think anymore on that problem we discussed a while back?"

"What? Oh, that. No, it, um, turned out not to be a problem after all."

"I'm glad to hear that."

"Yeah." They sat in silence for a bit while Andrew brought out a pair of cigars, offered one to Michael, and then returned it to his pocket when Michael declined. Andrew devoted considerable time and attention to the nipping, trimming, and eventual lighting of his smoke. He had to turn himself into a contortionist in order to manage lighting it, though. The sunlight coming through the leaves overhead was dappled and broken, and it was hard for him to find a steady source of rays so he could use the burning glass.

"More of that, what was it—Jamaican tobacco?"

"No, these are out of someplace else. I don't know where, but the English bring them in. They're good. Sure you don't want to try one?"

"Thanks, but it's a bad enough habit smoking the pipe. At least I can grow my own tobacco for that. I don't think I'd want to start smoking something that I'd have to go an' buy."

"Living in the city you have to buy any kind of tobacco. You kinda forget there's other ways to do things."

"You live in the city now, Andrew?"

"You know what I mean. This is still home. Houston darn sure ain't."

"And Austin? What will it be?"

"Pretty nice someday, actually. Good country up there."

"Yes, I remember it. But not with no city on it."

"Austin is laid out nice. Wide streets, everything planned and figured out from day one. As cities go, Austin is gonna be a good one."

"Manuel says folks have to stay indoors at night or risk getting caught by some skulking Indians."

"That won't last long. In fact, that's one of the things I wanted to talk to you about. James and Sly too, though. I'd rather not get into it until we're all together."

"All right, if you prefer."

"I do. As for Austin, Michael, I think you'll like it. I do. Enough to ask Petra to think about coming there with me."

"You'd give up the farm?"

"Not give it up, exactly. I'll want to be able to pass it along to

Ben one of these days. But I'd let it lie fallow while we live in a real house in the city."

"Your choice, of course."

"There's nothing wrong with cities, dammit."

"I ain't arguing with you."

"You are too."

Michael grinned at him.

"Okay, so you aren't. So what are we arguing about?"

"I didn't know we was."

"Good. In that case we aren't." Andrew puffed on his cigar for a while, then said, "I take it from what you said that Manuel did stop here like I asked."

"Of course. Why wouldn't he?"

"Did he tell you why he left Austin?"

Michael shook his head. "Not really. I figured he was just wanting to get home."

"He got fired off every job he could find on his own and every one I could find for him. It got so nobody would hire him no more, not even the Skinners, and that's why he left. He couldn't get work no more."

"Manuel?"

"Manuel," Andrew affirmed. "You know why he kept getting fired?"

"He never said a word to any of us about it."

"Fighting. Seems our young Manuel got turned into a tiger when Luke Blackwood beat on him that time. It was like he swore he wouldn't take any crap off any white man ever again. Not punches nor insults neither. And you know how a lot of fellows feel about Mexicans these days. Anybody say anything crossways or look at that boy cross-eyed and away he'd go. At first nobody cared so much because they could all beat up on him, and they thought it was kinda funny. Then they found out that Manuel kept coming at them. And he was learning how to handle himself too. They'd beat him up one day, the next he'd come back and whip two of them. It wasn't so funny after he learned how to do that. Job foremen pretty quick figured out if they had Manuel on their crew they were sure to have a fight before sundown. So they wouldn't hire him no more. Like I said, it got to where even the Skinner crews wouldn't hire him."

"That's twice now you've mentioned somebody named Skinner. Who is he?"

Andrew grinned and shook his head. "Now that one there,

Michael, is the question that has all of Austin awondering. If I could answer it for you I could answer it for them, and I'd be a mighty popular man at all the balls and galas indeed. That is, I would be if I wasn't already mighty popular. Which o' course I am."

"Of course," Michael agreed.

"As for Skinner, though, it ain't a him but a them. Brothers, I'm told, which is just about all anybody up there knows about these Skinners. Whoever they are, they had a land agent buy up a bunch of residential lots close to the business district that was being laid out. At that time most of the interest was in the business lots, y'see. A man could grab up a house lot for just about nothing. So these Skinners, by way of their agent, bought up three blocks' worth of house lots. The whole city blocks. Then they sent in a foreman who knows construction and a work crew made up of drunks and derelicts. Which you wouldn't think would work but it does. I'm told they don't pay but a few cents a day for their workers, but if a man asks they'll pay his wages in whiskey 'stead of cash, and figure the whiskey cheap instead of dear. They're crafty, I'll say this for the Skinners. And instead o' building regular houses like you might expect, they're putting up cheap cribs."

"For, um . . . ?"

"No, the city wouldn't allow nothing like that. Not right downtown. No, these cribs are for folks to live in, all right. But even when they're new these places are cheap and ugly and won't provide decent accommodations to live in. What they will do—and this is what makes me realize how crafty the Skinners are—what they will do is provide cheap quarters for all the low-paid people the government will be hiring once the capital is permanently in place an' working there. Think about it: there'll be all kinds of laborers and swampers and clerks and whatnot needed, and they won't be paid hardly nothing. They'll be able to rent a sleeping place off the Skinners at prices they can afford, and because there'll be so awful many of them the Skinners will be raking in profits by the bucketful for years an' years. And with as good as no costs for upkeep once the cribs are built. But ugly? I can't tell you how mad these places've made folks. The president himself is furious. Cribs like these aren't what he had in mind when he envisioned Austin. But what the Skinners is doing is legal. There doesn't seem to be anything that can be done about them."

"I know this is important to you," Michael said, "but I doubt I'll ever see one of these places you're talking about."

"Of course you will. You'll want to come to Austin sometimes. Why, if nothing else it will be a fine place for you and Marie to go to shop for the things you can't find close to home. Really nice things, I mean. Furniture or if you were to want a piano or a nice oil lamp or something."

"You know, Andrew, I can't think of a single thing that Marie and me might ever want that we can't either make for ourselves or get by way of Sly or else Marie's brothers back in Loosiana." He grinned. "An' I don't see neither one of us ever wanting a piano, thank you."

"It was just . . ."

"I know."

"If Petra decides to move there with me and let me build her a house in the city you'll come visit, won't you?"

"Andrew, you almost look serious enough to make me think it makes a difference to you if I would or if I wouldn't."

"It does, Michael. There ain't anything, not in Austin and not in the congress of this republic, that's more important to me than family. I, uh, thought that one through a little while back, y'know."

Michael reached over and gave his next-younger brother a squeeze on the shoulder. "Wherever you an' yours are, Andrew, I'll visit. Even if it's in Austin."

Andrew grinned, and then became sober again. "Now tell me how James is doing, Michael. Petra doesn't think he's doing so good. And she said *Jonathan* is here? Whoever would've guessed that to ever happen. Lordy, Michael, there's an awful lot I need catching up on. I hope you aren't in any big hurry to get home now."

"Not today, I ain't. Today I'm gonna sit right here and visit with my brother, by jiminy."

Andrew nodded happily and laced his hands around one knee. He exhaled a cloud of cigar smoke that wreathed his head. "I sure am glad I came home now, Michael."

"So'm I, Andrew. Now then, you was asking about James . . ."

☆ Chapter ☆

41

"Are we havin' fun yet?"

Mordecai's head snapped around at the sound of Jonathan's slow drawl. He bristled and was on the verge of making a sharp retort. Then he realized what Jonathan meant and Mordecai commenced to laugh. The laughter proved to be contagious, and Manuel joined in and finally Jonathan, who had started the whole thing.

And a fine measure of relief it was, too. They were all of them overdue for some letting down and some laughing.

Mordecai had a knee that had swollen to the size of a muskmelon, a foot that'd been stepped on twice and now felt like surely it must be broken, mesquite thorns driven so far into his one shin that they might fester and rot away in there without ever being seen again, a jagged scrape across his collarbone that'd bled until his shirt was surely ruined for all time, one elbow that hurt every time he tried to bend it, and a ringing in his ears left over from this afternoon when he'd gone and ridden full speed into a branch that he hadn't ducked low enough to quite get under.

And that was counting only the big stuff. Near about all the rest of him was punctured, torn, rubbed, ripped, aching, or otherwise damaged too.

And at that he had to admit that he looked in the best shape of the bunch.

Jonathan had been kicked in the face by a cow he was trying to hog-tie. In point of pure fact, Jonathan'd been kicked more than just once. Now the right side of his face looked like a red-and-purple pumpkin, and the left side wasn't a whole lot better, although it did look some smaller and less swollen than the right, Mordecai thought.

Manuel limped and groaned and muttered things under his breath every time he had to move, which he did with the help of a makeshift crutch whenever he wasn't horseback. Manuel's horse had tried—by accident or maybe not—to scrape him off against the trunk of a tree and managed to hit the immobile object hard enough to knock himself sideways. The dang horse first bashed Manuel's one leg against the tree trunk and then fell over sideways when it bounced off, dropping with all its weight on Manuel's other leg. It was just lucky neither horse nor man busted anything. As it was, Manuel wasn't feeling much like engaging in foot races.

None of that, though, had kept them from keeping on after the stupid, miserable, louse-ridden, fleabitten, buzzard-bait, SOB cows that'd brought them out here.

At this point they about had it down to knowing what they were doing.

The other boys would get themselves into position and then Mordecai would ride his horse, which didn't mind some brush busting, into a thicket where they suspected some of the wild and ornery ladino bovines were hanging out. In this part of the country, unfortunately, a thicket generally wasn't nice soft willow or scrub oak or what have you like so much of it back home along the Colorado. Here a thicket most likely was built of pale, whippy mesquite that had thorns like hat pins except thicker, stronger, and sharper. Then there might be prickly pear, which was covered with sewing needles instead of hat pins, smaller than the mesquite spikes but a thousand times more of them. And there was coma and agave and agarita and retama and . . . and ten dozen other darn things that even Manuel didn't know the names of. They all of them were nasty one way or another, and at that they didn't have decency enough to give a man a fighting chance against them. They wouldn't stand there and go *mano-a-mano* with a fella. No, what they'd do would be to gang up on him. They'd bunch up and grow together, and sometimes Mordecai absolutely swore that they'd weave their branches together as tight as any basketmaker could've done. And then they dare a fellow to come and try to break through them if he could. It was sometimes enough to almost seem daunting.

Still and all, inside those thickets was where the cattle hid out. So that was where the cattle had to be chased.

Mordecai's horse had a hard mouth and now Mordecai figured he understood why: the horse was just generally insensitive to any sort of feeling or pain, otherwise it couldn't possibly crash through brush and come out the other side bleeding, yet charge right on to crash into the next patch too. They would bust into the middle of a thicket and scare whatever cows was in there into a tail-high run for safety, which, the boys did hope, was nowhere to be found.

Soon as the bovines got out to where they could be seen, Manuel would pick out a likely-looking victim and run his horse up alongside it. Unlike the normal flat saddles that Mordecai and Jonathan rode, Manuel's was of the vaquero style and had an apple-sized horn built right onto the front. Once he got close to a cow, Manuel would do one of two things depending on his position, his mood, how far away Jonathan was, and maybe the phase of the moon, for all Mordecai understood of it. Either Manuel would rope the cow and drag it down with a riata that he kept tied fast to that funny-looking saddle horn, or he would bend down and grab hold of the cow's tail, then real quick straighten up and wrap the tail itself around the horn and rein his horse hard to the side. Either way he decided to do it, once Manuel got hold of a cow that critter was as good as lying flat on its side in a cloud of dust.

This was where Jonathan got in on the deal. It was his job to come flying along behind Manuel, and quick as a cow hit the ground so did Jonathan. He'd run up behind the critter and jump on top of it, wrestling its hind legs and holding on to them so the cow couldn't get up again, which, unlike a horse, a cow has to do back end first. So Jonathan would hold the bawling, kicking, twisting thing down long enough for Manuel and Mordecai to gather round and join him. That always took long enough for Jonathan to have plenty of opportunity to stick his face in front of a hind foot if he wasn't careful.

Then all together they would hobble the cow, tying the hind legs together and sometimes tying the tail to a forefoot too if an animal was especially snorty and wild. Once they did that they were pretty much home free. The cow could get up and limp around, and they could make it move in whatever direction they wanted without having to worry about it running off.

Once they had their cow they drove it back near the camp they'd set out and tied the thing by the horns to a good, stout tree. The idea of that was twofold: to keep the critter from running away again, and to let it pull and twist until its head was sore enough to make it sensitive around the horns. Soon as they were ready to travel they would tie the cows in pairs, tying their horns tight together so that each one would be wanting to follow the other and not pull back against this harness arrangement. Cows tied or yoked like that could be handled easy.

A drawback to the method, of course, was that a fellow couldn't get greedy about collecting cows this way. A cow tied to a tree isn't a cow that's able to go off to graze and drink, which helps up to a point, because a cow that's been gaunted down some is more docile than one straight outa the brush and feeling snorty. On the other hand a body can't keep on collecting a herd very long or the first ones caught start dying off, so a few days is about the limit of usefulness for the method.

That was all right by Mordecai and Jonathan and Manuel; they weren't greedy. The first day, learning how to do this under Manuel's tutelage, they'd caught and tied one cow. The second day they got three. And now at the end of the third day they'd collected three more, making seven in all. They could sell those seven in Bexar, Manuel thought, for probably four dollars apiece.

It seemed there was some point to all those squirming evenings at the table after supper, Mordecai found. He was able to work out that they could each of them hope for nine dollars in his pocket and a bit of change to boot.

Lordy! Mordecai didn't know about Manuel, but he'd never in his life held that much money in his hand at one time. Jonathan had, of course. He'd brought Frank's share of Great-uncle Benjamin's estate and'd had as much of his own once. Maybe Manuel was used to having such sums too, having worked for wages in Austin before. For Mordecai, though, the thought of nine whole dollars was mighty impressive.

He hadn't any idea what-all he might do with so much cash money. But he reckoned it was a difficulty he was willing to face head-on and try to overcome.

Mordecai thought about Jonathan's silly, grinning question as he looked around at the angry cows tied to trees nearby and at the stove-up, limping, scraped, and filthy fellows who were his companions on this venture.

He chuckled and nodded.

"Yeah," he said. "I think we're havin' fun now."

☆ Chapter ☆
42

Sly was the last one to arrive. He'd been off at San Felipe de Austin—or what was left of it after so many people pulled up stakes and moved on to the new town that was also named for an Austin, the new one honoring Stephen while the old one really had been named for Moses Austin—so they had to wait for Sly to get home and Annie to feed him and pass the message along: Andrew was wanting to visit with the menfolk at his place after supper. Sly finally showed up a good three hours past dark.

"Help yourself to coffee," Andrew offered. "You know where to find it."

"Thanks." Sly found a tin cup on a shelf and poured some of the by now very stout coffee. "Where's Petra and the kids?"

"They're over visiting with Marie."

Sly nodded and sat, joining Michael, James, and Frank at Andrew's table. Jonathan and Mordecai were off chasing cattle somewhere, and none of the women or children seemed to be wanted underfoot this evening. "You look serious this evening, Andrew."

Andrew smiled. "It isn't that bad, really. I just wanted to give you boys fair warning about something. I know we disagree about . . . well . . . about some things sometimes. But I think we all want what's best for Texas an' for Texans. So I wanted a chance to talk to everybody before you hear things from somebody else and maybe make decisions too quick."

"Hear what things?" Michael asked.

"If you want to jump right into the heart of the matter, all right. Fact o' the matter is, next week there is gonna be a call-up of the militia."

Michael frowned. "Mexico? Is Santa Anna coming again?"

"That's what we're trying to prevent," Andrew said. "They want another crack at us, and this time they want to catch us in between the two prongs of a nutcracker. That's why the president and the secretary of war want to strike now, boys, an' break one of those prongs before the two of them together can hurt us. If we protect our backsides now, then we can face Mexico an' anything they send against us without having to fret so much about our families an' our farms in the rear."

"I don't understand," James said.

"Really," Frank agreed. "Some national policy decision hardly seems cause enough for you to come running home and talk with us like this, Andrew."

Andrew cleared his throat. "Yeah, well, I'm getting to that. Does anybody want a cigar?"

"What we all o' us want, Andrew, is for you to come to the point here," Michael said.

"That's what I came for, dang it. I just . . . well, I just don't want any of my own family thinking he knows more than the president and all his cabinet. That's all."

"Andrew . . ." Michael prompted.

"All right, dammit, you want it in a nutshell so here it is: we're calling out the militia and we're going to march against the Cherokees."

"No," Sly exclaimed.

"We got to."

"But they ain't done anything."

"They've conspired with Mexico to—"

"Bull."

"They have. Lordy, you don't think this whole thing is on account of those few pieces of paper we found this past winter, do you? There's a helluva lot more than that involved, boys. An awful lot more. There's other proofs too, an' they all show that the Mexicans are intent on arming the Cherokees and stirring up a revolution in the north. With that to draw our people into a fight, the whole o' the south will be left wide open. While we're fighting Cherokees up north, the Mexican army will be pouring into the south. They plan to occupy everything from Bexar through Washington-on-the-Brazos and on across to Nacogdoches. Then once they got that consolidated, them and their Cherokee allies can squeeze in from both sides an' crush us."

"But if we know what they have in mind," Frank said, "surely we can just refuse to bite on the ruse. We can stand and fight them in the south, can't we?"

"No, because if we do that we still risk losing. If we concentrate our forces in the south, that lets the Indians run wild in the north and there'd only be the women and the stay-at-homes to fight them. Besides, once the Cherokees start showing some success, the other tribes are sure to come in too. The Mexicans have already been making overtures to them too, promising arms if they'll join in. If the tribes unite behind our backs and come at us while we're fully occupied with the Mexican army, we won't stand a chance, especially if those tribes have been armed with modern firearms. And that is exactly the risk we run if we don't do something to block this thing before it starts moving. We can't let that happen, boys. Not to Texas and not to our people. We can't let anything like that happen."

"I just can't believe it, Andrew. I just can't," Michael said.

"We have spies in Mexico, Michael. Good men, many of them. Too many of those good men are hearing the same stories for me to doubt the truth. Texas is in danger, and we have to move now to protect ourselves. We have to remove the danger of the Cherokees so we will be free to fight Mexico when that time comes again. Which it will, Michael. Which it most certainly will."

Sly tugged at his chin and made a face.

"Something chewing on you, Sly?" Andrew asked.

"There is, for a fact. When I was in San Felipe I heard we've sent a peace commission to treat with the Cherokees. If we're planning to go to war with them next week . . . I know, the call-up is next week; no telling when the militia will actually move on them . . . my point is, if we're determined to go to war with them anyway, why are we talking peace with them today?"

"The president is making every effort—"

"Don't play the politician with us, Andrew. Don't make us no speeches. We're your own kin, dammit. At least give us the courtesy of the truth," Michael protested.

"All right," Andrew said. But even so he hesitated for a moment before he spoke. "Vice-president Burnet's peace commission will draw the Cherokee all together. We'll be able to whip them hard and fast and get this campaign over with so we can all get back to our fields and our families where we belong."

"This isn't right, Andrew."

"But it is, Michael. It's necessary for the survival of Texas. That is what makes it right."

"No, sir. Those Cherokees are farmers, not marauders. They don't have any intention to fight us. Hell, they already got one treaty with us. General Houston made one with them when he was president."

"Which the congress of this republic never did ratify, Michael. Without ratification, there is no treaty in force. And anyway the Mexicans—"

"Dammit, Andrew, I don't care what some gold-braid Mexican general wants to see happen, those Cherokees aren't the danger your boy Lamar thinks they are. Why, even if Mexico *is* arming the Cherokees, what's to say that the Cherokees aren't just taking the free guns and then going back to their own business? Wouldn't be nothing wrong with that, if the Cherokees wanted to take gifts off the Mexican government and then ignore whatever Mexico wants in trade. I'd think that was kinda funny, actually. Have your people thought about that possibility?"

"We've thought about everything we conceivably can, Michael. We are doing what we think is right and proper. And I came down here to talk with all of you and to . . . well, to plead with you if I have to. Don't refuse the call when the militia turns out. Please. I'd hate to see my own people charged with desertion."

"You'd hate to see it, Andrew, or you'd hate for your constituents to see it," Michael spat.

Andrew stiffened.

"Dammit, Michael, you know better'n that," Frank said.

"I . . . you're right, o' course. I apologize, Andrew."

"Sure. It's all right." But it was not. Michael could see in his brother's shocked and deeply wounded expression how hard that accusation had hit.

"I'm sorry," Michael insisted, knowing it would do little good if any. "Really."

Sly stood and touched Michael on the elbow. "We'd best be going now. Thanks for giving us time to think this thing over, Andrew. We appreciate the warning."

"Yes we do," Frank said.

James stood too, shrugged, and shook his head. It clearly made little difference to him what the country chose to do right now. James had things on his mind other than questions of national policy. "See you tomorrow, Andrew. G'night."

Michael stood for a moment staring mutely at his brother, but Andrew did not look at him again, and after a minute or so Michael turned and went outside behind the others. Sometimes, he was thinking, a modicum of foresight can save a whole bunch of regret. The pity was that he hadn't thought about that five minutes earlier than this.

☆ Chapter ☆

43

Michael snatched his foot away barely in time to keep from being stepped on, then prodded the fool horse in the side to move it away. The animal was a sly one about stepping on unwary toes and was a leaner besides. Get too close and it'd try and lean on you. Pick up a foot to clean out the hoof or to set a new shoe, and pretty soon you'd near be carrying the critter attached to that foot. Still, it was a pretty fair animal, not fast but steady and tough. He made sure the horse was standing firm on all four legs and therefore couldn't manage to step on him without giving itself away, then once again he moved in close to the animal's side and finished tying his blanket roll in place behind the cantle.

"You are sure you have everything now, my Michael?" Marie asked.

"I'm sure I do, darlin'." But her question made him go over everything in his mind again just to make sure. In the bag tied on one side of his pommel he carried the food Marie had prepared for him: parched corn, acorn flour, coffee already roasted and ground ready to use, and a good supply of dried meat. He wouldn't be going hungry. In a bag on the other side of the pommel he had a picket rope, two spare horseshoes, a spare pair of moccasins, and a packet of thread and sewing needles that Marie insisted he take along. He also packed the small whetstone that he generally carried with him in the field for sharpening his scythe. When Mordecai finally got home from Bexar it would be up to him to mow and shock the oats, and the lack of the little stone would make that harder; Michael wondered if he should change his mind about taking it with him and borrow a stone if he needed to sharpen his knife. Inside the rolled blanket he carried extra stockings and a clean shirt. And of course in the possibles bag slung over his shoulder he had powder, ball, patching linen, bullet mold, and extra flints. Far as he could tell there wasn't anything more he could possibly need.

"Everything," he said aloud now, more sure of it this time after taking inventory.

To the north he could see James and Sly riding down. They would arrive in another five minutes or so. Then the three of them would go by Frank's place to collect him, and the Lewis clan would be on their way to San Felipe to be mustered in.

Michael quite frankly hadn't intended to go, not even after Andrew's pleading. Then Marie had said something that changed his mind. "You have never been wrong, Michael, and so you could not be wrong about this too? You, all of us, fought so very hard to make a free country of Texas, Michael. I thought you would give the government of your country more of a chance than this," she'd said.

Michael still believed he was right. He still believed the Cherokees wanted nothing but a chance to live and farm in peace. But the call-up was issued, and like virtually every other adult male Texan he was a member of the militia. Like it or not, it was his duty to go. Marie was right 'bout that.

One last time he checked the tightness of his cinch and then let the stirrup down. He stood awkwardly before Marie and cleared his throat. "James and Sly're on their way."

"You must be careful, my Michael."

"You too. When Mordecai gets home . . ."

"I know. I will tell him."

He nodded and fidgeted from one foot to the other. This standing here and waiting was much worse than simply getting on the damned horse and riding away would have been.

Michael motioned for Angeline, and she came to him and accepted the hug and the kiss he gave her. "You help your mama, hear. And keep your brother in line."

"I will, Papa."

He gave Angeline another squeeze and then took Marie into his arms. There was so much he should have told her when he had the chance to do so. Well, he hadn't said the words then and he wasn't going to say them now. But surely Marie would know what he meant without it having to be said. She always seemed to, bless her.

"Reckon I better go now."

"Yes."

Neither of them moved.

"No tellin' when we'll be back."

"We will watch over things until you are home, my Michael. Do not worry yourself about us."

"No, I know there ain't no need for that." He'd be worried half sick every night, and they both of them knew it.

"It is you who must take care."

"I will. Not that anything's gonna happen anyhow. Burnet, he'll come t' treaty terms without a shot havin' to be fired. I'm sure o' that. They say we're all just goin' t' put on a show for the Cherokees and let 'em see there's too many of us for them to fight. That way they're sure to agree t' the peace commission's terms."

"Yes, I understand," Marie said seriously. Neither of them believed a word of that cock-and-bull tale.

"I'll miss you."

"I will miss you too."

"Yeah . . . well . . ." He bent, gave her a fierce kiss on the mouth, and turned quickly away, swinging into his saddle with a fluid motion that belied the pain in his aching joints. He laid his old rifle across his lap and fussed with the reins for a moment, making sure they lay straight and even. "Reckon it's time," he said.

"Yes." Marie's face, lifted toward his as he towered over her atop the horse, was as unblemished and beautiful as it had been the first day he ever saw her, that day so very long ago now in a different country and seemingly a different lifetime.

"I love you, woman." He hadn't meant to say that.

Damn, now he could see bright tears welling up in her eyes and spilling down over her pretty cheeks. She was standing there smiling up at him and tears running like somebody'd dumped over a bucket.

Crazy damn female. How could a man ever figure them?

"Good-bye, Papa."

"Good-bye, my heart. '*Con dios, mi amor*."

Michael felt something solid and weighty lodge in his throat. He reined the horse away sharply and bumped it with his heels to set it into motion, preferring to ride out and meet James and Sly rather than wait any longer for them to reach him.

He didn't look back.

Chapter 44

Except for there being a want of comestibles and a glut of rumors, this campaigning business wasn't so awful bad, in James's opinion.

They'd been out the better part of three weeks now, and mostly the campaign consisted of lounging in camp with the fires and pipes alike sending smoke into the air. They were camped on the Neches not far below Williams Ferry, and the living wasn't bad here.

James was seeing fellows he hadn't run across since the War for Independence. In a way it was almost like a reunion.

Michael grumbled some about they oughtn't to be here. And Frank grumbled even more about missing Hope and his boys. But except for that things were pretty pleasant.

If nothing else, the campaigning was keeping James's mind off other things. That was a blessing of itself.

They'd passed the Fourth of July occupying themselves with drilling. It still seemed strange to not celebrate the Fourth, it being a holiday for the States but not for the republic. Still and all some of the boys were caught up in the spirit of old habit and loosed off gunshots toward the sky. James had fired a few shots with them. But that was more than a week ago, and since then it was mostly drill a little in the forenoon and forage some in the postnoon and visit all the rest of the time away.

John Hurley said the Cherokees were camped somewhere across the river, but James hadn't seen them. He hadn't particularly wanted to. Far as he was concerned, the peace commission could deal with them and then they could all go home. One of the rumors was that the Cherokees had already agreed to pull north past the Red, which would be out of Texas and back into the States for them, if Texas would agree to pay some sort of restitution for the farms that'd be left behind. That seemed a small enough price to most of the fellows James'd talked to about it. According to that one all that remained was for them to set an amount that would be agreeable to both parties. Then the Cherokees could move north and the militia go south and nobody have to worry about any part of it.

If any of that was true, that is. You never knew which rumors to believe and which not. Michael said you shouldn't believe none of them, but there'd been the one about the train of supplies being shipped out from San Patricio, and sure enough, soon after a detail was put together to go down to Anahuac by the mouth of the Trinity and collect the stuff off boats. Sly Shipman had been chosen to go with that bunch. They'd been gone near a week now and so should be back before too long.

James scratched the sole of his bare left foot, turned his head, and spat.

"Hey!"

"Sorry." There sure was an awful lot of people here; hundreds, some said thousands. James didn't believe there were thousands, but there had to be several hundreds at the least.

"Lewis."

"Yo." It was a man from Victoria named . . . it took James a moment to call it back to mind now . . . named Jeffers. "What d'you hear, Ray?"

"Not much. You?" Ray Jeffers hunkered beside James's fire and pulled a twist of tobacco out of his pocket. He offered a chew to James, then took one himself. "Some of the boys plan on throwing the bones over past the picket line after retreat. You want to join in?"

"I got no money."

Jeffers grinned. "Hell, man, ain't nobody got any money. We'll play for 'baccy, buttons, or beans, whatever you got. You want in or not?"

"I'll think about it."

"Did you hear the latest?"

"What's that, Ray?"

"They say the Bowl wants five hundred gold dollars for every family, else they'll press a claim in Lamar's own courts an' force the Houston treaty down the old man's throat like it or not. They say the general hisself is over in the Cherokee camp and has agreed to file the suit for them and represent the tribe in court."

"That sounds like something General Sam would do, all right," James said.

"Way I hear it, it's gospel. O' course Burnet won't let hisself be pushed around like that. Texas don't have that kind o' money to pay out to a bunch o' damn injuns even if we was of a mind to. Which nobody is that I know about. I'm thinking that Albert S. will put us in line an' take us across the river awhooping and ashooting before they agree to something like that." He was referring to Albert Sidney Johnston, secretary of war for the republic and a member of the peace commission that had been treating with the Cherokees. Jeffers chuckled. "Let the damn Cherokees put that in their bowl an' smoke it." He was engaging in a small play on words there. The chief of the Texas Cherokees, named Bowl, was an old man, at least eighty, and a longtime friend of General Houston, himself an adopted son of the Cherokee tribe.

"You think we're gonna fight, Ray?"

"I hope we are."

"It ain't everybody feels that way."

"Whenever there's fighting t' be done there's always some that're soft and some that're scared. Me, I don't figure to come up neither."

"No, but there's some don't believe we're right to be putting the Cherokees off their farms like this."

"Those farms ain't theirs without there's a treaty to say so," Jeffers countered. "Deny me that one." He shrugged. "Besides, they ain't but a bunch o' stinking injuns. It ain't like they was people or anything."

James frowned. "The whole thing is way too deep for me. All I know is that I'm here now. The best thing for me will be to draw my two squares a day and do whatever I'm told."

"You an' me too, Lewis. You an' me too." Jeffers stood, his knee joints cracking loudly. "Come along an' get in the game later if you've a mind to. You got the invite."

"Right. Thanks."

"After retreat it'll be."

"So you said. Over past the picket line."

"That's right."

"Thanks for the tobacco, Ray."

"Yeah, well, see you later, Lewis."

James decided he probably would go over later and join the game. It would be better than sitting around trying to puzzle out the right and wrong of things that he really didn't understand and didn't see how anyone else ever could either, unless they had a whole lot more true facts available to them than James suspected they did.

"What was that all about, James?" Michael asked, limping over from the direction of the nearly empty supply wagons and trying to pretend he wasn't sore. Sometimes it seemed to James that Michael was doing an awful lot of that lately, not that he ever said anything about it.

"Nothing, Michael. Just Ray Jeffers wanting me to roll some dice with him and some of the other boys this evening."

"Oh. I thought maybe he'd heard some news." Michael sounded disappointed. But then here lately Michael had become worse than Frank at trying to think things out. Either one of them was apt to take hold of some notion and gnaw the idea up, down, and sideways like a hound worrying a bone. And danged if sometimes James didn't think that old Michael was getting even worse about that than Frank always had been.

"Nothing important," James said, which was easier than starting a big explanation and maybe even an argument if Michael and that idiot Bauman from the next fire over got into it. Michael Lewis and Cully Bauman mixed about as smooth and slick as fire and gunpowder, and Bauman was bound to've overheard most of what Ray Jeffers said. "Is that some salt pork you've got there?" James asked, changing the subject.

"Yeah. It's a little green but not too awful bad."

"Tell you what then, Michael. You get the fire built up an' I'll cook us some supper."

"Fair enough."

It occurred to James that, all in all, he was pretty nigh enjoying himself on this bloodless campaign against the Cherokees.

☆ Chapter ☆
45

"Mount up, boys. Come on now, everybody up. Time to move." Lieutenant Stamm rode through the camp bellowing the call and waving his sword. Michael scowled. The timing of the lieutenant's order was most unpleasant. Michael had been boiling a midmorning pot of coffee—acorns parched and stone-ground, with a little of their hoard of precious real coffee tossed in to strengthen the flavor—and it was near about ready to drink. Now here came the darn lieutenant wanting them to mount up and move.

Michael had a choice to make. He could count on this being nothing but another drill and leave coffee and pot where they were to be returned to later. Or he could dump out the pot and pack it along with him, assuming that the call to horse was the real thing and that they might spend tonight in a new camp. He hated to lose the real coffee he'd put into that pot. On the other hand, he'd hate even worse to lose the pot itself, particularly since it belonged to Sly Shipman, who was still off somewhere down south with the supply party. "Lieutenant."

"Yes, Lewis?"

"Will we be coming back here tonight, d'you think?"

"No one has the answer to that, Lewis. All I know is that the peace commission has broken off talks with the Cherokees, and we've been told to pack up and form a column of twos."

"It's gonna be a fight then?"

Stamm shrugged. He was a young man, small and feisty and quite the dandy in his droopy-brimmed slouch hat with the feathers streaming off the hatband. The lieutenant had wide mustaches and a heavy dragoon saber that he was inordinately proud of. "That depends on the Cherokees, Lewis. If they want to march to the Red without offering resistance then I'm sure no fight will be necessary."

Michael grunted, and poured his precious coffee out onto the fire, raising a cloud of ash and hissing steam as the blaze was extinguished. He reached for his bedroll and bags and began to make his preparations for the move.

"Comp'ny . . . halt!" The command came back down the line, repeated from one pair of riders to the next even though anyone who could see more than ten feet in front of him could see that everybody in front was stopping and letting their reins go slack so the weary horses could gain a few moments of hip-shot relief and perhaps snatch a mouthful or two of graze from underfoot while they waited for the next orders to be delivered. It was the middle of the afternoon or slightly past it, and they'd been on the march for more than five hours steady, not even stopping for lunch or to rest the horses more than two minutes at a time. If any animal had been able to get a drink it was only whatever it could gain on the move while crossing the Neches several hours earlier.

"Now what," James mumbled. James was riding on Michael's right, the two of them paired in the middle of Lieutenant Stamm's column. Frank was somewhere behind them. Michael hadn't seen Frank to talk to since they broke camp this morning.

"More o' the same," Michael guessed. "Go like mad. Then set an' wait till you go mad. Seems it's always like that."

"I hear you."

Michael grinned. "Why, James, you do sound wore out. This should teach you t' stay up all hours throwing dice."

"I wish they'd let us step down a minute," James said, refusing to rise to Michael's taunt about his gambling—there wasn't, after all, much he could say to defend himself, particularly as he'd lost during each of the past several nights' play. He squirmed from side to side on his saddle and said, "I can't sit here much longer without I go find me a bush to get behind."

"Hold on then, I think the lieutenant is fixing to find something out." Up ahead in the clearing they'd just entered Michael could see a courier moving back down the line. The rider stopped beside Lieutenant Stamm and tapped his forehead in a gesture that was intended to be a salute. He said something to Stamm, then leaned closer to the officer and said something more. The lieutenant frowned and shook his head, and the courier frowned back at him and spoke again, his expression this time hot and impatient. It was plain the lieutenant wasn't liking what he was hearing.

"I wish we could hear what they're saying," James said.

"You ain't the only one." Michael glanced down to check on the leather cover that was tied in place over the lock of his rifle, protecting the priming powder from moisture and the lock itself from being bumped about. The leather thong that held the cover in place was tied in a fairly tight knot. On an impulse Michael loosened it. Better to risk losing a scrap of leather than not be able to get a shot off if he needed.

All around him he could see that the men—as James was also doing and as Michael found himself doing as well—were looking not at each other any longer but into the woods on either side, as if suddenly they were expecting to find painted savages lurking in the undergrowth, as if there could be an ambush laid or breastworks discovered. Horses fidgeted and danced as inattentive riders concentrated on matters other than horsemanship. Almost imperceptibly the column lengthened and grew wider as the men moved slightly apart from one another lest they bunch together and present too tempting a target.

The courier tossed a sketchy salute toward Lieutenant Stamm and cantered back along the line again, moving swiftly past Michael and James and on back to give his message to the units marching farther back in the long column. There would be a good many of them back there, almost a thousand men total, Michael had heard. Stamm's San Felipe company with Michael, James, Frank, and Sly as part of it was third or fourth in line today. Fairly close to the front, anyway. David Burnet, Albert Sidney Johnston, General Burleson, and a Major Jones were at the head of the column not a quarter mile forward. That was where the orders and the courier would have started.

"We gonna fight, d'you think?" James asked.

"You sound worried."

"Dang right I'm worried. They didn't give us time for lunch, and I'm hungry. It ain't right they shouldn't give us time for lunch."

Michael grinned. James was all right if his biggest concern at the moment had to do with a missed meal.

Out ahead of them Michael could see the next unit in line begin to move, at a walk to begin with and then lifting into a trot.

"Comp'ny . . . for'ard . . . harch!" Lieutenant Stamm motioned with his saber and bumped his horse into a walk. "At the trot . . . ho."

"I dunno what's fixing to happen," Michael said. "But something sure is."

☆ Chapter ☆
46

"Column, uh, column, uh . . . form a line, boys. Over there. Facing that way."

The men found that sort of order more comprehensible than a proper instruction would have been anyway. They complied with the lieutenant's direction, spreading out into a broad front in the rear of Lieutenant Bronfman's bunch from Refugio.

"That's good, boys. Steady now."

They had come out into a clearing in the brakes beside the Neches, and it was here that they were forming into a wide front.

Not that there seemed to be anything ahead for that front to face, as far as Michael could see. All he could see beyond the Refugio boys was another bright green glade of dancing leaves and slender sapling trunks growing close together. The clearing wasn't more than eighty, ninety yards across. The vice-president and secretary of war and general and all the rest were off to the left toward the river. It was late afternoon, soon evening, and already the heat of the day was moderating.

"Looks like you're gonna get t' eat finally," Michael observed.

"'Bout dang time," James said. "My belly's been growling since noon."

"Longer than that," Michael said. "Believe me, I know when it started. It's been so loud it scares my horse every time. Why, I like to been unseated fifteen, twenty times already this afternoon. I'll be gladder than you when you get something to eat, dang you."

James chuckled and reached into his pocket for a chew. A chew should give him some relief until they could get a fire started and supper on to cook. If they could find something to cook, that is.

They were about out of the rations they'd carried with them from home, and the government hadn't all that much to kick in either until Sly and that crowd brought the supplies up.

"For'ard, boys. Follow behind Refugio there, but keep your interval, don't close up on them. For'ard now."

Michael grunted and eased his hold on the reins, his horse moving forward to stay abreast of the others without having to be urged.

Up ahead the wall of leafy green foliage sparkled with bright points of light, and cotton balls of pale white blossomed and then quickly withered. A sound like dozens of twigs snapping reached Michael's ears, and several massive bee-drones sang close overhead.

"Well I'll be damn."

"Ain't that the truth."

The Cherokees were in the woods up there, and they were firing on the ranked Texans.

"I'll just be damn," Michael said.

There was a dull, moist sound like a chunk of fresh meat being thrown hard onto a wooden tabletop, and a man several places over to Michael's left grunted. "I been hit. Dammit, boys, I been shot." The man's name was Taylor. He was one of the many who'd come to Texas after independence. Now he was getting his chance to shed blood for the republic. "Is it bad, Taylor?" "Bad enough, by Godfrey. This here's my best shirt." Taylor stood in his stirrups and tried to take aim on the tree line, but he couldn't shoot for fear of hitting one of the Refugio men in the rank between them and the Cherokees.

The Refugio boys loosed off a volley and then broke back to reload, leaving a clear lane of fire now for the San Felipe company.

"Fire at will," Stamm shouted.

Michael had come here opposing the conflict, if conflict there had to be. His firm intention was to pay lip service to the militia call, put in his time, ride all the miles anyone wanted to him ride, but if it came to shooting aim deliberately high and get through the fight without having to shoot anyone. He didn't wish to participate in something that he considered to be morally wrong.

On the other hand, he hadn't given any particular thought to the idea that the Cherokees would be shooting too. He especially hadn't considered that the Cherokees might start the shooting. And they most certainly had been the ones to open the ball.

Michael let out a whoop and gouged his heels into his horse's side. He ripped the cover off his firelock and guided the horse at a run toward the tree line.

There wasn't a thing to see there, not any single identifiable target a man might aim at. The Cherokees were hidden within the trees.

But they had to be packed pretty close together in there, and that was good enough.

Michael swept his mount in a hard run that curved close to the thicket. He held his rifle one-handed in a bouncing, wavering, virtually unaimed direction that pointed indiscriminately toward the green wall.

"Eeeee-yahhhh!"

The rifle snapped, the primer powder sizzling in the pan and the propellant charge igniting a split second afterward. Michael had no idea what he hit, if anything. He yelled again and hauled hard on his reins to spin the horse back the way it'd just come, kicking into a belly-down run for the line of skirmishers that was now forming where moments before there had been orderly ranks of mounted militiamen.

"Lewis, what in hell . . ." Lieutenant Stamm sounded rather proud of his warrior, Michael thought. Certainly there was no condemnation in the officer's tone, more like a certain amount of disbelief. Well, that was all right. Michael wasn't much believing it himself.

Balls sizzled and zinged past his ears as he pulled rein back at his own lines. He dismounted and turned his mount over to one of the first-fight youngsters who were the designated horse holders.

"What the hell'd you do that for?" James demanded.

"I dunno." It wasn't much of an answer, Michael knew, but an honest one.

Quickly he reloaded, aimed once again in the general direction of the hidden Cherokees, and loosed off a round.

Michael thought the volume of fire coming from the Cherokees was less now than it had been in that first volley. But perhaps that was only his imagination.

"This is crazy. You know that, don't you?" he asked of no one in particular.

But no one answered.

"We got no business shooting these people an' they got no business shooting at us."

The puffballs of smoke continued to bloom and wither at the

near edge of the tree line, and the Texans continued to pour fire back at the hidden Indians.

Michael loaded and fired as quickly as he could, his rifle barrel growing hot and the thick, gummy residues of burnt powder building inside the barrel until it was difficult to force a patched ball down onto the powder charges. Since accuracy wasn't much account in a fight where you couldn't see what you were shooting at anyway, Michael resolved that little problem by loading unpatched balls and keeping on. When the gummy mess inside his rifle barrel was so thick he had difficulty seating bare balls he decided it was time to call it quits. Besides, it was getting on toward dark then anyway, so he turned and wandered down toward the river so he could draw some water and wash his rifle.

He hadn't seen or thought about James in more than an hour, and as he came out of the haze where he'd been, slightly divorced from reality there, it occurred to him to wonder if his brother was all right and where Frank had been all this time.

He was tired, he discovered, and thirsty, and his eyes burned and watered from the acrid fumes of the powder smoke.

All he wanted, really, was to get his rifle clean and then to find a place where he might lie down and rest. Just for a little while, that was all.

He found a patch of fern short of the slow-flowing river, and he sank down onto the soft, sheltered, sweet-smelling loam underneath the fern fronds.

Lordy, but he was tired.

He would rest, he thought.

Just for a minute.

Then he would wash out the rifle and after that he would see could he find James and Frank.

Just for one minute, though. That was all the rest he needed.

Just a lone minute.

Michael hadn't any more than closed his eyes before he escaped into the restless sleep brought on by sheer exhaustion.

☆ Chapter ☆

47

"Are you all right?"

Michael nodded, almost meaning it. He'd slept the whole night through, although somehow he had managed to do that without getting much real rest from it. Still, the night had been gotten through, and now the officers up ahead were ready to assault the Cherokee positions again.

As before, the San Felipe troop was mounted and in line. Hundreds of other mounted militiamen were nearby. Michael had no idea how many Cherokees there were in the thicket. But then any number is too many of an enemy you cannot see. He cleared his throat and licked at dry lips without accomplishing much. He leaned over and touched Frank's wrist. "Listen, thanks for taking care of things last night."

Frank nodded but didn't answer. When Michael stumbled away toward the river the previous evening it was Frank who tended to Michael's horse. Later on it was Frank who came down the path and located Michael snoring in the ferns and who boiled water and some of Hope's lye soap so Michael could clean his rifle. Michael had been in such a fog at the time that James'd had to remind him about all that this morning.

Now, though, it was Frank who looked as if he needed the tending to, looked as if he hadn't managed sleep nor rest either one during the night. He was ashen and haggard, with dark puffy circles under his eyes and beard stubble on his face. His nostrils flared wide, and the look in his eyes was like a doe's, startled beside a water hole and knowing she isn't quick enough to escape.

"Michael."

"Yes, Frank?"

"If anything happens today. T' me, that is. You'll tell Hope that . . . I mean . . ."

"Nothing is gonna happen, Frank. Not to either of us."

"But if anything does?"

"I'll tell her. That's a promise. And your sons too. They won't want for anything, Frank."

"Thanks."

Michael looked around. James was far off this morning, nearly to the other end of the San Felipe company line. Michael knew that James wasn't avoiding him or Frank. If anything, James would've chosen that position because it put him just a little bit closer to where the fighting would be. James looked eager and restive, and his intensity was communicated to his horse, which pawed the ground and tossed his head.

"It's comin' time, I think," Michael said. Out ahead of the lines of militiamen Vice-president Burnet and the adjutant general of the republic, Hugh McLeod, were squaring off toward the thicket as if they would be willing to charge it all alone.

"I got a bad feeling about this," Frank admitted.

"Stick close beside me, Frank. We'll be fine." Michael glanced down to satisfy himself that his frizzen hadn't come open and dumped the priming powder. The rifle looked fine. And this time Michael wasn't going to bother messing with patches. In this kind of fighting the volume of fire was more important than accuracy. Michael'd learned that yesterday. This morning he carried a handful of lead balls in his mouth, so to reload all he had to do was spill powder into the barrel and spit a ball in atop it, then reprime the pan and fire. Until the black, gooey gum started building up again, for the first three or four shots anyway, he wouldn't even have to fool with the ramrod; a slam of the buttstock against his foot would be enough of a jar to drop the ball down onto the powder charge. That way a man could reload while he was still mounted and shoot his way in close before he had to dismount. It was something the officers had gone around from fire to fire last night reminding everyone about.

"Watch out," Frank snapped.

Michael too saw the movement inside the thicket. Involuntarily his grip on the rifle tightened, and he leaned forward in his saddle ready to jump the horse into a run to meet any attack that might be coming.

"What the . . ."

A horse and rider breached the green wall of trembling leaves, then another and another.

But they weren't Cherokees riding out of the thicket, they were Texans. Michael recognized them as the same fellows James had been spending considerable time with lately, men from Hal Rush's ranging company. They were recognizable even from a distance by the braces of revolving pistols they wore tucked into bright-colored sashes at their waists. Nearly all the rangers, as they were coming to be called, carried cap-lock pistols like those Sly Shipman owned.

Beside Michael, cousin Frank gasped with obvious relief.

"They've run off," one of the rangers shouted. "They pulled out an' left their dead behind."

Michael wondered how many Cherokee dead there were inside those dense woods. Word around camp was that two whites died in the battle the evening before. But no one had any idea how good an account of themselves they had given.

Apparently no one was going to wait around to find out right now either.

"Let's get after them, boys," Burnet shouted. "Form into column and follow me." And he was off and moving without waiting to give the company officers time to move from line to column. Not that it really mattered. That sort of neat, precise drill was beyond the one-afternoon-each-month militia companies anyhow. If a column was wanted then it was pretty much a matter of expecting a brief melee that would sort itself out once everybody decided where he wanted to ride in the bunch.

"Come on, Frank. You an' me will ride together."

"Right beside you, Michael."

Generals plan on a grand scale and historians analyze and criticize afterward. All Michael knew about this fight was that the morning was hot, he was thirsty as hell, and his cousin was lying still as death on the ground not thirty feet away, which was as far as Michael could see through the ragged and increasingly shattered cornfield that someone had planted but would never harvest.

They'd caught up with Bowl and the Cherokees again in the cornfield after trailing them from the thicket, and here the Cherokees chose to stand.

Michael's eyes stung from the acrid smoke that hung in the air like winter's clinging fog, and his jaw ached from keeping it clamped hard shut lest he spit out a rifle ball before he wanted to.

He was beginning to think it wasn't such a fine idea to carry his ammunition that way after all.

He spat the few remaining bullets into his hand, transferred them back into his pouch, and then, peeved and feeling mulish, he stood upright and ignored the sounds of gunfire all around as he walked through the cockeyed and canted stalks of flint corn to reach Frank.

When he got there he smiled.

"I thought you was dead."

Frank blinked and sat up. "For a minute there, I thought I was too."

"What happened?"

"Tripped an' fell down, dammit. Knocked all the wind outa me and I couldn't draw another breath. I swear for a little bit there I thought I was shot." He scowled and looked down to examine himself. "You don't see no blood, do you?"

"Nope."

"Hadn't you ought to hunker down, Michael? You must make an awful good target standing around in plain sight like that."

"Yeah, I reckon I do." Michael squatted beside his cousin, who looked even more tired than Michael felt and even more wan and waxen than Frank had appeared earlier in the morning. "Look, d'you want me to get you back to the wagons an' check you over?"

"But I don't think I'm shot."

"You don't look good, Frank."

"If I go back now the other boys will think I'm a coward."

"Nonsense." Michael winked at him. "An' anyway, if I help you back then I gotta go back too. Me, I want to find somethin' to drink an' a bush to step behind. C'mon. We won't stay back long. Then we can come ahead an' fight some more."

"Yeah, we could do that."

Michael took Frank's hand and helped him up. Frank was wobbly but could stand on his own once he got his balance again. Michael bent down to get Frank's rifle and handed it to him.

"Thanks."

"De nada."

Michael carried his own rifle in one hand and with the other helped steady and support Frank as they made their way out of the cornfield.

"Over there. See that gum tree? No, that one. *That* one, dammit."

"Don't get yourself in a uproar. Just point where you mean an' I'll sight along your finger. That's right, hold steady now. Got it."

"I been trying to put a ball in there for the longest time, but every time I think I got 'er lined up my barrel slips an' I got to start over. Can't lay the damn thing down on a rest 'cause then I'm down too low an' I can't see where I gotta shoot. It's been frustrating, let me tell you."

"Let me try." Michael reloaded slowly this time, with a greased patch and a struggle with the ramrod. He took careful aim before he fired. Immediately after his shot there was a flutter of movement in the leaves that could have been caused by a stricken enemy dropping to the earth, or by the passage of Michael's ball as it sped harmlessly through the leaves, or by any one of probably a dozen other reasons. Whatever the cause, the fellow beside Michael smiled. "Thankee."

"Sure."

"Reload an' put one more there just t' make sure, will you?"

"Glad to." He knelt and began reloading once again.

Michael and his companion, whose name and origins had never been given, were taking shelter behind a dead horse. The fight had moved out of the cornfield, and now the Cherokees were lodged inside another dense thicket near a village where someone said a bunch of Delawares lived, or had lived. The village was deserted now. The thicket in front of the Texans was not. At this point Michael wasn't sure if they were fighting Cherokees or Delawares or who. For sure this fight was a brisk one, at least Michael's new companion was bound to think it so. The man had pleaded for Michael to do his shooting for him because a musket ball had shattered his right elbow, and he was having difficulty trying to load his rifle and aim his shots now. But he refused to go back to the wagons where there was said to be a surgeon. No, absolutely not until he got back at the Indian who shot him.

Not that Michael necessarily believed that the crippling gunshot would have come from that precise spot the man pointed to.

The thing was, as long as the man believed it, it was true enough for the purpose.

The fellow would be able to take little enough satisfaction away with him despite this tiny measure of perceived revenge. At best the fellow would have an arm stiff as an ax handle for the rest of his life. More likely he would lose the arm.

"Ever try an' shoot left-handed?" the man asked.

"Nope." Michael finished loading and once again fired at the point where the fellow had directed.

"That's good, that's good," the man said with cheerful enthusiasm. "Don't ever try an' shoot a flint gun left-handed," he went on. "Not without a left-handed firelock, don't. Damn thing'll burn the hairs right outa your nostrils, it will." The fellow was grinning and winking.

Michael laughed. "Come along. I'll help you get back to the sawbo—I mean, the doctor."

"Oh, I don't mind you sayin' it. But if one o' them butchers comes at me with a saw in his hand I reckon I'll have t' shoot the sonuvabitch. Mind you tell 'em that if I do something stupid like pass out on 'em. Will you do that for me, neighbor?"

"Glad to."

"All right then, friend. Drag me back there."

It wasn't until then that Michael saw the man was already shy of his left foot and that the peg he wore below a slightly truncated ankle had been broken somehow.

"Ever think maybe you oughta give up this business?"

"I'm commencing to, neighbor, I surely am."

"That's the Bowl, Michael. That there is Chief Bowl."

"How d'you know?"

"Fella pointed him out to me a while ago, but I missed him. Guys been shooting at him an' missing all the day long, I expect." James raised his rifle and snapped a shot in the direction of the elderly Cherokee chief, but once again he missed.

The Cherokees had been driven back into a swamp bordering the Neches, and here it seemed they must stand or be broken, because from here there was no place left to run. Here the Indians were trapped.

The chief of the band, old Bowl, was highly visible. He wore a top hat and what was left of a swallowtail coat. A bright scarlet sash circled his sagging belly, and he carried a battered sword in one hand that he waved overhead while he shouted encouragement to his warriors. As far as Michael could tell, though, the old man was unarmed except for his sword.

Word had spread through the militiamen that the sword was one General Houston captured from a Mexican officer at San Jacinto and later presented to Bowl as a gesture of friendship.

Now most of the men within Michael's hearing were declaring a desire to capture the sword back again.

Michael didn't want it. He only wanted this fight to end. Shooting at eighty-year-old men wasn't his idea of glory. And the old Indian had already had at least one horse shot out from under him. Michael had seen that happen himself, although he hadn't known at the time who the rider with the sword was.

"You aren't gonna try for him, Michael?" James asked.

"You go ahead."

But someone else hit Bowl before James could reload and aim again.

Bowl was struck in the thigh. He staggered, shouted something in his own language, and began limping away. The Texans were closing in on the Cherokees now. A bearded man wearing a fox-skin cap paused fifteen or twenty yards from Bowl and shot him a second time, the bullet striking the chief low in the back.

Bowl dropped into a cross-legged position and sat there leaning forward from the waist with his arms wrapped tight around his stomach.

The man in the fox hat ran forward to claim the prize of Bowl's sword, then charged off toward the remaining Cherokees, waving the sword and shouting.

Someone else trotted by, noticed Bowl sitting there, and came back. He leaned down and said something to the old chief, and Bowl said something back at him. The Texan took a pistol out of his trousers pocket, cocked it, and stepped behind Bowl. He placed the muzzle on the nape of the old man's neck and fired. Then the Texan trotted off into the swamp and the diminishing gunfire of the Cherokee warriors.

"Come on, Michael. They're breaking."

"Go ahead, James. I'll be along directly."

"You don't look so good, Michael. Something wrong?"

"I got a bellyache, that's all. Go on now. I'll catch up to you later."

"Okay." James held his rifle slanted across his chest at the ready and went running off after the others who were already pursuing the fleeing Cherokees.

Michael turned and began walking slowly back the other way.

☆ Chapter ☆
48

"I'm sure glad t' see you, Sly."

"I hear we missed the big fight."

"Ayuh, so you did."

"They say there's to be plenty more fighting," James put in.

Michael grimaced and spat into the fire. "No more fighting. Just a lot o' hatefulness. It's one thing to face a man who's shooting at you. But by God it's another to ride around setting fire to somebody's cornfields an' bean patches. And that's all we done the past two days."

"The general says—"

"The hell with what the general says. The Cherokees, what's left of them, are running for the Red as hard an' fast as they can. They already had to go off an' leave their homes and their fields for us to burn behind them. Are we gonna press them so hard they got to leave their women unprotected and run for the States separate from their families? This ain't right, dammit, and I don't mind who wants to listen to me say so." Michael raised his voice toward the end of that statement.

"Hush up now or Cully Bauman will be sneaking off to tattle on you with the lieutenant."

Michael snorted. He jumped up and stood with his jaw shoved forward and his chest puffed out. "Lieutenant! Hey! Lieutenant Stamm. You want to listen in on what I got to say here?" he shouted.

"Will you please set down an' hush yourself, Michael."

"What if I don't?" Michael challenged.

James gave him a dirty look but didn't object any further.

"I hope you brought us some of them eatables you took so long collecting," Michael said to Sly, quieting now and returning to his seat on the ground beside their fire.

"I think a sackful might've got mixed in with my stuff," Sly confessed.

"Good. I want it."

"Pardon me?"

"Did I stutter? I said I want it. Or if you want to keep it for your own self, just say so. I'll go steal me something from the commissary wagons. Whichever. It don't make no nevermind to me, Sly."

"My, ain't you the proddy one tonight."

"Can I have a slab o' damn bacon or not, Sly?"

"Of course you can have whatever you want, Michael. But excuse me, please, if I don't know what is eating at you tonight."

"Nothing. And come tomorrow I'll be eating at that bacon. That's the point."

"Should I be getting the impression that things are happening here that I don't know about?" Shipman asked.

"No reason you can't know about it," Michael said. "I'll be pulling out tonight, and I'm wanting something to eat whilst I travel home."

"We haven't been mustered out yet," James said.

"Nope, I agree that we have not."

"The lieutenant won't like it."

"Hell with what the lieutenant likes or don't like. I ain't deserting. I was here for every shot that was fired, dammit. Now the shooting's over, and I'm going home. Let somebody else burn farms an' destroy crops in the field. Me, I'm going home now."

"Mind if I go with you?" Frank asked. He'd been sitting in morose silence at the edge of the group. Now he perked up and for the first time in several days showed some animation and some interest.

"Glad for the company," Michael said. "How 'bout you, Sly?"

"Not yet, I think. Don't forget, I wasn't in on the fight. I don't wanta walk out until I'm satisfied there won't be any more shooting."

"There won't be. But I can see as how you'd want to see that for yourself. What about you, James, you want to ride along with me an' Frank?"

James frowned and sighed. "Actually, Michael, I been thinking about something these past couple weeks. There's nothing for me at home now. No reason why I should go back an' make believe

I'm happy when I ain't. So what I been thinking . . . that is t' say, some of the boys have made what you might call an invite to me . . . an' what I been thinking about doing . . ."

"You're fixing to enlist in a ranging company, aren't you?"

James smiled. "Hal Rush and some of his boys have asked would I want to come in with them. We'll be down along the coast, mostly. Chasing border bandits an' like that. They pay cash money, you know, an' supply a man with everything he needs but his horse and guns. The republic will pay for all the ammunition he can burn and a burial if one of them is needed. I, uh, already told them I'd go south with them when this thing with the Indians is done."

"I can't fault you, James," Michael said. "If that's what you want to do, by all means do it."

"I'm real glad to hear you say that. I been kinda worried about what you'd think."

Michael leaned forward and squeezed James above the knee. "Be all right if we worry about you sometimes?"

James grinned. "I'll let you get away with that now an' then. But not real often, please."

"Annie will be disappointed," Sly told him.

"I know. I'll miss her too. You tell her that for me, Sly. But this is something that I think I oughta do. And I'll be coming home to visit now and then. It ain't like I'm leaving permanent or that I won't never be coming back. I'll be back real often. That's a promise. You can tell it to Annie as gospel. Oh yeah . . . Michael, when Mordecai an' Jonathan get back I'd like you to tell Jonathan he can just stay in my place if he wants. Until he gets his own land claimed and a cabin up."

"I didn't know Jonathan wanted to claim any land," Michael said.

"He never mentioned that to you? Sure. He's a Lewis, ain't he? And the republic is offering ground to anybody who'll come in and take it up. Jonathan and Mordecai was talking before they left for Bexar about Jonathan claiming that piece of bottom land and the good woods below where the Blackwoods used to be. And Mordecai wants to take up the land next to it when he's old enough too. That way us Lewises will stand astride both sides of the Colorado. I thought sure those boys had talked to you about it."

"This is the first I've heard of it."

"You don't mind, do you?"

"I don't much care what Jonathan decides t' do."

Frank gave Michael a questioning look.

"That didn't come out the way I meant it," Michael apologized, although probably it had, denials aside. "What I meant was that he's free, white, an' twenty-one. Jonathan can do as he pleases without my say-so."

"And Mordecai?"

"He's welcome to take up his own land too, o' course. That way when I pass the home place to him he'll have all that much more." Michael stood and brushed off the seat of his britches. "If you're ready, Frank, let's be getting along now. I'd like to put some miles behind us tonight."

"What should we tell Lieutenant Stamm when he comes around tomorrow?" James asked.

"Tell him the truth, o' course. I ain't hiding and I ain't ashamed. I'm just going home now. Stamm or anybody else can find me there whenever they want."

Sly stood too. "Let me get that poke of supplies for you. We didn't get any coffee, but there's English tea and sailor biscuits and plenty of bacon and salt pork. You won't have to go hungry. Wait here while I fetch it for you."

"You're still welcome to come with us," Michael said when Sly handed him a bulging sack that must have weighed twenty pounds or more.

"Thanks, but not yet. Tell you what, though. You can give Annie the message that I won't be but a few days behind you."

"All right. And thank you, Sly." Michael turned to James and grasped his hand. "Little brother. You take care o' yourself."

"I will, Michael. You do the same."

They looked at each other for a moment and then, impulsively, James grabbed Michael in a hug, startling Michael but pleasing him too.

"We'll see you soon," Michael said.

"Real soon." Both knew they were lying.

"Yeah, well"—Michael cleared his throat and picked up his blanket roll—"see you later."

He and Frank made their way through the darkness to the picket line where the horses were tied and the saddles stacked. It was about two hours past dark, and Michael was pretty sure the picket line held significantly fewer horses now than when he had been here earlier to water and feed.

Even as he watched, a threesome of riders detached themselves from the shadows and began to drift away down the Neches toward the old Spanish highway.

Apparently Michael and Frank weren't the only militiamen who'd decided they had seen enough of this campaign and were headed for home now.

A sentry posted at the near end of the picket line kept his attention pointedly directed into the woods where an attack, improbable but perhaps not entirely impossible, could come from.

There was no challenge from the sentry when Frank and Michael mounted and began the long ride home.

☆ Chapter ☆

49

Andrew stood staring pensively down at the slow-flowing waters of the Colorado. He bent, picked up a round disk of white, clean wood left from where someone had cut a log section short. He skimmed the disk over the water like a flat rock, getting it to skip twice before it settled into the stream and began to bob along with the current. The scrap of wood, in a few days' time, would float past Andrew's farm. Even now, at this very moment and for some days to come, that piece of discarded timber would be closer to Petra and the children than Congressman Lewis was.

Funny, he thought, how he was always the most homesick after he was recently home again for a visit. It had been little more than two weeks this time since he was last able to break away from the new capital. And on this miserably hot August afternoon Andrew was more homesick, and heartsick, than he could remember being in a very long while.

He missed Petra and Rose and Ben, and all the others too. He missed being able to walk over and sit with his brothers in the cool of the evenings. He even missed the hard physical labor of farming—well, almost. After more than half a year of living in cities he was willing to concede that there could be value in service as much as in labor. But, Lordy, he did miss the closeness of family. Here in Austin he had no one. If he hadn't believed so strongly in what President Lamar and the Republic of Texas were trying to accomplish, more importantly in what they already *were* accomplishing, he would have chucked the whole thing and been on his way home long before now.

He heard footsteps on the path that led from the boardinghouse down to the river. Lexie's smile greeted him when he turned to see who was disturbing his reverie. Not that he minded the interruption; these were the sort of thoughts that badly needed shattering lest he start feeling sorry for himself.

The pretty half-caste stopped beside him and slipped her arm into his. The gesture was that of friendship and honest affection, however, and nothing more. That question was settled long before.

"What brings you down here, Lexie?"

"I come to find you, Andrew."

"How'd you know I was here?"

She laughed. "But this is where you always come when you have had the difficult day an' want to be alone, no?"

"Am I that easy to read?"

"Only to those who care about you, Andrew."

It was a compliment, Andrew knew, and a truth. Relieved of obligation and command, the lovely slave seemed to feel free now to give an affection of the spirit that Andrew did not demand from the body. And her affection was returned by Andrew. Had it been possible he would have told Petra about the mulatto girl and acquired her for the sole purpose of freeing her. In Texas, though, that would be impossible regardless of the best of anyone's will. Throughout the republic it was illegal for a person of color to be freed. Moreover, any free Negro entering Texas would immediately be impounded by the government and sold at auction. Those were among the laws with which Andrew disagreed, and among those he was powerless to change. But that too was something with which Andrew had long since come to terms, at least insofar as Lexie was concerned. He rarely thought much about it any longer.

"So," he said. "What is it that I've done this time?"

"There is someone to see you, Andrew."

"Really?" He grinned and smoothed down the lapels of his coat, wanting to present himself to best advantage if this was the visit he'd been hoping for. When he was home last, Michael and Mordecai were in the midst of planning a journey up the Colorado, more or less in search for the headwaters of the river but mostly in search of the pleasure of each other's company. They'd said they would leave after the beans were picked, and they would be free to travel for the next month or so until the corn was ready for harvesting. This seemed a little early for them to have gotten away. But then Michael had been mighty anxious. "Tall fella who looks a lot like me and a young one who looks like the both of us?"

"No, Andrew, I would have run fast like the wind to tell you if it was M'su Michael and your nephew Mordecai."

"How'd you . . . never mind. I keep forgetting. You hear everything and you don't never forget nothing. So if it isn't Michael, who is it? Mm?"

Lexie frowned.

"Somebody you don't like. I can sure see that."

"No, no, Andrew. I don' say nothing like that. Please."

"You know I won't carry no tales. Now who is it that wants t' see me, Lexie?"

"A M'su Pruett, Andrew."

"I never heard of him. But I take it you sure have."

The girl shrugged. "It is not my place to say."

"Not your place to volunteer anything maybe, Lexie, but now I'm asking. An' anyhow, we're alone down here. Nobody can hear whatever you an' me decide to talk about right now."

Lexie nibbled at her lower lip for a moment, then with much more relief than reluctance nodded. "This M'su Pruett, Andrew, he is a supplier of labor. He buys slaves, cheap. Everyone knows this man pays nothing. But this man, he buy any slave. No man too bad so that M'su Pruett won't buy him. Whip marks an' the branding? Pah! This man don' care, he buy anyway an' pay for them cheap, an' then he get plenty work from them."

"I kinda get the idea that he isn't able t' do that outa kindness an' a gentle touch with his people, Lexie."

"When this man buy someone the first thing he do is make heem too weak to fight. No drink, no food, big chain. This man make anyone do what he say. His people work hard or they die quick. Plenty people, good people, they die 'stead work for this man Pruett, Andrew. Every nigger knows about this man."

Andrew frowned. "And you say he's here to see me?"

"Oh, yes. He is in the parlor to wait for you. He tells me to run fast an' get you quick or he will have me punished." She turned her head and spat.

"That'll be the day," Andrew agreed. "But I wonder what somebody like that would want with me?"

"You really don' own no people for him to buy, Andrew?"

"Nope. Not me nor none o' my kin."

"I think you should do no business with this man, Andrew."

She dropped her eyes then and blushed, apparently overcome by the enormity of having volunteered an opinion.

"I suspect you're right, Lexie. But I got to admit that I'm curious now. I can't think of anything somebody like that would want with me. Look, if you'd be more comfortable, not having to be around this Pruett fella, like, whyn't you go over to the store and get me some tobacco. And some candy for yourself if you want. Tell 'em to put it on my account." He winked at her. "And don't be in no hurry to rush back. Anybody asks what you're about, you just tell 'em it's an errand for me."

The girl beamed. "Thank you, Andrew." She clapped her hands with delight and ran off along the footpath leading north beside the river while Andrew began the steep climb to the newly constructed boardinghouse where he and a half dozen other like-minded politicians stayed.

Pruett, eh? He grunted. He'd never heard of the man.

☆ Chapter ☆ 50

It didn't take much effort to work out the puzzle of what Oliver Pruett did with all the food he saved by not feeding any to his slaves. The man looked like a beer cask with a pumpkin set atop it. He could have been any age and not shown it because his skin was puffed so full it wouldn't have been possible for him to wrinkle. Andrew suspected anyone that fat would require a servant just to get his shoes tied in the mornings.

Still, the fellow should have been a politician himself. His smile was huge, his demeanor sincere, and his handshake firm. He came across as just the most friendly and likable fella you could ever hope to meet.

"I can't tell you how much I've looked forward to meeting you, Congressman," Pruett enthused as he prolonged the handshake by clinging to Andrew's hand with both of his. "This is a great treat for me, sir, truly it is. I've heard so very much about you."

Except for Lexie's warning, Andrew conceded, he very likely would have been taken in by the fellow's charm. Pruett had, come to think of it, the same sort of contagious effervescence that Christopher Campodoro did.

"Really?" Andrew countered. "Who'd you hear all this from?"

"Pardon?"

"I asked who it is that told you 'bout me."

"Why, um, many people, sir. Many. You have admirers, you know." Pruett smiled.

"No, I didn't know that. Name a couple for me so's I can thank them."

The smile faltered. But only for a moment. "Why, I should say that the most prominent among your silent supporters would be the Skinner brothers."

"Now I'll just be danged. The Skinners? Really an' truly?"

"Oh, yes, I assure you. They've told me about you quite often."

"You know them boys then, Pruett?"

"Yes, certainly."

"Face t' face?"

"Of course. We, um, have done a certain amount of business together."

That made sense, Andrew conceded. Cheap as the Skinners were, and as much construction work as they'd been having done, it only stood to reason that eventually they'd team up with Pruett or someone like him.

"I've never had the pleasure o' meeting those boys," Andrew said. "Though o' course I've heard plenty about them. Folks in Austin do like t' talk about the Skinners. But you want to know something funny, Oliver? I don't think I've ever even heard anybody say what their first names are. F. Skinner and L. Skinner, that's all that shows on the recorded property deeds. Did you know that?"

"I did not, sir."

"Yeah, it's true. But you say they know me?"

"They certainly know of you. They are quite complimentary when they speak of you, Congressman."

"I'll be dang."

"I assure you it is true."

"Oh, I take your word for it, Oliver. Yes, sir, I do." Andrew smiled at the chubby fellow. "O' course all of that is real interesting, but it don't tell me much about why you've been wanting so bad to meet me."

"To discuss certain, um, legislation, Congressman."

"Oh? Which?"

Pruett glanced around the parlor as if expecting to see eavesdroppers, even though they were alone in the room. "Could we discuss this elsewhere, Congressman? In, um, private? My home is not far."

Andrew shrugged. "If you'd ruther. I got nothing to hide, but I guess it don't matter where you want t' talk."

"Very good. Thank you." Pruett stood, having considerable trouble with lifting himself out of the deep chair that Lexie had showed him to earlier—with malicious intent, Andrew suspected, as that particular article was the softest and most awkwardly deep piece of furniture in the house—and rubbed his hands together in a display of eagerness to be off. "Over dinner, perhaps? Would that be satisfactory?"

"You bet. If you'll wait right there I'll go fetch my hat. I won't be but a minute."

"Good. Wonderful." Pruett bobbed his head happily and waddled in the direction of the front door while Andrew turned toward the staircase.

"No, thanks." Andrew and his host were seated at the dining table of a small but nicely appointed house on the outskirts of the city, the remains of the evening meal before them. The food and the service alike had been exceptional, and now pale curtains billowed softly at the windows, admitting a breeze so pleasantly cool that it belied the heat that had been in the air earlier.

"It's the very best quality, I assure you."

"Oh, I'm sure it is, but I don't care for any, thank you."

Pruett seemed disappointed, but only for a moment. He shrugged and set the whiskey bottle aside. He hadn't poured any for himself, Andrew noticed, but he was certainly interested in providing for his guest.

"That was a mighty good dinner, Oliver. Nice o' you to have me in."

"You hardly touched a bite." Which in comparison to Pruett's own rather prodigious intake was true.

"I had plenty, thanks."

"Cigar?"

Andrew accepted the offer. A servant girl, not as pretty as Lexie but even lighter in skin color, instantly was at his disposal with a silver device to trim the ends and a candle to warm and light the excellent panatela. "Mm." Andrew puffed on the cigar and smiled around it. "Nice."

Pruett winked at him. "The smoke, Andrew? You don't mind if I call you Andrew, do you? I didn't think you would. Or the girl, ha ha. Would you like her, by the way?"

"No thanks."

"Oh, that's right. The incorruptible congressman. Isn't that right, Andrew?"

"Not that I've ever heard anything about."

"Take my word for it, Andrew. That is the reputation you've acquired."

"Really? Is that one of the things the Skinner boys told you about me?"

"As a matter of fact, sir, it is." Pruett smiled. "But we are going to change all of that." His smile broadened. "Aren't we?"

"Are we, now?"

"Yes, actually, we are." Pruett reached into his coat pocket and withdrew a leather pouch. He tossed it onto the table. It hit with a telltale clink.

"Isn't this a little crude, Oliver?" Andrew sat back, enjoying the cigar and ignoring the bag. "I woulda thought better of you than this."

"Don't you even want to count it?"

"Not particularly."

"A hundred dollars, Andrew. And in specie, too. None of this weak paper currency that you people insist on printing. What are Texas dollars trading for now, Andrew? Twenty cents on the dollar? Less?"

Andrew shrugged.

"You are right, of course. Forgive me. The point is that what I offer you here is not currency but hard money. Gold, sir. Pesos, if it matters, but gold. Good anywhere in the world, never mind where the coins may have been struck."

"Just a hundred?" Andrew chuckled. "Lordy, I'd of hoped I was worth more'n that."

"Are you suggesting that you could be . . . persuaded, shall we say . . . by an amount larger than a hundred dollars?"

"No. But it woulda been less insulting if you thought I was worth more'n that."

"Ha ha. My dear Andrew. I do like you."

"You got kind of a funny way of showing that, Oliver."

"Nevertheless, sir, it is true. I like you very much. It's almost a pity to find myself the instrument of your destruction."

"Damn, Oliver. I didn't even know I been destroyed. Would you mind telling me how? I mean, I haven't so much as looked inside that bag. There could be lead slugs in there for all I'd know. An' surely you don't think one meal and a cigar are enough to compromise a fella in Austin these days. Give us some credit, man. Even those of us that can be bought don't go that cheap."

"Oh, but my dear fellow. There is something I should confess to you. While I might be willing to bribe you honestly, so to speak, I would also be willing to lie afterward. Whether or not you take the money. Think about that. If you fail to accept a little compensation under the counter, I shall simply go public with a claim that you did. On the other hand, if you do agree to take the money it will be in my best interests to remain quiet about it—and make certain suggestions now and then as regards your vote." Pruett was smiling now fit to break his face, which Andrew was considering although not by way of any smile.

"Your word against mine, Oliver."

"Actually, uh, no." Still smiling, Pruett pointed toward the doorway leading into the kitchen. "Harold? You can join us now." A man stepped into view there, a white man Andrew had never seen before. Earlier Pruett had said they were alone on the premises except for the slaves. "My word and his against yours, Andrew. And I assure you, both of us can lie quite convincingly. Are you sure you won't change your mind now and accept our little . . . gift? There would be more to follow later. Say, fifty dollars a month? It is either that, Andrew, or Harold and I go to the authorities and swear that you tried to shake us down, that you demanded bribes or else you would author legislation that would harm our business."

Andrew puffed on the cigar Pruett had given him. He shook his head sadly. "You make it difficult, Oliver. Mind if I ask why?"

"You don't honestly know?"

"No, I honestly don't."

"Goodness gracious, dear fellow. And you said you'd never met the Skinners."

"Nope. Never have."

"They certainly do know you, Andrew. I was not fibbing to you about that. They described in considerable detail what I might expect of you. I must say that they have been correct in every particular, right up to your refusal to accept a bribe. But to tell you the truth, Andrew, they seem to think you are stubborn enough and foolish enough that you will allow yourself to be forced out of office and see your entire family disgraced before you give in and let yourself be bent. Frankly, Andrew, I am hoping my friends the Skinners are wrong about that. I personally would hate to see you in disgrace, perhaps even in jail. I still hope you will do the sensible thing and put that pouch into your pocket." Pruett sighed and spread his hands. "You will do that, won't you? You will save yourself and your family that trouble?"

"I don't reckon I'd be comfortable doing that, Oliver."

"Dear me. My friends appear to know you all too well. I'm afraid this will only please them. And it won't even change anything, that is the saddest thing of all, Andrew. If they can't buy you, why, they shall only buy some other congressman. Wouldn't the sensible thing be for you to give in now? Or must Harold and I go swear out a complaint against you?" Pruett sat there looking something like a greasy-fat cat with canary feathers in its whiskers.

"The servants have heard what's gone on here," Andrew said.

"No matter. They wouldn't be allowed to testify in a court of law even if they were stupid enough to think about doing so. They can give you no defense, Andrew." The fat man leaned forward. "Please believe me, it gives me no pleasure to do this to you. I would much rather you take the money. Save yourself, Andrew. Pick up that pouch."

Andrew grinned.

"You won't take this so lightly tomorrow, Andrew. Harold and I shall place our charges against you immediately the courthouse opens for business in the morning. You have only that long to reconsider. Once we have sworn to our statements we shan't budge. Either of us."

"No, I'm sure you wouldn't. But there's no need for you t' wait all that long, Oliver. You can go ahead an' make your statements tonight. I ain't gonna change my mind."

"We can wait for regular business hours. It is only fair to you."

"Fair? Damned if I'd figured you boys for being fair. But really now, there ain't no need for you t' wait."

"I wouldn't know where to find the sheriff until morning anyway," Pruett said.

"Would a state officer do?"

"I expect so."

"Well, I know where you can find a major in the rangers an' a couple o' his boys. You can talk to them real quick."

"Oh?"

Andrew raised his voice. "You dang sure had best be out there, Tom."

"Right here, sir." The answer came from an open window not four feet away from Oliver Pruett's broad back.

"What!"

"It's what you might call a precaution. A little bird whispered in my ear, Oliver, said bad things about you. So when you were so worried about privacy this evening I kinda thought maybe I'd best cover my backside. Made the arrangements when I went to get my hat, y'see. Major Finley and his men have been posted outside where they could hear every word you said."

"As a matter of fact," Finley put in, "we were able to see quite a lot too. There will be no problem making a case against this one, Congressman. Extortion, attempted bribery—we'll see if there is anything else we can come up with. I suspect Mr. Pruett will be out of business for some time, sir."

By then two men with revolving pistols in their waistbands had come inside and were busy snapping manacles onto Pruett and the man he had identified as Harold.

"You and me are gonna have to have a talk about your friends the Skinners, Oliver," Andrew said.

But by then the fat man had his mouth clamped firmly shut. He refused to say another word to anyone as he was led out.

Lexie, Andrew thought, was owed one big debt after this night's work, and so were Major Finley and his men. Andrew knew what he could do for Finley. The rangers were lobbying to have another company enlisted for frontier service against Indian raids. The existing companies had all they could handle trying to keep the border calm and the Mexican incursions down to a minimum. Andrew's vote on the rangers' behalf would be thanks enough for them. As for Lexie, he would have to give that some thought.

Andrew drew deep on the cigar Pruett had given him—whatever other faults he might have, the fellow certainly knew quality when he found it—and headed back to the boardinghouse.

He was going to have to remember to ask Michael if he or anybody else in the family remembered running afoul of anybody named Skinner before now, he decided. For sure the name meant nothing to Andrew.

Still, there likely wasn't anything personal involved, just some shady businessmen trying to get their hooks into a legislator. He would try and remember to ask, though, quick as Michael and Mordecai got here.

His mood brightened as he thought about that soon-to-be eventuality, and his step became more lively. Seeing Michael and Mordecai here in Austin would be the next best thing to getting home again, and the sooner they got here the better he would like it. By the time he reached the boardinghouse Oliver Pruett and his bumbling bribery attempt were far from Andrew's thoughts.

☆ Chapter ☆

51

Nobody, not all the way since Moses and Meshach and Malachi, nobody had ever had as good a woman as Marie Villaret Lewis was.

Michael knew that and marveled at his own good fortune even as he was packing his things onto the horse that would carry him and Mordecai north and west for maybe as far as the waters of the Colorado ran

This was a trip Michael had wanted to take for an awful long while. He'd thought about it, talked about it, yearned for it, and even planned on it. But there was always something else that needed doing.

Now him and Mordecai were going. And it wasn't only that Marie agreed they should go, she'd as good as insisted.

Ever since Michael came home from the campaign against the Cherokees he hadn't been feeling right. He hadn't been settled in his mind about the drubbing the Cherokees had gotten, and he hadn't recovered in his body either. The hard ground and restive nights of the militia campaign had roused his rheumatism until it was worse than ever. Pains flickered and jolted through almost every joint and with almost every movement.

If he didn't take this long ride now, Michael was afraid he never would. If the hurting got any worse he wasn't sure he would be able to stay horseback more than a few minutes at a time.

Marie hadn't known any of this. She couldn't have, for Michael surely never spoke of his hurting, not to her nor to anyone else; he never expected to.

Yet somehow Marie had known of the longing that was in him. She was the one who'd insisted that Michael and his son go now before the corn needed bringing in instead of waiting for the fall when colder weather and the onset of the winter's chill rains would have made it all the harder for Michael to travel.

He didn't know why she had turned so insistent like that, but he was almighty glad she had.

"This would be the best time," she said. "There is nothing Angeline and I must do here but see to the garden and mind the hens. If more is required we have Frank and his sons to turn to. Or Dennis or Jonathan. We will be fine." Of them all, Marie was about the only one who so much as remembered that Sly had a real name; for sure she was the only one who sometimes called him by it.

And as for Jonathan, Michael even suspected that Marie had something to do with his staying back here as Michael wanted. When the idea of the adventure was first brought up, Mordecai'd been all hot and eager to bring his chum and part uncle Jonathan along to share the excitement. Michael hadn't wanted that at all. It was Mordecai's company he wanted on this long-awaited trip, not Jonathan's. Michael didn't even like Jonathan much, though that was among the things he'd never come right out and said, even to Marie.

But there again she'd known. Bless her, somehow she'd known. And Michael didn't have any proof of it, but he was mortally certain that it was Marie who put a whisper into Mordecai's ear, for after a couple days of not very subtle wheedling and suggesting, Mordecai of a sudden shut up on the subject of Jonathan riding with them, and after that the only mention of Jonathan was about his plans to build a cabin for himself before winter. While Michael and Mordecai were away Jonathan would finish laying out the boundaries of the land he claimed and would get a start on the cabin walls. Mordecai figured to help him with the roof after he and his papa got back from the source of the Colorado.

Oh, it was an excitement, Michael thought. A true and wonderful excitement.

They were traveling the way Michael used to as a boy—just a horse and a rifle and no more than could be carried wrapped in a blanket behind the cantle. They weren't even taking along a packhorse. As far as Austin they would live on what they carried with them. Beyond that, out where there weren't farms and people yet, they would carry gunpowder and salt and count on eating whatever came their way.

This wasn't Tennessee, of course. But Michael wanted his son to know as near as possible how it used to be for Michael and for his pa, for young Mordecai's namesake, in those long-ago times.

That, as much as anything, was what this trip was all about. It was a chance for Michael to have one last time with his son before the boy became the man—and wasn't that happening so quick that it seemed nigh impossible to accept—and for Mordecai to know firsthand the things that'd gone before.

So Michael packed the few things he would take along and watched out to make sure Marie didn't try to slip in so many extra goodies that the horses would be overburdened, and he found himself whistling light airs as he finished lashing his blanket roll in place and reached for the old rifle that had been his companion since he was younger than Mordecai.

"You ready, boy, or do I have to spend the day waiting on you?"

Mordecai was already on his horse and had been for several minutes. He grinned but didn't bother to answer.

"Old woman." Michael bent down and put a wiry arm around Marie's still-tiny waist. He drew her tight against him and kissed her slow and deep. "Take care, hear?"

"Take care yourself, my Michael."

The time had come for him to turn and mount and ride away. But for some unknown cause he felt impelled to hold on to her a moment longer, to squeeze her all the tighter and just one more time to enjoy the warmth of her sweet softness close to him. He nuzzled the top of her head, breathing in the scent of her hair, and he savored the feel of her taut flesh against his palm. "Damn, but I surely do love you, woman."

"Hush, Michael, or you shall see me cry."

He laughed and kissed her one last time, and finally swung up onto his saddle, able to do it smoothly and without wincing at the sharp spear-points of pain in his hips and knees.

Mordecai made his good-byes to his mother, and Michael leaned down to give Angeline a final hug.

"Don't expect us till you see us," he warned. "We might could take a notion to keep on agoing till we see the Californias and the ocean they say is beyond them."

Marie smiled. "Only if you can do that and be home again before the corn must be picked."

"There y' go, dang it, taking the fun outa things."

"All right then. See your ocean if you must, Michael. Only remember to come back to me."

"Always have, haven't I?"

"And this time too, my love. This is what I pray for every day you are away."

He sat for a moment and felt a lump that threatened to rise in his throat. For those few seconds he felt a reluctance to ride away. It was something Michael had never before experienced.

The moment was quickly, and welcomely, shattered. "Are we gonna set here in the yard, Papa, or are we gonna see some country?"

"I expect we'll go look at some country, boy. Now keep up with me." Michael grinned. "If you can."

He winked at Marie and reined his horse north along the river toward the easy ford above the Blackwoods' old place.

☆ Chapter ☆
52

Lordy, but he did love it, just love it. They were four days out of Austin, and Michael felt taller and stronger and better now than he had in . . . years.

Happier too, if the truth be known.

Not that he wasn't happy at home just from being with his beloved Marie.

But that was different. That was sweet and good and dear. But this here was . . . free. Wide open and deep breathing and free, free, free.

Lordy, but he loved it.

Just four days away from Austin and Andrew and all the restrictions of city living, and already the very country they rode through was changing right around them.

The soft, familiar hills of home were gone now, flattened out and disappeared. Now the Colorado trickled over rocks and wound through shallow gorges carved out of pale caliche. The land to either side was flat and grassy, marred here by thick mottes of scrub and pin oak and there by long, low buttes and mesas that were shaped like monstrous big bread loaves with flat tops and steep sides. Mordecai had never seen the like before. Michael rarely had, and then not for years past.

"Are you doing all right, Papa?"

"O' course. Why'd you ask?"

"Nothing, Papa. Just checking."

"I'm fine." It wasn't a lie, not exactly. He hurt. Bad. The hard sleeping and the day-long riding drove spear-points of fire into his hips in particular. But he really was fine. This country, and being able to see it with his own son at his side, was enough to make that and twice more like it worth the while and then some.

"Could we stop early this evening, Papa? I'd like to see can we catch some fish for supper."

"I reckon we can do that if you like. We got no schedule to keep."

Mordecai grinned and nodded and reined his horse off to the south, toward another of the countless low rises that lined the course of the river here. Had he had so much energy when he was that age? Michael wondered. He supposed he had; it just wasn't something you thought of at the time. It wasn't till you lost it that you even became aware of it, he decided. Now even Mordecai's horse had to have that much more energy, just to keep up with all the side ventures the boy wanted to make. There wasn't nothing they would pass by that he didn't want to see firsthand and to examine close up. Michael smiled, thinking that apart from the obvious rest Mordecai was wanting to give his daddy by stopping early this evening, the halt would be good for the horses too. It would give them that much more rest and grazing time.

And they truly weren't on any schedule. They had no obligations nor any plan but to see some country and have some good times. Far as Michael was concerned they were surely succeeding on all counts.

"Psst."

Michael's attention was snapped to the hissing signal. Mordecai had reached the west end of a thicket of low-growing scrub oak and was stopped there, his horse blowing and him leaning low over the animal's neck. Mordecai was grinning—whatever he saw over there it wasn't trouble—and motioning for his papa to come on.

Michael reined toward him but kept the horse at a walk lest the noise of its travel spook whatever it was that had Mordecai so tickled.

Mordecai silently pointed as Michael came near.

Then it was Michael's turn to grin some.

Buffalo, five of them. No sign of the great herd these five should have been a part of. But here were five, sure enough. Three cows and two calves that looked to be yearlings at the very least.

The calves had fairly slick hides, but even this late in the summer, with the winter coats soon to thicken on them, the cows were scruffy and ugly, with ragged patches where the old winter fur hadn't been completely shed. That, coupled with the clumps of dried mud they carried from the wallows, made them even uglier than they ordinarily appeared. A buffalo wasn't the most handsome of critters at the best of times, and here Mordecai was seeing them just about at their worst.

The wind was right, blowing from the quietly grazing buffs back toward the men, otherwise Mordecai never would have gotten so close undetected, and even from this distance of more than a hundred yards Michael thought he could smell the rank, ammoniac stench of the buffalo.

They were a purantee mess, these buffs were. They stank, with flies and gnats swarming about their heads like clouds, and they were splotchy and ragtag and nasty. Michael doubted he had ever seen worse.

"They're beautiful, Papa."

"Yes, they are."

"We could use some fresh meat."

"I'm not sure o' the charge in my rifle, son. Was thinking I'd best pull the ball this evening and put in fresh powder. Whyn't we not take no chances here. Whyn't you go ahead and knock one down. That calf on the left, say. It looks like it'll cut up nice an' tender."

Mordecai nodded and swung his horse's head a bit to the right so as to position himself at a good angle for shooting.

Michael watched with some interest. If he'd been doing the shooting he would have dismounted and fired from afoot. But then he never felt comfortable shooting from horseback. That was one of the many differences of habit and thought between father and son. In Tennessee, where Michael grew up, travel and hunting alike were mostly done afoot, and a horse was thought of as another form of sometime transportation but mostly as a tool for pulling things. Texas-raised Mordecai, who'd grown up with horses as a regular part of everyday living, never would have thought of getting down from a horse before he shot off a gun over its head.

Somehow—and Michael didn't pretend to understand it—somehow Mordecai and the boys like him could just sit atop most any horse and do whatever chore was needed, up to and including the firing of loud guns, while Michael or Andrew or someone like them could fork the same horse, shoot off the same gun . . . and get dumped onto his backside for his troubles. The horses seemed to accept from a relaxed horseman the things they'd leap and sunfish over if anyone else tried them.

Mordecai took his time about aiming, waited while the calf took a mouthful of summer-dry grass and then stepped forward, placing its foreleg at a better angle for the ball to penetrate the chest cavity to the heart and lungs.

The rifle cracked, its muzzle rising and spewing flame and white smoke.

Out on the grass the buffalo calf coughed and sank to its knees.

"Nice," Michael said. "Very nice." The light breeze caught the smoke from Mordecai's charge and drifted it back to Michael. The scent of it was clean and fresh and good on the open air like that.

Mordecai grinned and bumped his heels against his horse's flanks.

As soon as the horse and rider moved out from behind the scrub oak so they could be seen, but not until then, the cows and one remaining calf tossed their heads, rolled their eyes, and broke into a lumbering but deceptively fast rocking-chair gallop to the northwest. They ran with their tails held stiffly erect but their dignity, such as it was, intact.

Behind them the calf Mordecai'd shot was not yet dead. It struggled in an attempt to regain its feet and follow the others. Mordecai rode near, leaned low out of his saddle, and with one of the pistols Sly had given him finished the calf with a ball behind the ear.

By the time Michael came up, Mordecai was already on the ground and was busy reloading his rifle and pistol. Michael was pleased to see that. A man never knew when he would need a gun and an empty barrel is small protection. Mordecai was tending to first things first, and that was good.

"You can do the honors here, son, while I go back over beside the river and set us up a camp for the night."

"Yes, sir."

"Fetch the tongue and backstrap and a couple goodly hunks of meat. About what you figure we'll be wanting for the next three days. It might not keep that long, but if we find fresh in the meantime we can throw whatever is left to the coyotes and take more. But mind you bring the tongue and the backstrap. We'll be wanting those for supper tonight."

The boy's face was lit up bright as any lantern from the pleasure he was taking here. That was a good thing to see and itself was worth the trouble of the trip. Michael felt a welling sense of fullness deep inside his chest and knew that never in all his life had he been happier than he was these past few, fine days.

This right here was the salt that flavored a man's living.

"You done good, son." He reined away. "I'll have the fire going and some coals to cook over by the time you get in."

When he rode back toward the river in search of a perfect spot to camp—and perfect he would surely find on a day as good as this one—he couldn't feel so much as a twinge of discomfort in his joints. Even that was unable to intrude upon him right now, and he smiled to himself as he rode slow and content to start their fire.

☆ Chapter ☆ 53

Mordecai rode along behind his pap, reins loose and his horse given its head to follow behind the tail of Papa's mount. Mordecai had one leg draped over his pommel so that he was sort of riding sidesaddle. Behind him, everywhere they'd been, there were gray wisps of fluff drifting in the air and lighting on the grass. That was because in his lap he was carrying a turkey he'd shot this morning, and now he was busy plucking the underfeathers off the carcass. The bird, cleaned and packed inside a casing of fresh mud, would be buried in a pit with hot coals beneath it and around the sides and laid over top of it too. Then they'd put some green brush and a bit of dirt over all that and leave it to bake through the afternoon. By the time they got back to camp this evening they'd have a turkey roasted so sweet and moist that it would be as good as anything Mama could cook—or so Papa claimed. For sure Mordecai was willing to taste the proof that it was so.

They'd been camped at this spot for two days now. They hadn't seen any more buffalo since the calf Mordecai shot, but they hadn't gone hungry neither. There'd been pronghorn antelope and fat deer and now the turkey. In a bend of the Colorado there was a little glade where the grass was lush and soft and smelled nice, and it was shaded there by overhanging cottonwood branches. Just off the riverbank there was a deep pool where the swimming was refreshing on a hot afternoon and where trout so stupid they must never have seen a hook before could be found whenever a body wasn't wanting to swim.

There was wood all around, already down and dried out and ready to be busted up and thrown onto the fire, and it was dry so it didn't make hardly any smoke. Across the river there was a bank high enough to cheat the wind that came down off the empty plains so that they could sleep comfortable of a night.

All in all this was about as nice a camp as Mordecai could ever recall seeing.

The living was so easy here that Papa wasn't even hardly having to hold himself stiff and pretend that he didn't hurt when he moved. Papa was proud and didn't want anybody to know about that. They all knew, it was just that none of them let on to him that they did. And of course Mordecai made it a point to take on all the heavier chores around the camp, which was only right for him to be doing anyhow.

"Now you're for sure this ol' bird ain't gonna taste like mud when it's done?" Mordecai asked. That part of Papa's recipe seemed somewhere over the edge and onto the incredible side of things.

"I promise you it won't taste of the mud," Papa said over his shoulder. " 'Less you take the mud outa a buffalo wallow or a deer scrape. Then it wouldn't taste like mud neither, but you can guess what it would taste of."

"I think I'll let you choose the place where you want me to make the mud," Mordecai suggested.

"That might be a good notion."

"Shee-oot, Papa. I don't think there's anything uglier than a naked ol' turkey."

"You got that'un picked?"

"Pretty much."

"It don't have to be perfect. Any little feathers left on will stick in the mud when it bakes hard. They'll pull out clean when we crack it open."

"Now you tell me."

Papa laughed. "No point giving you an excuse to go lazy on me."

"Lazy? Who? You want to swap chores sometime?"

"Anytime you want, button. Just say the word."

"Yeah, an' I might too." He wouldn't, but he would sure threaten to. That was all right.

With the benefit of this new information Mordecai decided the turkey was clean enough. He held the carcass by the wings and took out his knife. Holding the bird well out to the side he made a cut and let the guts spill out with a wet, sucking noise. "Yuck."

"What's that, boy?"

"How can anything that ends up tasting so good stink so bad?

This thing smells as bad as a danged old chicken. We should of brought Angeline along to clean our birds for us."

Papa laughed again—he'd been doing that easy and often lately, and the sound of it was nice to hear—and agreed with Mordecai's opinion without offering any explanations. That one was beyond even Papa's abilities to explain.

Mordecai used the point of his knife to scrape inside the body cavity of the turkey, gave it a shake to make sure there wasn't anything clinging inside there, and decided the bird was ready for the baking. If it wasn't ready, dang it, Papa could do the rest. If there was any one thing that Mordecai hated it was butchering chickens. He didn't mind a bit being shoulder-deep inside a deer or a cow or a buffalo, but then none of them stunk like dang birds did. This turkey was as bad as any chicken, just bigger.

He was in the process of taking his leg back over the pommel so he could set his saddle straight on when Papa's horse stopped without warning and Mordecai's like to put its nose up the backside of Papa's. Mordecai had to move sharp to keep from losing his seat, and darn near lost his grip on the turkey carcass too. "Hey!"

"Hush a minute." Papa frowned. "D'you hear something, son?"

"No sir."

"Wait a second." Papa tilted his head to the side and squinted, as if that would make his hearing sharper. Maybe it did. "There it is again. Don't you hear that?"

"No sir."

"Come along then, but stay quiet."

"Yes, sir."

Papa eased over to his left and a little ways up a bit of a slope there, and Mordecai stayed close behind him. When he was just up far enough that he could see over without exposing himself to view from the other side, Papa stopped. There was tension in his body, which Mordecai didn't understand until he was up the slope to that same level and could see what Papa'd seen before him.

After all this time out on the grass—they hadn't seen so much as another man's smoke since their second day out from Austin—they'd run across other folks.

There was wagons out there. Carts, actually, or to be real right about it they were *carettas*, the big, slow, clumsy Mexican freight carts that had solid wheels and could be made by anybody who owned an ax and had himself some patience. Mordecai was used to seeing *carettas* around Bexar and in the south, not so often in the east, because Anglos didn't favor them.

There were a dozen or so Mexicans with the carts and a bunch of Indians gathered around close.

For a minute there, Mordecai thought he was seeing a bunch of Mexicans being attacked by raiders. For these were surely horse Indians down off the plains, not the tame Caddos and few remaining Tonks or Karankawas like you'd see around San Felipe or on the highway once in a great, great while.

He could see right off that these Indians were different. They dressed different and their horses were different and, mostly, they just plain held themselves different.

Most of the Indians Mordecai had seen before—there hadn't been so very many of them anyway—carried themselves shy and half scared all the time, like stray mutts that didn't know would they be fed or kicked but expected the kick more than the tidbit.

These Indians standing beside the Mexicans and the *carettas* stood straighter and kind of strutted when they moved. But the Mexicans wasn't scared of them. That was clear even from the distance, which Mordecai judged to be a quarter mile or better.

Even from that far away you could see that both the Indians and the Mexicans was getting along, visiting and talking and likely doing some trading.

"You know what I bet?" Papa said.

"No sir."

"I bet those fellows would have some chilis to trade. Maybe some vinegar too." He chuckled. "You know, son, I didn't want us to pack anything like that because I was wanting you and me to travel like I did when I was a boy. Just salt and gunpowder. Well, that was all right then. But I've got spoiled, son. I've got so used to your mama's fine cooking that I'm hankering for some spices for a change now. Why don't I see if those fellas want to make us a swap for something."

"You think that's a good idea, Papa? What about those Indians?"

"You can see that they're friendly."

"I can see that they're friendly enough with them Mexicans, Papa. But they don't know us. They might not feel so neighborly to a couple white Texans, Papa."

"I think you'll find, son, that most folks give back whatever you give to them. Starting with respect. I've fought Indians before, but only when I've had to. Mostly I've found them to be about like anybody else. Don't show either trouble nor fear and a man is generally all right with Indians or any other stranger."

"I dunno, Papa. There's something . . . I just don't like the looks o' that out there. It's like there's something wrong with it. I don't know what. But I ain't easy about this. I'd rather just go cook our turkey and leave them fellows alone if it's all the same t' you."

"Wouldn't you like some chilis, boy? And some vinegar?"

"We can get along without, Papa."

"That ain't the point. Besides, it never hurts to make another friend. No, I think what I want to do is ride over there and see if those fellas will make me a trade."

"We don't have anything to trade with, Papa. Nothing except our supper."

"We could spare a haunch off that doe you shot yesterday. Somebody might as well get the use o' that meat before it spoils. For sure you and me can't eat it all before it goes green. I'll offer 'em that." He turned in his saddle and nodded in the direction of camp, which wasn't more than a half mile away in the direction opposite the Indians and the Mexicans. "Go ahead in, son, and get started on the turkey. I'll ride out an' talk with these fellows. If they want to make a trade I'll come back for the deer meat."

"I don't think . . ."

"I know, son. But it's all right. Really." He smiled. "Go on now. I'll be along direc'ly."

"I don't know how to do this turkey by myself, Papa. Why don't you help me with it, then later if we want we can take that haunch with us an' ride over . . ."

"Mordecai."

"Yes, sir."

"Do what I told you now."

"Yes, sir."

Mordecai didn't like it. He had a hollow feeling in his belly and a taste of acid in his throat. Papa jigged his horse on up the slope so that he was in plain sight. He hadn't more than showed head and shoulders before he was spotted. Mordecai could see from all that distance the way the Indians reacted to the sight of a rider coming into view. Some of them moved to surround the Mexicans and others ran to their horses. There must have been thirty or more of the Indians out there and the dozen or so Mexicans.

Papa saw the reaction too and waved, holding his hand extended up at arm's length with his empty palm showing and waving it slowly from side to side to show that he meant no threat. Even so, the Indians that were going for the horses sprang onto their mounts and poised themselves like they were ready to wheel and run away if need be. The ones on the ground with the Mexicans stepped forward a few paces and stood there waiting.

Mordecai felt a little better after seeing that. Nobody, not Indian nor Mexican either one, was grabbing for guns.

Even so, Mordecai stayed where he was. Papa'd said he should go back to camp. Mordecai sat his horse without moving. It wasn't that he didn't trust Papa's judgment, exactly; what he didn't trust was some bunch of strangers out here in the middle of noplace.

That, he decided, was what he didn't like about this. If those Mexicans wanted to trade with some Indians, and if those Indians wanted to trade with some Mexicans, what were they doing here? Rightly speaking, the Indians should've gone to Bexar or Santa Fe or some such to do any honest trading. Or the Mexicans should've taken their carts north into the assigned lands up in the United States where the Indians were supposed to stay, and where they mostly did stay until they decided to break away on one of their wild, awful raids, striking south all the way into Mexico or sometimes down into the Gulf coast.

But . . . for them to meet here?

There was something that didn't seem real right about that.

"Papa!" Mordecai blurted it without thinking and spurred his horse up the way Papa'd just gone.

Papa was almost to the *carettas* now, and some of the Indians were riding out to meet him. He was still waving and so were they. The Indians waved as they came closer to him. They motioned Papa forward and held their arms out in welcome. Mordecai was closer too now and he could see more detail. In Bexar with Manuel and Jonathan they'd heard tales about the wild raiders from the north and how awful they were, and descriptions of the way those raiders decorated themselves and their horses. Mordecai felt a chill strike through him, and he jumped his horse into a run toward Papa and toward the Indians.

"Turn 'round, Papa, don't trust 'em. They're Comanche, Papa. Ride back. Ride back quick."

Papa must have heard. He stopped his horse and turned to look toward Mordecai.

While his attention was behind him like that the Comanches

whipped their horses at him in a sudden charge. They were close. Oh, Lord, they were close.

And there wasn't no welcome now.

They had bows in their hands and clubs with lumpy, rounded heads, and some of them had lances.

Mordecai saw their mouths open and moments later heard a quavering, high pitched, ki-yi yelping coming from them.

The ones riding in front were shooting now, loosing arrows while they rode. Eight, ten, a dozen arrows lifted into the air.

Papa's rifle came up.

He was close to them, so awful close.

Too close to miss if once he fired.

Mordecai felt the blood drain from his head and felt a dizziness sweep through him, sapping the strength right out of him.

Surely the Comanches would see Papa's rifle and turn back lest he shoot one of them dead.

Surely they would do that.

Yet the Comanches swept toward the lone man who stood his ground before them. Their horses' hoofs drummed the hard earth like thunder, and their war cries lifted across the grass to Mordecai's horrified ears.

And on they rode into the muzzle of Papa's rifle.

"Jesus!" Mordecai whispered. And it wasn't no blasphemy. It was a prayer.

☆ Chapter ☆

54

Papa's rifle barked and the warrior in the lead threw his arms out wide and toppled from the back of his charging horse.

Mordecai cried out. The others were coming on. They didn't slow nor even swerve to ride around their own fallen comrade, they were that deadly intent on their purpose.

They were close to Papa. So close.

Arrows from their bows were striking him, sticking into him. The shafts showed sharp and black against the cloth of his shirt.

"Run, Papa. Cut an' run."

It was too far away yet, a hundred yards or more. Papa couldn't hear. That didn't matter; Mordecai couldn't not holler it anyway. "Run, Papa. Please."

Heat stung his eyes and blurred his vision.

The Indians were all around Papa now. He never even tried to spin his horse away. There wasn't time. Or it could be that he knew what was coming and was set that he would take it face-on and not in his back. Damn them. Damn them anyway.

The Comanches swarmed about Papa's horse, too close for the arrows now. Clubs flailed and knives slashed. Mordecai could see Papa try and swing his rifle butt to bash one of them, but it was no use. The Indians were too close, and Papa was already too weak to hardly lift his gun, much less bash a Comanche with it.

Papa went down under the battering, and the Indians jumped off their horses, and now Mordecai couldn't any longer see what they were doing.

He brought his own horse to a halt, startled to realize of a sudden that he'd closed on the shrieking, yammering, ki-yiing Indians and that now he was within fifty, sixty yards of them.

Their attention, damn them, was on Papa still, on whatever it was they were doing to him on the ground there. Damn them.

Mordecai swung his horse half about and raised his rifle.

There was one Comanche in particular, a tall and muscular sonuvabitch with thick ropes of greasy hair falling in braids near about to his waist and with streaks of blood, Papa's blood, spattering his naked, sweaty chest. That one kept lifting his club high and pounding down with it, again and again, pounding and pounding.

Mordecai felt a sense of vaguely unreal detachment as he raised his rifle and took careful aim on the breastbone of that particular Indian.

He even took the extra time to touch the set trigger on his rifle lock, making the pull on the firing trigger so light the touch of a hair was said to be enough to trip it. It was slower to do that but more accurate, because there was less chance of the pull disturbing one's aim.

He touched the back trigger, and the rifle jerked in his hands.

Out there in front of him the tall Comanche with Papa's blood smeared on him was hit dead center. The Indian cried out and collapsed into the melee around Papa's body.

Mordecai felt a thrill of savage satisfaction drive through him when he saw the Indian shot and dead or damn soon gonna be.

The rest of the Comanches went to ki-yiing and yipping again all the louder, and now they remembered that their first victim hadn't been alone. They scattered, leaving Papa lying there in the dust, and ran to reclaim their horses.

Mordecai wondered if he had time enough to reload and get another shot off before they took him down the way they'd taken Papa.

Then he realized what he was thinking, realized he was setting there in his saddle waiting for those Indians to come kill him, and there wasn't reason for him to go and do that.

Never mind waiting for the Indians to surround him and swarm all over him and batter him to the ground in a bloody heap.

Papa'd been shot dead by their arrows and knew it, and stayed to fight his own murderers with his last breath. Mordecai was sitting untouched atop a stout, sound horse. It would only be stupid for him to play the brave fool and wait for the same to be done to him.

Mordecai wheeled his horse the rest of the way around, and while the Indians were busy catching up their mounts and starting after him he put his horse into an easy lope.

The temptation was in him—Lordy, but it was strong now that

he'd gotten started running—to throw his heels into the horse and take off at the hardest, fastest run he could wring outa the creature.

But that would just be another way of giving in and allowing the Comanches to catch him.

This wasn't gonna be some Sunday afternoon horse race where the prize was a coin or a hen or the right to brag. The stake this time was life itself, and there wouldn't be no second place awards given out.

A sprint would only wind his horse and let the pursuers catch up in ten miles, or twenty or forty if they wanted to press it that long.

What Mordecai needed here was a long run, speed balanced against endurance, nerve balanced against fear. The temptation to run was there. Thoughts of what an arrow would feel like jabbing deep into his back impelled him to speed. But good sense told him that what he needed to do was to keep ahead of those Indians . . . just barely. Just fast enough to keep from being shot, and slow enough to keep from using his horse up.

The Comanches had the advantage, damn them. There were so many of them. The first bunch of them could afford to sprint after him. If they used their horses up and dropped behind, no matter; there would be others coming behind to take up the chase where those first ones had to leave off.

For Mordecai there would be only one error, and then he would be dead.

Or, damn them, there would be no errors. And then he would live to kill more murdering Comanches. Someday. Please, God. If there was any one thing that Mordecai Lewis wanted to do, now and forever, it was to live himself so that he could kill Comanches. Damn them.

He reached behind him and felt of his cantle. It was bare, and that was good. He couldn't afford to carry any more weight than he had to. For a moment there he'd forgotten that all his stuff and Papa's was still at their camp. The last one Papa ever in his life made.

There was a small gourd of water tied at the pommel. Mordecai took it up and used his teeth to draw the corncob stopper. He drank from the gourd and then tossed it aside. Gourds can be easy replaced, and the weight of those extra few ounces of water wasn't wanted now.

The Comanches were screaming and yelling behind him. He hoped they kept it up, the sons of bitches. Their noise kept him aware of how far back they were without him having to look around all the time.

While he rode, and while he could, he held his rifle butt down in his left hand and with his other reloaded, going about it slow and careful so as to compensate for the jarring of the horse's gait.

He could hear an increase in the pitch of the yelling behind him, and soon he could hear the drumming of hoofs closing on him as the Indians saw that he was reloading the rifle. They lashed their horses, some of them anyway, into a belly-down run in an effort to catch and kill him before he could reload the rifle he'd already used to kill one of them.

Mordecai went on with what he was doing. He willed himself to finish before ever he looked back.

When he did, rifle charged and ready once more, he was pleased with what he saw.

There were only four Comanches that had charged out ahead of the pack. Four nearby and another dozen or so riding well behind. The pack of the dozen were moving at pretty much the same easy speed Mordecai was taking. The four were running hard in pursuit.

Mordecai leaned his weight forward just a little and gently squeezed with his knees. His horse responded with a slight increase in speed.

Just enough was what was wanted here. But what was just enough, anyway? Mordecai knew he wanted to get those four Indians well apart from the rest of them. But he didn't want to jade his horse to do it. Just enough could be hard to figure, dammit.

He let the horse stretch its stride a tiny bit more, and the Indians behind yelped and yammered like they'd gained a great victory. Likely they thought they had him boogered now and turning stupid-scared.

Mordecai dearly hoped those Comanches did believe exactly that. For there were a few things they didn't know and some lessons he wanted to teach them, damn them.

He tried to ride relaxed and easy now as he held on at this pace, allowing the four to come closer while all the while the pack was falling farther and farther behind.

Loose and easy was what was wanted here. Papa had taught him that.

Mordecai allowed himself to think about Papa now. There was no time for grief, but there was time enough for a little thought. Time enough to honor Papa and wish . . . no, dammit. There wouldn't never be time enough to wish for what wasn't so. A man had to deal with what was and not moon over the things that weren't. That too was something Papa taught him.

Lordy, Mordecai thought, nobody, not ever, had a father better than Michael Lewis was to his son. Nobody.

He could hear the hoofbeats of the racing Indians now. Could hear the horses clear and separate from the ki-yi cries of the Comanches.

They were close.

He glanced over his shoulder in time to see an arrow flicker past his right shoulder.

They were close, all right. But not too close.

Mordecai's lips drew back in a mirthless smile, and he twisted hard around in his saddle so that he was near about facing to the rear.

His rifle came up, held more or less level for a moment, and fired.

He was more lucky than good. The rifle ball struck the arm of the Indian closest to him and spun the Comanche half around with the force of it. The warrior lost his hold on the lance he'd been carrying, and the brief look Mordecai got made him think the Indian's arm was busted as well as bleeding. That Comanche dropped back, and now there were only three in close pursuit, the dozen of the pack much farther back now.

The three that were near howled all the louder. They knew the deadly rifle was empty, and they were much too close for Mordecai to be able to reload again before they would be onto him. The three of them screamed, no doubt cussing and taunting him, and whipped their horses to a lather in a final sprint.

Grimly and without haste, Mordecai slung his rifle muzzle down over his shoulder so that it would be out of the way.

Oh, the Indians did shriek and chatter when they saw him do that. They were in a frenzy now, using their bows to beat on their horses in an attempt to get just a bit more speed from the tiring mounts.

Mordecai held his horse's gait as it was, allowing the Comanches to close on him fast.

They were close enough that they were waving their war clubs and one of them, the silly SOB, seemed to be coming at him with a puny little bit of a stick that'd been carved and decorated with paint and feathers. It didn't look like any sort of weapon Mordecai had ever seen before. Certainly it didn't look like anything he ought to be afraid of.

The Indian that was the closest to him of them all was the one with the stick. The others had put their bows aside and intended using their clubs. From this close up Mordecai could see that the clubs were vicious things, with pointed stone heads heavy enough to bust a skull wide open or break whatever bones it encountered.

One of the clubs—damn the Indian that carried it—one of them was fouled with dark blood and matted hair. Freshly drying blood, it was. Papa's hair.

Mordecai felt a lurch of rebellion in his gut when he saw that.

But it lasted for only a moment, and then he was cold inside again the way he wanted to be now.

The Indian with the skinny stick came closer, almost close enough to grapple with, and leaned out as if he intended to touch Mordecai on the thigh with the feathered end of his silly stick.

The two of them, Texan and Comanche, were riding near side by side now and not five feet apart. Four. Three.

The Indian's face wasn't painted. But then this bunch had been trading with those Mexicans when Papa tried to ride friendly amongst them.

This crowd hadn't counted on making war today. They'd simply seen Papa openhanded and smiling and murdered him for the pure hell of it.

Mordecai felt a cold, steely knot inside his belly as he looked into the brown eyes of one of the Indians that'd killed his papa.

The Indian was definitely trying to reach over and tap him with that dumb bit of stick.

Stupid SOB.

Mordecai raised the pistol Sly had given him, thrust the muzzle into the Indian's face, and pulled the trigger.

"There. There, damn you. There."

The Comanche flopped over backward off his horse, his stick sailing high into the air.

Mordecai pushed the empty pistol into his waistband—there wasn't time to hunt around with the hook and hanger on the belt—and took up the other one while he wheeled his horse hard left and hauled back on his reins, pulling the animal down into a hock-down sliding stop.

The other two Indians couldn't react in time to avoid having their horses carry them right on by. Their momentum put Mordecai behind them and only a few feet away.

"Damn you," he screamed and urged his horse forward again.

His second pistol spat, and the ball smashed an Indian in the flat of his back and sent him tumbling.

"Damn you."

Mordecai had no loaded weapons left, but he had hate enough that he didn't much care. He charged the one remaining Indian and tried to brain the Comanche with the barrel of the pistol Mordecai was still holding.

The blow missed, almost unseating Mordecai when his striking arm swept through, so hard did he try to hit the Comanche.

"Damn you!"

The Indian cried out and reined away, turning back in the direction of the oncoming pack.

For an instant Mordecai was tempted to chase after him.

But only for that instant.

The dozen were still coming on at a dogged, muscle- and wind-saving lope, and he had no weapons at the moment save his own hatred.

He turned the nose of his horse east again and once more set out at an easy pace, just barely fast enough to stay ahead of his pursuers.

And once more too he began the process of reloading his guns while he rode.

The Comanches were falling farther and farther behind now as Mordecai's grain-fed American horse began to outdistance the grass-fed scrubs the Indians possessed.

Mordecai almost wished some of the Comanches would spur ahead and close on him again.

Almost.

Next time, if there was a next time, they would know better than to get close enough for sticks and clubs. They knew about the pistols now and that their quarry wasn't limited to a single rifle shot before all his fangs were pulled. Next time they would come no closer than bow-shot, he was sure.

And there again he would have no room for error. If he failed to survive this run there wouldn't be anyone left to carry the news back to Mama.

Damn them.

He reloaded his rifle last and carried it slanted across his pommel the way Papa always had, and after that the Comanches seemed to get slower and slower, until before dark he was no longer able to see them back there.

He commenced to get hungry then and wondered whatever he had done with that turkey him and Papa had wanted to cook just those few hours earlier. Mordecai had no recollection whatsoever about what he might have done with that bird.

Damn those Comanches anyway.

☆ Chapter ☆

55

She felt hollowed out and empty, like one of the cornhusk dolls Michael used to make for Angeline. How very many of those dolls he had made, his big, rough, work-hard hands twisting and tying and arranging sheets of carefully selected husk so that he could give joy to a child. Michael. Her Michael. It was so hard to believe. She did not believe it yet. She hadn't cried yet, not one tear. But then, cornhusk dolls don't cry. Later, perhaps. Now there was no time. Now there was only the emptiness.

She would try to fill the emptiness with the things that must be done. There were so many of them.

She walked out into the dogtrot of the house that her Michael had built for her, and she stepped down into the yard and handed to her son, to the son Michael had brought to her, the bag she had packed full with parched corn and dried meat and cold, dry corn dodgers.

They were not taking coffee with them. They would not take time enough to cook any, or so they said. They would not take time to hunt. They would stop only when they had to.

They. All of them. All the Lewis men. They'd all come, Andrew from Austin, James from Goliad. It was Jonathan who had ridden day and night to find James and tell him and bring him back so he would not be left out now.

Jonathan. Sweet Jonathan, who had loved Michael so much and whom Michael himself never was able to love. Perhaps because of this disparity, with Jonathan loving Michael so completely and Michael unable to give of himself to poor Jonathan, perhaps because of this Marie felt a special fondness for Jonathan now.

For Jonathan had wept at the news of Michael's death, and Marie herself had not. Not yet.

Later. When there was a whole person within this brittle shell again, this crisp and fragile husk that was left of herself. Then she might be able to weep.

"Thank you. Thank you all." She said the words and knew that she was saying them, and yet she heard them as if they came from the mouth of a stranger. She walked on the ground among the horses and clung briefly to the hand of each of these Lewis men as she passed through them and yet she felt like an observer, as if she were floating somewhere eight, ten, a dozen feet above the ground and could see herself standing now by James, now by Andrew, beside Dennis and Frank and Jonathan and finally now at Mordecai's side. She saw herself as if from above and slightly behind while she moved and spoke and did the things that were necessary.

"Thank you. Thank you so much."

"We'll not be long," Andrew promised.

"A week. Not longer," James said.

"Everything will be ready," Marie heard herself say. It was what she was expected to say. She had no idea if it would prove to be true.

"We've sent word. The Reverend Fairweather will be here before we get back with the . . . with Michael," Frank said.

A week. Longer. It did not matter. Time held neither comfort nor sting. Michael would never again share the passage of time with her. What other meaning could it possibly hold now? Now time was only a reminder of that truth.

Marie thanked each of the men, touched each of them, showed a gratitude that was real enough even if it was unfelt—a husk holds no feelings—yet true.

Poor Mordecai—he hadn't cried yet either, she suspected, and he would need the release of tears even more than she—had to go with them. She would have stopped him if she could. But without Mordecai to guide them they would never find Michael's body. Without Mordecai it would not be possible to bury her Michael here among those who loved him. Without this trip of the Lewis men it would never be possible for her to be buried beside Michael. She could not contemplate spending all of eternity without him. Life by herself would be cruelty enough without adding that to her sorrows as well.

So now the Lewis men would ride out together to find her Michael's shattered body and bring it back here to her.

How terrible it must have been for Mordecai then. Alone and far from home and surrounded by his enemies, yet he had found the strength to go back and to wait, and when the Indians and the Mexicans were gone—Comancheros, Mexicans such as those were called, or so James of the rangers explained to them—poor Mordecai had gone back and found his papa's body and buried him for safekeeping.

And now they all would ride together to collect this man they all had loved so very much.

How terrible for them all.

But how proud she was of them, these men who were so like her Michael.

"May God ride with you," she heard herself say. Once the words left her she could not have said in which tongue she had spoken them. Not that it mattered. Even if the words were not known they would be understood.

The men nodded solemnly and took up their reins, and Marie felt the women close in tight about her. The wee ones had been sent indoors, but the women were with her, and the older children. They drew near and lent unspoken courage to her.

"We'll not be long," Andrew said.

"We will be ready," Marie promised. She held her head high and her back straight, and her eyes were dry.

"Yeah, well . . ." James cleared his throat and licked at his lips. Jonathan looked like he might cry again; his eyes were huge and damp and his Adam's apple jerked up and down as he swallowed over and over again.

Marie stepped back and waited for these tall, strong Lewis men to ride out to claim her Michael's dear body.

It occurred to Marie to wonder which of them would take the lead among the Lewis men now. Always before it had been Michael who was the leader of the clan and the driving force who impelled the others forward. Michael was the one they all looked up to, their arbiter and their patron.

Andrew lifted his reins and looked around at the rest. Andrew, who was a congressman and a leader not merely in the family but among all the peoples of the republic. He might be the logical choice to lead the family now. Or James, who was a ranger and a warrior, might well have taken up the head of this terrible mission. Or Frank, who was the eldest of all the Lewises in Texas. Even

Dennis, who of them all had the most experience in dangerous and lonely pursuits.

Marie's chin lifted a fraction of an inch higher when she saw Mordecai move as if by right to the fore of these men.

It was Mordecai who would lead them out into the wilderness to claim his father's body, and if need be to fight again.

Michael's son Mordecai.

The men rode forward, Mordecai in the van and the others, grim and silent and fixed in their purpose, following close behind.

And as the Lewis men rode away, Marie felt the hollows fill. Pride and anguish welled hot and wet within her body, and she began to tremble. Her eyes began to burn and sting, and her throat closed tight shut against the low, keening grief that erupted without warning from the depths of her soul.

Loving hands surrounded and supported her, and she felt herself being caught up and lifted by the warmth of the women who pressed close about her.

Marie was able, finally, to cry for her Michael. And for his son, who so young had taken up the burdens of being a man.

"God help us all," she whispered.